Amish Christmas
ROMANCE COLLECTION

Three Novellas in One

D0054560

LINDA BYLER

Good Books

New York, New York

Good Books books may be purchased in bulk at special discounts for sales promotion, corporate gifts, fund-raising, or educational purposes. Special editions can also be created to specifications. For details, contact the Special Sales Department, Good Books, 307 West 36th Street, 11th Floor, New York, NY 10018 or info@skyhorsepublishing.com.

Good Books is an imprint of Skyhorse Publishing, Inc.®, a Delaware corporation.

Visit our website at www.goodbooks.com.

10 9 8 7 6 5 4 3 2 1

Library of Congress Cataloging-in-Publication Data is available on file.

ISBN: 978-1-68099-398-1
eBook ISBN: 978-1-68099-399-8

Cover design by Abigail Gehring

Printed in the United States of America

Contents

The
LITTLE AMISH
MATCHMAKER

Chapter One

HE GRIPPED THE HANDLEBAR OF HIS FLEET red scooter with one hand, reached up and smashed his straw hat down on his thick brown hair as far as it would go, hunkered down and prepared for the ascent.

Traverse Hill was no child's play, he knew. You had to stay sharp. Especially this morning, with the fine, hard snow just starting to drive in from the northeast, pinging against his face like midget cannonballs. They hurt.

His ears were two red lumps of ice. That was what happened if you didn't wear a beanie to school, but Dat frowned on them, saying he never wore one. In his day, you wore your Amish hat to go to school, not a beanie, which in his view, was still the law, or *ordnung*, of the church.

He said this in the same level way he said everything: that half smile, the gentleness, the genuine
kindness that was always in his voice.

Isaac had never heard Dat raise his voice in anger.
He was firm, but always kind. *Ordnung* mattered to
him. His family was raised to be conservative, strictly
adhering to the old ways, never judging others who
were less stringent.

Isaac thought Dat was a lot like God. He wanted
your obedience, but it came easy, being loved the way
Isaac was.

Sometimes, Isaac would have liked to have a beanie,
or a red shirt that had faint stripes in it, or a pair of suspenders with prints on them, gray or navy blue or red.
But it was not Dat's way. Or Mam's for that matter.

Mam was a lot like Dat, only she talked too much.
She said the same thing over and over, which usually
drove Isaac a little crazy, but Mam was just busy being Mam.

When Mam milked the cows, she lifted those
heavy milkers as handily as Dat, her red men's ker-
chief tied the whole way over her brown hair, her

cheeks round and flushed, her green eyes snapping, always whistling or singing or talking.

Isaac's eyes were green, like Mam's. His last name was Stoltzfus, and he lived in Lancaster County, where a bunch of Amish people lived, making up a large community of plain folks, all members of the Old Order. Isaac was the youngest son in a family of 10 children. All of them were baptized, the older ones married in the Amish church. Seven sisters and two brothers.

Jonas got married to Priscilla a year ago in December. Mam said wasn't that the most wonderful thing, attending your son's wedding, being the guest of honor and not having to do a single, solitary thing all day except eat and sing German hymns, which, after talking, was Mam's favorite thing to do.

The other Stoltzfus brother, Simon, was still at home. He was 21, and worked with Dat on the farm. The German version of Simon's name was "Sim," or "Simmy," but since he was older, they called him Sim. He was already a member of the church, so he was never very disobedient.

Isaac was in seventh grade, attending Hickory Grove School, a one-room parochial school nestled in a grove of maple trees on the edge of Leroy Zook's farm. There were 22 pupils. The teacher's name was Catherine Speicher, and she was about the prettiest, sweetest girl he had ever met.

Isaac didn't think girls were of much account. Not one of them had any common sense. They shrieked hysterically about nothing and sniffed in the most annoying manner when you traded arithmetic papers to check in class. They sniffed because they were mad that they had more wrong than he did. But they weren't allowed to say anything, so they drew air in through their noses and batted their eyelashes, giving their faces something to do if they weren't allowed to speak.

Girls were all the same, in Isaac's opinion.

Except this new teacher, Catherine Speicher. She could stay quiet. Common sense rested on her shoulders, and she wore it like a fine cape. She was excellent with those squirmy little first-graders. Isaac had to be careful or he'd get carried away, watching her animated face as she explained letters and numbers to the little ones.

She was fancy, in a way. She wore bright colors and combed her blond hair a bit straighter, not rolled in as sleekly as his Mam or all his married sisters. Her eyes were so blue he thought they could be artificial, but Dat said those Speichers all had blue eyes, so he guessed they were the real thing. She was also kind, like Dat.

You could hardly disobey Dat and feel right about it. That was why Isaac wore his straw hat on weekday winter mornings. Dat was very frugal. Straw hats didn't cost as much as black felt hats, so his and Mam's boys wore straw hats, even in winter, except for more important times like church and funerals and maybe school Christmas programs.

Isaac's plastic Rubbermaid lunch box rattled in the wire basket attached to his handlebars, and the wind whistled in his cold ears. The front brim of his hat jigged up and down. He closed his eyes to mere slits, enough to watch where he was going but nothing much besides. As he swooped to the bottom of the hill, his pace slowed, and he saw the dark forms of his classmates arriving from each direction.

The schoolhouse was hunkered down under the maple trees, its yellowish stucco walls withstanding the snow and cold, the same as it always had. There were paper candy canes and holly on the windows, the red and green colors looking so much like Christmas, especially now that it was snowing this morning. The Christmas program was only a month away, which sent little knots of excitement dancing in his stomach. School programs were nerve-wracking.

"Hey, Professor!" Calvin Beiler waved from his scooter, his gray beanie pulled low over his ears.

"Morning, Calvin!" Isaac yelled back.

Isaac was used to being called "Professor." It started as a joke, when he was fitted with a pair of eyeglasses, Mam taking him to Lancaster City to an eye specialist when he had trouble seeing the blackboard. His glasses were sturdy but plain, a bit rounder than he would have liked, but Mam said they were serviceable, strong and very expensive, meaning he had better be careful with them.

So because Isaac could multiply in his head, recite the Beatitudes in German, say "The Village Blacksmith" without missing a word ever since he was in fourth grade and was always at the top of his class, they started calling him "Professor."

He was secretly pleased.

He had found out early on you couldn't brag about it. That simply didn't work. You kept your mouth shut about your grades, learned to praise others and then everyone liked you.

"Didn't your ears freeze coming down that hill?"

"Oh, they're cold." Isaac grinned, rubbing them with his gloved hands.

Calvin grinned back, and nothing more was said. It was okay. Calvin's parents were more liberal, allowing more stylish things like different colored sneakers with white on them, which looked really sharp. But somehow it never bothered either of them that Isaac wore black sneakers, plain all over. They just liked each other a lot.

They both loved baseball, fishing and driving ponies. Calvin's parents raised miniature ponies, but he had a Shetland pony named Streak that was the color of oatmeal with a caramel-colored mane and tail.

Isaac had four ponies. He was very good with the ponies, Dat said, but only Calvin knew about Dat saying that, because it would be bragging to tell anyone else.

Best friends knew you through and through. You didn't have to be afraid of anything at all. Whatever you said or did was acceptable, and if it wasn't, then Calvin would say so, which was also acceptable. Or the other way around.

Like trading food. Isaac's Mam raised huge neck pumpkins, not the round orange kind that everyone thinks of when you say pumpkin. Neck pumpkins were greenish brown, or butterscotch-colored, shaped like a huge gourd. Or a duck or goose.

Mam tapped them, picked them, peeled and cooked them. Then she cold-packed the mounds of orange pumpkin, set the jars away in the canning cellar and made the best, custardy, shivery-high pumpkin pies anyone ever had.

Calvin would trade the entire contents of his lunch box for one large slice of that pie. Isaac never took it, of course, just taking one of Calvin's chocolate Tastycakes, those little packages of cupcakes Mam would never buy. Or his potato chips, and sometimes both. Then if Calvin got too hungry at last recess, Isaac would share his saltines with peanut butter and marshmallow cream.

When the bell rang, Teacher Catherine stood by the bell pull inside the front door, smiling, nodding, saying good morning. She was wearing a royal-blue dress and cape, her black apron pinned low on her waist. Her white covering was a bit heart-shaped and lay on her ears, the strings tied in a loose bow on the front of her cape.

Her cheeks were a high color, a testimony to her own cold walk to school, probably shouldering that huge, green backpack like always.

Isaac hung up his homemade black coat, putting his hat on the shelf. He ran his fingers through his thick hair, shook his head to settle it away from his forehead and slid into his desk.

Ruthie Allgyer slid into hers across the aisle, never turning her head once to acknowledge his presence.

Fine with me, Isaac cast a sidelong glance in her direction. He decided anew that girls were an unhandy lot. There she was, her eyebrows lifted with anxiety, a tiny mirror already held to her face as she scraped at a gross-looking pimple with a fingernail.

Yuck. He swallowed, looked away.

"Good morning, boys and girls!"

"Good morning, Teacher!"

The chorus from the mouths of 22 children was a benediction for Teacher Catherine, who glowed as if there was a small sun somewhere in her face, then bent her blond head to begin reading a chapter of the Bible. Her voice was low, strong and steady, pronouncing even "Leviticus" right. His teacher was a wonder.

Ruthie sniffed, coughed, stuck her whole head into her desk to find a small package of Kleenexes, extracted one after a huge rumpus, then blew her nose with the most horrendous wet rattle he had ever heard.

Isaac winced, concentrating on the Bible story.

They rose, recited the Lord's Prayer in English, then sang a fast-paced good morning song as they all streamed to the front of the classroom, picking up the homemade songbooks as they passed the stack.

Ruthie stood beside Isaac, so he had to share a songbook. She was still digging around with that dubious Kleenex, snorting and honking dry little sounds of pure annoyance, so he leaned to the right as far as he could and held the songbook with thumb and forefinger.

His shoulder bumped against Hannah Fisher's, and she glared self-righteously straight into his eyes, so he hove to the left only a smidgen, stood on his tiptoes and stared straight up to the ceiling, the only safe place.

He certainly hoped girls would change in the next 10 years, or he'd never be able to get married. Girls like Teacher Catherine only came along once in about 20 years, he reasoned.

He had a strong suspicion his brother Sim was completely aware of this as well.

For one thing, Sim had offered to bring the gang mower to mow the schoolyard back in August. A

gang mower was a bunch of reel mowers attached
to a cart with a seat on it, and shafts to hitch a horse
into. It was the Amish alternative to a gas-powered
riding mower, and a huge nuisance, in Isaac's opinion. By the time you caught a horse in the pasture
and put the harness and bridle on him, you could
have mowed half the grass with an ordinary reel
mower. Isaac had caught Sim currycombing his best
Haflinger, Jude, the prancy one. Then Sim gave Isaac
the dumbest answer ever when he asked why he was
hitching Jude to the gang mower instead of Dolly,
who was far more dependable.

Besides using Jude, Sim had showered and then
dressed in a sky-blue Sunday shirt which, to Isaac's
way of thinking, was totally uncalled for.

He even used cologne. Now if that wasn't a sure
sign that you noticed someone, Isaac didn't know
what was.

It was a wonder he hadn't taken a rag to the mower blades. Polished them up.

Sim stayed till dark, even. Got himself a drink
at the hydrant by the porch when Catherine was

sweeping the soapy water across the cement, just so he could say hello to her.

Isaac was going to have to talk to Sim, see if he could arrange something.

That whole scenario had been way back before school started, when all the parents came to scrub and scour, wax the tile floor, mow and trim the schoolyard, paint the fence, repair anything broken, all in preparation for the coming term.

They wouldn't have had to use the gang mower. Weed-eaters did a terrific job, especially if 10 or 11 of them whined away at once.

But Isaac supposed if you wanted attention from a pretty teacher, a prancing Haflinger and a blue shirt would help.

Before they began arithmetic class, Teacher Catherine announced she had all the copies ready for the Christmas program. Amid excited ooh's, quiet hand-clapping, and bouncing scholars in their seats, she began by handing the upper-graders their copies of the Christmas plays.

Isaac's heart began a steady, dull acceleration, as if he was running uphill with his scooter.

Would he be in a play?

Oh, he hoped. There was nothing in all the world he loved more than being in a Christmas play. He was as tall as the eighth-grade boys. Almost, anyway. Sim was tall. He was over six feet, with green eyes and dark skin. Isaac thought he looked a lot like Sim, only a bit better around the nose.

Sure enough. A fairly thick packet was plopped on his desk.

"Isaac, do you think you can carry the main part of this play, being Mr. Abraham Lincoln? Ruthie will be Mrs. Lincoln."

Isaac looked up at Teacher Catherine, met those blue eyes and knew he would do anything for her, even have Ruthie as his wife in the Christmas play. When Catherine smiled and patted his shoulder, he smiled back, nodded his head and was so happy he could have turned cartwheels the whole way up the aisle to the blackboard.

Yes, he would have to talk to Sim.

Chapter Two

Outside, the snow kept driving against the buildings, the red barn standing like a sentry, guarding the white house, the round, tin-roofed corn crib and the red implement shed on the Samuel Stoltzfus farm.

Darkness had fallen, so the yellow lantern light shone in perfect yellow squares through the swirling snow, beacons of warmth and companionship. A large gray tomcat took majestic leaps through the drifts, making his way to the dairy barn where he knew a warm dish of milk would eventually be placed in front of him.

Heifers bawled, impatiently awaiting their allotment of pungent corn silage.

The Belgian workhorses clattered the chains attached to their thick leather halters, tossing their heads in anticipation as Isaac dug the granite bucket into the feed bin.

A bale of hay bounced down from the ceiling, immediately followed by another. Then a pair of brown boots and two sturdy legs followed, and Sim pounced like a cat, grabbing Isaac's shoulder.

"Gotcha!"

"You think you're scary? You're not." Isaac emptied the bucket of grain into Pet's box, then turned to face Sim. "Hey, why don't you ask Teacher Catherine for a date?"

No use beating around the bush, mincing words, hedging around, whatever you wanted to call it. Eventually, you'd have to say those words, so you may as well put them out there right away. Sort of like that gluey, slimy, toy stuff you threw against a wall and it stuck, then slowly climbed down, after you watched it hang on the wall for awhile.

The long silence that followed proved that Sim had heard his words. All the lime-green fluorescence of them.

Isaac hid a wide grin, shouldered another bucket of feed, calmly dumped it into Dan's wooden box, then turned and faced Sim squarely. In the dim light of the hissing gas lantern, swinging from the cast-iron hook that had hung there for generations, he was surprised to find Sim looking as if he was going to be sick.

Sim's face was whitish-green, his mouth hung open and he looked a lot like the bluegills did after you extracted the hook from their mouths and threw them on the green grass of the pond bank. Even his eyes were bulging.

"What's the matter?"

Sim closed his mouth, then opened it, but no words came out.

"Nothing can be that bad," Isaac said over his shoulder as he went to fill a bucket for Sam.

"Why in the world would I do something like that? In a thousand years she would never take me."

Isaac had no idea Sim was as spineless as that. Why couldn't he just approach her and ask? If she said no, then that was that. No harm done. At least he had tried.

"You think so?" is what Isaac said instead.

"Yes." Sim jerked his head up and down. "What would a girl like her want with … well, me? She's way above my class."

That was stupid. "There is no such thing as class. Not for me and Calvin."

"Well, there is for me." Sim reached out and tipped Isaac's straw hat. "I live in the real world. I know when I have a chance and when I don't."

Isaac bent over and picked up his hat, stuck it on top of his head, then smashed it down firmly. It felt right. That tight band around his head, just above his eyes, was a part of him, like breathing and laughing. His hat shaded the sun, kept angry bumblebees from attacking his hair, kept the rain and snow off, and if he wore it at a rakish angle, it made him look like an eighth-grader.

"Did you ask God for her? The way Mam says?" Isaac asked.

Sim dug in his pocket for his Barlow knife. He found it and flicked it open before bending to cut the baling twine around a bale of hay. "It's not right to ask God for a million dollars or a mansion or something to make you happy."

"Who said?"

Isaac leaned against the hand-hewn post, tipped

back his straw hat, stuck a long piece of hay in his mouth and chewed solemnly.

"But the thing is, you don't know. If it's God's will for your life, he might consider it."

Sim shook his head, mumbled something.

"What did you say?"

"Nothing you'd understand."

"Are you coming to the Christmas program?" Isaac asked.

"When is it?"

Isaac shrugged. "You could offer to fix the front door before then."

"Look, Ikey, give it up. She'd—"

"Stop calling me Ikey!"

"She'd never consider me. She's … just too … pretty and classy and awesome. Besides, she was dating Rube King."

Isaac lifted a finger, held it aloft. "Was! There's the word. Was!"

"Well, if she'd say yes, it would soon be a 'was!'"

Isaac knew defeat when he saw it, so he went to help Mam with the milking. He was cold and sleepy.

He wished chores were finished so he could go indoors and curl up on the couch with his Christmas play.

The cow stable was pungent, steamy and filled with the steady "chucka-chucka" sound of four, large, stainless-steel milkers extracting the milk from the sturdy, black and white Holsteins. His mother was bent beside a cow, wiping the udder with a purple cloth dipped in a disinfecting solution. She straightened with a grunt, smiled at him and asked if his chores were finished.

"The chickens yet."

"You might need a snow shovel. It was drifting around the door this afternoon already."

Isaac nodded and then bent his head, prepared to meet the onslaught awaiting him the minute he opened the cow-stable door. It did no good. A gigantic puff of wind clutched his hat and sent it spinning off into the icy, whirling darkness. He felt his hair stand straight up, then whip to the left, twisting to the right. No use looking for his hat now. He had better take care of the chickens.

Isaac's heart sank when he saw the snowdrift. No way could he get into that chicken house without shoveling. He retraced his steps, found the shovel and met the cold head-on once more. His ears stung painfully as his hair tossed about wildly. This was no ordinary snowstorm; it was more like a blizzard. Likely there would be no school tomorrow.

He was able to wedge his way into the chicken house through the small opening, quickly opening the water hydrant and scattering laying mash into the long, tin trough. He fluffed up the dry shavings the hens had thrown in the corner. Then Isaac made a headlong dive out of the warmth of the henhouse, wading through knee-high snow to the house.

He was surprised to see Dat on the front porch, kicking snow off his chore boots.

"You done already?" he asked his father.

"No, Sim's finishing. Levi Beiler came over, riding his horse. They need help at the Speicher home."

"Speicher? Teacher Catherine?"

Dat nodded soberly.

"What happened?"

"I'm not sure."

That sort of answer was no answer at all, but Isaac knew it meant he did not need to know, that he should go into the house and ask no questions. When Dat laid a reassuring hand on his shoulder and Isaac looked up, Dat's eyes were warm in the light from the kitchen.

"You think you'll ever find your hat?"

Dat's hand spread a whole new warmth through him, a comfort, an understanding.

"I have another one. My school hat." He fixed himself a large saucepan of Mam's homemade hot cocoa mix and milk. The whole saucepanful ran over, hissing and bubbling into the burner, turning the blue gas flame orange. Isaac jumped up and flipped the burner off, salvaging his warm drink. He dumped the hot cocoa into a mug that said Snoopy on it. Mam loved yard sales. She had a whole collection of funny mugs which made Dat smile.

Mam came in, went to the wash house and kicked around to get her boots off, all to the tune of "God Rest Ye Merry Gentlemen."

He was proud of Mam. She was one smart lady. Not very many Amish people knew that song, but she did. She knew lots of things. She knew what Orthodox Jews were, and synagogues, and she knew who the leader of Cuba was. She explained dictatorship to Isaac, and Dat hid his head behind the *Botschaft* for a long time when Isaac said his teacher was a dictator. That, of course, was before Catherine Speicher.

He wrapped both hands around the Snoopy mug of hot cocoa, took a sip and burned his tongue.

Mam came through the door, taking off her apron, sniffing and asking what was burning.

"The cocoa ran over."

Mam frowned. She hurried to the stove, peered at the blackened burner, and then bent for her tall green container of Comet. "Tsk, tsk. Should have wiped it off, Ikey. This is quite a blizzard. There are no cars moving at all. The snowplow is going, though, so I'm sure they'll keep some of the roads open."

Mam was basically doing what she did best, talking. No matter if Isaac didn't reply, she rattled on anyway. "Sim went with Dat. They're having trouble with their water pump. At least that's what I thought he said. Don't know why Sim had to go. You'd think Dat and Abner could handle it. Well, see, they can't run out of water. Those calves and heifers they raise need water. Isaac, what are you reading? School stuff? Christmas plays, I bet. You know I'm not allowed to see it. Just tell me the title. Is it a play? Are you hungry? I'm going to eat a chocolate whoopie pie. I made them this afternoon. You want one to dip in your cocoa? Better not dip it. Whoopie pies fall apart, they're so soft."

By the time she reached the pantry, she was singing again, partly under her breath, a sort of humming with words. She was carrying a large rectangular Tupperware container with a gold-colored lid, one Isaac knew contained either whoopie pies or chocolate chip cookies. Sometimes she made pumpkin or oatmeal whoopie pies, but she always had to put some of them in the freezer for sister's day. Her boys just weren't so *schlim* (fond of) pumpkin or oatmeal.

"Guess none of these will last for sister's day, huh?" Mam said, as she kept talking while pouring herself a glass of creamy milk. Isaac raised his eyebrows, knowing Mam wouldn't expect an answer.

Sister's day was a regularly occurring hazard, in his opinion. First of all were those 18 nieces and nephews to contend with. All his Legos, model ships, harmonicas and BB guns had to be stowed into hiding. His sisters sat around the table and ate, drank endless quantities of coffee, discussed either people or food and didn't watch their offspring one bit.

Especially Bennie. That little guy could do with a good paddling from his dat, not his mam. Isaac told him a dozen times to leave that wooden duck decoy alone, the one that sat on his chest of drawers, but inevitably Bennie would climb up on his bed, then his clothes hamper, and get that decoy down. Every time. Isaac told Mam, which did absolutely no good. Mam's head was stuffed full of babies and recipes and songs and time on the clock and all kinds of troubles. Some things in life you were better off shutting your mouth about and not caring so much. It was only a wooden duck.

But if Bennie ran with the wild crowd in his *rumspringa* years, they couldn't say they hadn't been warned. He'd done his best.

He yawned, rubbed his eyes, then reached for a whoopie pie. Slowly, he dug at the Saran Wrap, uncovering half of it, then sank his teeth into the chocolatey goodness.

"Better get in the shower. Be sure and brush your teeth. Don't forget to brush for a whole minute," Mam called.

That, too, was a ridiculous thing. If you brushed your teeth for 60 seconds, you ended up swallowing all the toothpaste, which could not be good for your digestive system. So he never timed himself, just brushed awhile.

Isaac's last thought was wondering what was going on at the Speichers before he fell asleep.

Chapter Three

It was unbelievable, but in the morning, the light was still gray, the air stinging with brutish, icy snow. They did the chores swiftly, shoveling drifts from doorways, opening frozen water pipes with propane torches.

No school, of course, although Isaac knew they could have, so it would be a sort of holiday. Horses pulling a carriage or sleigh could get through deep snow, but most horses were terrified of snowplows. With this amount still coming down, those clattering monsters with yellow blinking lights and chains rattling would be plowing the drifting snow back into place. It was better to take the day off.

Isaac never found out when Sim came home, and he didn't bother asking about the trouble at the Speichers. Sim was a puzzle. His eyes were way too

bright, almost feverish, and yet he looked completely
miserable. Isaac figured he'd have all day to corner
Sim, which he fully intended to do.

Mam made fried cornmeal mush, stewed crackers,
puddin's and fried eggs for breakfast.

"*Mush und levva vosht.* (Mush and puddin's)
Nothing better on a cold winter day," Dat said, gazing warmly at Mam. Her cheeks flushed like red apples as she basked in his praise.

Isaac squirted homemade ketchup all over his
stewed crackers, then cut a bit of fried egg and laid it
on top. Shoveling it onto his fork, he wedged it into
his mouth, then bit off a corner of his toast spread
with homemade raspberry jelly and watched Sim's
face.

Seriously, that poor guy was in a bad way. He
didn't even talk.

Dat opened the subject, saying Abner Speicher
was taken to the hospital, with a bad case of pneu-
monia, only worse. He wasn't sure what it was; viral
something. A few hours later their water pump gave
out, leaving the calves in the veal barn without water.

Dat hated gossip. He never belittled anyone, but Isaac could see he was choosing his words carefully, trying hard not to disparage his neighbor. Not everyone had the same work ethic as Dat, nor owned three farms. Dat was very humble in that respect, teaching his sons to never speak of the farms he possessed.

He asked Sim if they wanted to have a working day at the Speichers, sort of a frolic.

When Sim choked on his mush and had to swallow some juice, then choked on the acidic drink, Isaac burst out laughing uproariously. Sim smacked his arm, but Isaac kept on laughing.

Dat and Mam were clueless, the expressions on their faces much the same as the duck decoy on his chest of drawers.

While their parents drank their coffee, Isaac and Sim went to the basement for some cider. As soon as they were out of earshot, Isaac crowed triumphantly. "Do you think you should have a frolic at the Speichers?" then scampered behind the Ping-Pong table before Sim could catch him.

Sim shook his head, telling him he was too big for his britches.

"Did she help you fix the water pump?"

"No."

"Did you go into the house?"

"Yes."

"Did you see her?"

"Yes."

"Did you talk to her?"

"Of course not. Her mother made coffee and set out some kind of cupcakes."

"Did you eat one?"

Without answering, Sim asked, "Is Catherine shy?"

"No. Not one bit. She's just right."

That was the end of the conversation. Sim would not say one more word, taking the jar of home-canned cider upstairs and heating it, his thoughts clearly a million miles away.

They hitched Pet and Dan to the bobsled, that ancient, hazardous rattletrap half hidden in the hay-mow with loose hay and cobwebs. They swept the bobsled clean, rubbed it with moist old cloths, spread clean straw on the bed, oiled the runners and springs, fixed the seat with two extra screws, then settled bales of hay covered with buggy blankets behind the front seat.

Isaac was allowed to wear one of Sim's beanies, Dat saying a storm like this was a rare and wonderful thing, but not to expect to wear one always. They were worldly, in his opinion, but you needed to exercise common sense on a day like this.

Isaac couldn't express his feeling of absolute happiness, sitting up there beside Sim, wearing the beanie he wore to play hockey. He felt like a true king reigning over his subjects. Not one thing could go wrong.

Pet and Dan were both the same color, a light caramel with lighter manes and tails. They were brushed to sleek perfection, the black well-oiled harness slapping against their rounded haunches as they broke into a heavy, clumsy trot, their hooves making a dull "thok-thoking" sound against the snow. Their manes were so heavy they broke apart on top of their massive necks, then jiggled back and forth with each step.

It was snowing still. Isaac bent his head to avoid the stinging flakes, but after a few miles he became used to it. They picked up Calvin and his sister Martha and gave them a ride, making a wide circle before depositing them on their driveway again. They picked up some chicken feed at the hardware store in Bird-In-Hand, then turned to go back home.

Isaac was checking out the new sign in front of the bakery when he heard Sim yell, "Whoa!"

He turned to look down into the astonished eyes of his teacher.

"Do you need a ride?"

In disbelief, Isaac watched as his beloved teacher's eyes filled with quick tears.

"Oh, I do. I'm so glad to see someone. Anyone! Our water isn't coming again. The calves are bawling, and I was going to walk to the firehouse for help."

Quickly, Isaac scrambled to the back and sat primly on a hay bale with his hands clasped jubilantly on his knees. Now she would have to sit beside Sim.

She took Sim's proffered hand, sat down gingerly, and turned to look at him, saying, "You have no idea how glad I am to see you. I'm just desperate. My mam can't go out in this, and I can see the roads are all but impassable."

Sim only nodded, and Isaac thought, Oh, come on now, say something.

"I hope we don't meet a snowplow," Catherine said.

"These horses should be okay. They're used to just about anything."

Isaac pumped the air with his fist, quickly folding it into his other hand when Catherine turned, saying, "Hey, Isaac! I took your seat."

In the distance, they heard the ominous rattling of chains, the dragon let out of his lair, that abominable snowplow. Sim tightened his grip on the reins; Isaac could tell by the squaring of his shoulders. The humongous yellow vehicle rolled into view, spraying a mountain of white snow to the side, chains squeaking and rattling. Pet and Dan lifted their heads, pricked their ears forward, while Catherine grabbed Sim's arm with one hand, stifling a scream with the other.

Perfect! Just perfect!

Isaac knew these Belgians wouldn't do much, if anything, and sure enough, they plodded on as the monstrous truck rattled by.

"Sorry! I'm so sorry," Catherine said.

Sim grinned down at her, saying, "That's all right, Catherine. I wouldn't mind meeting another one."

Yes!

Up went Isaac's fist, then he brought it down and banged it against his knee, squeezing his eyes shut as he dipped his head.

And they still had to fix the water pump.

Isaac had to walk to school the following morning. The sun was dazzling, the whole world covered in a cold, white blanket of snow. The wind moaned about the house, sending gigantic clouds of whirling snow off rooftops and trees, across hills and onto the roads, especially where there was an embankment to the west.

Scootering was out of the question, that was sure. He tied his lunch box to the old wooden sled. He had greased the runners with the rectangular block of paraffin that Mam used to stiffen her white coverings when she washed and ironed them. This sled used to be Dat's, and it was the undisputed leader of all the sleds at Hickory Grove School.

Teacher Catherine greeted him from her desk with the usual "Good morning, Isaac." He was a bit disappointed, the way she said it sort of quieter than usual, then dropped her head and immediately became quite busy.

Had she seen all that fist-pumping? He certainly hoped not.

Hannah Fisher had only one problem wrong in arithmetic class, and he had 100%, which sent Dora Esh into a spasm of sniffing and carrying on. She even raised her hand and asked if it was wrong if Isaac had boxes instead of cartons for a story problem, trying to make him lose his 100%. Then when Teacher Catherine said it was all right, that the problem had both boxes and cartons in it, she looked as if she was going to start bawling, blinking her eyes like that and getting all red in the face.

Someone should straighten these girls out.

All day, Teacher Catherine acted strangely. Even at recess while sledding, she seemed a bit stiff, her movements calculated, almost self-conscious. He caught her watching him do his English, and when he looked up, she quickly looked away.

That was odd.

But, he supposed, you couldn't get away from the fact that no matter how much he admired his teacher, she was a girl, and they all had a tendency to be strange at times.

You just couldn't figure them out.

Take last evening while they were fixing the pump at Speichers. Sim had soon become aware of the problem, but they had to pull the water pump. Catherine had helped gamely. She watched as Sim tightened something, primed it, stopped and started it, then lowered it and told them to open a spigot somewhere and let it run for awhile until the water ran clear.

She hadn't invited them in.

Just stood out there by the old windmill and talked to Sim. Isaac was freezing. He was hungry. Why couldn't they go inside and have a cupcake? They weren't laughing or having fun at all. They just talked boring stuff about hospitals and her dat and *all mosa.* (alms) He thought Catherine was sort of crying at one point, but he got cold and climbed on the bob-sled and covered himself up real good with the buggy blanket.

Once, he peeped out over, and they were still standing there, only closer yet, and Sim's head was going to fall off his shoulders if he leaned forward any more than that.

You couldn't date a girl without laughing, ever. Isaac's toes were so cold he stuck them under the hay bale and got steadily angrier. Just when he thought he was going to die of cold and starvation, alone on that bobsled, he heard footsteps, a "Good-night!" and they were off.

He told Sim what he thought, too, and Sim called him "little buddy" and put an arm around his shoulder. Sim said he was sorry it took so long, then burst into some hymn about how great is our God.

Isaac didn't appreciate being called little buddy, either. He was as tall as the eighth-graders, and told Sim so. Then Sim got all emotional about that, so

Isaac was thoroughly turned off by the time he got into the warm kitchen.

They ate by the light of the kerosene light: beef stew kept warm in the gas oven, thick with soft buttery dumplings, piles of sweet applesauce, and slice after slice of homemade bread and church peanut butter. Joes had church at their place, and his sister Naomi made a whole batch of the spread. She told Mam that was way too much, that next time she was going to use only two jars of marshmallow cream. Well, at least they had church peanut butter, which was by far the best thing ever.

They practiced for the Christmas program in the afternoon at school. Isaac sincerely hoped Abraham Lincoln liked his wife better than he liked Ruthie.

She acted so dumb. She was supposed to look at him when she spoke her lines, but she looked at his right suspender. He checked it to make sure there was nothing wrong with it, like a stink bug sitting on it, but it just looked like his left suspender, unless the stink bug had flown off. They could fly. He told Calvin that once, and he said, yeah, every time a stink bug flew around the propane gas lamp his mam would scream and point and back away, saying it would put a hole in the mantle and burn the house down. Isaac really laughed about that.

The practicing went terribly wrong.

He pitied Teacher Catherine. She kept a brave face, but no one spoke loud enough, they all droned their lines in a sort of monotone and Ruthie said "Heerod" for King Herod, then got all red-faced and muttery when Teacher Catherine corrected her.

It was a good thing they still had over three weeks to practice.

When Isaac yelled "Bye, Teacher!" at the end of the day, she was staring absent-mindedly out the window at the flying snow and didn't hear him.

Chapter Four

THE SUN SHONE, THE WINDS MELLOWED and the days turned into fine winter weather, the kind that are blissful for sledding.

Recess was never long enough. Teacher Catherine was kind enough to allow an extra 30 minutes on Friday, but told them the Christmas program was more important than sledding, and they still had a long way to go.

Isaac knew that was true. They didn't talk plainly. Most of the students spoke in resounding tones, but their words jammed together until no one could understand very well what the poem was about.

How to tell them to speak clearly without being insulting? Teacher Catherine took to pacing the floor, adjusting the shoulders of her cape unnecessarily, sliding her sleeves above the elbow and gripping one forearm with the other until her knuckles turned white.

When it was Isaac's turn to recite his 14-verse poem, he faced the classroom squarely, lifted his chin and spoke in the best way he could possibly muster.

It's Christmas tonight.

The hills are alight,

With the wonderful star of God's love.

On and on he intoned the words of Jesus' birth. They were well-spoken, perfect and he knew it. Teacher Catherine nodded her head, praised him for his clear speech and asked the rest of the class to follow his example. He knew his face was turning a hateful shade of pink as he made his way back to his desk, so he watched the glossy floor tiles closely, wishing his bangs were longer still. Calvin grinned openly and raised his eyebrows.

They practiced three songs, which went well, especially "Joy to the World," which started on a high note. Everyone knew most of the words, and the voices rollicked along together in holiday harmony, which really perked up Teacher Catherine's mood.

After that, little first-grader Eli said his poem in a voice only a decibel above a whisper, his voice shaking with nervous tension. Isaac knew the teacher would not be able to correct him, Eli being so close to tears.

Christmas programs were tough. You had to walk that delicate balance of praise and admonishment, nurturing and controlling.

Ruthie Allgyer sniffed, ducked her head and searched for the ever-present plastic packet of Kleenexes.

Isaac looked out the window and observed Elam King hauling manure with his mules, their large heads wagging in unison, their ears flapping back and forth in their ungainly fashion, as if they were much too big for their heads. He shouldn't be hauling manure. The snow was too deep, adding to the heavy load on the spreader.

Dat said it was hard for the horses to keep their footing, so instead they'd get ready to butcher the five hogs in the shed next week. Isaac knew he'd be cleaning the kettles, and sharpening knives and saw blades in anticipation of the butchering.

When he looked back to the front of the classroom, he was shocked to see Ruthie Allgyer standing in complete misery, her face red with exertion, her mouth working, devoid of any sound at all.

Isaac couldn't watch.

He heard a sob, and a wave of heat washed over him. His heart lurched, feeling her embarrassment keenly. His fingers trace a carved R on his desktop, as he heard Teacher Catherine say kindly, "Ruthie, you may go back to your seat."

Ruthie bent her head, held the white Kleenex to her face and pushed her feet along the floor in humiliation. She slid wretchedly into her desk, folded her arms on the top and buried her face into them as she cried softly.

Isaac couldn't believe it.

Ruthie Allgyer, of all people!

She stuttered?

When had that all started? She hadn't stuttered last year. He remembered everyone saying their poems, Ruthie among them.

Hannah Fisher was next, so she started in her singsong roar. She spoke so loudly you couldn't even hear the words, then plucked the shoulders of her dress in the most self-assured manner it set Isaac's teeth on edge. Well, that Hannah could be set back a notch, in his opinion. Dat said pride went before a fall, so she better watch it.

Isaac pitied Ruthie so badly. He would be extra kind to her, maybe even say something encouraging at recess if he got a chance.

Maybe she dreaded the Christmas program because she had a stuttering problem that was only visible if she had to speak to a crowd. Maybe that was why she looked so anxious and picked her face.

The students colored bells, candy canes and candles, and hung up letters that said, "Merry Christmas." They made paper chains with red and green construction paper and hung them from the four corners of the ceiling to the middle.

There was no Christmas tree and no Santa Claus anywhere. The Amish *ordnung* did not permit either one. Santa Claus was a myth, and Christmas trees were too fancy or worldly and were frowned upon.

The Amish believed in gift-giving because the wise men brought gifts to the Baby Jesus, and God gave the greatest gift of all when he gave the world his son. But presenting gifts was to be done *in maus und maz-ich-keit* (with common sense) and not to follow the ways of the world with very large gifts no one could afford.

That, too, varied in each household. Isaac's parents were conservative with their gifts, giving one package to each child, usually something useful.

Calvin got five or six packages, things Dat would deem frivolous. Calvin had a Game Boy with a pile of expensive games, something Isaac could only dream about.

It wasn't that he wouldn't have enjoyed having one, it was just the way of it. When you knew something was truly off limits, there was no getting around it. You just read the *Outdoor Life*, ate your whoopie pie and drank milk in the evening and didn't even think about a Game Boy.

Sometimes he felt left out, just a bit, when Calvin and Michael, the other eighth-grade boy, would discuss the games or bring one to school to trade with each other. But not for long. Calvin would always return to Isaac, saying he'd never have a sled that would beat Isaac's old wooden Lightning Flyer, and then Isaac's whole world righted itself.

At recess, Isaac was waiting in line to fill his drinking cup at the water hydrant when Ruthie stepped behind him. Turning around, Isaac faced her squarely and said, "Ruthie, you don't have to be ashamed. Did you know a whole pile of people struggle with not being able to talk in front of a crowd?"

At first anger flashed in her big brown eyes, but then she bobbed her head in acknowledgment. Isaac had never noticed she had freckles on her dark skin.

"Seriously, Ruthie, you can do it. Just don't get so nervous."

"I'm not nervous."

"What is it then?"

Ruthie shrugged her shoulders.

"Did you talk to your mam?"

"Of course not."

"Maybe she could help you."

"I'd never tell my mam."

"Why?"

A shrug of the shoulders and Ruthie fled. So much for that. He knew he could help her. He had read about that somewhere. He'd ask Sim, too.

On Saturday, they attended a Christmas horse sale in New Holland. Isaac had barely been allowed to go along, not having swept the loose hay in the forebay the way Dat wanted him to. He had been sternly lectured, the big calloused hand coming down on his shoulder afterward, saying there was no room in the buggy tomorrow morning for boys who didn't listen.

Isaac had blinked tears of humiliation and pushed the stiff bristled broom like a person possessed, bending his back low with the effort.

He hated displeasing Dat. It was just that he had practiced shooting at tin cans with his BB gun, hitting them dead center in the end, after the winter light had faded to gray. Then supper was ready, and he forgot about the forebay.

That, and Sim had really made him mad, mooning around the barn with his eyes rolling around in his head like a coon hound. He couldn't even focus them right, cutting his finger with his pocketknife when he opened the twine on the bales of straw. Then Sim blamed Isaac for taking too long watering the pigs.

"Do you have any idea how much water five pigs can drink?" Isaac had shouted, sending a good-sized snowball flying in Sim's direction.

When Sim turned around and started after him, Isaac clapped his straw hat on his head and took off, slipping and sliding, sheer terror lending acceleration to his booted feet. Sim grabbed his coat collar, hauled him back, rolled him in the snow and washed his face thoroughly, the snow melting in icy rivulets down his green shirt collar.

They sat together then. Isaac wiped his face with his coat sleeve and told Sim he was lucky he wasn't wearing his glasses, or he'd end up paying for a new pair. Sim laughed and asked how his day at school went.

"Catherine looked extra pretty, thank you very much," Isaac answered, narrowing his eyes.

"I didn't ask about her."

"You did. You don't care about my day one bit. Catherine is also having a hard time with this Christmas program. I'm the only one who says his poem right."

"I bet."

"I'm serious."

Sim smiled.

"But that poor Ruthie. You know, Levi Allgyer's Ruthie. She's in my grade, and she couldn't say her poem. Her face was so red, Sim. It was painful to watch. The words just wouldn't come out."

"What did Catherine do?"

"She was so kind. She just asked Ruthie to go to her seat, and I saw them talking at recess."

Then Sim's eyes got all stupid again, his mouth lopsided and wobbly, and he didn't hear Isaac when he asked if it was true that you could help someone with a stuttering problem.

"Right, you can?" Isaac asked louder.

"Yeah."

But Isaac knew Sim hadn't heard him, so on the way to the horse sale, Isaac scooted forward from the back seat, stuck his head between Dat's and Sim's shoulders and pursued the subject of stuttering once again.

They had stopped at a red light on Route 23 in the town of New Holland. There was traffic everywhere, boxing them in, and Sam the driving horse was a bit too energetic to hold completely still, waiting for that light to change. He hopped up and down on his front feet, so Dat had to hold a steady rein and didn't answer until the light turned green and they could surge forward with the traffic.

Dat reached down and turned the right-turn signal on after they had moved swiftly for about a block before he answered. "You'd think one of Levi's daughters wouldn't have that problem. He's quite a talker."

"I read somewhere that you can help people who stutter. You get them to talk very slowly. Or something like that." Isaac said this a bit hesitantly, afraid Sim would laugh, but he didn't, just nodding his head in agreement.

Horse sales were magical. The flat, long, white buildings were surrounded by vehicles, trailers and black carriages belonging to the Mennonites who drive buggies, the Joe Wengers, as they were known by the Amish. They lived side by side in unity, but the Joe Wengers were an entirely different sect of plain people. The Amish buggies were gray with black wheels; that's how you told them apart.

White fences divided the pens of horses and ponies. Motors hummed, people talked and the auctioneer could be heard from the vast sea of concrete that was the parking lot. The horses milled about, whinnying, tossing their heads.

Dat gave Isaac a five-dollar bill for his lunch. It wasn't enough, but Isaac was ashamed to tell Dat, so he asked Sim for more.

Sim raised his eyebrows. "You can buy a hot dog with five dollars."

"Not French fries and Mountain Dew."

Sim shook his head but extracted his wallet and handed him five one-dollar bills. "You can't go to a horse sale without buying candy and chewing gum."

Isaac couldn't believe it. Another five dollars! At the most he had planned on another dollar, maybe two.

"Hey, thanks, Sim." He ran off before Sim changed his mind.

He'd drink all the Mountain Dew he wanted. That was the best drink anyone had ever invented. He could drink a gallon and never tire of it. Mam said it was not good for little boys, rotting their teeth and supplying too much sugar and caffeine, but Isaac couldn't see the difference in drinking a few cans of the delicious soda, or sitting around at sister's day drinking pot after pot of coffee. They were like camels at a watering trough, never getting enough, those sisters.

Isaac sized up the dollar bill, turning George Washington's head the same way it was imprinted on the Pepsi machine. He held his breath as it gobbled the dollar, then whirred softly, and with a clattering sound his green and red can of Mountain Dew rolled into the little tray.

Expertly, he popped the top, and turned to see Catherine Speicher watching him.

Chapter Five

IT WAS UNSETTLING, SORT OF.

Teachers were teachers in the classroom, dressed a certain way, always professional, sort of untouchable, set apart.

Here she was, standing in the bright December sun, her hair as light as an angel's, wearing a black coat fancier than the one she wore to school, with a red scarf thrown loosely over one shoulder.

Isaac held his Mountain Dew, then returned her smile, and said, "Hey, Teacher!"

She looked at him a moment longer, and for one mortifying second, he thought she was going to hug him. "Isaac! It's good to see you!"

"Yeah. You, too. You buying a horse?"

She laughed, adjusting her scarf.

"Actually, I am helping at the tack shop today. My friend Liz helps her dat when they're busy before Christmas."

"That's nice."

She hesitated for only a second, then asked, "Are you here by yourself?"

"No, I came with Dat and Sim."

Was it his imagination, or did her face change color only a bit? Perhaps it was the red scarf that gave her cheeks that glow.

He'd have to find Sim, which he accomplished in short order, weaving his way in and out of the crowd, searching the seating area where you could pretty much find someone easily, the seats stacked up the side of the room like bleachers at English peoples' stadiums.

There he was.

Isaac plopped himself in the seat beside Sim, and said, "Catherine Speicher is helping her friend Liz at the tack stand."

That got his attention.

He looked very nice, with that narrow-brimmed

straw hat he wore, turned down in the front and back with a piece of rawhide knotted around the crown instead of the black band that belonged there traditionally. A lot of the youth didn't wear hats, but Sim was older, a member of the church, and Dat's ways were deeply ingrained and respected.

Maybe, though, Catherine wouldn't match. For one instant, this flashed through Isaac's head. She was definitely not quite like Sim, and maybe Sim was right that he didn't stand a chance.

No, you just couldn't think along those lines. God wasn't like that. You just took a chance, went ahead and asked the question to see what happened.

"So, are you going to ask her for a date?" he asked, after a long swallow of the sweet soda.

"No, Isaac."

"Why not?"

"Because."

"That's no answer."

"Go away."

"Oh, come on, Sim. You big 'fraidy cat. Just go down to the tack stand and act like you need a new halter, and when she hands it to you, say, 'Could I come see you on Saturday evening at 8:00?'"

"It's not that easy!" Sim hissed. "And don't talk so loud."

Isaac found Tyler, the neighbor boy, who was horse-and-buggy Mennonite. He wore jeans and a thick coat with a zipper and a narrow-brimmed gray hat. Tyler talked with a different accent, although it was the same Pennsylvania Dutch that Isaac spoke.

They clambered up on the wooden fences, perched there and watched the horses milling about. Tyler said the horse dealers drugged the ponies so everyone thought they were safe, and once the drugs wore off, some of them were wild and vicious. Isaac said Dat never bought ponies at an auction, and Tyler said that was smart.

They got to the food stand early, and bought cheeseburgers and French fries and more Mountain Dew. They tapped the glass ketchup bottle hard and a whole glug of it clumped on to their fries, but that was fine with them. They loved ketchup.

They talked about school and Christmas and sleds.

Someone stopped at their table, and Isaac looked up to find Catherine Speicher with a tray of food.

"May I sit with you? The tables are all full."

"Sure."

Isaac slid over immediately, and she sat beside him.

"I'm starved; no breakfast."

She ate hungrily, saying nothing. Tyler's father came to get him, so that side of the table was empty, until Sim came in with his lunch and slid in opposite them.

Catherine stopped eating, then, and got all flustered and acted so dumb Isaac could not believe it.

Sim took off his hat and asked if they'd prayed. Catherine shook her head. They bowed their heads for a short while, then Sim began eating his ham hoagie. He had coffee, too, which seemed awfully mature. Isaac was glad, him being so confident and all.

They talked, and Catherine's face turned pink, and then it turned a greenish-white, and sort of leveled off to the usual color as she finished her roast beef sandwich. Isaac sat in the corner and drew down his eyebrows and made "Ask her!" motions with his mouth, which did absolutely no good.

They talked about the snow and school, and who went to which crowd, all having names the way the youth did nowadays. There were Eagles and Pine Cones and Hummingbirds and what not. The wilder youth had their own group; the more conservative ones their own as well. Some of them had rules and were parent-supervised, which turned out well. Sim was with the Eagles, but not the same group as Catherine, since she was so much younger and all.

Oh, she and Sim could talk all right. Endlessly. Same as the night they fixed the water pump.

Well, this was enough. Sim wasn't even close to asking her for a date, so what was the use talking about all this other stuff? Who cared if there was a singing here, or a supper crowd there, or who was marrying who after Christmas?

Just when Isaac was seriously thinking of sliding down beneath the table and crawling out over their feet, Dat came by, looking for him. Catherine blushed again. She said "Hello," very politely, answered Dat's questions respectfully and then let Isaac out of the booth.

Isaac could see the pure elation on Sim's face when Dat said he bought a pair of Belgians, and would Isaac like to ride home in the truck with him?

When Isaac looked back on his way out of the dining area, Sim was leaning forward with that intent look of his, and if he wasn't careful he'd have to have his back adjusted at the chiropractor's office to put his head back in place.

But Sim just wasn't getting anywhere, that was the whole trouble.

At home, Isaac decided to talk to Mam about the impossibility of the whole situation. It was Saturday afternoon, and she was taking five loaves of whole-wheat bread from the oven. Her gray apron was pinned snugly around her ample waist, covering the front of her dark purple dress. Her covering was large and white, the wide strings pinned together behind her back to keep them from getting in her way as she moved effortlessly from table to stove and back again.

There were four pie crusts cooling on the

countertop, so Isaac broke off a tiny piece. Mam yelped and came bustling over, saying, "*Doo net! Doo net.* (Don't) They're for Barbara, for church. Don't touch them. I'm making coconut cream."

"Never chocolate," Isaac muttered.

Like a fluffy, warm comforter, her heavy arm enfolded his shoulders as she steered him to the refrigerator and opened the door, proudly producing a wonderfully high chocolate pie, crowned with an amazing amount of whipped cream and chocolate shavings.

Isaac turned his face to his mother's.

"For us?"

So often, these wonderful concoctions that Mam made on Saturday afternoons were for someone else. Chocolate layer cakes, loaves of bread, creamy vanilla pudding were usually all "for church."

"For you, Isaac! Just for you!" Her words were better than Mountain Dew. What a mother!

"Mam, did you really bake this chocolate pie for me?"

"Yes, for you."

Love looked and tasted exactly like that pie. It was cool and creamy, rich, the chocolate neither too light or too bitter. He ate two wide slices, then asked Mam what she thought of Sim asking Catherine Speicher for a date.

Mam's eyes opened wide, she threw her hands in the air, then folded herself into a kitchen chair and said, "Good lands! You make me weak." She shook her head.

"He likes her. He just doesn't have the nerve to ask her for a date," Isaac said, scraping up the last of the chocolate pudding with his fork.

Mam said there was more to it than that. Dates had to be prayed about and God's leading felt. It always took patience. She wasn't even aware of the fact that they knew each other, and besides, Sim was older, and she thought the teacher a bit fancy. For us, she said.

Isaac told her that had absolutely nothing to do with it, look at him and Calvin. Mam nodded and said maybe that was true, and that Abner Speicher's family was a nice family. It was just that Abner wasn't too good with money, and now he was sick in the hospital. She made that clucking sound.

Isaac told her money has absolutely nothing to do with it either. Did God check out money before he put two people together?

Mam wagged her finger at him and said he better watch it, he was getting too big for his britches. She would talk to Sim about this, he needed to be careful, Catherine was … then she didn't know what to say.

Isaac shrugged into his chore coat, slapped his straw hat on and went to start the chores. Sim was batty as a loon. He was either whistling or looking as if he would burst into tears at the slightest provocation.

Isaac ignored him.

Even when Sim showered, shaved, dressed up and left with his sorrel horse and buggy, he ignored him. He didn't talk to Mam about it again, either.

In the morning he tumbled out of bed and did all his own chores, plus Sim's, when Dat told him Sim was attending church services in another district. Well, that was a fine thing to do. Why would he go off to another church district if Catherine Speicher was in this one? So much for the budding relationship today.

But as these things went, Isaac forgot about Sim, dressed in his Sunday black suit with his white shirt, heavy black felt hat, gloves and boots. Isaac went with Dat and Mam to church at Johns. John was married to his sister Barbara, Bennie's mother.

By the time all the women had been seated on their side, and the men on the other side, and it was finally the boys' turn to file into the warm basement, his toes felt like 10 nuggets of ice. He was cold and sleepy and not in the mood to sit on that hard bench for three hours. Isaac slumped forward and put his chin in the palm of his hand, until he caught Dat's eye. Dat drew his eyebrows down and shook his head slightly, the sign of disapproval.

So Isaac snapped to attention, held his corner of the heavy *Ausbund*, and tried to look attentive and alert. The slow German hymn rose and fell, babies cried, fathers got up to take them to their mothers.

When the minister stood to begin the sermon, Isaac listened to his voice, hearing the usual German verses he heard most Sundays, followed by an explanation in Pennsylvania Dutch. The real German (*hoch Deutsch*) was still read and used in the sermon, but explained in the everyday Pennsylvania Dutch as well, for the children and those who found the German difficult. It was, indeed, an old and precious tradition, to be well-versed in both German and Pennsylvania Dutch. It came easy to Isaac, so he understood and recognized most everything from both sermons.

He fell asleep once, the minister's face swimming in a sea of black-clad men, and he knew nothing for awhile. He was dimly aware of his head drooping to the left. He was so glad to sing the last hymn, then shuffle his way out to the blinding white snow, free at last.

Isaac ate at the last table, after the men and women had already eaten. His stomach was so painfully empty that his head hurt. It was the most cruel thing to eat breakfast so early and dinner so late. He spread a thick slice of homemade bread with soft cheese spread made with white American cheese and milk cooked together, piled on a liberal amount of ham, speared two red beets and a sweet pickle and began to feel instantly better.

Teacher Catherine was pouring coffee at the boys' table, dressed in a purple dress and a white organdy cape and apron. Isaac thought what a golden opportunity Sim was missing. When she poured his coffee, Sim could ask her for a date, very quietly, of course, but he could.

If Sim never got it accomplished, it sure wasn't for lack of his younger brother's great ideas. Or his subtle scouting skills, for that matter.

Chapter Six

Hickory Grove school was a beehive of activity the following Friday. All lessons had been put aside, serious artwork taking up everyone's attention. The classroom must be decorated for Christmas.

They had already accomplished quite a bit, Teacher Catherine said, but they seriously needed to apply themselves, finishing the Christmas poster on the north wall between the two sets of windows. They hung navy blue construction paper for the back drop, which was the upper grade boys' assignment. Elmer's School Glue was used to attach all the pieces.

Michael took charge of the glue, applying it entirely too liberally. It squeezed out when he rubbed his fingers along the edge, so Calvin told him he was using too much, and Michael's face got red and he told Calvin he didn't know everything. That was when Isaac decided to work on the pond. It looked safer.

They leaned over the Ping-Pong table in the middle of the classroom, construction paper scattered everywhere, the tension crackling between them since Michael said that. As soon as Michael got up to get another bottle of glue, Calvin raised his eyebrows, Isaac pointed to the white construction paper and Calvin nodded. He glued the rectangular sheets of construction paper, then whispered to Calvin about the shape of the pond.

"Whatever you think, Professor," Calvin whispered back.

Yes!

Isaac knew he could do the shape of the pond very well, making it look realistic. After all the construction paper was in place, they'd draw in bushes and trees, stars and a moon, skaters, horses tied and blanketed and a bonfire. It would be a grand poster, one the parents would talk about all Christmas season.

The girls were making bells with cardboard egg boxes. They cut out the little cups that contained the eggs and punched a hole in the top. They covered them with crinkly squares of aluminum foil, strung red and green yarn through them and hung their "bells" from the roller shades by the windows. They were Christmasy looking, Isaac thought, especially with those brilliant red, green and white candy canes in the background.

The white construction paper was designed, cut and attached by Isaac, and then the three boys stood back and admired their efforts.

Teacher Catherine came over and said it was very well done, and that the trees would look great done with black and brown Magic Markers.

"What about snow?" Isaac asked.

Teacher Catherine put one finger to her mouth, tilted her head to the side and considered this.

"There's no snow on the pond," Calvin volunteered.

"Good thinking, Calvin. The snow may have blown off the branches," she said.

Isaac thought snow on the branches was an essential, mostly because the pine trees in the background would look so much better with snow on them, but figured he'd stay quiet. Dat often told him how important it was to give up your own opinion for a better one. It was more influential in the long run to keep your opinion to yourself, if it meant working together in peace and harmony as the end result.

Take barn raisings. Someone had to be the *fore gaya*, the one who ran the whole business. If each worker recognized this, contributed his share of talent, giving and taking, it worked.

One Sunday morning Dat explained the Scripture about the lion laying with the lamb, and he said it meant each of us must lay down our own nature to get along with others. Isaac had mulled that one over for days, and he still didn't get it, really, but figured he didn't have to until he was older.

Teacher Catherine was very pretty today, he thought. Her face shone with a soft light. Her red dress made her look like Christmas, her black apron just slightly lopsided from moving around, bending over desks, always trying to be at two places at one time. Well, the way these lower graders raised their hands was ridiculous. How could she be expected to get anything of her own accomplished?

Then Sarah started crying, rubbing her eyes, mewling like a lost kitten, her lips pouting, as she haltingly told Teacher Catherine that her puppy was supposed to be gray and it looked brown and wasn't nice.

What a *brutz-bupp*! (Crybaby)

Sarah should have used a gray color instead of a brown one. She was in third grade and old enough to know better. Isaac thought Teacher Catherine should straighten her out, but no, her ever-loving kindness and patience was unfurled like a pure white flag, an example for the impatient ones like Isaac. Putting a hand on Sarah's shoulder, she bent low, assuring Sarah that if she didn't like the color of her puppy, she could start over with a new copy. Sarah wiped her eyes, sniffed, then marched proudly to the teacher's desk for another copy, one woolen black sock falling sloppily over her Skechers. Third graders were an annoyance, no question. But if you went to a one-room Amish school, you just had to put up with them, that was the way of it.

So now. Night sky and pond in place. This was going to be awesome!

"Boys," Teacher Catherine announced. "The girls will soon be finished with their bells, so they may help you with the freehand drawing of figures, horses, whatever. Isaac?"

Before he could stop himself, his arm shot up. "Well, we can't have just anyone helping, can we?"

Then he was subject to the most awful glare of disapproval. It shot from her blue eyes, a laser of reproach. Not one word was necessary.

Isaac felt his face fire up to about 500 degrees. He wished he could turn into an ant and disappear beneath the baseboard.

He should have stayed quiet.

But these girls and their cutesy-pie drawings of flowers and butterflies and birds and stuff. How could they ever be expected to come up with anything decent? This poster was serious material.

Isaac cringed when Ruthie hung the last cluster of bells on the window shade and went to the cupboard for art paper. He had to admit, though, they had done a real good job on those handmade bells.

"Put your books away for lunch," Teacher Catherine announced. Instantly there was a rustle of paper, heads bent to put things in their desks. "Davey, is it your turn to pass the waste can?"

Davey nodded happily, picked up the tall Rubbermaid waste can and slowly wended his way down the aisle as everyone hurried to throw their crumpled paper, bits of crayon, and colored pencil shavings into it before he moved on.

The wooden desks all had a hole cut on top, to the right, where pupils had kept their inkwells in times past. There were no more antique ink pens, of course, so that hole was perfect for stuffing crumpled waste paper.

Hickory Grove School was an older one, so they still had those desks, but the newer ones were made without the hole. Dan Stoltzfus and his helpers made school desks now, sleek and smoothly finished, the steel parts painted black, all glossy and shiny like the buggies.

Some of the Amish schools got the desks the English schools no longer needed. They were not attached to the floor, the lids opened and you could see your whole cache of books and stuff at once. Nothing fell out of those desks, which was nice, but the teachers complained about them being noisy, saying the tops were propped up too long while bent heads did a lot of whispering behind them.

Dora got the teakettle from the stove top, poured the steaming hot water into the blue plastic dishpan, then carried it to the hydrant beside the porch to add cold water. Why didn't she fill it half-full with cold water first, then add the hot? If she thought, she wouldn't have to carry all that hot water out the door.

You simply couldn't get past it. Girls had very little common sense.

She set the dishpan on a small dry sink, added a squirt of anti-bacterial soap, and washed her hands, drying them with brown paper towels from the dispenser on the wall.

"First row," Teacher Catherine said. Row after row, the scholars filed in an orderly fashion, washing their hands, drying them, grabbing their lunch boxes from the cloakroom and returning to their seats. Teacher Catherine bowed her head, the pupils followed suit and they sang their dinner prayer in a soft melody.

When they finished, the "amen" fading away, most of the pupils made their way to the front of the room, where the propane-gas stove held dozens of foil-wrapped sandwiches, hot dogs, chicken patties, or small casseroles containing the previous evening's leftovers. Tiny Tupperware containers of ketchup were scraped over hot dogs and chicken patties and put on a roll. Juice boxes or containers of milk washed down the good, hot food.

Calvin opened his lunch and produced a ham sandwich loaded with lettuce and tomato. He popped the top of a can of grape juice and grinned at Isaac, who was wolfing down his sandwich made of homemade wheat bread, sweet bologna and mustard. A pint jar of chocolate milk, made with the good creamy milk straight from the bulk tank in the milk house and flavored with Nestle's Quik, accompanied his sandwich. Mam bought the chocolate mix in large yellow cylinders at Centerville Bulk Food Store. Sometimes he wished Mam would buy fancy Tupperware drink containers the way other mothers did, but she said all her children used glass pint jars for their chocolate milk, and she had no intention of stopping now.

There was a gasp from Ruthie, as Daniel and Reuben started to tussle, spilling Daniel's juice all over everything.

Teacher Catherine laid down her sandwich deliberately, her mouth set in a straight line as she got up, grabbed Reuben by the arm and marched him back to his seat. "You know you have to stay in your seat at lunchtime," she said firmly. Isaac didn't know whether Reuben was pinched, or if the reprimand alone was enough, but he bent his head and cried softly.

The classroom became devoid of sound as Daniel was marched to sit in an empty desk, without his juice. Dora helped mop up the sticky mess with paper towels, but it was Teacher Catherine who had to use warm water and soap in a bucket, get down on her knees and wipe it all up properly, while her sand-wich got cold.

It served that Reuben right. Daniel, too. Those little second graders couldn't hold still one minute, not even long enough to eat their lunches. The pupils had to remain seated for 15 minutes, which was the most cruel thing the school board had ever invented. You could easily eat a sandwich in five minutes, drink all your chocolate milk, grab your bag of pretzels and be out the door.

Recess was only 45 minutes, which wasn't long enough at all. Especially now, with all this snow. So they ate in a big hurry, sat together with their feet in the aisle, traded snacks and talked.

Calvin said there was a fire on the other side of Georgetown; the fire engines had made an awful racket. Isaac asked him how he knew already, and Calvin shrugged his shoulders, so Isaac figured one of his brothers who was at the *rumspringa* age had a radio or a cell phone, maybe both.

You just didn't talk about those things in school, those objects being *verboten* (forbidden)the way they were. It was not a good subject to discuss, especially with the more conservative children like Isaac, whose family would never own anything the church frowned on. It was called respect.

Isaac knew Calvin's brothers were not like Sim. They each had had a vehicle for a short time, even. Isaac and Calvin never talked about it, though, which was good. That was a separate world, and to avoid that subject meant they could like each other tremendously. They lived in their own young world of friendship, discussing only matters of importance, like horses and sleds and scooters, and really awesome ideas like making a better scooter, how to fire up a stove with the right kindling and who was the best skate sharpener in Lancaster County.

When the long hand on the clock finally reached the three, they moved fast and efficiently, throwing their lunch boxes on the shelf with one hand, grabbing their coats and hats or beanies with the other, and moving to the front door with long strides that were not really running, but certainly not quite walking, either.

The minute their heads popped out the door, a nanosecond ahead of their feet, yells of pure elation broke out. They dashed to their sleds, grabbed the rope handles and raced out of the schoolyard, around the fence, and up Eli Esh's slope.

Sledding was the only time they were allowed out of the schoolyard. They had to be closely supervised, staying off the road until they were safely in the field, which was free from traffic. But the "big boys" were allowed to go ahead, before Teacher Catherine appeared with the smaller ones.

They had already reached the top of Eli's hill and were on the way down. The paths they had cut to smooth perfection on Monday, now slick from the sun's rays, had frozen and melted and frozen again. It made for glorious sledding.

The sun, the flying bits of snow, the absolute speed, the cold, all filled Isaac's mind. So when the horn sounded, the brakes screeched, the children screamed and screamed without stopping, it took a while until he knew something wasn't right.

In fact, something awful had just occurred.

Chapter Seven

Isaac was off his Lightning Flyer before it stopped, left it and began to run.

The vehicle had skidded to a haphazard stop, sideways on the road. A small black figure lay inert on the cold, hard macadam.

A middle-aged couple emerged from the car, the man reaching for his wife's hand. Her gloved hand was held across her mouth, her eyes wide with terror.

Teacher Catherine reached Raymond first. She bent, put out a hand, then looked up as the English man reached her. He got down on one knee. Isaac was relieved to hear a moan, followed by an ear-piercing scream.

It was Raymond! He was conscious.

Isaac was joined by Calvin and Michael, then Jake and Danny, the fifth-grade boys. Teacher Catherine got up, spoke sternly, loudly, as Raymond's screaming continued.

"Take them all inside. Ruthie. Dora. *Nemmat die kinna ny.*" (Take the children in.)

With one wild look at Raymond, the car and the English man and his wife, they obeyed, herding the sobbing huddle of black-clad children back to the schoolhouse, where they promptly stationed themselves on the bench below the windows, watching.

An approaching car stopped. The man got out, assessed the situation and pulled his cell phone from his coat pocket, as Raymond continued his screams of pain.

The English lady dashed back to the car, returned with a crocheted afghan in red and green, then bent to lay it gently over the child.

Teacher Catherine was on her knees beside Raymond, stroking his hair, talking to him in Pennsylvania Dutch, but nothing helped. Raymond just went on screaming.

Isaac could hardly take it. He felt sick to his stomach, and the white, white world went crooked for an instant. He swallowed and was all right.

Why did the fire company take so long? Surely it shouldn't take the medics that much time.

Teacher Catherine left Raymond only long enough to step over and tell the boys to scooter to Jesse Kauffmans' and tell them to come, fast.

The boys ran, grasped their scooter handles, bent low and pedaled furiously, one leg flung back as far as it would go to build momentum.

Raymond's mam was eating her lunch. Her face turned white, but she remained calm, instructing her older daughter Ella Mae to run to the phone shanty and call her dat, who worked at the welding shop in Gordonville.

"*Bleib yusht do,*" (Just stay here.) she told Ella Mae, then hopped on a scooter and followed the schoolboys.

The medic had arrived. Raymond was sedated and put on a stretcher before his mother got there.

Isaac was relieved, glad Jesse *sei* Anna did not have to witness that horrible screaming.

They opened the back doors of the ambulance and loaded Raymond into it. His mother was taken with the English people who had accidentally hit him.

The police swarmed about, their yellow lights whirling on top of their vehicles, their radios crackling, asking questions, jotting down information.

Teacher Catherine remained calm and effective, answering questions. Her face was white, her blue eyes huge, filled with liquid her pride would not allow to spill over. Isaac admired her so much. He sure had a story for Sim.

They went back to the schoolroom and sat in their desks. No one wanted to continue sledding, work on the poster or practice for the Christmas program.

Teacher Catherine asked each family whether their parents were home, and then dismissed the school at one o'clock. She said as soon as she received any news about Raymond's condition, she'd leave them all a message on their voicemail, so they should be sure to check their messages later in the day.

The children nodded soberly. They wended their way quietly out of the schoolyard. Concerned parents wiped tears, hugged their own little ones and were thankful. To be able to hold their warm, healthy little bodies was something, now, wasn't it?

Edna Beiler went to the phone—hers was in the shop on her husband's metal desk—and called her sister Esther, who often heard her phone. Esther had a bell rigged up to it, which was louder than the high insistent whine of an ordinary telephone.

Esther always got her way, that Amos being the kindhearted soul he was. Edna knew her Paul would never rig up a bell to her phone. He said women didn't need to sit there yakking and gossiping all day, so she set her phone in an aluminum cake pan, which increased the sound quite a bit, deciding if Paul didn't like it he could just get her a bell like Esther had.

Thankfully, Esther answered after about six rings, and they had a breathless conversation about Teacher Catherine not watching those children.

Edna said maybe Catherine had been there, and Raymond didn't listen. You know how first-graders are. Barely off their mothers' laps.

Edna said it was a good thing it happened to Jesse Kauffmans, they could afford a hospital bill better than some, and Esther snorted and said nobody could afford a hospital nowadays, no wonder there were so many benefit auctions and suppers.

Edna promptly told her that Paul said maybe they should stop, too much going on all the time, when we're told to live a quiet and restful life. What's quiet or restful, going, going, going the way everyone did?

That really irked Esther, so she hung up before Edna finished, leaving Edna staring at the black receiver in disbelief. Not knowing what else to do, she took the tip of her apron and cleaned the dust off the black telephone.

Then she dialed Esther's number again.

That was just wrong. She wasn't one bit mad. She had only voiced an opinion. Not even her own, but her husband's. Oh well, they were both upset, felt helpless in the face of this tragedy. What if poor little Raymond died?

When Esther didn't answer the phone, Edna decided she was just as *dick keppich* (thick headed) as she had always been, left the shop in a huff, then cried in her dishwater.

Voicemails were filled with the news much later that evening.

Raymond was home. His collarbone was broken, and he had a bad brushburn on one thigh where the car had thrown him on the rough macadam, but Eli Esh *sei* Barbara was already at Jesse Kauffmans with burdock leaves and B & W ointment. The collarbone would heal on its own, although he came home wearing a stiff, white neck brace. The doctors at Lancaster General allowed the B & W ointment to be used, although Jesses had to promise to report any infection.

The children returned to school a subdued lot, the accident still embedded in their memory, a thorn of pain along with Raymond's.

Esther and Edna forgave each other on the phone the following morning and got together a Sunshine Box, sending messages to dozens of voicemails. Each family was given a letter of the alphabet, and they were to buy a gift starting with that letter. Then the gifts were placed in the Sunshine Box, so that each day Raymond would open one, starting with the letter A.

Poor Sarah ended up with three poems to recite since Raymond couldn't say his, which greatly upset her. She went home and told her mother she felt like she had too much to do at the Christmas program. So her mother sent a note along to Catherine asking her to reduce Sarah's load. Teacher Catherine asked everyone if they felt they had too much to say. Isaac volunteered to say another poem, so he was allowed to say the one everyone considered too difficult.

The plays were going much better. The pupils only needed to glance briefly at their copies to get it right. Isaac's version of Abraham Lincoln was perfect, Calvin said, especially after they crafted a top hat out of black construction paper.

Then, the front door broke. Jake went flying out, slammed it back against the brick wall and busted the glass. Teacher Catherine's face got red and she made Jake go sit in his seat.

She wrote a note for the school caretaker but he was down with a herniated disk, his back causing him awful grief. Isaac stepped up to the plate, offering Dat's services, secretly plotting not Dat, but Sim's expertise. He knew Sim could replace that window. He'd watched him plenty of times at home.

Gleefully, he cornered Sim in the forebay when he was leading the Belgians to the water trough that evening.

"Hey, the door—the window in the door—at school broke. Henna Zook broke his back, or something like that, so I told Catherine Dat would fix it. You will though, right? Right, you will?"

Sim looked at Isaac, then said he wasn't going to go there when all the children were there, and Isaac said that was fine, Catherine stayed later in the day, he'd go along.

"Maybe you need to stay home."

"If I do, will you ask her?"

Sim showed up at school the next day with a tape measure, while the children flocked around him wide-eyed, watching every move he made. He went off to the hardware store and returned just after everyone had gone home, with Isaac lingering on the front porch.

Perfect!

While Isaac watched, offering advice, Sim worked to remove the broken glass, and then the frame.

Teacher Catherine stayed at her desk, checking papers, and nothing happened. Not one thing.

Sim whistled low under his breath, not even glancing in her direction.

She kept her head bent, her blond hair neatly combed back beneath her white covering.

The sun fell lower in the evening clouds, a red orb of inefficient heat in the winter sky, night-time fast approaching, the cold beginning to flex its muscles as Isaac sat on the cement steps.

"Why don't you go on home, Isaac?" Sim suggested.

"I'm going with you."

"You'll freeze your backside, sitting there."

"Will not."

Finally, Sim tapped one last time and bent to retrieve his tools. Then he stood up, fixed his hat, adjusted his coat collar, opened the door, and walked into the classroom.

Isaac followed, eager to watch the action, his eyes bright pools of curiosity.

"How are you, Catherine?" Sim asked, in his deep, manly voice.

She looked up, smiled and didn't look away. She didn't answer, either. She just looked.

So Isaac scrambled happily up on Calvin's desk and sat there.

"I'm fine," Catherine said, and her voice was not shaky and flustered. It had music in it.

"How's your dat?"

"Much better. I haven't seen him with this much energy ever, I don't think. Did I thank you for picking me up that day? In the sled?"

"I don't remember, I'm sure you did."

She laughed, sort of soft and low, and so did Sim, which made absolutely no sense to Isaac. They hadn't even said anything funny, so why did they laugh?

They talked about the accident, and Catherine said she felt bad, still, that if only she would have been quicker she may have prevented it. Sim told her that was total nonsense, no one could have stopped Raymond if he darted into the path of a car that fast.

Catherine shook her head and her blue eyes turned darker and she looked sad, in a way.

Isaac said to Calvin the next day that he thought his brother Sim might like the teacher. Calvin said lots of guys did, but his mam said Catherine was terrible picky; that's why she was still single.

So Isaac figured everything he'd gained pretty much shifted out of his grasp again, Calvin making that comment and Sim looking so dull these days.

The poster was looking more wonderful each day. Ruthie surprised him most. She drew a girl skating backward, going in a tight circle, her skirt and scarf blowing so realistic and all, that Isaac admitted to Michael he didn't know girls could draw freehand like that.

Hannah drew two horses that looked like camels and were about the same color. Isaac told Teacher Catherine they couldn't have those horses on there, and she said they could not hurt Hannah's feelings, the horses had to stay. Maybe he could draw blankets on them.

Isaac did, then, and the horses looked like camels with horse blankets, but when he colored them a bright shade of red, it looked Christmasy, decorative and colorful enough. Hannah was insulted anyway, sniffing and parading around like a cat that fell in the water trough, saying the horse blankets ruined her horses, so Isaac told her to cover them up with snow.

That really got her going.

Chapter Eight

Ten days they had.

Teacher Catherine really cracked down on the procrastinators. There was no putting off what could be done today. Those that did not listen and learn their parts would have to give them to someone else.

That got the ball rolling.

No more copies were allowed. The plays had to be memorized, the parts said at the right time with the proper expression, and loudly enough. Teacher Catherine stood against the wall at the back of the classroom, a formidable figure, her lips set in a grim line of determination. The pupils sat up and took notice. She praised, cajoled, stopped the quiet ones and made them do it over, always goading them on.

The only pupil that seemed hopeless was Ruthie. She desperately wanted to speak. She had a lovely poem, but so far, had been totally unable to finish it. She picked her face, cleared her throat, reached behind her back to pin and re-pin her apron, stalled for time, but nothing worked.

Isaac talked to Mam one evening, the best time of the day to approach her when she had just gotten out of the shower. She smelled of lotion and talcum powder. She wore her homemade, blue flannel bathrobe, buttoned down the front with leftover pants buttons, a *dichly*, that triangular piece of fabric she wore to cover her head at night so that when she woke in the middle of the night, she would have her head covered so she could pray for her family, starting with the first and going all the way to Isaac. Her gray hair was wavy after she washed it, loose and wavy, even when it was bound by the ever-present *dichly*, making her appear more girlish, safer, somehow.

"Mam, what do you think of trying to help someone overcome stuttering?"

Mam looked up from the *Blackboard Bulletin* she was reading.

"Why?"

"You know Ruthie? Lloyd's Ruthie?"

Mam nodded.

"She just can't say her poem this year." He described in vivid detail Ruthie's nervousness, her unwillingness to talk to her mother.

Mam shook her head.

"Well, Isaac, I don't want you to think this is looking down on someone, but Ruthie probably doesn't have much of a home life. Her mother and, well … she has reason to be nervous."

"So what could we do? Is it true that you can help someone stop stuttering, stammering, whatever you want to call it, by speaking slowly?"

"I've heard of it."

"How could we do it?"

"Why don't you start a support group? Sort of a system where all her friends work with her? Ask Teacher Catherine to help you."

Isaac thought that sounded just wonderful. He pitied Ruthie and told Mam so.

Mam said she was glad Isaac had a soft heart. It spoke well for his character.

Isaac usually fell asleep soon after his head touched his pillow, having to get up at 5:00, the way he did.

Tonight, however, was different. He was thinking.

Ruthie could just give up her poem. But he knew for himself, he would be ashamed to be without that solo piece of poetry, everyone expecting it the way they did.

She was about as decent as any girl could be. For one thing, she could draw stuff other than hearts and flowers. She had drawn most of the figures skating on the pond, some of them looking real. And she liked dogs. She had an English Setter of her own named Shelby. That was sort of cool. Shelby. It had a nice ring to it.

He also liked the way her freckles were spattered across her nose, sort of like God put sprinkles on the icing of a cupcake. If he had to pick any girl as his wife, it would have to be Ruthie. He didn't know when he'd heard her sniff last. Or blow her nose.

The next day at first recess, Isaac approached her, after talking to Calvin and Michael.

"How would you like to be helped with your problem of stammering?" he blurted.

"You mean stuttering?" Ruthie asked. Her eyes were watchful.

"Yeah."

"Who would help me? Who would even know how?"

"Me. Me and Calvin and Michael and Hannah and Dora."

"You would?" She sounded surprised and a little pleased.

"Sure."

"When?"

"Every lunch hour, 'til the program."

"Give up sledding?" She asked, considering.

"Mm-hm."

"Ar-aright." Ruthie's eyes shone.

So that was how it started. They called themselves the SOS group. Support Our Stutterer.

Ruthie giggled, twisting her apron. Isaac began by having her read long sentences from a book, anything, as long as she spoke. She could speak perfectly as long as she read from a book, but when she was placed on the stage in front of the blackboard, she could not face anyone and speak a word without stumbling horribly.

When she felt the constriction in her throat begin, they asked her to stop. At first, she was close to tears. She grabbed a corner of her black apron and twisted it, then released it, clearing her throat, blinking her eyes, doing anything she possibly could to avoid eye contact or holding still.

Isaac took charge. Barking instructions, pacing, his voice carrying well, he asked her to look at him. If she wasn't comfortable looking at him, she could look at Hannah.

She shook her head.

So Isaac met her eyes, told her to watch his face, and repeat this sentence.

She got nowhere, her mouth twisting, her throat swelling with the effort of making just one coherent sound. After that, they stopped.

"Okay, Ruthie, let's start by saying sentences while you are sitting with us."

Patiently, they started over. If she read from a book, she was fine, but when she faced anyone, the words stayed in her throat as if someone had closed a gate.

It was time for the bell.

Isaac's shoulders slumped. Michael walked wearily to his desk, Calvin rolled his eyes in Isaac's direction and even Hannah lost a bit of her swagger. They could not accomplish this in nine days. It was hopeless.

Isaac hung around the schoolyard until the last pupils had pushed their way home on their scooters, then returned and entered the classroom.

Catherine was surprised to see him.

"Yes, Isaac?"

"Sorry to bother you, but is there nothing we can do for Ruthie? Do you know of anyone who has overcome this problem? Any books we can read?"

Catherine said nothing, just looked at Isaac without seeing him. Finally she sighed.

"Isaac, can I trust you to keep this bit of information to yourself?"

He nodded.

"Ruthie has a sad life now that her mother is ... well, she's in the hospital for ... help. She has problems with her thinking. They just found out a few weeks ago that she may have either a tumor on her brain or Alzheimer's."

"What's that?"

"It's when your brain is diseased, in a way, and you no longer function normally."

"Oh."

"I think Ruthie is very afraid. She's trying to go about her life as if nothing is wrong, hoping none of her classmates find out. She carries a deep sense of shame. Her mother has always been ... an excitable woman, to put it mildly, and those children have suffered seriously, in ways you can't imagine. So ... perhaps, Isaac, you could reach her? Maybe if she found out ...."

Catherine's voice drifted off.

"You mean if I told her that I know about her mother and tell her it's all right, stuff like that happens to people all the time, she'd loosen up?"

Catherine nodded.

Isaac pushed himself home, flinging his leg energetically, happy with this bit of information. Teacher Catherine was the best, most beautiful, sweetest person he had ever met. She treated him as her best buddy, letting him in on that secret, doing it in a way that didn't make Ruthie's mother appear mean, just pitiful. Now he believed Ruthie might be able to overcome her crippling stutter, if he did this right.

At home, he grabbed two chocolate chip cookies and ran out the door to find Sim. It was very important that Sim knew about this, especially about Catherine being so wise and pretty, and if he didn't get around to asking her for a date soon, it would be forever too late, the opportunity evaporated like mist from the pond. It was time Sim straightened himself up.

He found Sim loading manure in the heifer barn. The acrid odor met his nostrils before he saw Sim, but he was used to the raw stench of fresh manure, so he climbed the gate and walked over to him.

Hatless, his everyday shirt sleeves rolled up above

the elbow and his shoulders bulging beneath the seams of his shirt, Sim was forking great quantities of the sodden stuff with each forkful. He stopped, ran the back of his hand along his forehead, stuck his pitchfork into the remaining manure and smiled at Isaac. "What's up?"

"Hey, you know Lloyd's Ruthie? The girl that stutters? She can't talk one tiny bit. And you know what?" He related the entire afternoon's visit with his teacher, watching Sim's face, emphasizing Catherine's part.

Sim didn't show any emotion, just scratched a forearm and looked out the door at the snowy landscape.

"And, you know, Sim, if you don't make yourself do it, she's not going to wait around much longer. You need to ask her for a date. Get going oncc!"

Isaac was surprised at Sim's reaction. Sim looked as if he was going to cry. When he spoke, it was quietly, seriously, almost like a preacher in church.

"All right, little brother. I hear you. And I wish I could tell you okay, I'll ask her. At your age I probably would have. A schoolboy hasn't seen much of life, of love or loss. It's not as simple as you think. And, Isaac, a lot of children your age would not talk the way you do. You're too smart. You see, God comes first. If I pray to him first, ask him for his blessing in my life, then maybe, just maybe, someday, he will allow me to have her. But I have to wait. Wait on his answer."

Isaac snorted loudly, scaring the heifers in the corner watching the pair of Belgians hitched to the manure spreader with frightened eyes.

"Well, and just how does God go about speaking to you? You a prophet, or what? Catherine likes you. You're too dumb to see it."

With that, Isaac climbed back over the fence, popping the last of the chocolate chip cookies into his mouth, and let Sim finish cleaning the heifer barn by himself. If he got out of there fast enough, Sim might not remember the chicken house needed to be cleaned.

Just his luck, he ran into Dat.

"Hi, Isaac! Home from school so soon? How was your day?"

"School."

"That's not much of an answer," Dat said, smiling broadly.

"Same thing. It was just school."

"Christmas program ready yet?"

"Yup."

"Good! I'm looking forward to it."

Isaac smiled at Dat and was rewarded by the warm kindness in his eyes, the same as always.

Dat was like a rock-solid house you could go into and never be afraid of anything or anyone. He was always the same, sometimes busier than others, more preoccupied, but never angry or hateful or rude.

Now he looked at Isaac with a shrewd expression.

"So, do you think a boy like you should be getting a pony spring wagon if he forgets to scrape the chicken house?"

He looked up sharply and found Dat's smile.

"How would you like to drive Ginger to school every day?"

A new spring wagon for ponies! It was hard to grasp.

"You better get busy, Isaac."

Dat reached out, lifted Isaac's torn straw hat and plopped it back down, a gesture of affection.

While Isaac cleaned and scraped, shooing chickens away, he kept repeating, "Wow! Wow!"

Chapter Nine

ISAAC FAIRLY FLEW TO SCHOOL, THE thought of the new spring wagon goading him on, his energy buzzing and humming.

The sky looked dark and heavy enough to fall right down on his head. Big piles of iron-gray clouds were flattening themselves into the fish-bone shape Mam always spoke of. She said if gray clouds looked like a fish skeleton, gray and flat and straight, there was a wet air from the east, and a rain or snowstorm was approaching.

Dat clucked over the morning paper. "There's another big one coming."

"*Ach, du lieva!*" (Oh, my goodness.) Mam set down her cup of coffee, broke another glazed doughnut in half and took a generous bite, hungrily. And she just had breakfast. "You mean we'll have two storms before Christmas?"

"I would say so. Whatever you do, Isaac, if it gets to *rissling* (ice coming down), wait at school until someone comes to get you. Your scooter isn't safe on the road in those conditions."

Dat was very serious, so Isaac sat up and listened.

At school, he told Calvin about the approaching storm, Calvin nodding and saying already there was a winter storm watch for Lancaster, Berks and Dauphin Counties.

It was dark in the schoolhouse. Teacher Catherine got a lighter out of her desk and lit the propane gas lamp, its warm glow and soft hissing sound wrapping the pupils in homey, familiar light.

It was the only light they were used to at home. A propane tank was set in a pretty oak cabinet, sometimes painted black or off-white or red, depending on the housewife's preference, with a long pipe attached to the head where two mantles were tied. When a tiny flame was held to the mantles, a bright light burst forth, illuminating a whole room easily. It was the best alternative to electricity.

Mam said years ago they didn't have propane lamps. They used naptha gas in a lamp hung from the ceiling. They were right dangerous, in her opinion, but back then you never thought about it. You could burn kerosene in the same lamp, except you had to heat the head with a torch, or use the little cup that was provided for a shot of lighter fluid, ignite it, and then a small, steadily burning blue flame heated the mantles until you could turn the lamp on, which was even more dangerous and time-consuming. So they had come a long way.

Dat shook his head about the fast moving solar and battery operations that were creeping into homes nowadays. Some of the more liberal households no longer used propane lamps, but a 12-volt battery in the oak cabinet attached to a bulb on a real electric lamp that was converted to battery use.

You had to wonder where it would all end, Dat said, stroking his beard and looking very wise. It was important to keep the old traditions, he said. They meant a lot.

Sim said change would come, though, it always had. Look at the milking machines and bulk tanks. Propane gas stoves and refrigerators. Some change was good. Dat agreed, but admonished Sim to be *trick-havich* (hold back) and it would never spite him, reaping the benefits in later years.

As Isaac settled into his desk, he shivered. Normally, the classroom was warm, but the farthest corners were cold this morning. He gazed out the window as Teacher Catherine read the Bible, waiting for those first icy snowflakes to ping against the east side of the schoolhouse. He glanced at Ruthie, appalled to find her blinking, her eyes bright with unshed tears. As he watched, her brown eyes overflowed, the tears leaving wet streaks through her freckles.

He looked away.

When he returned from singing class, he got out his arithmetic book as usual. Now he inserted a piece of paper, and wrote,

> *Ruthie, it's O.K. Teacher Catherine says it is. I know about your mam. I feel sorry for her. Hang in there. You're strong.*
>
> *We're all here for you.*

Isaac knew it was against the rules to pass notes, but when he exchanged his arithmetic paper with her, he put the note inside, then watched steadily out the opposite window while she read it.

That day was a turning point.

It was as if Ruthie had been slipping, unable to gain a foothold. Now, a shaky attempt had paid off. She had found the strength to shake the crippling defeat in her young life.

At the recess SOS group, she repeated sentences, stuttering, straining, sometimes having to be completely quiet. But she spoke.

Then the snowstorm came at suppertime, all right.

It started like granules of salt, so fine and hard, piling into every crack and crevice it could find. It sifted along the cow stable's windowsills, a place Isaac could not remember ever finding snow.

The hen's water froze. They pecked holes into the ice and drank anyway. Dat said to feed the pigs and hens plenty; they'd need extra to keep themselves warm. Isaac and Sim put straw bales around the pigpen, wrapped sheets of insulation, that pink, itchy, fiberglass stuff, around the water hydrants and put a heater in the milk house.

Their Barbara came down with bronchitis, and needed Mam to send over Numotizine.

"What a night!" Mam fumed and fussed. No driver wanted to go out in this weather. She'd be ashamed to call one.

Sim said he'd make the five-mile drive. He had a heater in his buggy. When Isaac offered his company for the ride, Sim grinned and nodded.

Mam put a glob of that vile salve from her own blue and white container in a glass jar. It was an old, old remedy, containing something so awful smelling you could hardly stand to watch Mam put it in a jar, let alone having it applied to your chest with a steaming hot rag slapped on top. It was enough to suffocate a person, having to sleep with that stench, but Mam showed no mercy with her administration of Numotizine. She stated flatly that it had saved her hundreds of dollars in doctor bills, spared her children from antibiotics, and why wouldn't you use these old home remedies from the past?

So in the cold and dark, the snow zooming in through the opened window, Sim and Isaac started out.

With a horse like Sim's you had to keep the window latched to the ceiling for awhile, allowing the cold and snow its entry. There was no other way to do it. For one thing, the small rectangular holes cut in the window frame to allow the leather reins to pass through, were actually too small to handle a spirited horse. Horses always needed a firm hand starting out, and Saddlebred Fred was no exception, the way he hopped around. He shied, he ran way out around the driveway, making a large circle in the alfalfa field, and then dashed down the road as if a ghost was after him.

The steel-rimmed buggy wheels lost traction, swaying and zig-zagging across the quickly disappearing road, as Sim strained to control Fred. Isaac wrapped himself tightly into the plush buggy robe, and hoped the snow plows would hold off until they got home. The way Fred was acting, they'd end up in Philadelphia if they met one.

Sim didn't talk, so Isaac said nothing either. Then, sure enough, the twirling yellow light of a snowplow showed through the gloom, bearing down on them.

"Yikes!" Isaac wasn't planning on saying that; it just slipped out of its own accord.

"Hang on!" Sim shouted.

Isaac couldn't do that, as the buggy went straight down a steep bank. Grimly, he bit down on his lower lip, slid off the seat and socked into the corner of the buggy. Sim was standing up, leaning way back, his gloved hands working the reins, Fred galloping across someone's field out of control.

The buggy swayed and lurched, Isaac cowering in the corner, his eyes squeezed shut, waiting for the moment the buggy would fly into a thousand pieces, his body exploding out of it into the wild black night. It didn't happen. They just slowed down. Fred stopped his headlong gallop.

They made it safely to Barbara's house, who looked as if she needed a hospital more than she needed this Numotizine. She was on the couch, her breathing raspy, her cough sounding like a piece of wood falling down the stairs.

The house was a royal mess. As usual, Bennie wasn't behaving, sitting on the table spreading Ritz crackers with peanut butter. He had everything all over his pants, the table top and his sister Lydia. When Isaac told him to put the peanut butter away, he lifted his face and howled. John came rushing over carrying the baby, who set up her own high-pitched yell, her bottle of apple juice suddenly disappearing as her dat rushed to the rescue.

John glared at Isaac, got a wet cloth and told Bennie to clean up the peanut butter, which was the same as asking a pig to clean up his pen. Isaac sat on the recliner by the stove, disliking Bennie.

He was glad to leave with Sim.

These things, of course, were not talked about. He couldn't tell Sim how much he couldn't stand that Bennie. Sim would say it was a sin, which Isaac knew, but sometimes you could hardly help it.

Sim chuckled to Isaac, saying now that was marriage, and didn't that take the fairy story out of it?

This was the real thing.

Isaac hoped fervently Bennie would get a licking from his dad, although he couldn't see that happening.

"Bennie was sure making a mess," Isaac said drily.

"They probably didn't have any supper."

Sim, too!

Everyone stuck up for that Bennie, Isaac told Sim, and was happy to see him nodding his head in agreement. "You have a point there."

Isaac was glad he had spoken. Sometimes schoolboys observed things from their lowly vantage point that adults like Sim would be wise to learn.

"You know if Barbara doesn't watch it, that little Bennie is going to be a handful, the way no one makes him listen," Isaac said.

Sim agreed.

Isaac was convinced Sim would make a great father. He was just humble enough, and agreeable, too. He took advice, and took it right. Yes, indeed, it would be a pure shame if Catherine and Sim never started dating.

On Friday, Ruthie stood by the blackboard, wringing her hands, her eyes clearly terrified as she lifted her head.

"I ... h - h - h."

She stopped, searched for Isaac, found his face, then his eyes.

Come on, Ruthie! You can do this! He didn't say a word. His belief in her came from his eyes.

"H - hope m - m ... my h ..."

She stopped.

Isaac's eyes never left her face.

He was aware of Hannah and Calvin beside him. They all waited and waited. Ruthie took a deep breath. He watched as she clasped and unclasped her hands. That day, she spoke two whole sentences, haltingly, with exhausting effort.

At third recess, Isaac left sledding and found her sitting the porch, her feet dangling down the side.

"Ruthie, why don't we talk about your mam?" he asked.

"Who told you?"

"Teacher Catherine."

"I told Hannah and Dora today. It feels good. It's … everything feels easier now."

Isaac grinned encouragingly. So she told him. The struggles at home, trying not to hate her mother, the relief now, knowing her problem may actually be physical.

The following Monday, Ruthie made real progress. Teacher Catherine was beside herself with excitement. The Christmas program was shaping into a good one, molded by days of practice, pleading, cajoling, praising, the teacher at the helm guiding her Christmas ship.

Isaac wondered if her energy and enthusiasm had all been because of Ruthie. He doubted it. Didn't Sim have something to do with it when he came to pick Isaac up Friday afternoon? Late on purpose, then yet. Teacher Catherine was sweeping the snow from the porch, her cheeks red, her eyes sparkling as they exchanged greetings.

Well, Isaac was done. They could just keep up all this nonsense. He was out of it.

If Sim wanted to wait on God, he could. Hadn't God always been slow? Look at Methuselah. He was

900 and some years old. Let Sim wait until they were both 60 and then they could go visit the eye doctor together. He was thoroughly tired of Sim's *ga-mach*. (way of doing things)

Christmas was coming, and the program and the spring wagon were much more important, anyway.

Chapter Ten

RUTHIE STOOD BY THE BLACKBOARD NOW, the only sign of agitation her interlaced fingers, which she loosened, then hung her arms at her side for only a second before entwining her fingers again.

Endlessly, they had practiced sentences, words that began with the letter B, or H, or C, the hardest ones.

Hannah and Dora spent nights at her house, listening to her amazing stories of the past when her mother had been ill.

Ruthie no longer picked her face. Her eyes seemed quieter, somehow.

The parents had their invitations to the Christmas program, stamped holly with brilliant red berries on a gold card, inviting them to Hickory Grove School at 1:00 P.M. on Friday, December 23.

One more day to practice, then two other schools were coming to see their program on Thursday, a day before the real one, when all the parents would attend.

The plays were shaping up. Four white sheets hung from the wires suspended from hooks in the walls and on the ceilings. Bright tinsel was draped from the curtains.

The poster was magnificent. It was the finest piece of freehand art work Hickory Grove School had ever shown. Isaac knew that, but didn't say so. It was bragging, which was wrong. It was a form of pride. He could be pleased with it, though; he just couldn't say so. He told Calvin, however, who said he agreed 100 percent. It was a great poster.

Teacher Catherine drew camels and wise men on the blackboard, and the upper-grade boys helped color them with colored chalk.

Isaac had to bite back his observance of the similarities between these camels and Hannah's horses on the poster. They looked exactly alike. The noses, especially.

Teacher Catherine's apron, even her *halsduch* (cape) was covered in colored chalk dust, but her blue eyes radiated her enthusiasm. She talked non-stop, even chewing gum at recess, which was sort of unusual. Chewing gum wasn't allowed in school.

Thursday morning, Isaac leaped out of bed, flicked the small blue lighter and lifted the glass lamp chimney on his kerosene lamp. The small flame traveled the length of the wick.

He yanked open his dresser drawer, hopped into his denim work trousers and shrugged into his blue shirt as shivers chased themselves across his cold shoulders.

It had to be zero degrees outside.

It was! The red mercury hovered at the zero, and if you stood on your toes and looked down, it was colder than zero degrees. No doubt Calvin would have the real temperature, though.

Isaac rushed through his chores. The minute he walked into the kitchen, Mam said he needed to shower before breakfast. His black Sunday pants and his green Christmas shirt were laid out. He was supposed to wear his good shoes, not his sneakers.

If Mam would give him time to catch his breath when he walked into the kitchen, it wouldn't be so bad. But barking orders when you were cold and hungry and wanted to sit by the coal stove and think of fried mush and dippy eggs just didn't work very well.

So Isaac grumbled under his breath, scalded himself in the shower and shivered into his Sunday clothes. He brushed his teeth, watching the blue foam from the Crest toothpaste splatter the mirror. His face looked pretty good this morning. He liked his green eyes. He thought they looked nice, but you couldn't tell people that. Not even Calvin.

He bowed his head over his plate. He had to rearrange his thoughts away from the Christmas program to thank God for his breakfast before digging into a pile of stewed saltine crackers, fried mush and dippy eggs. Now he felt much better, fueled to meet the day. Mam's eyes approved of his clean appearance, but nothing was said. It wasn't Mam's way.

"Did you get my name-exchange gift ready?" he asked Mam, as he bent to pull on his boots. His

Sunday shoes were in his backpack, reminders of the importance of the day.

"Yes, indeed I did. Why would I wait till the day before the program?" she replied tartly.

Isaac laughed, knowing that was an insult. Mam prided herself on her good management.

The schoolhouse was fairly bursting at the seams, with Red Run and Oak Lane schools there at the same time. Teacher Catherine was flitting about, trying unsuccessfully to remain calm, unflappable.

Isaac could hardly wait to get started. This was Ruthie's chance to prove herself, and the SOS group's chance to savor their success. Isaac was confident, eager to get out there and show these schools what they had done.

The program went very well. The singing rose to the ceiling and swirled around the room, lighting on each pupil, bringing Christmas cheer to everyone.

Because the curtain divided the schoolroom, Isaac only became aware of Ruthie's absence when the program was almost over.

What had happened? Why had she failed to appear?

After "We Wish You a Merry Christmas" and the goodbye song were sung, the pupils of Hickory Grove rushed out the back door, one stream of exulting, yelling children, relieved to be free of restraint and tension.

Ruthie slunk along the side of the schoolhouse, her head bent, Hannah and Dora clustered around her. Isaac wasted no time.

"What happened, Ruthie?"

She shook her head. "I don't know."

Oh, boy.

There was nothing to say. Calvin and Michael's disappointment hung over their shoulders, a cape of black defeat.

Well, at least we won't expect her to say her poem tomorrow, Isaac thought. We failed. But it's only a Christmas poem.

Mam says acceptance of failure is a virtue, which is sort of hard to fathom, but I know now what she means, he thought. To lose with grace and dignity.

"Ruthie, it's okay," he told her, his voice kind.

She nodded.

"You want to practice?"

She looked at him, her eyes pools of fear. The monster called "I can't" had caught up with her.

The Hickory Grove pupils talked to some of the visiting school's children, only the ones they knew, who attended the same church services. The teachers soon herded the children into waiting vans, whisking them off to their own schools, allowing Teacher Catherine time to clean and prepare the classroom for the most important event of the Christmas season.

No matter how careful they had been, the upper-graders had erased parts of the camels' legs on the blackboard by leaning on the chalk tray in singing class. So Isaac and Calvin were put to work, filling in the erased spots.

Suddenly, Isaac was aware of Ruthie with a can of furniture polish and a dust cloth, viciously swiping desk tops, polishing them until they shone. In time to her ferocious swipes, she was singing, in jerks, but singing.

"I. Hope. My. Heart. Has. Heard." And on and on.

Isaac jabbed an elbow into Calvin's side, producing a puzzled expression and an "Ow!"

"Listen to Ruthie," Isaac hissed.

They stopped their work, their ears straining to the sound. They both knew it was her Christmas poem. Isaac shrugged his shoulders, turned to the blackboard and continued fixing the camels' legs. He was done with that SOS thing, same as he was done with Sim asking Catherine for a date. You could only do so much, and that was it. If Ruthie couldn't do it, then that was that. If Sim wanted to be a bachelor, then that was that, too.

He had other things in life to enjoy. Like a pony spring wagon. Imagine!

He told Calvin he might be getting one, which was a great surprise to Calvin, since Isaac's Christmas gifts usually amounted to less than half of his.

"What got into your dat?" he asked.

Isaac shrugged his shoulders, grinning happily.

At home, the house smelled of gingerbread, date and nut pudding, and chocolate, all mixed together in anticipation of Mam's Christmas dinner.

Dat brought home a whole quart of oysters for oyster stew on Christmas Eve. It was a tradition, to open gifts the evening before Christmas, and then savor the rich stew Mam made with that expensive jar of oysters. They only had oysters at Christmas-time.

The stale bread was brought from their freezer at the neighbor's garage and cut into cubes with the best bread knife to make *roasht*, that delicious holiday dish of bread cubes, celery, egg, and great chunks of turkey or chicken. Isaac was put to work chopping celery, the old wooden cutting board a sure prevention from cutting into Mam's countertop. He looked up when Sim came into the kitchen, sitting down to unlace his boots, humming softly under his breath.

"What are you doing?" Isaac asked, scooping up a handful of chopped celery.

"Oh, I might go watch the hockey players on Abner Speicher's pond for awhile."

"Is the pond fit?" Mam asked quickly.

"Should be."

"Not with 30 hockey players on it."

They went through this same conversation every year. Ice on the pond was a subject of great controversy, according to Mam. Six inches was sufficient, she'd say, until all those people started skating on top of it. Then what? She'd move around the kitchen wagging her head, finally giving in and saying if someone fell through the ice they would never forget it, and don't come crying to her, she'd tried to warn them.

"Wanna come along?" Sim asked Isaac.

Isaac jumped off his chair, raced around the kitchen searching for gloves, boots, and his coat, shouting his elation. Of course, he wanted to go!

He grabbed his hockey skates, clunked them into a corner of the *kessle-haus* (wash house) and raced back upstairs for an extra pair of socks.

His room was pitch-black. He groped on his night stand for his lighter, found it and flicked it on above his sock drawer. It took only a second until he located a pair of heavy wool socks and ran headlong down the stairs.

He didn't even think of Teacher Catherine. He didn't know girls came to these hockey games. He'd never been to one.

So when he saw Teacher Catherine sitting beside another girl he didn't know, warming her hands by the fire, he felt shy, unable to look at her.

Teachers belonged in a classroom, not at a hockey game.

"Hello, Isaac."

"Hello."

Quickly, he ducked his head as the other girl stared at him, smiling. He turned his back and prepared to pull on his skates. The schoolboys weren't allowed to play hockey with the big boys, but they had a small section of the pond roped off, and this was where Isaac was going as soon as he got his feet into his skates.

Sim's voice made him very still.

"Hello, Catherine. Kate." Sim nodded in the other girl's direction.

Well, no use hanging around. Sim wasn't going to do anything at all about having a date with Catherine anyway. So Isaac tiptoed on his skates through the snow, hit the ice and skated smoothly across the pond to Calvin and Michael.

What Isaac completely missed was the "King's Florist" truck that had crept slowly down Traverse Hill earlier that day, looking for Hickory Grove School.

And the brown-clad driver who hopped out with a gigantic poinsettia in a lovely, woven basket trailing dark green ivy, with a Christmas card inserted on a plastic spike that said, "Merry Christmas, Catherine. A friend, Simon Stoltzfus."

He never knew his teacher pulled out the plastic spike, tore at the card with trembling fingers, her face tense with unanswered questions.

He didn't see her read the words for only a second, then fling the card to her desk, crumple into a second-grader's desk and laugh and cry at the same time, then get up and whirl between the desks until her skirt billowed out, aflight with genuine happiness.

Isaac had been at home chopping celery.

Chapter Eleven

Isaac was stiff, sore and extremely tired at 5:00 a.m. when his cheap, plastic alarm began its nerve-wracking little beeps. It was one of the dumbest alarm clocks anyone had ever invented for five dollars at Walmart. Mam could at least have picked a better color.

His hand groped for the too-small button that shut off the hysterical beeping, gave up and threw it against the wall. When he remembered this was the day of the Christmas program, he retrieved the still-beeping alarm clock and shut it off this time.

Why should he have noticed any heightened color in Teacher Catherine's face? Or her extraordinary good humor, for that matter?

It was Christmas, after all. The program had gone well yesterday, and today was the season's crowning glory, with parents, friends and relatives cramming into the schoolhouse, craning their necks to see better.

Mam had brushed his coat well and washed his green Christmas shirt and hung it by the coal stove in the kitchen to dry until morning. She had polished his Sunday shoes and hung out his black Sunday vest. He felt very fine, wearing all those Sunday clothes.

Calvin looked fancy, he thought, wearing a red shirt with a hint of plaid design in it. Michael wore a green shirt, with a swirl in the pattern of the fabric. Isaac's was a plain, flat-out green. The girls wore red or green, but he couldn't remember who wore what.

Teacher Catherine looked especially fine. She wore a festive red dress, her usual black apron, Sunday shoes, and a very new white covering that looked just a bit better than the ordinary ones she wore on weekdays.

Isaac guessed playing baseball was what really got those coverings wrinkled and brown, the way the covering strings flapped and fluttered behind those girls dashing to first base. When they went sledding, the coverings stayed in the cloakroom in a Tupperware container, the girls throwing head scarves of rainbow hues on their heads and tying them below their chins, jutting out their faces to secure them firmly.

Isaac had a small black plastic comb in his vest pocket, which he used repeatedly throughout the forenoon. He wanted to appear neat and orderly, showing his green eyes to their best advantage.

They exchanged their gifts in the forenoon since the program didn't start until 1:00. Isaac had Henry's name and was proud to see how pleased Henry looked to find two Lewis B. Miller books and a pair of heavy gloves in his package.

Hannah had Isaac's name. He received a picture of howling wolves, an LED headlamp—he had three at home—and a package of Dentyne chewing gum. He was pleased. The howling wolves were cool. You could always chew gum or use another headlamp. Isaac thanked Hannah, and she ducked her head and wouldn't answer. He should have been nicer about those horses on the poster.

Teacher Catherine presented each of the boys with a small cedar chest with horses decoupaged on the lid.

It was one of the neatest things Isaac had ever owned. When he opened the lid, the contents took his breath away. It was full of root beer barrels! His absolute favorite! He thanked her fervently, and Teacher Catherine's eyes twinkled at him. He thought her the most wonderful person he had ever met.

The big girls were each given a hand-carved, wooden mirror with a lovely, smooth, rounded handle. Ruthie said it was a *hinna-gook schpickel.* (mirror to look behind you.) Calvin and Michael said their sisters all had one on their dressers, and they worked great to get your fighter fish going crazy. That really got Isaac's attention. A fighter fish? What was that?

Michael had a small aquarium in his room. It was rectangular, filled with smooth stones and plastic plants, but it contained only one grayish-red fighter fish. The reason they had to live alone was because they were so angry they killed any other fish that was in the aquarium. They swam around thinking they were the boss, always. But if you held up one of those *hinna gook schpikla* and the fish caught sight of himself, he instantly propelled himself into a frenzy, slamming against the side of the aquarium repeatedly.

Isaac listened, amazed. That was really something.

Hannah said that was cruel, then turned up her nose, inhaled mightily and stalked off.

Dora agreed.

Sarah said at least the fish had a bit of excitement in its life, swimming around like that all by itself.

Isaac informed her fish couldn't think.

Dora asked, how did he know?

Calvin said if you read about fish in the encyclopedia you could know.

Ruthie didn't say anything. Isaac looked at her and smiled. He thought that was a good quality, staying quiet the way she did. For a girl, anyway.

The little boys got wildlife books from Teacher Catherine. Big hardcover ones. With the longest Reese's Peanut Butter Cup Isaac had ever seen.

The little girls each received a pretty little chest, white, with a lid that opened and was lined with pink or lavender. It played music if you opened it. There was a handkerchief and a tiny, sparkly bag of red and silver Hershey's Kisses inside. Isaac thought Teacher Catherine must be rich, the way she spent money for Christmas.

All the children were agitated, the impending program, and the exchange of Christmas gifts goading them on. They raced outside to the playground, and then talked too much and far too loudly in the classroom. Before lunchtime, quite a few of the pupils had forgotten to put their foil-wrapped food on the propane gas heater. Little Sally cried, wanting her pizza warmed, so Teacher Catherine put her arm around the little girl's waist and pulled her close, then turned the heater up as far as it would go, heating her lunch in five minutes.

No one was really very hungry, although they did their best to hide that fact. Nervous fingers pressed sandwiches flat, bits of iceberg lettuce were torn to shreds and finally stuffed back into plastic sandwich bags. Apples were put back into the colorful Rubbermaid lunch boxes, with only a few bites missing. Pretzels stuck in dry throats.

The boys spent a great deal of time in the horse shed, their shoulders hunched as they rammed their hands in their pockets, shifting their weight from one foot to the other, talking nonsensical things, laughing nervously about things that really weren't that funny.

They all heard the arrival of the first horse and buggy. The unmistakable rumbling of steel-rimmed wheels on macadam, accompanied by the dull clopping of a fast-paced driving horse.

The boys beat it to the schoolhouse porch, a flock of nervous black-clad boys like frightened starlings. It was Levi Stoltzfuses already. It was barely 12:00. The program wasn't scheduled to begin until 1:00.

The boys moved in a huddle to the side of the porch as the team pulled up to the steps.

The buggy door opened, and Levi *sei* Rachel stepped down lightly, holding her baby wrapped in a blue blanket.

"*Vit mit da Dat Koinma?*" she asked. (Want to come with Dad?) The little boy clinging to the glove compartment nodded, and the buggy moved off.

Rachel was holding the diaper bag, the baby, and a large plastic container.

Isaac stepped forward. "*Brauchtsh hilf?*" (Do you need help?)

Rachel nodded gratefully. "*Denke.*" (Thank you.)

Proudly, Isaac carried the red container, lowering his eyes to look through the clear plastic lid. Chocolate-covered something! Oh, the wonderful things mothers brought to the Christmas program!

There were plates of cookies and trays of bars and cupcakes and homemade candy. Potato chips and pretzels and cheese. Party mix and popcorn, mounds of tortillas spread with cream cheese and seasonings, crammed full of ham and cheese, cut in little pinwheels of pure pleasure. There were paper cups of fruit punch, iced tea, coffee and hot chocolate.

No one thought of healthy food at Christmas-time.

Isaac was always pleased with Mam's contribution. She was a fine baker. This year she made extra peanut-butter tartlets for the Christmas program, which made Isaac especially glad. They were a buttery, rich crust shaped into miniature muffin tins, with a small Reese's cup pressed into them. Calvin and Michael loved them.

Second-grader Sally spied her mother and moved to her side quickly, reaching for her little brother

Jesse, bursting to show her classmates how cute he was, what a capable helper she was, uncovering his face, pulling on the strings of his pale blue stocking cap as her friends watched enviously.

Isaac's heart began to race in earnest when a white 15-passenger van slowed, then turned into the snow covered driveway.

Fremme! (Strangers!)

The boys jostled each other from their elevated position on the porch, then stood respectfully, watching. A few young girls hopped down, then turned to open the second door, allowing more room for the remaining passengers.

Doddy and Mommy Stoltzfus! (Grandpa and Grandma) Isaac was pink cheeked with high spirits. What a treat!

It was interesting to see who the people were that had to hire a driver, living too far away for their horse and buggy to bring them. Isaac knew Doddy Stoltzfuses lived in *die unna Beckveh* (lower Pequea) which was below Kirkwood and Quarryville, very seldom making the long drive to Gordonville.

It took awhile for Mommy to step down. She had to go backwards, grasping the arm of the second seat. Her black shawl and bonnet and the lower half of her skirt were the only things visible, as Doddy guided her feet to the running board of the van, then handed her the wooden cane with the black rubber tip she always used.

She grasped his hand as he steered her to the porch steps. His wide black hat brim hid his face, and only his white beard was visible in sharp contrast against his *ivva-ruck*. (overcoat)

"*Boova!*" (Boys) he said, as he maneuvered Mommy past them.

"Hello!" Mommy said, smiling widely, as she followed Doddy through the schoolhouse door.

There were other grandparents and aunts and uncles Isaac did not know. The van emptied itself one by one, everyone clad in the usual black. The boys greeted each visitor politely, then unanimously decided it was too cold on the porch, when, really, they were simply curious.

Teacher Catherine's face looked a shade whiter now, her mouth a grim line. That put fear in Isaac's own heart. Would everything go well? Would they remember their parts? Steely resolve replaced the fear. Of course, they would. Hadn't they practiced endlessly? They all knew their parts backward and forward, didn't they? It was like a repetition now. They said their parts without thinking very much at all.

Yes, everything would go well.

More teams turned in and unloaded their occupants. Little preschoolers followed their mothers up the steps, their eyes wide with curiosity, shyness mixed with anticipation.

Teacher Catherine's desk had been pushed to the back of the classroom, so that was where mothers deposited their offerings of Christmas treats. Fathers carried large five-gallon plastic orange containers of tea and punch, and one marked "ice water." Rectangular green coffee urns were brought in. Some mothers hurried over to make sure no spigot leaked, and put a few paper towels beneath them to catch any drips.

Isaac thought mothers must be the same, every last one of them. What did it matter if coffee dripped on the tile floor?

The whole classroom looked as if a hurricane blew through it after a Christmas program. He had seen it often enough. It never failed: half a dozen of those little preschoolers—who were never properly supervised—spilled their fruit punch. The other children ran through the sticky liquid before mothers—who talked entirely too much—saw it, leaving Teacher Catherine to clean up the whole unbelievable mess by herself.

A few weeks ago, Isaac would have tried to get Sim to stay and help Teacher Catherine clean up. Wouldn't that be an excellent opportunity to ask someone for a date?

But he had moved on. He no longer cared. If Sim wanted to be a bachelor and think himself a prophet, then he'd just have to do that. Isaac's services were over.

He looked at the clock.

12:45.

His pulse accelerated. He felt a bit skittish inside.
He needed to find Ruthie. Even a shot in the dark
was better than no shot at all.

Chapter Twelve

HE FOUND RUTHIE IN THE CLOAKROOM, standing by the window with Hannah, watching the teams pull up to the door.

He caught sight of Sam, Dat's superb black Standardbred driving horse. So they were here.

"Ruthie."

She looked over at Isaac, her eyebrows lifted.

"You going to do it?"

She took a deep breath. Her shoulders squared visibly. She looked straight into Isaac's eyes and said clearly and firmly, "Yes, Isaac, I'm going to do it."

Isaac's eyebrows danced way up, and his grin was so wide it changed the shape of his face. "You can do it, Ruthie! You go!"

She nodded, her face a picture of radiance. What had happened? Gone was the hand-wringing, the miserable expression.

Well, same as with Sim and Catherine, he wasn't going to expect too much. Stay levelheaded. Expect her to do it, but accept failure if it came.

The classroom was filling up now. Church benches had replaced the Ping-Pong table in the middle, which had been placed along the side of the room. The cloakroom was piled high with coats, bonnets and shawls. Babies cried. Mothers hushed them nervously, hoping they would fall asleep, or at the very least, remain quiet with some toys or a graham cracker.

Fathers held on to squirming little boys, bending to whisper words of discipline. "*Bleib sitza.*" (Stay sitting.)

A steady hum of voices, laughter, greetings, a kaleidoscope of faces, white coverings, colorful dresses, shirts accentuated with black vests. English people came to the program, too. Vans came, bringing friends of Teacher Catherine, friends of parents, all seated side by side, their colorful coats in stark contrast to the black.

Teacher Catherine herded the children into their curtained-off square of space. She spoke a few words of encouragement, made sure the necessary items for the plays were all in order and warned them all to be absolutely quiet behind the curtain.

"Do you want the windows up or down?" she asked.

"Down!" everyone whispered.

"It gets too warm in here."

"Too many people."

"Put them down."

Teacher Catherine nodded, smiled and said, "Do your best."

1:00. She tapped a small bell. The signal to begin!

Total silence now, as faces strained eagerly toward the open space in front of the blackboard, their stage.

The pupils sang a resounding chorus of Christmas songs first, the 21 beautiful voices blending into that special innocent harmony that only children can produce.

The emotional individuals in the audience sniffed, lifting spectacles to wipe eyes with meticulously ironed Sunday handkerchiefs.

Isaac stood in the back row between Ruthie and Hannah, singing with all his might. He knew their singing was good. In the guest book they passed to visitors to sign their names, almost all of them praised their singing. Isaac didn't like Hannah much, but she could sing. Her voice carried well with Isaac's, although he'd never tell her. Likely she'd take it as an insult.

After the singing, the smallest boy in school welcomed the audience to the Christmas program. Standing all alone, his head lifted high, his voice carrying well, he said clearly,

> *I'm very small, and very scared,*
> *But this job I have to do:*
> *Welcome you all on this glad day,*
> *Plus, "Merry Christmas," too!*

Smiling shyly, he turned on his heel and hurried behind the curtain.

There was a skit after that. Second, third and fourth grades came onstage with their skates and winter clothing.

Isaac's poem followed. He stood straight and tall and spoke in his usual crisp voice that carried well. His poem had 14 verses, which streamed from him effortlessly.

He spied Sim, lounging along the back wall in his red shirt, a head taller than his friend Abner. So he was here. Good.

Laughter followed the humorous parts. Babies became restless, were taken outside or given to another person.

The Abraham Lincoln play went well. Ruthie spoke with confidence, using her best voice, with Isaac supporting her.

The play about the wise men was flubbed a bit when Matthew forgot to finish his lines, confusing Rebecca, who bravely soldiered on, acting as if nothing out of the ordinary had happened. Good for her!

The first-graders wouldn't hold still behind the curtain, so Isaac snapped Ephraim's suspenders and shot them all a vicious glance, which did wonders. The little chap was always the one who stirred up everyone else. Like Bennie, probably no one made him listen at home.

The upper graders sang two German songs, "*Stille Nacht*" (Silent Night) and "*Kommet Alle*" (Come All).

That was always touching for Dat. Being conservative, he was touched by the continual teaching
of German in the schools. He fervently hoped that
the *Muttasproch* (mother language) of the forefathers
would not be neglected and that the old, but precious, tradition would be kept. So when these young
people sang the old hymns in the beloved language,
it meant much to him, and his respect for Teacher
Catherine was heightened.

Isaac saw Mam lift her glasses, unobtrusively extending a forefinger to wipe the wetness that had
pooled beneath one eye.

Little, first-grade Daniel's part was to sit in a
Christmas cake, accidentally, of course, while wearing an extra pair of pants, of course, which was always funny. The classroom erupted into unabashed
laughter. Very loud, Isaac thought, which was good.

A soft footfall, and he heard Ruthie. Isaac froze.
Chills chased themselves up his back. He became
warm all over. Her voice was strong. The words came
slowly, but they were absolutely distinct. He caught
Calvin's eye. Calvin shook his head in disbelief. From
the first line to the very end of her poem, she spoke

without faltering, her voice rising and falling in time to the beauty of the words.

No one in the audience knew there was anything unusual about the fact that Lloyd Allgyer's Ruthie spoke her whole poem slowly and clearly.

Only the SOS group and Teacher Catherine, who were bursting with Christmas joy.

The hour and 15 minutes flew by, as the plays and poems mixed with singing filled up everyone's senses. The spirit of Christmas swirled about and infused everyone who was in the room. Many of the guests were sorry to hear the closing song, telling each other it had been an outstanding program this year, that someone had spent a lot of time putting all this into the students.

Amid hearty hand-clapping from the audience, the pupils poured out of the back door into the clear cold air, relieved of the pressure to perform well, relieved of the month of practice, the hard work of memorizing and delivering the lines just right.

The upper-graders were pulled to Ruthie as if a gigantic magnet's force drew them there. Hannah and

Dora hugged her and squealed high and long. Isaac found that a bit overboard, but what else could you expect from girls?

"Ruthie! You did it!" Calvin yelled.

Isaac wanted to know how. "How could you do that?"

They all huddled together in the cold, cold air, as Ruthie crossed her arms tightly around her waist to stay warmer and keep from shivering. She told them she had practiced in front of a mirror, over and over and over, finally grasping the concept of speaking slower. "When I stutter, I'm afraid I can't say it, so I go too fast. Sort of like someone falling down the stairs. When they feel themselves slipping, they go too far in the opposite direction to stop themselves and roll down the stairs."

They all laughed about that description, which surprised Ruthie, who joined in whole- heartedly. It was a dose of Christmas spirit multiplied by 10, all brought about by Ruthie's success. It felt good.

Teacher Catherine met them inside the door, gathered Ruthie into her arms and held her there. Only the upper-graders knew why. Isaac felt his nostrils sting with emotion, but shook his head to straighten his hair, then looked out the window and blinked furiously. He got out his little black comb and pulled it through his hair, very hard, to get rid of that teary feeling.

They had to wait in line to fill their plates. Mothers bent over little ones grasping paper plates teetering dangerously with cookies and potato chips. Everyone was talking at once. Smiles were everywhere, faces shining with good humor.

Teacher Catherine moved among her pupils, thanking, congratulating, praising their efforts. Her face was absolutely radiant. Isaac could tell her praise was genuine. She was so pleased. That made it all worthwhile.

Finally, he reached the stack of paper plates. He helped himself to a large square of Rice Krispie Treats, pushed it to one side of his plate and added a monster cookie, three chocolate- covered Ritz crackers with peanut butter, a large scoop of Chex Mix and three or four of Mam's tarts. He was ravenously hungry. He had been too nervous to eat much of his food at lunchtime.

First he ate the monster cookie. Every year, Ben Zook *sei* Annie made these cookies. They were rough-textured with oatmeal and loaded with red and green M & M's for Christmas, of course. They were soft and chewy and buttery and perfect, every time.

Calvin was chomping on a handful of Chex Mix, sounding like a horse munching oats, spilling a lot of it on the floor, too hungry to worry about the excess.

Michael ate whoopie pies, one after the other, as fast as he could cram them into his mouth. Icing clung to his chin and the side of his mouth, but he didn't seem to mind, until his sister came bustling over with a handful of napkins and told him to wipe his mouth, and where were his manners? She had her eyebrows in that position, the one that meant he had overstepped his boundaries, and if he didn't straighten up it would go all the way to the Supreme Court named Mam.

Michael kicked carelessly in her direction and told her to mind her own business, he could take care of himself. Isaac giggled behind his Rice Krispie Treat.

Then Dan Glick brought the propane lamp stand out for Teacher Catherine, followed by Aaron Fisher who carried the propane tank and accessories. The lamp stand was made of cherry with a magazine rack on one side. It was beautiful.

Catherine put both hands to her mouth, her blue eyes opened wide and she said nothing at all for awhile. When the women crowded around, she began thanking them, saying it was too much, just way too much.

Dat went around with an envelope, collecting the money from each family.

Twenty-eight dollars. That wasn't bad, they said.

Who made the cabinet? they asked.

Sol King?

Oh, he was one of the best.

Wasn't that cherry wood different, now?

Did Teacher Catherine have other cherry pieces?

Levi *sei* Rachel thought her bedroom suit was cherry, but she wasn't sure.

The women nodded their heads, pleased. It was a good choice. Teacher Catherine was worth it, that was one thing sure. She had such a nice way with the children, didn't she?

The blanketed horses were becoming restless, stomping their feet in the snow at their stand where they were tied to the board fence. Mothers collected gifts, stashed them in bags or leftover cardboard boxes, and herded their children into their coats.

Fathers carried the boxes and empty trays and containers, stuffing them under buggy seats, as children clambered in, still munching that last piece of chocolate.

Doddy Stoltzfus pulled at Isaac's sleeve. "Isaac, *vee bisht*?" (How are you?)

"*Goot. Goot*!" Isaac answered, grinning happily.

"You did good!" High praise from Doddy. Isaac grinned, basking in the kind words from his grandfather.

Sim walked up, extending his hand, greeting Doddy. Doddy beamed as he lifted his head to meet Sim's eyes.

Isaac walked away, irked at Sim. Sim would be as old as Doddy and still would never have asked Teacher Catherine for a date.

Oh, well.

Chapter Thirteen

DAT AND MAM WERE ONE OF the last ones to leave. Sim, of course, the now deeply entrenched bachelor, was one of the first to hitch up his horse and head home.

Mam bustled about the classroom like a puffed-up little biddy hen, clucking about the mess. She had no idea this is what it looked like after a program. My goodness!

Catherine seemed a bit flustered, her cheeks about the color of her dress, but she remained polite, laughing frequently.

Mam noticed the gorgeous poinsettia, asking who gave it to her. "Oh, someone," was Catherine's answer, same as she told her pupils when they clustered about her desk in the usual way.

So Isaac rode home slouched in the back seat, his eyelids becoming heavy, rocked to a blissful state by the motion of the buggy.

It was all over now. He could relax and look forward to the Christmas dinner at home. He'd do his chores, then make himself comfortable with one of Calvin's books.

Dat talked to Mam about the singing. He'd never heard a school sing better. It must be that Catherine had a *gaub* (talent) in bringing out the best in her pupils. Mam said yes, it wasn't often you heard something like that. It seemed the children put their heart into it, didn't they?

Isaac grinned, wondering if they forgot he was in the back seat.

Back at the schoolhouse, a lone buggy retraced its steps, the horse a high-stepping sorrel Saddlebred, his ears bent forward in the typical heart-shaped fashion.

Sim got out slowly, led Fred into the buggy shed, slipped the neck rope around his neck and knotted the rope securely in the ring attached to the wall.

After throwing a blanket over the horse's back, he wiped down the front of his coat before striding purposefully to the front door.

Teacher Catherine was pouring hot water from the kettle on the stove into a plastic scrub bucket, when she heard a knock.

Was it a knock?

She froze, then tried to get ahold of her fear. It was still broad daylight; no one was going to hurt her; no one knew she was here; it was the Christmas season; she would be fine.

With her heart beating heavily, her eyes wide, a hand to her throat, she answered the knock. She couldn't think of one word to say, so she didn't say anything at all. She just stood there and looked at Sim Stoltzfus, all six feet of him, and thought there was simply no reason for him to be there.

"I thought maybe you would appreciate a bit of help," he said.

She looked into his green eyes and could form no words, so she stood aside and ushered him in.

Sim whistled, soft and low.

"What a mess!"

"Yeah." She had found her voice. "If you don't mind, you could burn the trash."

"Sure."

Eagerly, he grabbed the plastic garbage bags.

She added a dollop of Pine-Sol to the warm water in the plastic bucket, while trying to calm her racing heart.

Sim came back and took over with the mop, shedding his coat as he spoke. She watched him with large blue eyes and wondered if she should say something about the poinsettia or wait until he mentioned it first.

She began unpinning the curtains, taking them down. He talked of everyday, mundane things that put her at ease in a surprising way.

He said it was a shame to erase the camels and wise men, but she said she was glad to do it. There was a time for everything, and she was glad the Christmas program was over, that it was a lot of work.

Sim nodded his head and watched her stretching to reach the pins that held the curtains to the wire.

He told her she was a bit too short for the job and proceeded to help.

That was when her heart went all crazy again, and she could hardly breathe. She became so flustered she went out and swept the porch. When she returned, he had folded the sheets and was back to mopping floors.

He talked about the program, then asked why everyone was hugging the one eighth-grade girl. What was her name? Ruthie? He leaned against the wall and held the mop handle, while she forgot herself and launched into a vivid account of Ruthie overcoming her stuttering problem, the SOS group, and the grand way she had grasped the concept of speaking slowly.

Sim watched her face, the way she moved her hands when she spoke, and knew this was the girl he wanted to marry and live with for the remainder of his days.

When he finished mopping the floor, they moved the teacher's desk back to the front of the room. They washed the blackboard. Catherine stood back admiring the smooth blackness of it.

They found two containers of cookies someone had forgotten, so they sat by the teacher's desk and ate.

Sim asked her what she thought of the poinsettia. He watched her lovely face light up, listened to her blushing thanks.

She said, "You shouldn't have."

"I wanted to let you know I was your friend."

"Thank you. It was nice of you to remember me."

Sim's one eyebrow lifted.

"Remember you? I never stop thinking about you, so how could I remember you?"

He laughed easily when she became flustered. Then he became very sober. The classroom was silent. The winter sunlight was fading fast as the sun became veiled by cold gray clouds, then slid behind Elam's windmill, putting it in stark contrast to the evening light.

Out on Route 340, a diesel engine shifted gears. The cry of a flock of crows echoed across the stubbles of the cornfields as an approaching horse and buggy chased them off. A child cried out at the adjacent

farm, all sounds of a thriving community, lives inter-
woven, a reed basket of old traditions and new ways,
yet so much remained the same.

For hundreds of years, young men had sought
God's leading in asking for a young girl's hand. The
world turned on its axis, and life was continually rein-
vented. New hopes, new dreams, a young man seeking
a worthy companion, someone to love, to share their
lives, the cycle was still moving from seed to harvest,
to every season under the sun.

And so Sim found the God-given courage to tell
her what was on his mind and in his heart.

"I know I don't stand much of a chance, but I
won't have any rest until I ask. Will you accept
my offer of friendship? Will you allow me to take
you to the Christmas supper on Sunday evening?"
Catherine sat very still, her hands folded in her lap,
her head bowed.

As long as Sim lived, he carried the sight of her
face as she lifted it to the sun's last rays, her brilliant-
ly blue eyes holding a light of gladness. Before she
spoke he knew. And when she spoke, he carried the

remembrance of her words in his heart always.

"Oh my, Sim Stoltzfus."

Then, she laughed, a soft, happy sound.

"Yes."

That was all she said.

When he helped her into the buggy, he wanted to crush her light form to his, but he didn't. He could wait. Sitting beside her in the coziness of the buggy's lap robe was more than enough. He was blessed beyond anything he deserved.

He held her hand much longer than was necessary when he helped her from the buggy. Was it just his own craziness, or did her hand linger as well?

That evening, in the barn, Isaac was tired, grumpy and in a hurry to finish the chores. He had no time for Sim. When Sim asked him to take the baler twine to the burn barrel, Isaac said no, Sim could do it himself.

Dat heard him and said sternly, "Go, Isaac."

So that was the reason Isaac had nothing to do with Sim at the supper table. Life wasn't fair, when you were the youngest son. You always had to do what no one else wanted to do. Just being the smallest made everyone naturally assume it was his chore.

Taking out Mam's slop pail from under the sink, for instance. That vile little plastic ice cream bucket with a lid on it, setting there for days with apple peelings and cold, congealed oatmeal or Cream-of-Wheat, bacon grease, and spoiled peaches. No one had to smell it except the person taking it out and dumping it in the hog's trough.

His Christmas spirit was all used up, fizzled out, sputtered, and cold.

There was potato soup for supper, on top of all life's other atrocities. And the potato soup had hard-boiled eggs in it, which made him shiver. Gross.

Sim acted as if the potato soup was the finest thing Mam had ever cooked, opening his mouth wide to shovel the filled spoon into it.

Isaac ate bread-and-butter pickles, then felt slightly sick to his stomach. He swallowed hard when Sim cleared his throat and asked Dat if it was proper to bring Catherine to the Christmas dinner.

Dat looked up, surprised.

Mam's spoon stopped halfway to her mouth, then

resumed slowly.

"Since we're dating now, I wondered if you'd object?"

"You're …? What?" Dat said.

"I asked Teacher Catherine."

Dat smiled, Mam became all flustered and teary, and Dat nodded soberly and said he guessed it would be all right. Then he tried to look stern, but failed completely.

Isaac's mouth fell open.

"Did you ask her?"

"Yes, Isaac, I did. She said yes."

Isaac said nothing at all.

Later though, he said a lot. He said it to Sim, his Christmas spirit flaming brightly as he congratulated Sim in the best way he knew how. He hit him in the back of his head with a snowball, then took off running, Mam's plastic slop pail abandoned in a snowdrift, where Catherine found it in the spring.

The End

Christmas Reflection

I hope my heart has heard the song
The shepherds heard that night.
I hope my heart has found the star
The wise men kept in sight.
Then maybe I will find my way
To the quiet manger, too.
So my heart can kneel in worship,
Bringing gifts sincere and true.

THE Christmas VISITOR

Chapter One

IT WAS THE ROCKING CHAIR'S SQUEAK that started the tears. The high, annoying chirp would have driven him to find the WD-40, turn the rocker upside down, and liberally spray the irritating spot, satisfied only when it was completely silenced.

She could smell the WD-40. She could see him kneeling there—his dark eyebrows drawn down in concentration, his eyes flat, the perfect nose beneath them, his wide mouth unsmiling, but only for a short time. He was known to talk a lot and smile as much, his hands moving, alive, so animated, so interesting.

She didn't realize right away that her tears were falling on little Benjamin. They dampened the downy hair of the five-week-old son she was holding, darkening and flattening it in sections. Clucking and crooning, she moved a thin finger delicately across the wet spots, trying not to wake him, and then bent her head to kiss the warm, rounded cheek.

Here in her arms lay Ben's final gift to her, born three months after Ben had fallen at the barn raising at Elam Glick's down along 896 near Christiana. Ruth never had a chance to say goodbye.

Life went on, she found. It moved right along, whether she decided to go with it or not. It was impossible to speak of her grief and express it properly when it was a twisting, tumbling void that threatened to swallow her up the minute she didn't move along with life. Her children were the motivation that got her up and moving after she'd been chewed up and spit out after the viewing and the funeral.

The rain that day had been so fitting. The weeping pines bent their fragrant green boughs to allow the fresh April showers to drip from one branch to the next below. The black umbrellas sprouted like grieving mushrooms with the black-clad members of the Old Order Amish huddled beneath them.

Rows of horses and buggies were tied along the well-kept white painted fence. Numbers had been chalked in white on the sides of the gray buggies. Ruth had ridden in the buggy marked with a simple 1. The first buggy. His wife and children following the coffin, a plain wooden box laid reverently in the horse drawn hearse.

Back at the farm, where the services had been held in the shop, the women had packed sandwiches of Lebanon bologna and white American cheese with mayonnaise on wheat bread. It was a token of *sark feltich* (caring) hearts, as was the custom, a snack to tide them over after the long services and a boost of nutrition for the children before the burial.

She couldn't keep him, although she'd tried, touching that lifeless face just once more. In the end, as the minister's voice droned on in a singsong cadence and the pines wept, they had closed the coffin and lowered it, and the granules of Lancaster County soil hit the wood with a sound that was now a permanent part of her.

The smell of wet soil would always remind her of that day. So would Lebanon bologna.

"Mam!"

The call pulled her abruptly back to reality. Struggling, she tried to get out of the chair and then answered, "Lillian, *ich komm*! (I come!)"

Tenderly Ruth settled little Benjamin, pulling the soft baby blanket up to his waist, no farther, for in August the nights were warm. She moved swiftly down the short hallway into her bedroom where Lillian, the rowdy three year old, sat straight as a small tree trunk, saying she was thirsty. She wanted chocolate milk, but Ruth said, no, no chocolate milk, just water. Even when Lillian kicked off the covers and threw a fit, she remained firm, gave her a cold drink of water, and promised chocolate milk in the morning.

She checked on the older girls. Barbara was on her side, her shoulders rising and falling beneath the thin, handed down nightgown, the one Esther had worn for many summers.

She listened at the door of the boys' room, but all was quiet and peaceful, the darkness a comfort somehow. Roy was nine and Elmer ten. They were lively young boys with energy to spare, now that they'd been transplanted to the small rancher with vinyl siding on Hoosier Road.

She couldn't have kept the farm, with the depressing economy, so they said. A recession. Land prices had fallen—were falling. So she'd sold out to the highest bidder. The amount fell short of the accumulated debt. As was the custom, the people stood by her with donations, alms, and benefit suppers. It had all amounted to an amazing sum.

Levi King had provided the house. She had no income, other than her quilting. There was nothing else she could do, with six children to care for. If she did get a job, which she would need to do—and soon—she would simply need to hire a babysitter, the way the English people did. She didn't have much choice.

The church "kept" their widows as did kind relatives. Her parents, his parents—they all gave and *sarked* (cared for) Ben *sei* Ruth (his wife, Ruth). But she could not go on sponging off of others forever.

She showered and shampooed her thick brown hair, donned a thin nightgown, and pulled a hairbrush through her heavy, wet tresses.

Ruth Miller was only thirty years old—small, pe-
tite, and much too young in appearance for her thirty
years. She leaned over the bathroom sink to fasten
the snaps of her cotton robe, pulled back her hair,
and went outside to sit on the porch to allow her hair
to dry, if only for a moment.

The crickets were noisy, and the katydids noisier
still, shrieking their plaintive cries from the locust
tree by the shed. The sky was alive with twinkling
stars, but the leaves of the old oak tree hung limp
in the hot August night with hardly a breeze to stir
them. Somewhere a lonesome dog howled, starting
up a series of sharp yipping from a neighboring one.

Ruth lifted her face as she loosened her hair and
ran her fingers through it to help dry faster.

Well, Ben, it's been a long day. I think little Benjamin will be very much like you. Active, alert, quick
to speak. Lillian just drives me crazy. I never was good
with her. I can't start pitying myself now, but you were
so perfect for her. I think that is part of her problem.

Elmer had a bad day. He helped Priscilla pull corn
for the roadside stand, and she wouldn't allow him

to sell any—just sent him home with five dollars for three hours of work. Is that fair?

Ben, how am I going to make it? Coal is up to two hundred and some dollars a ton. I could burn wood, but is it really much cheaper? I can't afford propane.

Esther needs to have her eyes examined, I feel sure, but there is no extra money. I'm too proud to beg. And I'm afraid I'm not very good with the money I do have. I bought two rugs at Walmart, along with my groceries, and now I feel I shouldn't have.

What about Esther's eyes?

Ruth watched the stars, as if one might answer, then closed her eyes and prayed to the One far above the stars, the Presence in whom she placed her faith from day to day.

"*Unser Vater in dem Himmel* (Our Father who art in Heaven)," she murmured.

Later, she fell asleep the minute her head touched the pillow. She slept dreamlessly until Benjamin became restless and woke her with his soft little grunts, turning his head from side to side as the hunger in his little belly disturbed him.

Ruth sighed, knowing it would do no good to try the pacifier. She rolled out of bed, gathered him up, and cuddled him beside her.

The sun soon emerged above the horizon, and she knew the pulsing orange ball of heat would send the mercury on the old plastic thermometer up to well past 90 degrees.

She was up and dressed by six o'clock, wearing a blue, short-sleeved summer dress with a black bib apron tied over it and her washed and well worn white organdy covering pinned neatly on her head.

It was always good to get an early start. Quietly, her bare feet whispering across the floor, she picked up the plastic Rubbermaid hamper from the corner of the bathroom. She grabbed the dripping washcloth she saw dangling from the side of the white bathtub and threw it on top. She carried her load to the laundry room, where the Maytag wringer washer stood solidly attached to the floor, the plastic rinse tubs beside it.

As quietly as possible, she opened and closed the screen door, then hurried to the diesel shanty at-tached to the barn. There she flipped a switch, turned the key, and was rewarded by the grinding sound of the Lister diesel engine coming to life.

Blue smoke puffed from the gray exhaust pipe, staining the cement blocks around it with a black ring as usual. She closed the diesel shanty door and hurried back to the house.

There was always pressure on wash day to hurry and finish before the little ones awoke. She should be okay today—Benjamin's last feeding had been at four thirty—if Lillian stayed quiet.

Water gushed out of the hose with a turn of the spigot, filling the large washer. She added a cup of Tide with Bleach and opened the handle on the air line, allowing the compressed air from the tank behind the diesel shanty to power the air motor beneath the wringer washer with a rhythmic movement.

Quickly, she separated the laundry. Whites went in first. She closed the spigot after the rinse tub was full and added a capful of Downy, then went to put the teakettle on for her coffee.

She could already feel beads of sweat forming on her upper lip and glanced at the thermometer. She resigned herself to the heat but sighed when she heard Lillian's grumpy howls from the bedroom. Tying on the apron filled with clothespins, Ruth scuttled back the hallway saying, "Shh!"

Lillian was not happy. Her eyes were heavy with drowsiness from waking up before she was really finished sleeping, and she was every bit as ill-tempered as usual. Ruth swept her up, wrapped her arms around the small form of her daughter, and held her tightly, raining teasing little kisses on her sticky face.

Lillian fought, turning her head and grimacing, her pigtails stuck out in every direction, her muffled laughter emerging.

"*Do net!* (Don't!)"

"My funny girl! You're going on the couch!"

Dumping her unceremoniously on the blue sofa, Ruth pulled the lavender nightgown over Lillian's bent knees and pressed down on her legs, making her bounce slightly.

"*Do net!*"

But she was giggling, her round face wreathed in

smiles, her blue eyes creased at the corners, and Ruth smiled back.

"I want chocolate milk!"

How could one mighty little three year old re-member, through eight hours of sleep, that she had wanted that chocolate milk the night before and was refused?

She never gave up, often being "chastened" for outright disobedience. If she was told repeatedly not to get into the pea patch, that was exactly where she was fifteen minutes later, like a little rabbit, hunkered down and eating peas as fast as she could, her blue eyes completely innocent.

Ruth would not allow the despair to penetrate her sense of well-being. She pushed back the sinking feel-ing of being completely incapable of handling her six children, her life. It was one day, one hour at a time.

If Lillian had been promised chocolate milk the evening before, that is what she would have. Ruth stirred Hershey's syrup into the cold milk in the Sip-py cup and took it to Lillian, who smiled widely, without remembering to say thank you.

Ruth hung the whites on the wheel line, pushing the clothes out over the back yard after pinning them securely with wooden clothespins from the apron around her waist.

The air was still and already humid. She heard the purring of the diesel back on the farm, the rhythmic clip clopping sound of an approaching team, robins scolding from the electric wire beside the road.

She'd mow the grass today after she finished her cleaning. It was Friday, the day she usually accomplished all three major tasks of cleaning, laundry, and yard work. The boys would pull weeds in the garden and push the hand cultivator through it.

The door opened only a sliver, and bright blue eyes peeked out. The door was pushed open wider, and a tousled head appeared, followed by "Hi, Mam!"

"Well, good morning, Barbara!"

"Are you good?"

"Yes, I'm very good."

"Did you sleep good?"

"Oh, yes!"

Barbara came over and laid her head against Ruth's waist as her arms went around her mother. Ruth held her close, a wet washcloth clutched in her hand. She inhaled the sun and dirt and not quite properly rinsed hair.

"Mmm, Barbara. *Ich gleich dich so arich* (I love you so much)."

Barbara was the one endowed with a caring spirit, loving and gentle and kind to all, except for Roy. Roy was the one single irritant of her life, the fly in her chicken corn soup, the rain on her parade, the fingernail across her blackboard.

"Esther's awake."

"Good. Is she with Lillian?"

"Yes. Lillian wants Trix."

"Did she get her some?"

"They're all gone."

"Would you please check on the baby?"

Barbara left immediately, and Ruth shook her head, always appreciative of her five year old's willingness to obey.

They ate dippy eggs, stewed saltine crackers, and buttered toast for their breakfast as they sat gathered around the kitchen table near the sunny east windows. The windows sat low in the wall, allowing all that morning light to enter.

The table was a solid oak extension one, made by Noah Fisher down below Atglen before Ben and Ruth were married. The chairs were wheat chairs, the spindles on the back splayed out so that they resembled sheaves of wheat, all made of solid oak.

The tablecloth on the table was a durable double-knit fabric from Lizzie Zook's Dry Goods Store in Intercourse. Ruth had hemmed it herself, and it was a fine red and white gingham, serviceable for years, as long as she used her dependable Shout spray on the grease spots before immersing it in the hot water in the wringer washer.

Ruth's dishes were Corelle, the set her sisters had given her on the day she became Ben's bride. She still had most of them after eleven years, which was remarkable considering what they'd been through.

The kitchen cabinets were oak as well, fairly new, with the gas refrigerator set neatly in the space created for it. A healthy green fern sprouted from a brown pot suspended above the sink by a macramé holder, and the canister set was brown ironstone to match. By the low windows, there were more potted plants—a fig tree, another fern, and a few African violets.

The hutch against the west wall was made by Noah Fisher as well and contained the china that Ben had given her a few weeks before the wedding. He'd been so humble, almost shy.

Ruth loved pretty things, her artistic touch showing in her ability to maintain a nice home, although it was all done in simplicity, with common sense, the way the Amish *ordnung* (rules) required.

She felt blessed, having this small single story house and being able to live in it without paying rent. Levi King simply refused it, and Lizzie told her in whispered tones they wouldn't feel right taking her money, then closed her eyes and kept them closed for so long that Ruth had a terrible urge to laugh. Then she felt like crying and wringing this dear, plump woman's hand, but she just gave up and hugged her. Without the support of the Amish community, she'd never make it—that was one sure thing.

Her family's support was tremendous, her bank
account still containing the last of their generosity.
Her emotional support was bolstered frequently by
caring relatives and was as essential as the air she
breathed. But some things can only be spoken in solitude, things other people need not know.

Chapter Two

ELMER AND ROY DID A GOOD job in the garden, for all of thirty minutes, before they gasped and staggered toward the old oak tree, flopped down on their backs, and flung their arms across their foreheads—each movement seemingly synchronized, like swimmers.

"Mam!"

The howl was in unison, too.

Ruth stopped pushing the reel mower and wiped the perspiration from her forehead as the blood pounded in her ears. She answered with a calm, "Yes, boys."

"It's too hot! It's cruel to make us work in the garden."

"Oh, come on! You're men. You're tough!"

Elmer's head flopped back and forth as if it hadn't been properly attached.

"It's 100 degrees," Roy wailed, his despair bringing a deep mirth from someplace Ruth had almost forgotten.

It would soon be five months since Ben had fallen, leaving her to journey alone. She had never thought she would laugh ever again, certainly not within five years. But life kept on going. And it was the children that mattered. They gave her reason to go on living. And here was Roy, making her laugh, deeply and sincerely.

Flopping down to sit beside them, she bowed her head and gave in to her laughter, squeezing her eyes shut, lifting her face, and howling with it. She didn't cry hysterically at the end either.

Roy and Elmer looked at their mother, then both sat up and watched her with serious concern.

"Oh my!" Ruth gasped, wiping her eyes. "Sorry, I wasn't *schputting* (mocking) you."

Roy eyed her warily.

"Yes, you were."

"Nah-uh!"

"What else was it?"

"I guess it just struck me funny, because I'm hot and miserable, too. It is too warm. But I'm almost finished. We'll come back out this evening, and you can finish the garden while I run the weed eater."

Elmer looked as if he couldn't believe his good luck.

"Can we go swimming?"

Ruth considered his question.

"Would it be possible to pick the green beans and take them to Mrs. Beadle first?"

"I think so."

Completely rejuvenated, they bent their backs to the task with the plastic buckets by their sides. The sun suddenly seemed much more comfortable than it had ten minutes before.

Esther was in the house filling her usual role as the bossy older sister. She had her little bib apron tied around her waist and was caring for Benjamin while scolding Lillian for getting beads in the baby's face.

"Lillian, now get away from him!" she screeched, her dark hair wet with the sweat from her forehead, her dark blue eyes intense, her hands on her hips, for all the world a replica of a little biddy hen protecting her chicks.

Ruth washed her hands at the sink and dried them on her apron.

"Your face is red!" Lillian shouted.

"It's hot outside," Ruth answered, smiling.

"Mam, you have to stay in here. That Lillian is a mess. She won't listen to me. She just keeps getting at Baby Benjamin. She's driving me nuts!"

"Now, Esther. Don't say it like that. That's going a bit overboard."

"Well, I don't know how to say it so that you'll listen."

Ruth hid a smile as she stooped to pick up Lillian, buckling down yet again to the responsibility of raising this brood of six children alone without ever showing the worries that threatened to overtake her.

When Ben was alive, they had been busy. The farm required physical labor day after day, but the responsibilities and the decision making had been shared. It made a difference. There was so much to be shouldered alone.

The first thing to go had been the battery lamps. It was easier to fill a plastic can with kerosene to fill the lamps they used in the bathroom and bedroom than it was lug those heavy twelve-volt batteries around. Yes, the kerosene was smelly, and she had to wash the glass lamp chimneys each week, but it was easier to manage. She had also learned to change the propane tank for the kitchen lamp, a job she had never accomplished before Ben died.

Now she also had to harness Pete, the driving horse, all by herself, and with Elmer lifting the shafts, hitch him to the buggy to drive to church or the grocery store herself. She had become used to it, and it wasn't so bad, though she did often worry about driving alone with the children.

The responsibility of making decisions about the children was not easy, ever. Should Elmer be forced to return to Priscilla's corn patch? Would it be best to make him continue to work hard at a job he despised?

Or should she take pity on him and allow him to stop? Which was best—building character or understanding his total dislike of Priscilla and her weedy corn patch? That was when she needed Ben so badly. That was when she felt defeated, but only as much as she allowed herself, she soon learned.

All her life, courage had just been a word—much like virtue or hope or fear or any other word—until she'd been alone. Courage was now a noun. She had to buckle it on, like a harness or a back pack, click the plastic fasteners into place, take a deep breath, and just get going with it.

Dealing with Esther and Lillian took courage. Dealing with perfect little Barbara and her abrasive, yet sensitive, brother took courage as well. And on and on.

But this day ended with a perfect late summer evening, and as the sun slid behind the cornfields and the twilight folded itself softly down around them, they took a pitcher of iced mint tea out on the front porch and a bag of Tom Sturgis pretzels with some ranch dressing to dip them in. The lawn was clipped evenly, the edges of the flower beds were trimmed, and the garden contained no weeds—at least as far as Ruth could tell from the porch. Benjamin was settled for the night, and Lillian curled up on her lap, her tousled little head quiet at last. And Ruth knew she was not alone. God was right there with her and the children, supplying backpacks full of courage when she needed it.

The Lord giveth, and the Lord taketh away. Yes, of course. It was God's will to take Ben, for reasons we don't know, her mother had said. So had Aunt Lydia and Eva. The true test of faith is in accepting and trusting God when life's events leave us without understanding.

Why her? Ruth had questioned many times in her heart, but only once to her mother.

Dear Mam. Ruth's rock of comfort. When all else failed, her Mam was there with her large blue eyes and wrinkles and crow's feet that all somehow reflect- ed her life—the garden, the wringer washer, the har- rowing, hay making, cooking and baking, laughing and crying, teaching, and being stern in the way only

Mam could, living her life with Dat, her life's partner for more than thirty-five years.

Tomorrow, Mam would come for the day, bringing a spring wagon loaded with corn. Incredible, her specialty.

"Did you know Mommy (Grandmother) is coming tomorrow?" Ruth asked the children.

"Is she?"

"Yes, we'll be freezing corn."

"Goody!" Esther clapped her hands.

"Can we eat all we want all day long?'

"Of course!"

The prospect of having Mommy Lapp come to their house the next day provided a sense of anticipation. Their happiness replaced the usual melancholy that often settled over them at night, when the children missed Ben most.

Mommy Lapp might let the boys drive Ginger, her trustworthy driving horse, if they needed something at the store. Ruth glanced at Elmer, knowing what he was thinking, and grinned.

"You might be allowed to drive Ginger."

Elmer laughed, then watched his mother's face before saying, "Mam, I worry about training a horse.
Who will buy me a buggy, or teach me to drive my
own horse if…Dat is…." He stopped and swallowed,
then reached self consciously for another pretzel as if
that act of normalcy could cover his embarrassment.

"Oh, that's a long way off, Elmer."

But after the children were in bed, Ruth returned
to the porch. She aimlessly rocked in the wooden
rocker and thought of what he'd said.

Who would? She didn't think about being married
to someone else. How could she ever be unfaithful to
the memory of Ben? He lived on in her heart and in
her mind. It wouldn't be right.

She'd teach Elmer. Somehow they'd acquire the
money for a horse and buggy. Elmer had always been
a serious thinker, well beyond his years, and now,
without Ben, he was especially so. They would manage.

No, she could not imagine subjecting these children
to a new relationship. It would not be fair to them. It
would be entirely different if she had only one or two

children who were too young to understand. But at the age of ten, it would be too hard for Elmer and even the others—except perhaps her little Benjamin.

In the morning, the children were up and dressed, except for Lillian, who hadn't slept long enough the night before, when Ruth's mother drove up to the barn with the corn piled high on the back of the black spring wagon.

Ruth hurried out to help her unhitch, followed by the children, leaving little Benjamin howling in his bouncy seat.

"*Ach* (Oh) my!"

Ruth hurried back into the house, crooning as she took up the unhappy newborn and cuddled him against her shoulder, bouncing him and patting his back. She looked out at her mother, surrounded by the children, her back bent slightly, her gray apron lifted to one side as she reached into the oversized pocket sewn on the side of her dress and extracted a heaping handful of Tootsie Rolls—every flavor imaginable.

Ruth smiled, knowing the sugar-laden candy would just have to be consumed before breakfast as Mommy Lapp pooh-poohed the idea that candy wasn't healthy. Ruth figured scrambled eggs and toast could aid its digestion.

Her mother entered the kitchen. She was a small woman with a rounded stomach and a bit of fullness around the hips, having borne eleven children of her own. She said she needed the extra padding. It was what kept her going. Her hair was pure white, neatly rolled at the sides, and pinned in the back beneath her large, white covering.

Mam was a *dienna's frau* (minister's wife). Her coverings were large, and she wore a belt apron pinned around her waist. Her clothes were conservative as a good example for the younger generation. Radiating kindness and caring, her work-worn hands were always ready to be laid on a suffering one's shoulder or slipped about the waist with whispered words of condolence that were always as available as the air she breathed.

Mam sat down. She gathered Barbara in one arm and Esther in the other, stroking their backs and saying, "Oh, girls, it's so good to see you again. It's been too long. I make myself too busy in the summertime, *gel* (right), Ruth?"

"Well, no Mam, you still have Emma and Lydiann at home, plus all those big boys who should be dating and getting married. I declare they are spoiled with you for their mother."

Highest praise, Ruth knew, and she was rewarded by a smile of pure benediction.

"Oh."

That was all she said, but Ruth knew her mam loved having her boys around her, cooking huge breakfasts for them with fried mush and dried beef gravy and applesauce and shoofly pie and hot chocolate.

"Couldn't Emma come?"

"No, she goes to market with Lydiann on Saturdays now, too."

"Really?"

"Yes, David Kind gave her a job at the produce stand."

"Well, that's good."

"Yes, she'll be glad for some spending money.

Lydiann was so busy she could hardly keep up with the customers, so she said something to David about it, and he said Emma could start last week."

"Is that market so busy already?"

"Well, in New Jersey fresh produce from Lancaster is quite popular."

Ruth nodded.

Farmer's markets were a way of life for many single Amish girls who worked long hours on the weekends selling produce, baked goods, meats and cheeses, or prepared foods like chicken, pulled pork, and a variety of barbeque. They were huge, indoor markets with many different vendors, bustling places filled with homemade or homegrown food, mostly within a 100-mile radius of the Amish farms of Lancaster County.

There was a high-pitched shrick from Ruth's room, and dutiful Barbara went to find Lillian, reappearing with the crying three year old on one hip. Lillian was indignantly wailing and hitting her sister.

"Lillian, *do net*!" Ruth called from her rocking chair where she was feeding Benjamin.

Instantly, Ruth's mam was on her feet, trying to take Barbara's heavy, writhing load from her and saying, "*Komm*, Lillian. *Komm. Mommy iss do* (Grandmother is here)."

Lillian's shrieks only increased in volume, so Barbara let her slide to the kitchen floor, where she resumed her howling. When Mommy tried to pick her up, Lillian twisted and turned, her legs flailing, her nightgown revealing the large disposable diaper she still wore.

"*Ich vill my tootie!* (I want my pacifier!)"

Quickly, Barbara scuttled down the hallway to look for the missing pacifier, which, when presented, was refused. The shrieking resumed. Without a word, Ruth rose from the rocking chair, handed the baby to her mother, and bent to pick up her struggling daughter. She took her directly to the laundry room, where she administered a firm "reprimand," letting Lillian understand that such behavior was completely unacceptable by using the age-old method of the Plain people, who still honored the meaning of molding a young child's will.

Later, with Lillian's head on her shoulder and her
pacifier in her mouth, Ruth explained to her that
throwing a fit was not allowed as she was a big girl
now. Lillian hiccupped and sniffed but stayed quiet,
watching her grandmother warily.

Mommy cooked a large pan of scrambled eggs and
filled the broiler of the gas stove with slices of homemade bread. She sadly noted the absence of bacon or
sausage in Ruth's refrigerator that contained so little,
but she said nothing.

"I brought a coffee cake. Elmer, can you go get it?
It's under the seat."

"I'll go!" Roy yelled, almost upsetting his chair in
his urgency to please his grandmother.

Later the women drank coffee alone as the children unloaded the corn outside. Mam asked Ruth
how she was managing, her large, blue eyes round
pools of love and caring, which always and without
fail produced tears she did not want to show.

Ruth nodded, struggling for control. She got up
and grabbed a handful of Kleenex as she drew her
upper lip down to help stay the onset of emotion.

"Alright," she said.

No, Mam, actually I am not doing well. I'm afraid I'm not doing the right thing with Lillian. I'm weak and tired, and I miss Ben so much I want to die sometimes. I'm afraid my money will soon be all gone, and I feel guilty for everything I spend because it's really someone else's hard-earned money.

But she did not say that.

"Just alright?"

Ruth nodded, unable to speak. She was afraid one word would strangle her and open the floodgates of self-pity and grief and helplessness and inadequacy.

Mam cut a slice of coffee cake with the side of her fork, put it carefully in her mouth, and chewed, wisely allowing Ruth time to salvage her pride.

"It's Lillian, isn't it?"

Ruth nodded, avoiding her mother's eyes. Down came those mother's hands, the hands of a *dienna's frau* like the hands of an angel, taking up both of Ruth's and accompanied by healing words of praise and encouragement.

"Ruth, you did exactly the right thing. You amaze

me with the quiet way you have with these children. Lillian is different, but you know as well as I do that not one child is the same as the others. They are all given a different nature, and Lillian is just…well."

Ruth lifted her eyes to her mother's, saw the humor, those little stars of goodwill, and laughed.

"Mam, you know what she said the other day? She said she is going to put Benjamin in the rabbit hutch where he belongs."

Mam laughed heartily.

"I know, Ruth. She's a character. She's jealous, likely, of the new baby. And on top of that, she doesn't really understand about Ben."

"You noticed the Pamper?"

"Yes."

"She's three, Mam. I've never had a problem training any of my children. Till now. She's so stubborn. She knows better, but she just doesn't care. It simply tries me to the limit."

"And she will often continue to do so—throughout her life, no doubt. She reminds me so much of your sister, Betty."

"Help us all!" Ruth said, laughing.

Betty was Ruth's sister, who had taught school for many years. She often spoke her mind to distraught parents, roiling the calm waters around her with blunt remarks that were not always well received. She had finally married a bachelor at the age of twenty-seven, and her marriage was less than peaceful now, even after only a year and a half together.

"Poor Reuben."

"Oh, he takes care of himself."

And so the conversation carried on throughout the day as only the chatter of mothers and daughters can. They hopped from one subject to another as they sat on folding lawn chairs under the oak tree in the backyard with wheelbarrow loads of corn and piles of husks surrounding them. The dishpans were piled high with the heavy ears of yellow corn, brushed clean with vegetable brushes.

The two-burner outdoor propane cooker bubbled away as it cooked the corn, which, after being heated through, was plunged into the cold water in the cooling tubs. Roy manned the tubs, and the cold water from the hose often strayed, spraying his sisters or Elmer.

When the corn was completely cooled, the dishpans were filled again and set on a bench where Mam and Ruth cut it from the cobs with sharp knives. Some of it was creamed by sliding the cooled ears of corn across the stainless steel corn creamer. The device had a long, rounded shaft with jagged teeth built into the center, which tore the kernels into small pieces and creamed it for baked corn or just to be eaten with butter and salt.

They set up the corn eating station on the wooden picnic table with salt and butter at each end and a Corelle platter of sliced tomatoes, a jar of mayonnaise, and a loaf of sliced whole wheat bread in the middle.

For a small woman, Mam could eat so many ears of corn that it was almost alarming. She applied the butter with a liberal rolling of the ear of corn, over and over across the cold goodness of it. She poured on the salt with the same generous hand and continued by lowering her head, her teeth crunching. She stopped only to roll her eyes and voice her pleasure before buttering another ear.

Ruth agreed. Corn, especially the variety called "Incredible," was exactly that—rows of perfect yellow kernels bursting with flavor and a sweetness so good it was impossible not to look for another good ear after finishing the first one.

They wiped away their perspiration and cooled themselves by drinking cold beverages and plunging their hands into the cold well water, which also helped tremendously.

"Lillian, *voss huscht* (What do you have)?" Mommy called.

Ruth shrieked and grabbed at the fat, green tomato worm Lillian was laying gently on top of the cooled ears of corn.

"My worm!" Lillian cried. She quickly picked it up and deposited it in the sandbox, where Ruth decided if she wanted to give the worm a ride with the plastic dump truck, she could.

And Mommy allowed Elmer to drive Ginger the whole way to the freezer, the electric one kept in an

English neighbor's shed. Other Amish families also paid a set fee every month for the privilege of having a large chest freezer there.

Mommy told Elmer he was a good driver, even though he almost upset the spring wagon by turning too short. Later she sprouted a summer cold sore where she'd bitten down hard on her lip so she wouldn't yell in fright and perhaps hurt Elmer's feelings.

Chapter Three

AFTER THE DAY OF FREEZING CORN, Ruth also made spaghetti sauce, pizza sauce, salsa, and tomato soup, turning bucket after bucket of brilliant red sun-ripened tomatoes into row after row of colorful Ball jars of goodness, which were stored in the cold cellar with the pickles and red beets, the corn and zucchini relish. There was still applesauce to be done, and peaches and pears and grape jelly and grape juice.

School sewing, though, was on top of Ruth's list. It glared at her from beneath the square silver magnet on the refrigerator—the yellow slip of paper where she had written what she needed. Ten yards of Swedish knit, three yards of black apron material, shirts for the boys, buttons, black thread, sewing machine needles, hair pins.

School would start in a few weeks. The baby was crying from what seemed to be an angry case of heat rash that had developed overnight. Lillian had been stung by a carpenter bee—those wood borers that hovered around the barn's entrance like little bombers protecting their territory. Ruth was unsure if Lillian needed to see a doctor, the way her face was swollen and puffed up on one side so her eye had become a mere slit.

The heat had been unrelenting. It sapped Ruth's energy, so she often slept later than intended and then battled frustration, unable to accomplish all she wanted to.

Her steps were lighter now, coming in from the phone shanty, after having received a message from Aaron *sei* Hannah. Oh my. They were all coming on Thursday. The buddies. They were a precious group of women who had grown up with her. They had gone through their *rumspringa* (running around) years together and attended each other's weddings. They would bring their sewing machines! It was to be a covered dish gathering, and they would all bring something.

In the cool of the morning, Ruth slid onto the bench of the picnic table and folded her arms on the table. She lowered her head and cried just long enough to thank God for the gift of dear friends who were coming to pluck her out of discouragement.

Thursday arrived with the many teams turning into the driveway. They came bearing smiling faces, piles of little ones her own children's ages, casseroles, fruit, desserts, and salads. The women carried in their Berninas and Necchis and Singers and lugged along their twelve-volt batteries and inverters. The heavy blades from the Wiss scissors flashed as they cut into the fabric using the patterns Ruth kept in her folders in the bureau drawer.

The talking kept pace with the whirring of the needles, humming along as pair after pair of black broadfall trousers appeared like magic, and the ten-yard roll of Swedish knit quickly disappeared.

Elmer and Roy each had a blue shirt and a red one. The ladies decided that wasn't enough, so they cut up the dusty green, too.

The buttons were sewn on, and the buttonholes done by the machines. The women made quite a fuss about their mothers—or some of them—still making buttonholes by hand.

"Well, if you ask me, that is just dumb."

"My mother says it's her porch job. Sitting and relaxing in the evening."

"Seriously."

"*Unfashtendich* (senseless)."

"Why would you do that?"

There was talk of David Petersheim's new home being sold at auction.

"Four hundred and some thousand."

"That shop and all, no wonder."

"Who bought it?"

"Stop your sewing machines. Who?"

"A Mennonite?"

"Car Mennonite or Team?"

No one seemed to know. Somebody said the chap was English. Pretty old. They came to no conclusions.

Ruth wondered why Petersheims had sold out. It was a beautiful home set in the woods, all level land. She couldn't imagine living there. It looked so perfect.

"You're sure the last bidder wasn't Amish?"

"It's an Amish home."

And on and on.

They clucked over Lillian's face. Rachel said to put Swedish Bitters on it, without a doubt. Others were less sure with it being around the eye like that.

When they left, the new garments were all pressed and hung in the closets, but her whole house and lawn were a disaster.

No matter.

Ruth sang while she worked, sweeping, wiping Jello off walls, washing fingerprints from the windows, emptying trash cans. The boys picked up sandbox toys. Barbara and Esther hosed down the porch. Ruth got out the blue can of Raid and sprayed the walls around the doors, then slapped at flies inside the house and wiped them up with a tissue.

Later, they discovered the water trough in the barn contained more hay than water. It was soaked and slimy. Elmer voiced his opinion about buddies day, saying they all sat there and talked non-stop and let their children run wild.

But when school started, Ruth could send her three scholars down the road on their scooters, wearing the neon green, reflective vests she required. And she was thankful for her friends whose hearts had overflowed with love and kindness towards her and her family.

September brought cooler nights at least, but the heat persisted during the day. Her sister, Emma, helped her can peaches and pears. She made grape jelly after that, surveyed the stocked shelves in the cellar, and knew God was good.

Church services would be held at her parents' home the follow Sunday, in a *freme gegend* (a different district), so she ironed her Sunday covering with special care but was undecided about what to wear. Should it be her older black dress or one of the two newer ones she had made after Ben's death for her year of mourning? The older one was a bit too big around the waist, so she always felt as if her apron was falling off, no matter how tightly it was pinned.

She decided on the newer one that had a subtle swirl pattern in the material. The girls could wear their matching green dresses.

She laid out the boys' white shirts and their black vests and checked the trousers for any damage. One could never tell what might happen, the way boys played after services—especially at the homes of parents or relatives, when they stayed for the evening meal.

She buffed the boys' shoes, being careful to undo the black laces. Then she checked their drawers to make sure they had black socks, as she did not want them wearing white ones.

Her woven Sunday *kaevly* (basket) was packed carefully with Pampers on the bottom, an extra onesie, additional white socks, bottles, a pacifier, burp cloths, a small purse containing Goldfish and Cheerios, a keychain attached to a small plastic book, and three rolls of Smarties, enough to keep Lillian occupied at least for a short time.

Yes, she had her hands full with Esther, Barbara, and Lillian seated beside her and Benjamin, who was now two months old. But she learned it was possible to get through, with capable little Barbara as her helper. If only Lillian would cooperate, she'd be fine.

The morning was brisk and invigorating with the air bearing a hint of fall. The leaves were still green but hung tiredly, as if the summer's heat had made them weary and resigned to their coloring and final demise. The goldenrod was brilliant. The sumac had just begun to change color.

Pete was eager to go, so she let him run while half listening to Elmer's constant chatter as they passed homes, farms, and cornfields. He sat beside her, holding Benjamin, who was wide-eyed as the rumble of the steel wheels on the road made him aware of a change in his little world.

Ruth looked at him and smiled.

"*Voss? Bisht bye gay?* (What? Are you going away?)"

When a wide smile illuminated his face, Ruth bent sideways and kissed the top of his head.

"You're going to be good today, right?"

"You better watch where you're going."

"You want to drive?"

"Sure!"

"Give Benjamin to me."

So for the next few miles, Elmer was the attentive

driver, carefully pulling on the right rein to keep Pete on his side of the road.

When they pulled into her parents' farm, there were already quite a few buggies parked in neat rows along the fence back by the corn crib and the implement shed.

"My goodness! No one going in the lane? I hope we're not late."

"Nah," Elmer assured her, handing over the reins. He did not want to be responsible for the parking, which was sometimes a difficult thing to do with so many buggies already taking up a lot of the space. Of all the things that were changed by Ben's death, this one was one of the most difficult. Driving alone, a woman, so unaccustomed, having to worry about unhitching, even with Elmer's help. It was not exactly a humiliation. It was more the effort of staying calm and brave despite the appearance of being alone, different, the widow, the recipient of people's sympathy. She hated being alone in the buggy without Ben, always.

Where to go? Oh dear.

"Mam, over there," Elmer said, pointing a finger helpfully.

"All those boys," she said quietly.

"They won't look."

But they did. They all turned to watch as she pulled Pete up beside the silo and said, "Back!" as she tugged on the reins.

Pete had other ideas, of course—the cranky beast—so she was getting nowhere. Handing the reins to Elmer, she slid back the door of the buggy and was surprised to see one of the young men stepping out from the crowd and coming over to help her park.

Taking a firm grip on the horse's bit, he applied steady pressure, and Pete, who must have known he was in experienced hands, leaned back against the britchment and put the buggy right where Ruth had wanted it.

Then he stepped around to Ruth's side of the buggy. She stepped down from her seat in her black mourning dress and looked at him.

"*G'mya* (G'morning)."

"Hello."

"Shall I put your horse away?"

"You may, yes. Thank you."

There was a question in his eyes as plain as day, but he said nothing further. Ruth just went to the other side of the buggy and held out her arms for Benjamin as the young man reached under the seat for the halter and the neck rope. He went to release the buckle on Pete's bridle and looked at her, this small, young woman with all these children.

Ruth saw he had no beard, and his hat was well shaped, low in the back and pulled low over his eyes in the front. Someone had said at buddies day that Paul King's Anna was dating someone from the Dauphin County settlement. Oh, but it couldn't be him. Anna would be at her parents' church in a neighboring district.

Her helper was forgotten as Ruth was caught up in greeting relatives including some of her sisters she did not see on a regular basis. They had moved to neighboring counties and lived in smaller settlements of Amish folks.

Quite a fuss was made of little Benjamin's growth

and his likeness to his father, though not without quick glances of kind sympathy and questioning her with their eyes.

Are you doing okay?

Did we say too much?

It's been nearly six months, hasn't it?

She shook hands with many friends and some women she did not know but who were all a part of the faith she was so accustomed to. By the time the first hymn was announced, Benjamin had had enough, and his wails became loud and urgent. Bending to tell Esther to remain seated, she made her way past her sisters, crossed the yard, and went into the house.

This was the home of her youth, the dear old stone house with the high ceilings and deep window-sills. Mam's wringer washer stood all by itself in the cement-floored laundry room with the drain in the floor beside it, like a milk house floor. Most younger women's washers were put in a closet or fastened to the floor, with drains underneath the washer and the rinse tubs and a lever to open or close them.

Not Mam. What would happen if there was a clog
in there, she'd say, a hairpin or a safety pin? No sir.
She let her water out of the wringer washer the old
fashioned way—by unhooking the drain hose and letting it run across the floor and down the drain. Then,
if there was an object in the washer that shouldn't be
there, it came flying out in full view and could be
picked up and thrown in the trash can.

Ruth smiled as she fed Benjamin, her eyes devouring the cabinets, the corner cupboard, the old extension table, the braided rug in front of the sink. The
smells were identical to the ones of her youth with
evidence of Mam's Shaklee products everywhere.
The laundry soap, bath soap, dish detergent, window
cleaner—all Shaklee.

The house was spotless, as usual, but then church
services were here today, which had meant extra
cleaning even if it wasn't entirely needed. The services were actually in the shop across the lawn, where
Dat tinkered with woodworking or implement repair. It had been hosed down, the walls and windows
washed, carpet laid, and benches set out. And now

the services were beginning.

Rocking Benjamin, Ruth's head felt heavy, her eyelids began to close, and she longed to take a nap. She had been awake at four that morning and was unable to get back to sleep with thoughts of driving Pete to her parents' house for church crowding out any possible slumber. Voices in the *kesslehaus* (wash house) brought her back from her slide into actual sleep.

"No, that's Jake's Sammie's Davey's boy. You know, *Huvvel* (planer) Dave, the one who has a woodworking shop somewhere up in Manheim."

"So is this guy the one who bought that property at the end of Hoosier Road?"

"I don't know."

"This guy's not bad looking. Why isn't he married?"

"Oh, he has a girlfriend. Paul's Anna."

"I see."

After Benjamin was satisfied, Ruth headed back to the shop, where she scooped up Lillian and held her close. She looked around at the congregation and saw Dat seated in the ministers' row, his gray hair and beard neat and clean, his head bent, likely sending up a prayer for the young minister who had the opening.

Her gaze found the single boys as she searched for Elmer and Roy. Were they behaving? Turning her head, she found her nephews, Allen and Ivan, and yes, there was Roy, whispering to his cousin. Hopefully, he'd remain quiet after he said what he deemed necessary. She'd try to catch his eye to remind him of the fact that she could see him and knew if he misbehaved.

He looked up, guileless as a rabbit, his eyes open wide. Quickly, Ruth sat up straighter, put a finger to her lips, drew down her eyebrows, and shook her head ever so slightly. When Roy, her generally soft-hearted one, looked as if he would burst into tears, she smiled, only a bit, and gave him a slight wink as a reassurance of her love.

A small smile smoothed out Roy's humiliation, and she felt better, until she looked straight into a pair of very dark brown eyes that didn't turn away from her face. He had seen her wink. There are lots of words for humiliation, but none served to describe her shame.

Oh please don't let him think.... Then the thought struck her that, of course, she had nothing to be ashamed of. He didn't know her, and she had no idea who he was, so they'd never meet again. If he wanted to be so bold as to let her know he was watching, then, well, so be it. Sorry.

She told her sister, Verna, about it after services. They were busy putting red beets and pickles in small Styrofoam bowls to be put on the table with the rest of the traditional food that was served every other Sunday at church.

Verna watched her sister's face—the soft rose of her blush—and tried to laugh. But her mouth took on a squarish quality, and she became quite hysterical as she turned her face away. Her shoulders shook as she cried.

When Verna finished, she lifted her apron and dug out a wrinkled, not-so-white handkerchief and honked mightily into it. Then she lifted red-rimmed eyes to Ruth and said, "Ruth, I don't care if you think

I'm not quite right, but you need to think about marrying again someday. Your row is long, and the sun is hot, and you have it tough. I would wish for you a nice and decent young man, a special one for your children."

She again honked her nose into the questionable handkerchief, blinked her eyes, and lifted her apron to return the cloth to her pocket. Then she turned back to the task of fishing sweet pickles out of their brine with a spoon that had no slots in it. Silently, Ruth handed her a slotted spoon. Verna took it, and they finished filling the bowls.

The next time Ruth looked at Verna, she nodded her head ever so slightly, and they shared a watery smile of sisterhood and love and understanding.

Chapter Four

As the late summer sun burned the cool mists of September mornings into glorious fall, the leaves turned slowly into vibrant shades of red, yellow, and orange. The garden was cleared of its tomatoes and brown, rustling cornstalks and diseased marigolds.

Ruth gathered an armload of cornstalks, walked to the white board fence, and flung them over. Then she stood to watch Pete hungrily bite into one, allowing Oatmeal, the small round pony the color of her name, none of the tender evening snack.

"Pete, come on. Stop being greedy. Get over here, Oatmeal. He'll let you have some."

She turned in time to see Roy chasing Barbara across the lawn with a cornstalk held aloft, a banner of intended harm. Barbara was not crying out. She simply lowered her head in determination and outran him, her blue dress flapping as her knees pumped and her brown legs churned. She dodged Roy with the agility of a small rabbit.

Triumphantly and clearly the winner, though her chest was heaving, Barbara turned to face him. Roy swung the cornstalk futilely, accepting defeat, until she charged after him, neatly swiping the offending stalk and racing off with it. Roy took pursuit once more.

Ruth watched, laughing to herself, until Lillian ran directly into Roy's path, where he crashed into her. She fell back, hitting her head on the corner of the wooden sandbox and sending up a series of shrieks and howls, her face turning burgundy, her mouth open wide.

"Stop! No, no, Lillian. Don't cry," Roy said, bending to help his youngest sister, rubbing her head, sliding her onto his lap as he sat down.

Barbara dropped the cornstalk and came running to see how bad it was. She told Roy it was all his fault, because he had started it. Roy asked who had been running away when this happened, and Barbara retorted that that was not what she had said.

When Ruth reached them, Lillian was still emitting howls of outrage. Good-natured Barbara was bristling with anger, while Roy was determined to prove his point and trying to drive home the blame with his words.

Calm. I will remain calm, Ruth thought. She scooped up Lillian and checked her head for injuries. Her searching fingers found a large goose egg protruding from her daughter's scalp.

"Hush. Hush, Lillian. It's alright," she said softly, which did no good as her words were buried under a fresh supply of howling.

"Roy. Barbara. Stop. Go sit on the bench until you can be quiet."

"It was her!"

"It was Roy!"

"It was not. She started it!"

With Lillian on her hip, Ruth grasped Roy firmly by his shoulder and steered him in the direction of the wooden bench by the back door. Barbara followed, shamefaced.

As she went through the laundry room door, she could hear little Benjamin crying lustily from his playpen, and by the look of his tired, wet face, he had been crying steadily for some time.

Setting Lillian on the couch, Ruth crunched a few saltine crackers beneath her feet as she made her way to Baby Benjy, as they'd come to call him. She had to kick a plastic bucket of toys aside before reaching to extract him from the confines of his playpen.

What was most important here? She put Benjy in his baby swing and pressed the button to set it into motion as she mentally reviewed Lillian's fall, wondering if she should be taken somewhere. The ER was the only service available if she had a serious injury at this time of the evening.

Hadn't she heard somewhere that if a child yells and cries, it's not too serious? Or if a bump appears on the skull? Was that a myth? She could hear her mother saying that if the lump goes in but is not visible on the outside, it can be fatal.

A stab of fear made her cringe, the reality of Lillian's head injury looming ahead of her. She had fifty-seven dollars in her checking account. That was all. The ER would send a bill, and then there was the amount she would have to pay the driver she'd need to hire.

She held Lillian and felt the lump, undecided. She looked up to find Roy and Barbara entering the kitchen, followed by Elmer and Esther, their eyes wide with concern.

"Is she hurt seriously?"

"Is she okay?"

Ruth nodded, assuring them, but she was still unsure about whether Lillian should be seen by a doctor. The last thing she needed was another bill to pay, but her daughter's health was her first priority, she knew.

Oh, Ben.

She held Lillian, and Esther reached for Benjamin, who was not settling down. Ruth maintained a calm appearance as she tried to think rationally while watching Lillian's face, where the color slowly drained away until even her lips were alarmingly pale. What should she do?

She decided to watch her for an hour, then take action. She put a cool washcloth on Lillian's forehead and gave her a dropper filled with children's grape flavored Tylenol. The generic brand at Walmart had been half the price, thank goodness. Lillian swallowed dutifully, sighed, whimpered, and lay very still against her mother's breast.

Don't let them sleep. She could hear her old family doctor's voice as clearly as if he was in the room. Lillian's eyelids sank lower, and Ruth shifted her position to keep her awake.

"Lillian!"

She began to cry.

"Elmer, go get Mamie. Please?"

"Alright."

Instantly, he was out the door. Ruth was thankful for Elmer's obedience and wanted to remember to tell him so.

"Esther, would you please pick up toys? Roy, please get the broom and sweep up these crackers."

They both did her bidding quietly, with reverence for their injured sister worrying them into obedience.

Barbara brought a light blanket, and Ruth smiled at her as she covered Lillian's legs.

When Lillian's eyes began to close again, Ruth sat her up, saying, "Lillian!"

She was immensely grateful to see her neighbor, Mamie Stoltzfus, wife of Ephraim, come through the front door with her youngest, Waynie, hanging haphazardly on her plump hip. His thin blond hair was matted, his nose running, his blue eyes alight with interest—a small replica of his mother.

Mamie was what Ruth lovingly called "roly-poly." She was a heavy woman, though tall, with thinning hair and bright blue eyes. She viewed the world through rosy lenses, an extension of her heart overflowing with love and compassion toward every person she had the pleasure of knowing.

"*Ach* (oh) my, Ruth."

She bent to look at Lillian with Waynie bobbing along on her hip. She felt the large lump, stepped back to look at Lillian's face, and lifted the eyelids to look for contraction in the pupils. Then she clucked.

Ruth was assailed by odors of cooking and baking,

twice weekly baths, Waynie's unchanged cloth diaper, and other smells associated with Mamie's relaxed approach to life.

"What happened? Here, Waynie, you sit here. Look, there's a car. You want to play with the toys? Look, there's a teddy!"

Waynie gurgled happily and crawled across the floor, his questionable odor following him. Mamie grunted and straightened her substantial frame before sitting down beside Ruth, who promptly leaned against her as the cushions flattened under Mamie.

"The children were playing and knocked her over. She hit her head against the corner of the sandbox. She really cried."

"Oh, she looks aright. Some color's coming back to her cheeks. *Gel*, Lillian? *Gel, doo bisht alright. Gel?* (Right, you will be fine. Right?)"

Nodding and smiling, Maime reached for her neighbor's daughter, her arms and hands and heart needing to be about their business. She gathered Lillian against her greasy dress front and kissed her cheek.

"*Bisht falla*? (Did you fall?)"

Suddenly, Lillian sat straight up and said, "I broke my head apart."

"You did? Just like Humpty Dumpty?"

Lillian nodded and giggled, watching Waynie crawl in pursuit of a rolling ball. She pushed against Mamie's red hands and slid off her lap. She walked steadily over to Waynie and patted his bottom, giggling.

Tears sprang to Ruth's eyes, and her knees became weak with relief. Mamie beamed and said Lillian had quite a bump there but by all appearances would be fine.

"You wouldn't have a doctor examine her?"

"No. She just had a good tap on her head."

"Tap?"

Ruth shook her head, laughing.

As the sun made a glorious exit behind the oak tree, Mamie settled herself into a kitchen chair with a cup of hot spearmint tea and a plate of chocolate peanut butter bars.

"You didn't need to do this," she chortled happily, immensely pleased at the prospect of visiting with Ruth.

"No, no, it's okay. I need something to pick me up after that scare," Ruth assured her.

"I can't imagine life without Ephraim," Mamie said, quick tears of sympathy appearing in her happy eyes.

Ruth nodded, then sent the older children out to finish the removal of the cornstalks. After they'd gone, she turned to Mamie.

"It's not always easy, although I can't complain. I have so much to be thankful for, in so many ways."

Mamie dipped a bar into her heavily sugared tea, then clucked in dismay when it broke apart and the wet part disappeared into the hot liquid. Quickly, Ruth was on her feet to get a spoon, but Mamie held one up, laughing, and fished the wet particles out of the tea.

"Drowned my chocolate chip bar! Oh well."

She slurped mightily as she bit into another half of a bar. She nodded her head in appreciation and shook her spoon in Ruth's direction as she chewed, an indication of the volley of words that was to follow.

"I don't know how you do it. Everything so neat and clean. Your work is always done. You just glide seamlessly through your days and never complain. Waynie, no. Don't. As I was saying, how can you handle all your children, and get your work done? Waynie, no."

She heaved herself off the chair and extracted her young son from a potted plant, as Ruth winced at the trail of potting soil spreading across the linoleum, which was apparently invisible to Mamie.

Mamie settled Waynie on her lap and began feeding him chunks of the chocolate chip bar.

"You know Mert Ordwich died?"

"Who?"

"Mert. You know, the feed salesman. Oh, I forgot. You're not on the farm. Well, he had hardening of the arteries and wouldn't go to the doctor. That's how thick headed he was. Ephraim says he's stubborn as a mule. He was. I doubt if he is now anymore. We went to his viewing last night. The line was so long, and my feet hurt so bad. There we stood and stood, on and on. He didn't look like Mert. His face was so puffy."

Mamie looked at Lillian.

"She seems perfectly alright. Anyway…Waynie, *komm*. As I was saying, they say the David Petersheim place is sold. Eli Kings were standing in line with us. They said a young bachelor bought it. We…I don't know if he's a bachelor. I shouldn't say. He's single, but he's going with Paul King's Anna."

Ruth chuckled.

"He's single, but he's dating?"

Mamie laughed uproariously and thumped the table solidly in a most unladylike manner. Ruth watched her and felt her spirits lifting. She was also relieved knowing Lillian would be alright, and she was glad.

"*Ach* Ruth, I'm getting old. I say the dumbest things. You know what I mean. He's pretty old—to be unmarried. Anyway, he must have money, or his father does, paying four hundred and some thousand."

Mamie paused as she reached for another cookie bar.

"I'll just eat this one, and then I have to go. Oh, I meant to ask you. We have a shopping trip planned at the end of October—early Christmas shopping.

Would you want to go with me and a few others?"

Ruth simply didn't know what to say. How could she respond honestly and yet keep her pride intact at the same time? So she hesitated, pulled Lillian onto her lap, and checked the lump on her head to buy time. Then she answered Mamie.

"I'll see."

"Good! Oh, I hope you can go! We'd love to have you."

Later that night, when the late September moon had risen above the oak tree and bathed the small house in a soft, white glow, Ruth lay in her king sized bed, her eyes wide, her mind churning with endless questions and possibilities. What to do?

No one was aware of the state of her bank account. No one would need to know. Times were difficult for many people. They all had enough to do, simply staying afloat, paying mortgages, and providing for their own large families.

"*Arme vitve, vine nicht* (Poor widow, do not cry)."

Is that really what she was? How had it happened? How had she been toppled from her pedestal as Ben's loving wife? Toppled and broken into a million pieces. Would she ever find a way out of this labyrinth of personal fear of failure? Could she survive financially, as a lone parent, raising these fast growing and maturing children? And these boys. They so desperately needed a father figure in their lives.

Well, the fifty-seven dollars would hold them a few weeks. Then she'd either have to beg from her parents, or…or what?

The quilt was almost finished. She had four hundred yards of thread in it so far. At seventy-five cents a yard, that would be three hundred dollars. The gas bill was almost a hundred and forty dollars, and the telephone maybe fifty or sixty.

She'd go to B. B.'s Store, the bent and dent grocery in Quarryville. If she was especially careful, she could make do on seventy or eighty dollars.

The horse feed was about all gone. Well, they'd have to wait till another quilt was finished. In a few more years, the boys would be fourteen and fifteen and able to earn a few dollars, but until then…she didn't know.

She rolled on her side and punched her pillow into a different shape. Then she stretched out her arm, her fingers searching for Lillian's small form, and checked the rise and fall of her daughter's breath, feeling that comforting, even rhythm that assured Ruth she was alright.

Mamie was a treasure, asking her to go Christmas shopping with the others. Should Ruth have been honest with her? So far, she had no clue how they would celebrate Christmas—with gifts, anyway. Perhaps this year she would tell the children they would receive gifts from their grandparents and the teacher at school, but since their dat was no longer here, they wouldn't have Christmas gifts at home.

How could she manage?

Elmer and Esther would understand. She pictured Elmer with his shoulders held too high and his hands in his pockets, the "little man" stance he'd developed in the past five months. Ruth ached with love for her eldest son.

How could she—if she had a chance—replace Ben? How did one go about procuring a replacement for a husband? She guessed she couldn't. At least not outwardly.

There came a time, though, when she had to wonder what God had in store. Did He think it was best to stay alone? Was there anyone who would even consider taking the wild leap into the chaotic lives of six children and their mother?

She remembered the emotion her sister, Verna, had shown. But that Vern was something else—slightly unstable. Ruth thought of the wrinkled, yellowing handkerchief, knowing it wasn't laundered properly and had never seen an iron.

None of the sisters knew why Verna was that way. Verna herself claimed she was adopted. She didn't care one whit about her yard or garden or housework. She bought all her canned goods at B. B.'s Store in Quarryville, saying she could buy them cheaper than she could can them herself.

She pieced quilts and bought Little Debbies for her children, or Nutter Butters or Chips Ahoy. Her oldest, named Ellen—Mam had a fit about that fancy name—did the washing just as fast as she could without paying much attention to the outcome.

The thought of her sister and her questionable laundry was the deciding factor between sleep and more tumbling thoughts of worry. Ruth barely had time to pull Lillian's softly breathing form against her own before giving into asleep.

Chapter Five

RUTH WALKED TOWARD THE HOUSE, LEAFING through her mail as the October wind caught her skirt and whipped it around her knees. The gas bill, a few cards from folks in the community who remembered to send lines of encouragement—sometimes containing crisp twenty dollar bills—some junk mail, an offer for a credit card, which was tempting.

Hmm.

A letter with no stamp? Without her full address? She struggled to pull the storm door completely shut and then laid the mail on the kitchen table before hanging her black sweater on the row of hooks by the wringer washer.

Shivering, she sat down to open her mail. She found nothing unusual, but she was grateful for the cards with the usual verses, a token of care sent by people she did not know.

She saved the one without a stamp for last, some-how savoring the mystery of it. She blinked and caught her breath. The envelope contained a plain sheet of notebook paper from an ordinary compo-sition book with the loose fragments of paper still hanging from the holes where it had been torn from the notebook.

One, two, three….She almost stopped counting as her heart started beating wildly in her chest. Ten. There were ten one hundred dollar bills. There was no greeting and no name.

She hadn't planned on crying. It just happened, starting with her nostrils burning and a huge lump in her throat that was relieved only when the splash of tears began. She folded her arms on top of the mail on the oak table and let the wonder of this generous gift overtake her.

"Mam?"

Elmer's concern forced her to lift her head. She felt guilty now to be indulging in these senseless tears.

"I'm sorry, Elmer."

"What's wrong?"

Silently she handed the money to him and watched through blurred vision as he counted, then whistled softly.

"We're rich!"

"What?! What?!"

Roy came bouncing over with Barbara at his heels. That was the one thing Ruth would never understand—the way Barbara did that, always going where Roy went, only to be constantly irritated by his antics.

"Somebody gave us a bunch of money!"

"Let me see."

It was October eleventh, the day most Amish people set aside as a day of fasting and prayer in order to prepare themselves for the fall communion services. Ruth had always relished this rare day of relaxation to spend with Ben and the children. The day was an uninterrupted one, sanctioned for the reading of the German articles of faith or the prayer book, the traditional books read and re-read by generations of Old Order Amish.

There was no breakfast for Ruth on fasting day, but she prepared buttered toast and Honey Nut

Cheerios for the children. Lillian, of course, refused them, saying she wanted Trix. In her frustration, Lillian kicked the bench from her perch on the blue plastic booster seat and cried, squeezing her eyes shut and turning her head from side to side until the other children laughed at her. Then she lifted her face with her eyes closed and just howled because they were laughing, and Ruth had to shush the older ones. She took Lillian away from the table and talked to her firmly, saying there were no Trix in the house and if she wouldn't eat Cheerios, she would have nothing at all and would be just like the three little pigs who were lazy and the wolf blew their house away.

That made Lillian sit up straight and open her eyes. She told Ruth that a wolf could not blow houses away, but the story had served to get her mind off the Trix. She ate her Cheerios, and general peace was restored.

Ruth read her *Luscht Gartlein* (Love Garden), her soul blossoming and unfolding, as it received the simple German words about the wise ways one could live a good and Godly life. The reading of the German took more of her time, but she savored the pronunciation and the meaning of these words, remembering the agelessness of them.

At noon, she fried corn meal mush, cutting the squares from the aluminum cake pan and frying them in vegetable oil. It was Elmer's favorite for *fasht dag* (fast day) lunch. Ruth heated milk in a small saucepan and then poured it over a bowl full of saltines and covered them with a plate while she fried eggs.

Esther set the table, adding salt and pepper, ketchup, butter, and strawberry jelly to the spread with plates, knives, and forks. There was no orange juice, and grapes had been too expensive to can juice, so they drank cold water for their lunch on *fasht dag*.

When Ruth bowed her head before they ate, she remembered to thank God especially for the gift of one thousand dollars that had come with the early morning mail delivery.

The cornmeal mush was delicious. The boys devoured every last slice and ate two eggs each and all the buttered toast they could hold.

Esther didn't like mush, so she wrinkled her nose

and said it was greasy and disgusting. Elmer said that was great if she didn't eat it so he'd have more. Roy nodded his head in agreement, his straight brown hair sliding back and forth with each movement.

Esther said just doddies (grandfathers) and mommies ate mush. Roy said they did not either. Anyone could eat mush if they felt like it.

Esther said rich people ate bacon, and Elmer said they *were* rich. Roy nodded his head again. Esther looked at Ruth and said, "Right, Mam, we're not rich?"

"We are rich, Esther. We have each other and God takes very good care of us."

After that wonderful *fasht dag*, the coal bin was filled with three tons of coal, the gas bill was paid, and Ruth planned to go Christmas shopping with Mamie.

A few days before the shopping trip, the boys hitched Oatmeal to the cart and went back to the farm for two gallons of milk. It was a gray sort of day, chilly and overcast with the clouds bulging with rain that hadn't started to fall. Elmer said later that was why he didn't see the oncoming truck—it was gray, too.

Ruth saw the whole thing from the kitchen window and clutched Benjamin with one hand as she clapped the other across her mouth to stifle a scream. She was completely helpless as she watched Elmer pull out directly in front of a pickup truck. She saw him come down hard with the leather reins on the pony's haunches, scaring poor Oatmeal out of her wits. The driver also hit the brakes, and Oatmeal lunged forward, spilling both boys out onto the road.

Roy came screaming and crying, completely beside himself with pain and fear and holding his left wrist with his right hand. Ruth laid crying Benjy into his playpen and asked Esther to watch him, please. She'd be back.

The driver of the truck was middle aged, lean, and sensible but most definitely shaken up and unhappy with his circumstances at that moment. Elmer was running down the road after his surprised pony, Roy was yelling senselessly, and some very black tire marks stretched along Hoosier Road. But thank God, no one was seriously injured.

The driver's name was Dan Rogers, and he offered to call the police, although his truck wasn't damaged. Ruth grasped her sweater at the waistline and shivered as her teeth chattered. She told him it was fine, she'd have the wrist checked by their family doctor.

Dan stayed long enough to watch Roy spread his fingers, lift and lower his hand, and rotate his wrist. Then he waited until Elmer returned with Oatmeal and the cart, apparently unharmed, although Elmer had telltale streaks of gray where he'd wiped fiercely at his little boy tears.

Ruth hugged both boys together, gathering them close in a thankful embrace. That night she spent a very restless night as Roy woke up continually, calling for his mother because of the pain.

In the morning, resignedly, she took Roy to Intercourse to Doctor Pfieffer, who did a quick diagnosis and said it was only a bad sprain as the x-ray showed no fracture. He put a splint on the wrist and wrapped it over and over.

Ruth wrote out a check for two hundred and fifteen dollars, signed her name, and took Roy home again. She settled him on the couch with a few books and then took Benjamin and walked down the road to Mamie's house. Ruth knocked on the front door and was greeted by the usual insane yipping of Mamie's brown Pomeranian.

Mamie opened the door, a men's handkerchief of a questionable cleanliness tied around her head, a torn bib apron sliding off one shoulder, and Waynie, as usual, stuck on one hip like a permanent fixture.

"I don't know why you think you always have to knock," she said as her way of greeting Ruth.

"It's polite, Mamie."

"Who's polite? What is that? Here, give me your precious bundle. Waynie, go play now. Trixie, shoo. *Gay*! (Go!) Waynie, Trixie!"

Waynie sat down and howled. Trixie continued yipping, and Benjamin's eyes grew very wide and uncertain.

"*Ach* my! My house is a total circus. Johnny, come get Trixie. Put her in the *kesslehaus*. Fannie, come get Waynie. Susan, where's Fannie? Well, here, Susan, give him a graham cracker in his high chair. Trixie!

Johnny! Come get this dog!"

Ruth couldn't stop smiling, the warmth spreading through her like bright, summer sunshine. She loved Mamie so much she wanted to send her a card with a funny saying about friends or a bouquet of flowers, but as it was, she knew she could afford neither, so she unwrapped Benjamin and handed him to an eager Fannie. She was Mamie's oldest daughter, tall and slim, with a splattering of freckles and brown eyes. She had magically appeared after Susan, her younger blonde-haired sister, had taken away the wailing Waynie.

"He's teething," Mamie sighed.

"Poor Waynie, he looks unhappy."

"He is."

"Well, Mamie, I came to tell you that I'll have to back out of the shopping trip. The boys had a near accident yesterday, pulling out in front of a pickup with Oatmeal, and I had to have Roy's wrist taken care of."

"Oh no! Are they okay?"

"Yes, just a bad sprain in Roy's left wrist."

"Well, good, but it really spites me you can't go with us. Do you want me to give you some money? Of course, I better not say that. Eph would have a fit. He can hardly get forty hours in down at the shed place, this time of year. Trixie!"

Mamie got up and lumbered after the tiny Pomeranian. Ruth had to wonder what kept the dog alive, being underfoot all the time.

"I don't know where that Johnny is. Now, as we were saying, if you can't go, will you be able to have Christmas gifts this year? *Ach* Ruth, I simply pity you so bad. I'm going to tell Davey that you're out of money."

"No! Mamie please. Our deacon has enough to think about."

"You want coffee?"

"No, I have to get back. Roy might need me."

Ruth glanced around, trying not to notice the piles of dirty dishes, the messy stove top, the fly hanger above the table dotted with dead houseflies—not to mention the clutter all over the floor.

"Stop looking at my house."

Ruth laughed. With Mamie, everything was easy. You could always be yourself and say what you wanted without having to attempt any unnecessary niceties.

"Why don't you wash your dishes?"

"You know why?"

"Why?"

"Because I don't like washing dishes. Ever. I have to force myself to tackle a sink load of them. They need to come up with a dishwasher that runs on air."

"Tell Ephraim to start designing one. He could."

"Ppfff!"

Ruth smiled and then laughed.

"Mamie, you are the dearest best friend in the world. I just have to tell you how much I appreciate you."

"*Ach* Ruth, now you're going to make me cry. Well, I feel the same about you. Just so you know." Then Mamie held her head to one side, eyed Ruth shrewdly, and asked if she loved her enough to wash dishes.

"I'd love to wash your dishes."

"I bet."

Still smiling, Ruth walked home, richer in friend-ship than in money. That was sure.

All through the rest of the month of October, Ruth tried not to plan ahead unnecessarily or build up mountains of worry.

Of course, Mam and the sisters planned shopping trips for November, in between weddings and all the usual events planned around them.

Ruth had received three wedding invitations. She put them back in the envelopes slowly, absentmind-edly letting her fingers trace the embossed lettering.

How could she attend a wedding alone? If ever there was a single event that would cripple her sense of being even slightly courageous, it had to be a wed-ding. How could she endure a whole day surrounded by couples, dating ones or married ones? The absence of Ben was a painful handicap, even just thinking about it.

No, she would not go.

Chicken pox spread through the community all through November. The boys went to school as usual, having had them when they were much younger, but Esther and Barbara were feverish, achy, and irritable. They argued and fought over toys and crayons and books. And relentless, cold rain pounded against the east windows, ran down the panes, and puddled between the wet, swaying bushes. The bare branches of the old oak tree looked cold and black and slick, etched against the weeping sky.

Benjamin fussed in his swing. Lillian somehow found a permanent marker and scribbled all over the hallway, and Ruth felt as if she would not be able to tolerate one more day alone without Ben.

The pustules from the chicken pox broke out all over the girls' little bodies, and they finally felt better. When they became itchy, Ruth patiently filled the bathtub with warm water, added baking soda, swirled it around well, and let the girls play in the tub.

She scrubbed the hallway walls with Comet and Soft Scrub, but a faint gray line remained. Well, it would have to stay that way. There was no money for paint. She could ask Mam, she supposed, but she was always asking her for things like mantles for the propane lamp or batteries or rubber bands, things she never quite had enough money to buy.

But it's my life, she thought, as she sat rocking little Benjamin after she had rubbed his gums with teething lotion and given him a good hot bath and some Tylenol. Poor baby, she thought. He couldn't help it if those hard, little teeth pushed against his soft, tender gums and made them ache.

She wrapped him in a warm blanket and inhaled the smell of him, that sweet baby lotion smell that never failed to bring her joy.

When he was asleep, she laid him in his crib with a soft, white cloth diaper spread over the crib sheet, just in case he threw up during the night. She covered him to his ears and then folded the comforter back so she could kiss him one more time before tiptoeing out.

Lillian was lying on the couch, her pacifier in her mouth, her eyes wide and anxious as they always were when she felt sleep trying to overtake her, though she desperately tried to avoid it.

"*Komm,* Lillian."

Gratefully, Ruth gathered her three year old in her arms, savoring the comforting routine of smoothing the flannel nightgown, taut and neat, over the rounded little form. She did love her mighty Lillian, so pliant and adorable now.

"*Bisht meet* (Are you tired), Lillian?"

She nodded, her eyes wide.

"Shall I sing?"

"No."

"Why not?"

"I don't want you to. I want my Dat."

"But Lillian, your Dat is in Heaven."

"No, he isn't."

"Yes. His part that is alive went to Heaven—his soul."

Softly, Lillian began to cry, but Ruth remained strong, showing no emotion of her own. Soon, Lillian stopped crying and went to sleep. Tomorrow was another day, and she'd forget. Till the next time.

Ruth held the warm, sleeping form. Outside she heard the wind rattling the downspout at the corner of the house and playing with the loose shutter by the front door. She hoped the boys had remembered to close the barn door after they'd fed Pete.

She stroked Lillian's *schtruvvels* (stray hairs) away from her face and prayed for strength to carry on.

Chapter Six

THE THANKSGIVING HYMN SINGING WAS TO be held in Ephraim's shop, and Mamie was a complete wreck for an entire week beforehand. She waved her arms and almost yodeled with apprehension. Daily life overwhelmed her, let alone cleaning that shop and getting all that coffee going.

"I know just how this will go. Everyone says, oh they'll bring bars and cookies and potato chips and cheese and all the dips and pretzels and stuff, but what do they bring? I'm going to bake my Christmas cookies now. All of 'em, just in case it goes the same way it did last year. Why in the world that husband of mine offered, I'll never know. He knows I don't get around the way some women do."

But she was pleased to be an important member of the community, hosting this hymn singing for the youth and their parents, or some of them, as it usually turned out.

Ruth walked home with a promise to return to help bake cookies, something she genuinely anticipated. She enjoyed being in Mamie's company. The cookies, too, would be phenomenal, she knew.

Mamie mostly did what she liked, and baking was at the top of her list. Her specialty was raisin-filled sugar cookies. She used an old, old recipe that had been handed down for generations. She also used fillings other than just raisin—raspberry, blueberry, cherry, even lemon—and they melted away in one bite.

So the week flew by with Ruth helping Mamie and joking with her friend's good-natured husband. As he sat dipping cookies in milk, he seemed happily oblivious to the unbelievable mess around them.

They filled the sugar cookies with the various kinds of fruit fillings. Then they baked oatmeal raisin and chocolate chip cookies and date pinwheels. They made gingersnaps and molasses cookies with one side dipped in white chocolate. Mamie wanted to make chocolate cut out cookies, but Ruth refused, saying the singing was only three days away and when did she think she was going to clean?

Mamie plunked herself down on a flour-dusted kitchen chair and said she'd never get ready, that was all there was to it. Ruth eyed her neighbor's girth and imagined every extra movement of hers was balanced by plenty of extra calories. She'd guarantee Mamie had eaten ten cookies in the past few hours. It was actually scary.

"You know you're going to become diabetic?"

"What? Me?"

Mamie was horrified, till Ruth assured her she was joking. In truth, she wasn't completely.

At the end of the day, the smells, the sounds, and bustle of baking at Mamie's house put Ruth's home in stark contrast as she headed back with her tired children to a cold, dark house, the absence of Ben felt in every room. She'd stoke the coal stove in the basement, light the warm propane lamp, and bravely go ahead for the children's sake, getting them to bed without fights as best she could.

Thanksgiving was spent with her family, a day of

feasting on roast turkey and sweet potato casserole, surround by all of her dear family with every face a homecoming for her spirit.

Mam glided smoothly between stovetop and table, serving and barking orders. Her daughters scuttled to obey, pushing children aside in the process.

Twelve o'clock was not allowed to arrive until everyone was seated, the water poured, and heads bent in prayer. As always, Mam accomplished her goal and even ahead of time—the long hand on the clock pointing to the ten, the short hand to the twelve.

The children had a great time at Doddy (Grandfather) Lapp's, but anticipation ran high to continue their wonderful day at Ephraim's. They put Pete in the barn at home, unharnessed him, and fed him a good amount of oats and hay. In the house, they stoked the fire, washed a few faces, combed hair, dabbed at a few spots on the girls' pinafore-style aprons, and waited till Roy dashed to his room to change into a pair of black school trousers—he had spilled gravy all over his legs. Then they were off down the road to the neighbors' Thanksgiving hymn singing.

The wind was spiked with wet coldness, the fore-
runner of a chilly November rain, so they wasted no
time getting to the brightly lit shop at Ephraim's.
Buggies were being parked with teams approaching
from either direction, so Ruth huddled the children
to the side of the road, out of the way of approaching
hooves and steel wheels.

She could always tell the difference between the
young men's teams and the teams belonging to families. The youth drove horses with plenty of speed
or style, sometimes both, and their harnesses were
decked out in flashes of silver or chrome. The bat-
tery-powered lights on their buggies also outnum-
bered those of their parents, whose teams had only
the necessary headlights, blinking orange taillights,
and the reflective, slow-moving vehicle emblem—a
triangle of orange in obedience to Pennsylvania laws
of the road.

Often the youth decorated their slow-moving
vehicle signs with stickers from amusement parks
or their favorite football teams, which was tolerat-
ed in varying degrees. Some older members of the

community smiled knowingly, while others frowned.

The shop at Ephraim's was a haven of warmth and light. Some of the glossy church benches had been set on trestles to form a long table with the remaining benches on either side and the German songbooks stacked neatly along the makeshift table.

Off to the side, Mamie had set up two folding tables end to end and covered them with her good tablecloths. Then she had loaded them with Tupperware containers and plastic ice cream buckets full of her Christmas cookies. Large containers each held five gallons of piping hot coffee, and there was Coffee-mate creamer and sugar and a basket containing napkins and plastic spoons all set out in a manageable order.

Bags of pretzels and potato chips, deep bowls of homemade Chex Mix, platters of cheese and German ring bologna, dips and vegetables—loads of food appeared as if by magic as happy, festive women offered their contributions and delivered them to their proper places on Mamie's tables.

"Ruth!" Mamie bore down on her, a locomotive of

suppressed energy bristling with excitement.

"Mamie! Everything looks so nice. Your table is all decked out, and the coffee ready. You must have worked hard."

"Oh, I did. I'm ready to drop. Then Waynie was a mess with his teething, and Fannie had to go wash for Elam *sei* Katie. She has Lyme disease, you know. Hiya, Benjamin! Hiya. Come here, you sweet bundle. Oh Ruth, he's so cute. *Gel*, Benjy? Hi, Lillian. How's her head? *Komm*, Lillian. I want to see your head. *Gooka-mol* (Let me see)."

Lillian stood stock-still as Mamie's fingers explored the surface of the little skull, her eyes lifted solemnly to Mamie's kind face.

"The bump went away now, so it's better," she announced solemnly.

"*Ach ya, gel?*"

Mamie sat down, unwrapped little Benjamin, took Lillian's proffered coat, and left Ruth to search the room for other familiar faces.

The men were assembling on folding chairs, their beards wagging as they talked. They were dressed in colorful shirts, pastel blues and beiges with an occasional navy or burgundy. They smiled as they greeted one another with firm handshakes or familiar claps on the shoulder.

Ruth turned away, the loss of Ben—the raw absence of him—so unbearable when his brother, Sam, arrived. He smiled, then caught her eye and waved. So much like Ben. No one could ever replace his memory, she knew now. That knowledge was engraved into her being, like the words that were etched on his perfect gravestone.

"Ruth, what? A shadow just passed across your face. You're missing Ben, *gel? Ach* my, Ruth. Maybe you shouldn't have come. You poor thing. I can't stand it. *Komm, sits ana* (sit down)."

Mamie slipped a heavy arm around Ruth's drooping form, and the hurt was replaced by her friend's pure kindness along with the scent of her lack of a good antiperspirant—the only blight on their friendship. Ruth had never worked up the audacity to mention it. She winced now but resigned herself and chose to accept the kindness, regardless of the less than fresh Mamie.

"It's okay. I'm just being childish," Ruth whispered.

The two greeted others who came by to shake hands, give an occasional hug, and offer words of friendliness. They asked how she was, always. And always, Ruth would smile and say, "*Goot* (Good)," nod her head, and hope the person holding her hand would believe it.

No, I'm not always *goot*. My money is all but gone once again, Lillian is driving me batty, and I miss Ben so much right this minute, I could just run home and wrap up in a blanket and turn my face to the wall. My spigot leaks—the one in the laundry room—and a section of spouting is loose. So don't ask me how I am, because I'll just have to put on that false veneer of shining goodness that comes from generation after generation of pasted smiles and hidden suffering.

Ruth knew the Amish were always expected to be *goot*. It is bred in them, this taking up of their crosses, bowing of their heads, and repetition of "Thy will be done." They carry on, and when the load becomes unbearable, they still endure it. It is the Amish way. The Lord giveth, and the Lord taketh away. Ruth allowed a small sigh to escape.

As the girls filed in, shaking hands and greeting the women with polite smiles, Ruth turned her attention to look with interest at the different colors and styles of the dresses as well as the hairstyles. She noted which ones were neat and which could use a little work.

How well she remembered the anticipation of each hymn singing when she was young. Would this be the evening Ben would notice her? Would he be seated close by or much too far away toward the other end of the table?

Always, there had been Ben. She was fifteen when she spoke to him that first time. She'd fallen hard and had never been the same. It was at a volleyball game on a lovely summer evening. She was not yet sixteen, so she wasn't actually *rumspringing*, but he'd come over to her and Rachel and said, "Hello, Ruth, how are you?"

Their time together had been so short, and yet her mind was packed with many memories of their love. It remained a wondrous thing to file away those golden mental files that hung neatly in her special place labeled "Marriage, a heaven on earth." For she had loved him, given herself to him, and adored the ground he walked on.

Could she ever love again, in that same way? No. A steely resolve closed her heart to the thought. It seemed wrong somehow. She felt sure Ben would not want her to consider a second love.

You need to care for our children, Ruth.

Ruth blinked, frightened, her eyes wide. Who had spoken?

She looked left, then right, and then straight ahead and directly into the deep brown eyes of that bachelor who was single but dating Anna—Paul King's Anna. Ruth tried to look away, but she was held by his gaze that was asking her questions again.

How can eyes speak? she wondered much later that night. Those eyes had asked, Who are you, Ruth? How can I ever get to know you?

At the moment, because she had felt flushed and brazen and was still pondering whose voice she had heard speaking to her about the children, she had finally lowered her head. Her downcast eyes and the heavy lashes sweeping her softly blushing cheeks—none of it was lost on Mamie, who sat straight up and blinked. She pursed her lips, clasped her hands firmly in her lap, and knew.

The singing rose and fell. The lovely old hymns of the forefathers were coupled with choruses of English songs as the men's deep voices blended in complete harmony with the lighter tones of the women.

Ruth cuddled Benjamin, bent over him, and kissed his downy cheeks as she pondered her explosion of emotion, masked, of course, by her steadiness of character.

The coffee was piping hot, and the assortment of cookies and bars and pretzels and cheese and popcorn passed from person to person in a steady stream as the voices of young and old raised in cheery banter during the fellowship that always followed *an shoene singin* (a nice singing).

Eventually the horses were brought and attached to cold buggies, the headlights illuminating the person connecting the britchments and leather pulls to shafts. Friends called out their well wishes, and a few men hurried to help an insecure sixteen year old with a rowdy, misbehaving horse. This was common on cold, late evenings when the horses were tired of standing tied side by side in unfamiliar barns or along cold fences.

Ruth hurried the children along, careful to hold Benjamin close, warning Elmer to keep hold of Lillian's hand.

Suddenly a dark figure emerged and stepped in front of her, blocking her way.

She stopped, hesitant.

A deep, craggy voice spoke out of the blackness.

"May I ask your name?" He was breathing too fast.

Startled, not thinking, she said quickly, "Ruth Miller."

"These are your children?"

"Yes."

"Sorry if I appear rude. I'm John Beiler."

He extended a hand. Ruth shifted Benjamin, found the stranger's hand, and shook it politely.

"I would offer a ride, but I think your house is not far away."

"No."

"John!"

An irritated voice broke through the stillness as a tall, dark figure appeared, threw herself at John, and clasping his hand and looking up into his face, said, "Where were you? I've been ready to go for a long time."

"I'm sorry."

Nodding his head at Ruth, he moved off, firmly pulled along by his fiancé, evidently, leaving Ruth shaking her head at the boldness of girls in this modern day.

Ruth couldn't fall asleep. She finally got up, took down the flashlight that hung from the hook in the pantry, and found the trustworthy bottle of Tylenol P.M. Sleeping pills or not, sometimes they were a necessity to help her cope with the problems as they approached. Lack of rest was her biggest hurdle. She had learned that the hard way.

Thoughts tumbled about, turning a labyrinth of normal thinking into a hopeless puzzle. Why had she heard that? Those words? Were angels among us, she prayed. Please God, why? "You need to care for our children." As if it were Ben. It wasn't his voice, exactly, but more like a loud thought. Or a thought out loud. Was she losing her mind?

And those eyes. Oh, dear God. She was so ashamed. But, yes, they were like Ben's. Too much so. Heavenly Father, please keep me from falling in love. It's wrong for me, now.

In the morning, when Roy went to feed Pete and Oatmeal, he came back immediately, saying there was a box on the porch, a banana box, the kind they got from B. B.'s Store.

Quickly, Ruth lowered her hands from brushing Esther's hair, telling her to wait, and hurried after Roy. She lifted off the lid of cardboard box with its blue and yellow writing.

A hand went to her throat. Roy was the first to look, turning the large John Martin's ham on its side, touching the Butterball turkey, and poking at the large bundle wrapped in white butcher paper.

"Mam! Look! A turkey! What's in the paper? Let's take it to the kitchen table."

Elmer joined them, and the boys strained to lift the box with Ruth's help. Esther and Barbara stretched on their tiptoes, peering in to see for themselves as Ruth unwrapped the white parcel. There was a mound of fresh ground sausage, and her mouth watered thinking of the crisp fried patties she could make to eat with scrambled eggs.

The ham was enormous, and already she planned to bake it, freeze portions of it, and make soup and homemade potpie and ham salad. Oh, the wonder of it! Christmas was all taken care of now, at least the dinner here at home.

There was another package of ground beef and one of chicken breast—something she had not bought since Ben died. She would marinate it and then sauté it for only a few minutes—so good. She'd make a wonderful pot of chicken corn noodle soup with chunks of celery and slivers of carrot and parsley.

"Oh my goodness!" Barbara exclaimed.

"We're going to eat like kings!" Esther said and went twirling around the kitchen, her skirts flying in a circle around her and her partially done hair in disarray.

Lillian gave a whoop of pure excitement and followed, copying every move of her older sister.

Elmer, however, looked very grave as he pinched his mouth into a serious line, his eyes concerned. "How do we know who left it? How do we know it's safe?" he asked.

Ruth stopped. She noticed the way he held his shoulders, so erect, so…just so much more mature than his age with responsibility weighing on the thin boyish shoulders long before they were round enough or strong enough to support it. It broke her heart, the way he felt he needed to protect them—her oldest child and yet still so vulnerable.

"Listen, Elmer, I do understand your point. There is always that danger. But we need to have faith in our fellow humans. I think it was given to us by someone who was directed by God to do so. I think it's good, clean, wonderful food. Can you imagine our Christmas dinner with all of this?"

She smiled widely, held up one palm, and raised her eyebrows in question. Elmer nodded, grinned, and then sidled up to give her a resounding high five, followed by a leaping Roy who slapped her palm so hard she cradled it with her other hand and faked a serious injury.

"Hooo-boy!"

Barbara and Esther giggled and laughed before they caught sight of the clock and shrieked.

"Ten to eight!"

"Oh my goodness!"

That day the children went to school after shoveling cold cereal into their mouths at the very last minute. They rushed out the door still pulling on their coats and smacking their hats onto their heads before racing down the road on their scooters. Their journey to school that day was filled with more merriment than they'd had since their father passed away.

Chapter Seven

WHO HAD DONE IT, THOUGH? SOMEONE with plenty of common sense and knowledge of a poor widow's needs, Ruth thought.

The banana box of delicious meat was soon followed by another one that was mysteriously delivered on the same night Lillian became terribly ill with a sore throat. How could a mother be rocking her child in the living room with the blinds halfway up and not see someone leave a box outside in plain view?

Lillian was so sick, her little body racked with pain and fever that no amount of Tylenol would touch. It was a long night with an abundance of fear and unanswered questions. The small kerosene lamp by the recliner provided a small, steady flame of reassurance, while the shadows along the wall brought doubt and sorrow. The flickering gloominess reflected Ruth's constantly shifting emotions as Lillian's little heart pounded in her thin, little chest and her breathing became shallow and ragged. The little patient repeatedly cried out in pain when she tried to swallow.

Mam arrived in the morning, an angel quickly transported by an English driver. Her blue eyes filled with tears of understanding as she carried in her Unkers salve, Infection Aid, and liquid Vitamin C along with her knowledge of onion poultices and vinegar baths.

As always, Ruth meant to stay strong, but her resolve crumbled the minute she met with the kindness in her mother's eyes. She handed Lillian over to Mommy, soothed a crying Benjamin, and knew it was time to admit she wasn't *goot*. She was completely overwhelmed and underfunded. And, yes, she had bought those two rugs at Walmart, but now her money was all gone, and she just wanted to buy Christmas gifts and be normal with a husband who provided for her.

She did not want to be the poor widow who people watched with sympathy and pity. She wanted to hold up her head and say, "Stop it. I am Ruth. I am still human, and I want to be accepted as one of you and laugh when I want to or say silly things if I feel like it. Just stop looking at me." Oh, the thoughts that tormented her when she was exhausted!

First, Lillian was lowered into the bathtub, though the smell of apple cider vinegar was so strong that she cried and clung to her grandmother. The miracle occurred when the fever dropped after the Unkers salve was applied to Lillian's neck and she had swallowed a dose of Infection Aid, a potent mixture of herbs.

Lillian was dressed in a clean flannel nightgown with an old cloth diaper tied around her neck, where the salve was already doing its work. They pulled warm socks onto her feet, and she rested well, sleeping soundly for most of the forenoon as Mam busied herself doing the washing and then holding Benjamin.

Ruth suddenly remembered the box and brought it in, excitement in her eyes, a wide smile on her face. Her joy brought a tender look to Mam's own face as she remembered her daughter in easier times.

Slowly, Ruth lifted off the cardboard lid and found this box filled with groceries. Staples. Good, common sense pantry food. There was mayonnaise, ketchup, mustard—all expensive name brands.

"Oh, Mam! It's as if someone followed me around the bent and dent store and wrote down everything I couldn't find. Seriously. Coffee! Folgers. Just my favorite. I couldn't find it last time. Even pancake syrup! Mrs. Butterworth. Who is doing this, Mam?"

There were cans of navy beans and kidney beans, boxes of elbow macaroni and spaghetti, cake mixes and brown sugar, rice and flour and oatmeal.

"No name?"

"No clue."

Mam clucked her tongue and said she hoped the giver would be richly rewarded.

They used more of the ham that day, made bean soup with the broth, and ate large bowlfuls for lunch with grilled cheese sandwiches.

When Lillian woke, Mam said to try feeding her a bit of the bean soup, but she refused, turning her head from side to side, her lips squeezed tight. They opened a can of Campbell's chicken noodle soup instead, and Lillian ate spoonful after spoonful. She was extremely pleased with herself and all the praise they heaped on her, but she only smiled and promptly fell asleep before she could say a word.

When Mam's driver came late that evening, there was a mutual reaching for each other, a hug born of necessity. It expressed the great appreciation Ruth had for her mother and was absolutely essential for Mam to communicate her love and support for her daughter.

And so they stood, these two slight women, their coverings as white beacons of their subjection to God, and they drew strength from the warmth of human touch.

Ruth stood by the door and waved as Mam got in the car. Then she turned to go inside, knowing she would need to face the emptiness again.

Ruth's table had a round, brown placemat in the middle with a candle on it. As she headed back to her kitchen, she noticed a scrap of paper stuck beneath the placemat and tried to brush it away. Instead, she pulled out a check written to Ruth Miller in her mother's cursive hand, spaced perfectly as usual, and signed with her father's scrawl.

Again, Ruth got out her box of thank you cards and wrote her parents a note of heartfelt appreciation, grateful to know this time who to thank for the blessing. Then she put a stamp on it and hurried to the mailbox without a coat, her skirts flapping as she ran.

The air was invigorating, bringing color to her cheeks as she thrust the card into the mailbox and flipped up the red flag. She shivered and turned to race back to the house before she noticed a builder's truck bearing down, then slowing to a stop.

"Hello again."

She looked into John Beiler's eyes and smiled. Maybe it was the air nipping about her. Perhaps it was the fact that she was alone, the children already asleep in the house, or perhaps it was just the wonder of having to—no, wanting to—smile back at him, completely without guilt or wondering what anyone would say. No one would need to know. Not Mam or Dat or Mamie Stoltzfus.

"So you have a habit of going to the mailbox without a coat in the evening?"

"I'm afraid so."

He laughed then, and she continued smiling until the driver waved and John Beiler said, "Take care," as the truck moved off.

So. He was a builder. A carpenter, a contractor, or maybe a roofer or framer or mason. There were so many different occupations that all fell under the general term of builder.

He was not a farmer. More and more, the Amish were moving away from farming since they were simply unable to complete with the huge dairy operations. However, many people Ruth knew still made a good living milking cows.

She had so enjoyed her life on the farm and still missed the satisfying "ka-chug, ka-chug" of the clean stainless steel milkers hanging from the cows' udders as they filled with creamy milk, the cash flow of the dairy farmers of Lancaster County.

Her main concern was Elmer and Roy. The boys needed chores—everyday repetitive responsibilities that build character—the way she was raised.

Times changed, and she needed to change with them. Still it troubled her the way Roy came home from school, sprawled on the recliner by the window, and read anything he could find, or fought with Barbara, or picked on Esther. He needed a job, more chores.

Well, there was nothing to do about that now.

When the boys came home from school the next day, their trousers and shoes were covered with mud. Elmer's hat was torn along the brim, and Roy sported a long, red scratch on one cheek.

"Football!" they announced when questioned.

"In the mud?" Ruth squeaked helplessly.

"It wasn't raining."

"Out! Out! To the *kesslehaus*. Get those pants off."

Laughing, with towels wrapped around their waists, they zoomed through the kitchen and down the hallway to their bedroom, soon reappearing in clean black trousers and white socks.

"That's better. Why did Teacher Lydia let you get so dirty? You shouldn't have played football in the mud,"

Ruth fussed as she picked up the mud-covered pants and placed them carefully in the wringer washer.

Roy eyed her quizzically. "Well, Mam, I'll just tell you one thing. You're not the teacher."

"Yeah, Mam. At least in school we're allowed to drag dirt into the classroom and no one yells at us."

Ruth eyed her growing boys and said they shouldn't have such a disrespectful attitude. They were not to talk like that to her. Boys enter a house with clean shoes or leave their shoes at the door, and if they couldn't respect their mother or her clean floors, then she guessed they should never get married. This statement was met with a great enthusiasm about how cool that would be. Girls weren't anything they cared about, and they were both going to be builders like John Beiler and never get married.

Ruth's head came up. "What do you know about John Beiler?"

"He is cool."

"He's awesome."

"Well…but…" Ruth hated the way she was stammering and hoped the boys wouldn't notice.

"He fixed the roof at school today. He was asking me and Roy all kinds of stuff."

"Yeah. He asked if we want to come help him lay stone along his flower beds."

"No, he didn't say flower beds. He said landscaping."

"What's the difference?"

"He said in the spring."

"Yeah. When it gets warmer."

Ruth stirred the bean soup and hid her face. She told the boys to get their chores done before supper. She was relieved when Lillian cried and she could turn her attention from all the confusing emotions the boys had stirred by talking about John Beiler fixing the schoolhouse roof.

Esther became Lillian's nurse as she recovered, spoiling her so thoroughly that she resorted to a babble of baby talk. The little nurse fixed a plastic tray of doll's dishes containing yogurt and chicken noodle soup and a few gummy bears, a small vase of plastic flowers, and a Kleenex folded in a triangle for a napkin.

Later, while Ruth washed dishes, Elmer stood

beside her, snapping a dishcloth nervously and clearing his throat.

Ruth stopped washing dishes, looked into his eyes, and asked gently if there was something on his mind.

"No."

It was said much too quickly.

"Elmer, tell me."

He snapped the dishcloth, opened the silverware drawer, and closed it again. Then he said to the wall, "Mam, are you ever going to think about another dat for us?"

"Oh, Elmer." That was all she could say, his words having completely knocked the breath out of her.

"What does that mean, Mam?"

"It's just...."

"That if you did meet someone, he'd be stuck with all of us, too, right?"

Ruth knew Elmer had ventured into some turbulent, emotional waters. So she sat down at the kitchen table and asked him and Roy and Esther to join her.

"Elmer, I want you to know I would never, ever consider marrying again if that person did not want any of you. Besides, it's much too…soon. Your dat is still in my heart. He always will be. But he's not here now. You are. And you are a part of him, and the only thing I have to live for. I can never tell you how precious you are to me. The whole day I live to see you come home from school."

Roy's face shone with inner happiness.

"Boy, Mam!"

"You serious?"

"Of course I am. I don't have a husband, just you, and right now, you're all I need." Her smile was tremulous.

"But Mam, if you ever do want a husband, I think John Beiler's eyes look an awful lot like…" Elmer's voice dropped to a whisper as he finished saying, "my dat's." Then he put his head in his hands and the cried sweet, innocent tears of a young boy who missed his own father tremendously.

The next evening they decided to make Christmas lists, just for fun, pretending they had an unlimited supply of money.

Esther said she wanted a real playhouse—not the kind they could set up in the living room, but the kind they made at the shed place where Mamie's Ephraim worked.

"Oh my! That would be wonderful, wouldn't it? In the back yard, under the maple tree, by the row of pines. Okay, write it down. Let's pretend. What color, Esther?"

"White with black shutters."

"To match the house?"

Esther nodded happily.

"A porch!" Barbara announced.

"With a porch," Ruth wrote.

They wanted new scooters, a Gameboy, Monopoly, and all the books that Nancy's Notions had. Every single one. Elmer wanted bunk beds. Roy wanted a bow and arrow. Esther wanted a skateboard. And on and on until Benjamin started fussing, the clock struck eight, and it was time for their baths.

For their bedtime snack, they made popcorn and sprinkled it with sour cream and onion powder. They stirred chocolate syrup into their milk and discussed many silly subjects, along with some serious ones.

After Ruth had kissed the last soft cheek and collapsed on the recliner for a moment of rest before her shower, she realized she wanted a playhouse for the back yard so badly she could physically feel it.

Just as quickly, that dream's bubble burst, the pin named reality doing its job well. Ruth knew that a playhouse wasn't attainable and wouldn't be for a long time. That was okay. As Mam said, "*Siss yusht vie ma uf gebt* (That's just how things go)."

When the next box appeared on the front porch, the children squealed with excitement. Their enthusiasm turned quickly to disappointment when they opened it and found nothing inside except a small wooden box with a slot in the lid.

Elmer extracted an envelope from under the wooden box, tore it open hurriedly, unfolded the paper, and read, "Christmas wish lists. Please fold papers and insert in box. Put box on porch. Thank you!"

They gasped and lifted their round eyes to Ruth, questions flying as they reasoned among themselves. Who in the world? Well, they'd stay up all night.

They needed a dog, that was what.

Ruth, who had returned to her quilting, smiled and burst out laughing after Roy devised a plan to trap the "box person," as they began to call him or her.

"I bet it's Mamie."

"They don't have extra money."

"Maybe they do."

"It's Helen."

"The driver?"

"No way."

Ruth looked up from her quilt binding and said they may never know, but they didn't really need to know. The giver would be blessed for his or her generosity, regardless.

She told the children to make new wish lists, but she asked them not to write down large expensive gifts. She did not want the person to feel obligated to fulfill every wish.

Esther gnawed her pen, glancing at her mother with cunning eyes, and then wrote in very small letters at the bottom of her list, "Real playhouse with porch. White with black shutters." She slipped it smartly into the slot cut in the top of the wooden box, right under Ruth's nose. After the children were in bed that night, Esther whispered to Barbara about what she had done.

Barbara was horrified at Esther's disobedience but said maybe it wasn't too serious, knowing Mam would love to have one, too. She had said so herself.

Chapter Eight

CHRISTMAS WAS FAST APPROACHING, AND THE children marked each day with a large black X on the calendar, completely changing its appearance.

It was December thirteenth when they decided to hitch up Pete and go shopping together with the small amount of money they had. It was a Saturday, the sun was shining, and excitement hovered over the house as the children danced rather than walked, yelled rather than talked. Ruth barked orders, combed hair, and bundled everyone into clean coats and hats and scarves and bonnets.

They brushed Pete till he shone, cleaned the harness, hitched him to the buggy, and were off to the small town of Bart, which everyone called Georgetown. No one knew why Bart was the official address, since no one ever said Bart—just Georgetown—but that's how it was.

They were all snuggled into the clean buggy under the winter lap robes. Roy, Esther, and Barbara sat in back with Esther holding Lillian. Elmer sat in front beside Ruth as usual, holding Benjy.

Pete stepped out eagerly, and the buggy moved along smoothly around bends, past farms, up hills and down. They waved to oncoming teams, pulled to the side to allow cars and trucks to pass, and were very careful when they approached a narrow bridge. Ruth pulled firmly on the reins to allow a car to cross first.

As they approached the hitching rail at Fisher's Housewares, the row of parked horses and buggies left no room for them, so they drove past and pulled up to the fence beside it.

"You think it's okay to park here?" Ruth asked.

"Do you want me to ask someone?" Roy offered.

"No, we'll tell someone when we get inside."

The store was filled with so many things. The boys went off in one direction, and the girls in another, leaving Ruth with Benjy and a bit of time to buy some gifts for the children. It wasn't much, but it was all she could afford, and she wanted to be content.

The store was filled with others of Ruth's faith—some folks she knew, others she didn't. She tried hard not to be envious of the mothers with their carts piled high or a young couple discussing a purchase together.

Row after row of dress fabric, heavy pants material, bonnets, shawls, coats and sweaters, housewares, toys, beautiful sets of china, all sorts of kitchen wares, Christmas candy, books, and canning supplies—an ongoing display of every Amish family's needs.

Ruth chose a Monopoly game for the boys and a set of Melamine dishes for the older girls. Lillian would receive a small doll that boasted a 4.99 price tag. That was all she could afford this year.

She bought two serving dishes for her mam, two red handkerchiefs for her dat, a set of wooden spoons for Mamie, and some coating chocolate. She would make fudge and Rice Krispies treats.

Elmer and Roy begged for a set of books that was marked 29.99, and Ruth had to swallow the lump that formed in her throat. Oh, how she would have loved to buy them, wrap them in colorful Christmas wrap, and watch their faces on Christmas morning, the way it had been when Ben was alive—just last Christmas. But not this year.

Bravely, she handed her meager purchases to the clerk, smiled, and made small, cheerful talk, trying hard not to look around and want the items she could not have, the many things that were clearly out of her reach.

The children were quiet on the return trip, sharing the small bag of Snickers bars wrapped in red and green wrappers. Ruth courageously told them that Christmas was all about the baby Jesus being born in the stable and not about worldly possessions or large gifts.

"Is that all we're getting, though?" they asked.

"Oh, no, your grandparents, your teacher, you'll get a lot more," Ruth assured them.

It was no wonder that Ruth cried that evening, the silent tears running unhindered down her cheeks as she allowed herself the luxury of letting her guard down for just one evening.

She found she could only be courageous for so long before her white flag of defeat went up. She allowed herself to roll around in self-pity and longing and all the stuff she was supposed to avoid but just couldn't help.

It was cleansing and solidifying to accept and admit that she was just one very lonely woman. She knew these were the times that eventually helped her to move on. This plain down honesty was refreshing.

She looked at her reflection in the mirror with her swollen eyes, the red blotches on her cheeks, and her scraggly hair, and she burst into a snort of hysteria before she moved out of the bathroom and away from the brutally honest mirror. Ruth reminded herself that God was still in His Heaven, so all was right with the world. She accepted her lot in life once more and was comforted by His presence.

Hadn't He provided a miracle in the form of that large sum of money that had appeared in a plain, white envelope in her mailbox and in the banana boxes and the generosity of her parents? Surely God was good, and here she was, whining and crying, ungrateful, and asking for more when she already had been given so much. Deeply ashamed, she knelt by her bed and asked the Lord to forgive her *undankbar* (unthankful) thoughts, remembering to thank him over and over for the Christmas miracles she had received.

Yes, He had chosen to take Ben, and yes, she was an *arme vitve* (poor widow), but even she could be caught unaware in the devil's own snares, the same as everyone else, perhaps even more so, if she tried to cloth herself in self-righteous robes of martyrdom.

Her spirit revived, her thoughts at peace, Ruth tucked her slim hands beneath her soft cheeks that had been cleansed by her tears, and drifted off to sleep. She slept like a baby, with Lillian creeping dangerously close to the edge of the bed as she tossed and mumbled her way across the expanse.

After her good cry and a solid night of sleep, Ruth enjoyed the Sunday day of rest with her children. On Monday morning, feeling refreshed, energetic, and more alive than she had for months, Ruth shivered on her way down to the basement to stoke the coal fire.

They had a good system. She shook the grate and watched the ashes for red coals, which were the signal to stop as all the cold, dead ashes had already fallen to the pan below. Then she pulled out the pan and slowly dumped it into a small metal bucket, where the few live coals would soon be extinguished in the pile of ashes.

Elmer and Roy took the ashes out and scattered them across the garden or beside the old tin shed. Then they filled the coal hod every evening and placed it by the stove, so she had coal in the morning to get the system going again.

She grunted a bit as she lifted the heavy hod of coal, watched carefully as the pieces slid into the hopper of the stove. She shut the lid, adjusted the thermostat at the side to three, and went back upstairs.

She had developed a habit of stopping by the back door every morning to peer through the window, checking the sky for the starlight—or blackness without them—that signaled a sunny day or a cloudy one.

She opened the door and stepped outside for a better view, peered into the early morning gloom, and found not one star. She could hear the traffic plainly, over on 896, so that meant the air was heavy, and rain or snow was just around the corner.

She missed the daily paper. Every morning, Ben had read the weather forecast to her as she stood by the stove frying eggs. Daily newspaper service was too expensive for her now, so she just checked the atmosphere and the stars before sorting clothes for a day's washing.

Not a nice wash day, she thought, but the boys wouldn't have enough pants to last until Friday, so she'd wash. She filled the stainless steel Lifetime coffeemaker half full of water, set it on the gas range, and flicked a knob to turn on the burner. She got down the large red container of Folgers coffee and spooned a portion into the top of the coffeemaker before quietly gathering hampers, dirty towels, wet washcloths.

She frowned as she entered the boys' room and stumbled on soiled clothes strewn across the floor, a sure sign of a significant lack of respect. How often had she asked them to please scoop up all their dirty clothes and throw them in the hamper? She'd even put a plastic laundry basket in their room—one without a lid—so it would only take one second to carry out this small act of obedience instead of two or three. Time for another pep talk.

Her hand slid along the top of the nightstand, searching for the small flashlight Elmer kept there. She grimaced when the alarm clock slid off the edge and crashed to the floor. Elmer lifted his head and blinked, his hair sticking up in all the wrong directions, a scary silhouette from the dim lamp in the hall.

"Sorry," Ruth whispered. "Getting your clothes."

He flopped onto his stomach, hunching his shoulders to pull up the covers, made a few smacking sounds with his mouth, and went back to sleep.

No flashlight. Well, she'd try and get everything although, inevitably, she always found a dirty sock or a crumpled t-shirt under the bed when she cleaned.

Now to start the diesel. No time or need for a sweater as she'd only be out for a minute. She stepped briskly out into the dark morning and took a few steps across the wooden porch floor before the toe of her sneaker connected with a solid object. With a startled cry, she pitched forward.

The old boxwoods by the porch softened her landing, crackling beneath her weight as she came to a stop. She rolled off the breaking shrubs, leapt to her feet, and brushed bits of mulch and leaves off her apron.

Ouch. Her shin was throbbing, painfully bruised from connecting with the edge of the porch, or…was it? Yes, it was another banana box. Well, she'd wait until the children awoke to let them experience the thrill of the box's contents.

When the first load of whites was being churned back and forth by the washer's agitator, the hot water and clothing rhythmically slapping the sides of the machine and the frothy suds appearing and disappearing, Ruth went to the kitchen, turned off the burner, and poured the boiling water over the coffee grounds. She set the top part of the coffeemaker over the emptied lower section and put it back on the stove to drip. The rich, flavorful aroma from the dripping coffee gave her a boost of energy and well being.

They'd likely have snow today. Wouldn't it be wonderful? Maybe they'd even have a white Christmas! The children could go sledding at Doddy Lapp's.

She went to the boys' room and whispered loudly, "Elmer! Roy! *Kommet* (Come)."

"Esther!"

Sleepy little sounds of denial met her voice, and she smiled, anticipating telling the children of her clumsy tumble into the bushes. Lifting her foot to a chair, she pushed down the black knee sock and examined the dark, angry bruise that had appeared there, surrounded by a faint bluish ring. She certainly had slammed that leg. Well, nothing to do about it now. Gingerly, she pulled the sock back up and went to feed the first load of clothes through the wringer.

After the water had been squeezed from the clothes, Ruth took up her hanging ring, a clever handmade item that was exactly that—a ring made of white PVC piping with wooden clothespins dangling from it, a few inches apart and attached by a sturdy nylon cord. All the socks, underwear, handkerchiefs, bibs, baby onesies, and numerous other small items were attached to the clothespins and, in the winter, carried to the basement to be hung above the coal stove, where they'd be dry in a jiffy. Those rings were a housewife's dream, and every wash day Ruth appreciated hers with her six children and all the piles of small, wet items to be hung up.

Back and forth she hurried with the Rubbermaid clothesbasket, up and down the basement stairs, making sure the boys and Esther were up and starting to pack their lunches.

It was an unspoken rule. If they heard the air motor and knew their mother was washing, they'd have to finish packing lunches for school. She set the brightly colored plastic lunchboxes side by side on the countertop each evening, put their pretzels in sandwich bags, and chocolate chip cookies, too. All they needed to do was make their own sandwiches and add an apple or canned peaches or pears.

Sometimes the children spoke wistfully about their classmates' food—the Gogurts with cartoon characters on the tubes or the Fruit Roll-Ups they wanted so badly that their mouths watered as they watched the other children eat. Their schoolmates sometimes had chicken nuggets or frozen pizza slices wrapped in tinfoil to put on top of the gas heater, and they smelled so good.

In response, Ruth had devised her own recipe for the children's lunches. She bought outdated packages of English muffins and spooned generous amounts of spaghetti sauce on top, using a jar of sauce she had canned herself. Then she laid a slice of white American cheese on top of each muffin. One day, Esther proudly told Ruth that Rosanna had wanted a taste of her pizza muffin, and now Rosanna's mother made them for her and her brother, Calvin.

Ruth poked her head through the kitchen door. "There's ham salad, if you're tired of the pizza muffins."

"Nope!"

"Pizza!"

Smiling, Ruth carried the last load of laundry to the basement. When the clothes were hung, she placed the clothespin apron on its hook and rinsed the washer, hosing it down well with hot water. Then she got down on her hands and knees and wiped up any spilled water with a good, thick rag. There. Now let it snow. The laundry was all hung snugly in the basement, drying in the good heat radiating from the coal stove.

"Guess what?"

Roy was spooning spaghetti sauce onto three muffins, biting his tongue in concentration. Esther peered past his shoulder, disapproval written all over her face.

"Not so much!"

"Guess what?" Ruth said again.

"What?" Elmer asked, intently prying apart the slices of American cheese.

"Another box!"

"Nah-uh!"

"Serious?"

"Where?"

"Follow me!"

There in the cold, snow-laden air, they crouched, bending over the box with disbelieving eyes. There was another banana box, the same kind with Chiquita written in blue and yellow lettering and a picture of bananas. This one contained every item they had ever dreamed of putting in their lunchboxes. And some they hadn't even thought of—not knowing they existed.

"Jello already made!" Esther gloated, holding the small plastic containers high.

"Gogurt! Oh, I love these things!"

"Real candy bars!"

"Fruit snacks!"

"Crackers and popcorn and cheese curls."

"What's this?"

"String cheese."

"What's string cheese?"

There was ham from a real deli at a real grocery store and sweet bologna and a thick round of German ring bologna. The box was so heavy that Ruth took one side and Elmer the other so they could carry the box between them.

Quickly, she scrambled eggs for the children, hurriedly combed Esther's hair, and pinned her black apron around her tiny waist as she also goaded the boys along. "Brush your teeth!" she called over her shoulder as she hurried to her bedroom, responding to the morning sounds from Lillian and Benjamin.

Instead of opening the door the whole way, Ruth peeped through the small crack and said, "Peep!"

Mesmerized, Lillian sat straight up, watching the narrow opening. Up came Benjamin's head, his eyes wide with surprise.

"Peep!" Ruth said again.

Lillian bounced happily and then pitched herself onto her stomach, knowing Ruth would fling open the door and pounce on her, which was exactly what happened. Shrieking, she scrunched her little form into the farthest corner, and Ruth grabbed her warm, cuddly body and kissed her cheeks soundly.

"Morning, Lillian."

"Look, Benjy's awake!"

When Benjamin saw his mother approaching, he laid his head back on the crib sheet and kicked his little legs in anticipation. Lifting him, she inhaled his sweet baby smells and then carried them both out to the rocking chair for some cuddling, glad they had both slept through the washing.

As the school children went out the door, Ruth told them to be good and listen to the teacher. Their lunch boxes each held one of the containers of Jello. Ruth had told them they could only have one special treat each day. That way the food would last for a month, perhaps longer. They solemnly agreed, and Ruth was so proud of them.

Pride was something that wasn't named, since they were Amish. It was wrong to be proud of anything—one's home, husband, children, quilt-making abilities, baking skills, whatever.

So if Ruth was pleased, she didn't name it as pride. Compliments were often met with a shamefaced dip of the head or a word of denial. Even if true humility was actually in short supply, there was still an outward show of it.

Yes, this small ray of pride she would allow herself. She often felt inadequate and overwhelmed, raising these six children, so when the school aged ones readily agreed to make the treats for their lunchboxes last longer, she felt rewarded by their grave acceptance of her wishes. And she was proud of them.

Today, she would quilt. She would pin the new quilt top into the frame, the one her mother had given her when Ben died. It was a sturdy, wooden one with two rails resting on a stand at each end, allowing the quilt to be rolled as one side was completed.

She loved to quilt. It would be nice to have Mamie pop in to help her pin the back of the quilt to the fabric on the rails, but Ruth supposed she was still resting up from that hymn singing.

Ruth smiled. She loved Mamie. She was the epitome of every verse or poem ever written about friendship. Those words all held much more meaning since Ben had left her alone, to carry on raising the dear little ones on her own.

Not so little now, though. Elmer was turning into a miniature Ben with his shoulders held so high, his stance one of premature obligation as the man of the house.

And then, because the thought of Elmer's shoulders made her cry, her whole living room blurred and swam, and she couldn't see Mamie's form very clearly when her friend knocked on the storm door. Ruth thought it must be the UPS man and couldn't think what she had ordered that she'd be receiving a delivery.

When Barbara emerged from the girls' bedroom, rubbing the sleep from her eyes, she looked at the door and asked why no one let Mamie in.

Chapter Nine

"Hey!" Mamie decided enough was enough. That air was cold, and she let herself in through the back door into the kitchen.

"I'm here," Ruth called. "Just come in, you don't have to knock."

Mamie walked over, looked closely at Ruth, and said gruffly, "You were crying."

"Now, I wasn't."

"Yes, you were. I can tell."

And Ruth was wrapped in a compassionate embrace—never mind the odor of Mamie's sweater or the fact that her headscarf had once been white but now appeared gray and its fringes were hanging in Ruth's face. The love from her friend was the purest kind, bathed in glory.

"*Ach, siss net chide* (Oh, it isn't right), Ruth. *Komm,*

Lillian. Come to Mamie. Hiya! *Vee bisht doo?* (How are you?)"

Sitting down, Mamie's motherly hands explored Lillian's head as she peppered her with caring questions, Lillian nodding or shaking her head no in response.

"Hiya, Benjy. You little corker! You're growing! *Ach*, Ruth, such beautiful children. Hiya, Barbara. Did you just get out of bed? Hey, I smell laundry soap. Don't tell me you washed already? If you did, I'm going straight home. Did you?"

When Ruth nodded, Mamie grinned shamefacedly.

"You know what? I'm fat and lazy. I have to go home and wash and go on a diet. But, oh my, it felt so good to roll over and sleep till seven. Eph has a dinner down at Stoltzfus Structures, so he said he'd eat Corn Flakes this morning. He's a wonder, that man."

She realized her mistake too late and clapped a hand across her mouth, her eyes widening in dismay.

"Ruth, I'm sorry. Here I go rambling on about my husband, and you having *zeit-lang* (loneliness and longing) for Ben. Don't listen to me."

"No, Mamie. It's okay. Don't worry about it. I'm happy that you love your husband. It's as it should be."

"Oh, Ruth. I wish I could....*Ach*, I don't know what I wish."

"How's Waynie?"

"Beside himself with his teething. I put that teething stuff on, but it hardly makes a difference."

Ruth nodded. There was a space of comfortable silence as they sat, Ruth pondering the significance of Mamie's earlier comment, and Mamie's eyes drifting to the coffeepot, nodding her head toward it.

Ruth put Benjamin in his high chair, made toast and scrambled eggs, and filled a plate for Mamie. Mamie said she wasn't one bit hungry, but she managed to finish the last of the eggs as well as three slices of toast and two cups of coffee laden with sugar and milk.

She stayed, of course, to help pin the quilt to the frame, saying she simply had to go home as Fannie had a sore throat and Waynie might need her.

"Here, pull this over this way," Mamie said around the pins in her mouth.

"Is it crooked?" Ruth asked, realizing they'd have to unroll the whole backing of the quilt if it was.

"Stop pulling!"

"Which way?"

"My way!"

"I'm not pulling!"

"Yes, you are, too. Here, you go give Benjy some cereal or yogurt or something. Let me do this alone."

Ruth laughed out loud and said over her shoulder, "Do it your way."

"You know what? You may be a much better *everything* than I am, but you aren't as good with quilts as I am. You can't pull on the backing. You have to roll it in naturally."

"Really?"

"Now you're *schputting* me!"

"No, I would never do that."

They both grinned, and Mamie took the pins out of her mouth and told Ruth she was closer to her than her own sister, that she was the best friend she ever had.

Ruth told her about the boxes that had been appearing on her porch, and Mamie's mouth started to wobble.

Her blue eyes filled with tears, and she ran her hands across her large forearms and said it gave her chills.

"Who could it be? I'm afraid whoever it is doesn't realize how they're spoiling us," Ruth said, sitting down to spoon yogurt into Benjamin's mouth, which he opened eagerly, like a ravenous little bird.

"Who? Who would do something like that? Maybe a group of people. Maybe English people. Like a Sunday school class or something."

"Don't they go to Haiti or Africa or places like that? They have mission fields. You know—serious, big projects. Why would they bother with us? They don't know I'm a widow."

"Maybe they do."

"I don't like the word 'widow.' It sounds so lonesome, or sad…or something."

"I agree, Ruth, but that is what you are now. And before we know it, it will be a year. That's the proper time for remarriage, you know. I think you need to be reminded of that. Or do you?"

Never in her most intimate thoughts had it occurred to Ruth that Mamie would ever suggest the unspeakable. Her face flaming, completely at loss, she knocked over the container of yogurt, and it plunked solidly to the floor, splashing the thick, creamy mess all over the linoleum.

Leaving Benjamin in his high chair, she went to the pantry, grabbed the Cheerios box, and shook a few onto his tray. She kept her face hidden from Mamie as she got a clean rag from the drawer and proceeded to wipe up the yogurt without saying a word.

Wisely, Mamie busied herself with the quilt until Ruth had composed herself. Then she looked up.

"Well?"

"Well, what?"

"You know what I mean."

"I don't."

"You do."

"Alright, if I do, then who? Mamie, now come on. In all of Lancaster County there is not one man who would be....Well, think, Mamie, think about it—six. I have six children. A five-month-old baby. It's just too soon to speak of these things. And who would want all seven of us."

"Well, it's not too early."

Ruth looked up quickly.

"You are one determined lady."

"I sure am."

Then Mamie added, "You need a dog. If Trixie were here, you wouldn't have had to clean up that yogurt. She would have lapped it right up."

"All I need is a dog in this house, Mamie."

"If you had one, you'd know who is setting those boxes on your porch."

Ruth laughed.

"There. Now help me with this batting."

The soft, white middle part of the quilt was spread evenly across the rolled up backing. Then the actual quilt was tugged neatly across the top and pinned securely.

An appliquéd Rose of Sharon pattern in deep purple and shades of green was a sight to behold, they both agreed. The intricacy of the needlework was mind boggling, and the person who appliquéd was far more talented than the quilter, they confirmed.

"Oh, I just have to quilt a few stitches before I go," Mamie said longingly.

"You can stay."

"I have to wash."

Ruth knew, inevitably, that Fannie would do the washing, but that was none of her concern.

"I have a bit of a secret."

Mamie spoke as she was threading her needle, so she wouldn't have to look directly at Ruth. When Ruth was afraid to answer, Mamie went right on talking.

"Do you know who John Beiler is?"

"John Beiler?"

Ruth's voice was calm and quiet and so poorly disguised that she may has well have turned eagerly and pelted her friend with a thousand questions about him.

"You know who I mean."

Mamie drove her needle rapidly up and down through the quilt. She suddenly sat back and held up her thimble.

"This thing is too small. It pinches my finger."

"Here."

Ruth went to the sewing machine, located a larger thimble, and handed it to her friend.

"Yes, I know who he is," she admitted.

Seriously now, her face shining with concern and care, Mamie laid down the needle she was using and said, "Ruth, I saw at the singing, okay? I saw how he kept noticing you. And you were looking at him. Now, you need to know that he broke up with Paul King's Anna. They say it was him."

Ruth nodded weakly, the color leaving her face.

"Yes. They say it's awful hard on her. You know she's been a schoolteacher all these years. She's an attractive girl, gets along so well with the pupils, even the parents. I pity her. My heart just goes out to her."

"Yes," Ruth whispered, which was about the only sound she could manage.

"You know he's a brother to *Huvvel* Dave's Elam?"

Ruth nodded.

"Can't you talk?"

"Yes."

"Well, then act *chide* (right)."

They both burst out laughing, and Ruth cried a little. Mamie pushed back her chair and hugged her hard. She smelled of bread and butter pickles and

Waynie's diaper, and when Mamie went home to do the washing, Ruth sat staring numbly out the window, her hands hanging limply at her sides. Barbara had to tell her two times that Lillian was in the candy drawer.

How can one lonely widow ever sort out her feelings? It was wrong to forget the memory of Ben, wrong to let another man into her life. Besides, what did Mamie know? No man—in his right mind— would consider her.

Ruth's emotions bounced back and forth for the remainder of the day between this new longing and her old loyalty. The emotions were coupled with the humiliating thought of putting herself through all these conflicting feelings when it was all probably just a crazy idea of Mamie's. Mamie was a bit of an airhead, anyway. But a compassionate, loving one at any rate, and she truly wanted what was best for her. Ruth knew Mamie was completely genuine—not even remotely capable of any cunning motives.

By the time the children came home from school, Ruth was an unstable wreck. She heated leftover spaghetti for supper and didn't answer their questions when they asked.

When the clouds settled low in the sky just before darkness blanketed the countryside and small flakes of snow started steadily falling through the cold, damp air, Ruth was surprised to see a truck pull in the drive.

That driver better get home, she thought. It looked like some serious hazardous road conditions would soon be developing. She turned back to the dishes, her mind elsewhere, and never gave the truck another thought since nobody ever came to the door.

Elmer and Roy burst back into the kitchen, their faces red with the cold, yelling at the top of their voices.

"Hey! It's snowing and *rissling* (sleeting)!"

"No school!" Esther cried.

Later that evening, Ruth read the story of Mrs. Boot, the farmer, at least three times. Lillian listened attentively, completely fascinated by the thought of the littlest pig being too small to get any breakfast and having to break into the hens' pen to eat theirs.

After her youngest daughter had drifted off to sleep, Ruth tucked her carefully into bed before rocking Benjamin to sleep.

The boys studied their parts for the Christmas program, which was supposed to be a secret but hardly ever stayed that way. Then they yawned, took their showers, and dressed in clean sets of flannel pajamas. With their hair wet and faces shining from the soap and hot water, they each had a large serving of graham crackers and some milk.

Elmer said Roy had had to stay in for recess, but Ruth didn't hear what he said, so Roy kicked his brother under the table, hard. They went to bed, with Ruth answering them in quiet, absentminded tones when they wished her a good night.

In the morning, her tired eyes showed that sleep had evaded her. The fire was out, and she realized she'd forgotten to shake down the ashes and put more coal in the stove. The house was cold, but the darkness was alight with the white glow of the freshly fallen snow. Ruth did not bother opening the door to check the weather. It was too cold.

Making her way between the rows of dried laundry that hung from the line her dat had helped put up, she carried the ashes up the stairs, dumped them, and went to the tin shed to find a block of wood and a hatchet.

Setting the propane lantern on the floor of the shed, she brought down the hatchet, clunking into the piece of wood. She was rewarded by a splitting sound. Good. This would make perfect kindling.

"You want me to do that?"

In spite of herself, a scream rose to her throat, her hand went to her mouth, and she stared, horrified, at a dark form standing in the doorway. Clutching the hatchet, she straightened, without realizing what she was doing.

A low laugh was followed by, "Go ahead."

She looked down at the hatchet and then at John Beiler, who was also looking at it.

"Sorry. I really didn't mean to frighten you this way."

Finding her voice, Ruth asked weakly what he was doing here so early in the morning. She clutched her coat around her waist and realized she was still dressed in her ratty, flannel bathrobe, the one that had most of the buttons missing.

"I came over to put the key on the little hook by the playhouse door. I remembered last night after I got home."

"What playhouse?" Ruth did not understand.

"You didn't see the playhouse?"

"No. The…fire is out, and I hurried out here to chop kindling."

"Okay. Let's get the fire going. I'll show you later."

After a few masterful whacks, there was a pile of neat kindling that was then scooped up by the large capable hands that also picked up the lantern. He uttered a gruff, "Lead the way," and they were in the basement, where she found herself apologizing for the lines of dry clothes and wishing with all her heart she could take down the laundry ring suspended above the stove.

They said very little—at least not much that Ruth could later remember—till the fire crackled and burned. John added coal and then led the way up the stairs and out the back door. They crossed the newly fallen snow to the maple tree, where a small white playhouse with black shutters and a porch was set like a mirage. Ruth actually had to touch it before it appeared real.

"Oh, my word!" she said very softly. She was aware of him standing close behind her, and he bent his head and asked what she had said.

Softly she said, "But, who? I mean, why would someone put this playhouse here? How did it get here?"

Her hand traced the windows, the shutters, the posts that supported the porch roof, and she laughed, a happy response to receiving a gift and being glad of it.

"Do you like it?"

"Oh my!"

"Look inside."

She opened the unlocked door, and by the light of the lantern, she found a small room with a loft and a short ladder reaching up to it. The floor was covered with sturdy indoor-outdoor carpeting.

John followed her inside, and she held up the lantern, feeling very much like a child herself. The wonder of this perfect playhouse set in the clean, new snow provided the happiest moment of her life, at least since Ben had died.

"How soon can we wake the children?"

"We? Wake the children?" she asked dumbly.

"Can I? I mean, since I'm already here?"

She looked up at him, in the glow of the snow and the lantern light, and he looked down at her. And they smiled, a sort of shared conspiracy, as they thought of waking the warm, sleeping children and propelling them rudely out into the cold snow.

"Let's!" Ruth said.

"Should we let the boys sleep?" he asked.

"Oh no! They'll be excited just to watch Esther and Barbara."

"It is 6:30."

"Already?"

Everyone was rousted out of bed and bundled into coats and boots. Esther demanded an explanation, and Barbara yawned and sighed. Nothing could be worth getting out of bed before she was finished sleeping.

In the snow, they stood frozen, their faces broadcasting their disbelief—especially Esther, who appeared to be in shock.

"But, I didn't mean it," she stammered.

John put a hand on her shoulder, saying there was nothing to explain. Ruth was visibly puzzled.

They opened the door and examined every inch of the wonderful little house, climbing up the ladder, sitting in the loft, and becoming quite boisterous, the way children do when excitement runs high.

As the first light of dawn broke through the sky that was still spinning with snow, they all trudged back to the house. Ruth became flustered when Benjamin awoke, crying lustily from having been disturbed from a good night's sleep by the older children's chattering.

But John held out his arms, saying "*Komm*. May I hold you?" as naturally as if he'd had ten children of his own. Ruth handed Benjy over.

Benjamin sat sniffling but content, while Ruth got

the children's breakfast on the table, lunches packed, and hair combed. All the while, she was miserably aware of the horrible old housecoat she was wearing and the fact that her hair was uncombed, her face unwashed. But it was a school morning, and there was a time limit.

John would not tell them who gave them the play-house, in spite of repeated questioning, and only said it was snowing playhouses during the night. Elmer watched John, and they shared a man-to-man grin, one that made Ruth glad.

When the children left for school, Ruth put a hand to her hair and tried to salvage the scrap of pride she had left. John went down to the basement and put another hod of coal on the fire. When he came back up, he twisted his hat in his hands, cleared his throat, and asked if he could bring the children the rest of their gifts on Christmas Eve.

She said she supposed he could, but she had nothing for him.

"I don't need anything."

"Well, let me make supper for you then."

"That would be great."

"Would Saturday evening suit you?"

"Of course."

When he smiled at her, it completely banished the tortured thoughts in her mind. His eyes never left hers. There were long moments of shyness and kindness and understanding.

Would it be possible it could work? Before she lowered her eyes, she believed she knew the answer. It was up to him to lead her now.

Chapter Ten

MAMIE HAD A FIT. IT WAS the only way to describe her gasping and hand throwing and head shaking and shrieks of glee.

"We're not dating."

"What else are you doing? Huh? Answer me."

"No, Mamie. You said he...they...I mean, they broke up only a few weeks ago."

"No, it was longer than that."

"How do you know?"

"I just do."

And so began an afternoon of cookbook searching, the likes of which Ruth had never seen. Mamie kept insisting that the way to a man's heart was only accessible through his stomach.

They spoke seriously then of the near sleepless night Ruth had spent after Mamie had spoken to her about John Beiler.

"For me, Mamie, it was a sort of Gethsemane, a giving up of Ben. It was deeper than I ever realized. The letting go is so much more difficult that I thought. I cling to Ben, or rather to his memory, to get me through the days. I have to let that go now if I want to have another chance at…having a husband."

"So you have feeling for John?" Mamie asked, her hand stroking little Waynie's hair.

"Yes."

No hesitation, no pride, just a calm acceptance of something sent into her life that God had intended should be so. He knew when He would take Ben and knew when the time was right for John to be in her life, so there was nothing left but a spirit of willing acceptance, she told Mamie.

"But you're not dating."

"No. He's coming over for supper, that's all."

"Mmm-hm."

The turkey. It had to be turkey and stuffing, gravy, and mashed potatoes. Salad? Coleslaw? Red beet eggs?

Mamie made the best biscuits in Lancaster County, and her dinner rolls were perfection, but her whole wheat bread better than either of the two.

"Which one should I make?" she asked, never questioning whether or not Ruth wanted her to help.

"Dinner rolls."

"Men like biscuits."

"Do they?"

It was only Ruth's threats of never speaking to her again that kept Mamie from leaving a message on her sister Hannah's voicemail. They parted with the understanding that Mamie would promise to stay quiet about this.

"It's completely different, being a widow. Everything is top secret, and I can't trust you very well," Ruth had told her, which hurt Mamie's feelings a bit.

The secret didn't last long. Within just a few days, Mamie had told her mother, Hannah, and Ephraim, but they all promised to keep their mouth closed. Not a word. No sir.

Not until good-natured Ephraim *fa-schnopped* (gave away) himself down at Stoltzfus Structures. Before

Saturday night even arrived, at least fifty people knew that John Beiler was having supper at Widow Ruth Miller's house. They all said they wouldn't tell a soul.

So, trusting and innocent, Ruth cleaned her house until it sparkled, polishing furniture, washing windows, moving from room to room, caring for the little ones in between scrubbing floors. That was on Friday.

On Saturday morning, she mixed the stuffing and put the turkey in the oven after packing it full of the fragrant mixture. Then she shredded cabbage across a hand held grater, mixed mayonnaise and sugar and vinegar, stirred it lightly, and scraped it all into a Tupperware container to chill in the refrigerator.

She cooked eggs for seventeen minutes, cooled them, and went to the basement for a jar of pickled red beets, one of applesauce, and one of raspberry preserves. She peeled potatoes, checked the turkey, watched the clock.

She made two pumpkin pies and one pecan, using her grandmother's recipe for both, hoping and praying they'd turn out okay.

She jiggled the pumpkin pies only a bit, to see if they were set in the middle, and breathed a sigh of relief when they stayed firm an hour later.

Elmer and Esther set the table, Roy folded napkins, and Barbara pushed Benjamin around in his walker. Lillian was the only problem, cranky and uncooperative all day, until Esther wisely observed her lack of motherly attention. The instant guilt provoked by her oldest daughter's attentiveness guided Ruth to her favorite rocking chair and the Mrs. Boot book.

The children were bathed and dressed, the potatoes mashed and the gravy made, so Ruth left Benjamin in Elmer's care while she showered and dressed, choosing a deep plum colored dress, dark and demure enough for someone who'd lost her husband not quite nine months before.

She was grateful for the God-given gift of peace she possessed, somehow. The doubt and anxiety about the future was pushed aside, the darkness banished by the light of her new understanding. It was a gift, the best Christmas gift she had ever received.

She took a deep breath, though, to steady herself when the knock on the door did finally come.

"Do I look okay, Elmer? Roy, do I?"

"Perfect!"

"Yep. What he said!"

So with a smile on her face, partly a grin in response to her boys, she swung open the door and welcomed this kind man into her home.

His dark hair was neatly combed, his shirt a rich blue, his shoes clean and neat. If he was nervous, he did not show it, remaining relaxed and at ease with the boys.

It wasn't until they were ready to sit at the table that Ruth remembered the bread, or the lack of it. She said nothing, and when there was a knock on the back door, she wasn't a bit surprised. She knew her friend through and through.

Mamie entered without being told, her coat pinned over her ample stomach with two large safety pins, her grayish white headscarf tied beneath her plump face. Ephraim's camouflage hunting boots flopped on her feet, and she proudly bore a hot-cold bag from Walmart containing warm, crusty dinner rolls fresh from the oven.

"Thank you so much, Mamie."

She never heard or acknowledged Ruth but bent completely sideways in her strange attire and peered through the kitchen, searching desperately for a glimpse of John Beiler.

"I thought you were making biscuits," Ruth hissed.

Mamie was smiling, wiggling her fingers daintily at John. "Hiya, John."

"Hello, Mamie."

Mamie ducked her head shyly, then stepped back. "Men like dinner rolls," she whispered.

Ruth rolled her eyes, smiled, and said she'd talk to her later. But to her chagrin, Mamie stepped forward through the archway into the dining room, her safety pins prominent and gleaming silver on the black fabric of her coat. With a hand at either end of the scarf tied around her head, she jutted out her chin to tighten it and spoke very slowly and clearly.

"Well, John."

Oh please, Ruth thought frantically.

"So you bought the Petersheim place. Good for you. Now surely you know that house is much too big for one person to ramble about in all by himself. I mean, my goodness."

She tightened the scarf again, her face reddening a bit from the pressure, before resuming.

"Sorry to hear about you and Anna. But you know, sometimes things aren't meant to be, *gel* (right)? It's so nice to see you here at Ruth's table. Well, I certainly hope you have a wonderful evening."

She wiggled her fingers at John, who thanked her and wished her a good evening in return.

The evening was ruined for Ruth. She'd never be able to look at John after that. Mamie let herself out, while Ruth busied herself doing absolutely nothing at Benjamin's high chair.

The turkey was browned and golden in the lamp-light with the celery and onion stuffing sending up a rich, aromatic goodness. The gravy was creamy and full bodied, the chicken base giving it a golden color as it draped beautifully over the mounds of mashed potatoes.

The coleslaw was chilled to perfection with the shredded carrots making it colorful and the red beet eggs piled around it in a festive circle on Ruth's egg plate.

There was a moment of silence before John tried to put Ruth at ease saying, "You have done much more than was necessary."

Ruth found it too hard to meet his eyes.

"Ruth, don't worry about Mamie. I'm not embarrassed by her remarks. So please don't be."

It was only then that she looked up, met his understanding gaze, and felt the tension leave her body. She was comforted immensely. The remainder of the meal was a pleasure. John included the children in his easy banter, and they exchanged bits of news about the community.

Did they hear about the herd of cows that escaped their barnyard? It was the farmer's own forgetfulness as he was hauling manure and left the gate open.

Elmer was rapt, Roy completely taken. Esther ate her turkey and stuffing, her eyes shifting from one end of the table to John and then back to the other end where her mother sat, flushed and pretty. Barbara spilled her water and became so self-conscious that her eyes filled with tears. This did not go unnoticed by John, who jumped up quickly, snatched a tea towel from the countertop, and dabbed at the wet tablecloth while he teased her, saying she'd have to wash all the dishes. He continued smiling at her, winning her over so completely that she forgot to eat as she was so busy watching his face.

Lillian ate a bit of turkey, pulled up her legs, and yanked off her socks. She sang her favorite song quietly to herself and thought nothing very unusual was happening. They simply had a guest for supper that evening. She was waiting for dessert. That was all.

When John saw the pecan pie, he told Ruth there was no way she could have known that was his favorite. When he tasted it, he sighed in appreciation and told her it was just like his mother's, and he wasn't kidding. He'd tried every restaurant in a twenty-mile radius, and none—not one—had pecan pie with that particular taste.

Ruth's eyes shone with gratitude. "It's likely the green-label Karo," she said.

He helped with the dishes, standing too close. What else could it be that made her throat constrict with emotion? She wanted to make a cup of tea and sit with him on the couch and tell him about Ben's death and the months that had followed. She wanted him to share her fear and worry and *zeit-lang* (loneliness and longing). She wanted to lay her head on his wide shoulder and feel the solidness of him.

Furiously, she scrubbed plates, berating her lack of control. These thoughts were shameful. Or were they? She was only human, wasn't she? Yes, she was only one lonely person with Ben's memory sliding slowly away, fading into the background, whether she was willing to admit it or not.

They played a lively game of Sorry, Roy's favorite. They made hot mint tea, and John ate his second slice of pecan pie, adding a dip of vanilla ice cream. Lillian ate two servings of ice cream, which Ruth doubted had been balanced by very many potatoes or vegetables. But for tonight, it was alright.

When it was an hour past the children's usual bedtime, Ruth announced the end of the evening, which was met with the usual whines and claims of unfairness. After a few minutes, they all accepted their mother's wishes, took turns brushing their teeth, and told John good night.

John looked at Ruth. "Should I leave now, and let you get your rest?"

No, John, don't go. Stay with me. Let this evening go on and on for all eternity. But what she said out loud was entirely different.

"That's up to you."

Looking at him, though, was her undoing. He held her eyes with his own, so dark and kind and compelling. I would love to stay, they said.

She smiled and asked if he would like another cup of tea or perhaps coffee. He smiled and said coffee would be great.

"Another slice of pecan pie?"

"I was hoping you'd ask."

She laughed and relaxed as they sat at the kitchen table. She helped herself to slice of pumpkin pie. He looked kindly at her and asked how she managed so well—all on her own.

She shook her head, a hand going to her throat. "Oh, it's not the way it appears, believe me. I have my times."

"You would have to."

"I do."

"But you carry on so bravely. I...You know, I'll never forget when I met you that first time. I thought you must be babysitting your sister's children, or perhaps you had company and were taking your siblings to church...."

"Oh, come on now!" she broke in.

"I'm serious. You were...are so small, so young. I may as well be honest, Ruth. You look barely of age."

"What? I do, too!"

But she was smiling, a blush creeping into her cheeks, her lashes spreading against them as she lowered her eyes.

"Anyway, I asked plenty of questions, dug information out of anyone willing to answer. I was a real pest."

He grinned. He had a shadow along his chin, where the black stubble showed only a bit. My, he would be so handsome with a beard, the style required of an Amish husband.

"So when I found out the children were your own, I...."

She watched his face intently.

"I prayed. I asked God to show me the way. I truly meant every prayer. You see, I was dating Anna King, but...." He stopped, searching her face.

"Ruth, do you believe it's good to push two people together? When someone thinks two others would make a perfect match, so why not give it a try? I'm thirty-five, and everyone means well. They all want to help out. You know the way of thinking—poor guy, he just doesn't have the nerve to ask a nice girl out, so they try to play matchmaker."

Ruth laughed.

"So, I was dating, yes, but I think deep down I never really planned on marrying...her. Then, when I saw you...I saw Rebecca, all over again."

Ruth lifted questioning eyes.

"Once, long ago, I was in love, the kind of love that is rare. Completely head over heels. The romance book kind of heart throbbing love. And I thought, without a doubt, I would ask her to become my wife and live happily ever after.

"She was the type of girl who—let's say she had a roving eye. She kept flirting with other guys, but I would overlook it, thinking it was just Rebecca's way.

"I saw it coming—should have seen it long before I actually did. When she broke off the friendship, I vowed to never love again. I imagined myself the tragic martyr, the pitiful one, and for years, I thought wallowing in my lost love was sufficient. I didn't need a girlfriend, though Dat would have loved to marry me off."

He laughed, a rich baritone chuckle that brought joy to Ruth as well.

"So then I started my own roofing business. That became my life, my love, and...of course, God has blessed me, and I was able to buy the Petersheim place. I still feel God is richly blessing me far beyond anything I could ever deserve. It amazes me."

Ruth sipped her coffee but remained quiet. He smiled at her and told her she was a good listener, a rare quality in girls.

Ruth said she wasn't a girl. She was, at the age of thirty, practically a middle-aged woman—especially with her six children. And after having all them, she better know how to listen.

He laughed again, a repetition of his first joyous outbreak. And then he did something Ruth would never forget. Reaching across the table, he took her mug of coffee from her hand and set it carefully to the side before grasping both of her hands firmly in his own calloused ones. He questioned her with his eyes while maintaining a firm hold on her.

"Ruth you are an attractive and capable young woman, and I would love to know you better. If you believe it's possible that anyone else can take Ben's place, would you let me try?"

Her hands held in his strong, perfect ones, his voice saying the perfect words. All the loneliness of the past months had been turned into a blessing. It amazes me, he'd said. Yes, it amazes me, too, John.

Arme vitve, weine nicht. Jesus will dich trosten. (Poor widow, do not cry. Jesus wants to comfort you.) Was this God's way of sending comfort? Or was she unchaste—thinking thoughts that were uncalled for before a year had gone by?

The simple clock on the wall ticked loudly. A drop of water escaped the confines of the faucet, followed by another, and still he held her hands, patiently watched her face, noted the conflicted emotions crossing the tender features.

"If...if you don't think it's too soon." She whispered the words, so great was her humility. He had to ask her to repeat them, leaning forward to hear the quiet words as she repeated them.

When he heard what she had said, he released her hands, and shook his head. "No Ruth. It's not too soon. We'll take it slow. The children need to have time to adjust. I'm very concerned about Elmer and Roy."

Ruth nodded.

"Let me hear your story now."

"Would you be more comfortable in the living room?"

"We can sit there, of course."

So she told him of meeting Ben at age fifteen and

never having any doubts. She told him about her marriage when she was nineteen, life on the farm, the devastation of his fall, the difficult times since then. All was spoken in her quiet, even tones, and as he listened, the ashes of Rebecca's love sprang to life, lit by the Master's hand, and he knew he would not have to journey alone any longer.

At the door, there was no awkwardness, no hesitation. He stood and held out his arms, and she stepped into them. His shoulders were as solid and as comforting as she had imagined, and she smiled against them.

It amazes me.

And he did not kiss her.

Chapter Eleven

JOHN PROMISED TO BRING THEIR GIFTS on Christmas Eve, although they felt as if they'd already received so much. The teacher at school had given them pictures to hang on the walls of their rooms. The boys received a wildlife photograph, and Esther a beautiful poem with a yellow rose along the side. From Doddy Lapps, they'd received books and games and puzzles—far more than they'd thought possible.

And still the banana boxes appeared frequently and mysteriously in the night, sometimes dusted with powdery snow, but mostly just cold and always filled with useful items like fabric or towels, rugs, groceries, books, anything they could imagine. It became a ritual, the discovery of the banana box, a sort of race to see who would see the contents first.

Excitement ran high the day before Christmas. Their own meager presents were placed on the bureau in the living room, the absence of a tree so normal no one gave it a thought. A Christmas tree was unusual in any Amish home, so the bureau in the living room was the perfect place for the brightly wrapped gifts to bring cheer to the entire room.

It wasn't that Ruth didn't decorate at all. She pulled the box marked "Christmas decorations" out of the hall closet and distributed the red pillar candles around the house on windowsills and tabletops. She washed the plastic rings and placed them carefully around the candles.

A few snowmen were set beside the candles, and when the wicks were lit, the little snowmen seemed to come to life. There were no Santa Claus ornaments or any references to his coming down the chimney. Amish people had never believed in teaching children that myth, so there was no Santa Claus in sight.

The house was clean and bright, the cookies and candies set out on attractive trays. There was coffee, hot chocolate for the children, apple cider, seasoned pretzels, and popcorn balls.

Mamie, of course, had sent a huge platter of candy and cookies—so many, in fact, that Ruth considered not making any of her own.

She thought about inviting Ephraim and Mamie, but decided against it, afraid they simply wouldn't leave when it was time. Ruth smiled to herself as she set out the chocolate covered peanut butter crackers. She was ready to admit that she wanted time alone with John, and Ephraim and Mamie were notorious for staying up till four in the morning.

"Lillian, no!"

Ruth's words were sharp, bringing the busy three year old to a halt, halfway up the kitchen chair she'd pushed over to the bureau as she reached for the snowman by the burning candle.

Rushing over, Ruth grabbed Lillian around the middle, hauled her off the chair, and set her firmly on the floor.

"You may not have the candle. No, no."

"Candle so *shay* (pretty)!" Lillian protested.

"You just let it alone, okay? It will burn you, make an ouchy."

Lillian pouted and flounced off. She leaned against the couch, watching the flickering light on the little snowman.

There would be no supper that evening, they all agreed. Elmer did chores early, carefully sweeping the forebay in case John drove his horse and buggy. Esther said he didn't need to sweep as John would probably walk, but Roy asked how he would bring all the presents if he didn't bring his horse and buggy.

Elmer asked Ruth if she and John were.... His voice trailed off, and he lifted embarrassed eyes to his mother's face.

"Elmer, I was just waiting till you asked!" Quickly she slid an arm protectively around his shoulders, squeezing him affectionately, and looked into his eyes. "Do you wish I would not like John?"

Elmer shook his head.

"I won't think of doing this...I mean...well, Elmer, I hardly know how to say this. John did not ask me to marry him or anything. But if he did, and you would object, I would say no."

"I know you would." Elmer was very solemn, a mature soul in a child's form. His eyes searched Ruth's face intently.

"I would say no, Elmer. For you."

"But, Mam, if he does ask you, don't say no. We really need a dat."

"Does Roy think so, too?"

"Yeah. We talked about it a lot already. We think John Beiler is so much like we remember Dat."

"Really?"

So Ruth learned that her boys approved of John, which was a comfort. Esther just giggled and shrugged her shoulders when she was asked for an opinion, and Barbara said her mother needed help with the coal stove and removing the propane tank when it needed to be changed.

They all burst out laughing.

These dear children would always need to come first, Ruth thought. They may be facing another time of transition, but it would be made easier by generous amounts of explaining, understanding, and patience as she tried to ensure an atmosphere of stability in their young—and recently tumultuous—lives.

Yes, they approved, but she knew they would all have times of rebellion or disobedience. And yet her heart soared with newfound love.

The banana box came through the door first. There was no knock, no warning, just the door being pushed open by the cardboard box.

"Merry Christmas!"

"John!"

"Hey, are you the banana box guy?" Elmer burst out, unable to conceal his eagerness.

"You are!" Roy yelled, pointing his finger with a gleeful expression on his face.

"What are you talking about? I don't know a thing about banana boxes."

John took off his black coat, hung it on a hook in the laundry room, tucked his red shirt tail in his black trousers, and grinned.

"You left a banana box full of stuff on our porch. Every day almost!" Roy shouted.

"Shh!" Ruth was a bit embarrassed now.

"Why would I do that?" He caught Ruth's eye and

winked broadly, and she knew.

Esther said she recognized his footprints in the snow, which actually made him pause and look questioningly at Ruth.

The boys were hopping up and down now, their brown hair flopping, their white socks like springs propelling them up and down, exultant in the knowledge of his discomfort.

"Gotcha! We gotcha!"

"It was you!"

"We know it was!"

"You have no way of finding out!" John said.

"Take off your shoe."

"We'll measure the tracks!"

"Tracks? What tracks? You can't do that. Tracks widen with the sun's heat. When snow melts, it changes the shape of the shoe's mark. Or suppose I wore my boots?"

Too late, he caught himself, then threw back his head and laughed uproariously. Elmer and Roy pounced on him and tried to make him sit down so they could remove his shoes.

It all ended with Elmer and Roy overpowering him, landing him on his back on the living room floor, where he laughed as Roy held him down and Elmer undid the laces of his black shoes. Happily, they raised them high in the air, then slipped out the door, standing in the snow in their stocking feet to carefully evaluate the length and width and pattern of the footprints. They burst into a gleeful cheer and gave each other a high five before rushing back into the house.

"Yup, they match. It was you!"

John conceded, and the children suddenly became shy, watching him with careful expressions.

"Was it really you?"

"Why did you do it?"

The questions flew thick and fast, till John put up a hand and said if they all hushed, he'd tell them about it.

"I saw you driving the horse to church at your Doddy Lapp's house and asked many, many questions afterward. I decided your mam could not have an easy life and no doubt could use some help. It was my pleasure. I have no children, you know."

"So, what about the playhouse?" Barbara asked.

"It snowed playhouses that night, I told you!"

"You're *schnitzing* (fibbing)!"

"Mamie's husband works at Stoltzfus Structures, remember?" Elmer watched John's face, saw the seriousness.

"He does, that's right. I bet it was Ephraims."

"It would be just like Mamie," Roy agreed.

Ruth met John's eyes and played along. She knew Eph and Mamie could not afford a new playhouse, but she'd let John trick them, for now. What fun!

"Wow, I didn't know Eph had money."

"Well, you know how Mamie bakes. I bet she made five thousand dollars making Christmas cookies."

"Nah, Roy!"

"Hey, two thousand! Three!"

There was a discreet knock on the door, and Ruth's heart sank. Oh please don't let it be Ephraims. How could a person love a friend the way she loved Mamie and cringe at the thought of having her and her family there with John?

It wasn't right. As the Bible said—actually Jesus had said—it was wrong to give high seats to classy people, or those of high status, and barely acknowledge those of lower class.

Mamie was not lower class. She was just relaxed and dear to Ruth's heart. And Ruth knew she was only being selfish, desperate to have John to herself, so she flung open the door, letting in a blast of cold air and a tumble of children and Mamie and Ephraim and Trixie, the dog.

John looked surprised, then pleased. Ruth let out a quick sigh of relief. It was okay.

"Trixie! *Ach* my! Trixie!" Mamie raised embarrassed eyes to Ruth's face.

"Children! Fannie! Why did you bring Trixie? She wasn't supposed to come. Ruth, *fa-recht* (for real)!"

As usual, Mamie fussed and explained, taking coats, pushing children forward, as Eph stood smiling eagerly, saying nothing.

"Well, here we are, crashing your party. *Siss net chide, gel net* (It isn't right, is it)? But our noses grew steadily longer all day. I told Eph I can't stay at home.

Trixie! Fannie, get Trixie. Put her in the *kesslehaus*. Waynie, no. Mam will smack your patty. Waynie!"

Moving with remarkable speed, she flung herself at her ambitious little boy, who was scuttling along, intent on the potted palm tree in the corner. She grabbed him by the waist band of his black Sunday pants, swung him to her shoulder, and patted his bottom a few times.

"Here, Eph. Take him."

Waving a hand to cool her reddening face, she scooted back to Ephraim who received little Waynie with a solid thunk, whereupon the small boy set up an awful howling.

Ruth watched and smiled, catching John's eye. Yes, the evening would be extremely interesting.

John and Ephraim got along fine, of course. Mamie whispered to Ruth that everyone liked Eph. He didn't know what it would be like to meet someone and not have them like him.

Then she spied the presents, and said, oh my, you didn't have your gifts yet? Ruth assured her it was alright. They would exchange gifts in spite of them being there.

So Mamie settled herself on the sofa, eager anticipation shining from her generous blue eyes. Trixie
repeatedly yapped from the *kesslehaus*, very effectively
driving Ruth to distraction.

The children were seated now, on the floor or on
chairs. Esther clasped her hands in her lap—dutiful and restrained like a much older child. Barbara
was trying hard not to bounce up and down, but
she kicked one foot constantly. Lillian squirmed and
wiggled and bounced and squealed. She clapped her
hands and tried to lift the lid off the cardboard boxes, until her mother sternly told her to sit down and
hold still for a minute.

Elmer was very grown up, holding Benjamin, trying
to hide the excitement he must be feeling. Meanwhile,
Roy let his spill out all over the place, bouncing and
hopping from one end of the living room to the other.

"Now your children don't have anything," Ruth
told Mamie quietly.

"Oh, they will in the morning. They know that."

First Ruth gave the boys their package. Eagerly, they tore off the inexpensive wrapping paper,

crumpled it, and held up the new Monopoly game, exulting in the game they knew they would play with every single evening.

Barbara and Esther were equally pleased to receive the set of dishes, explaining to Mamie's girls that their dishes were either lost or broken, and this was exactly what they wanted.

Lillian gazed in disbelief at the doll in the box, the wrapping paper in shreds at her feet. "*An dolly* (A doll)." She could only whisper the words, so great was her delight. Mamie watched her tenderly and had to put a hand to her eyes to hide the ever-present tears of love that lay just below the surface.

John watched quietly. Then he got up and slowly lifted the lids of the boxes he had brought in, extracting one neatly wrapped package with a huge red bow on top. Ruth saw the bow and stored it away mentally, knowing it would adorn the gift that she would give to her parents on Second Christmas.

For the Amish, the day after Christmas is called *Ztvett Grishtdag* (Second Christmas). It is merely a continuation of Christmas Day, allowing for additional gatherings and festivities with the typically large extended families. Ruth looked forward to the time with her parents and siblings.

These days of Christmas always meant large meals, plentiful and generous gifts, afternoons of singing Christmas songs, and eating lots of snacks and delicious pastries. There was homemade candy, cookies, and trays of fruit, and the children playing endlessly with their cousins as the tempo of the day was fueled by their sheer exuberance along with a good dose of sugar.

"Elmer!" John said and smiled as he beckoned the boy to him.

Shyly, blinking self-consciously, Elmer went to receive his gift, muttering a quiet, "*Denke* (Thank you)," before returning to his seat, where he held onto it, unsure of what to do.

"*Machs uf!* (Open it!)"

Mamie gave him clear orders but then felt she was being bossy, if only for a second, Ruth could tell. Elmer looked at Ruth, waiting for her approval. She nodded her head.

It was unbelievable! Ruth could tell by his numb expression that the contents of the box extended far beyond his belief. An entire set of bird books and real binoculars! What a gift! Elmer couldn't say a word. He just picked up the binoculars and turned them over and over in his hand, tracing his finger over the sturdy field glasses before lifting them to his eyes.

Eph said he'd be up to borrow them right before hunting season, then slapped his knee and laughed very loudly, bringing a smile to John's face. Ruth thought he would, likely.

When John called Roy's name, the boy catapulted from his seat, scooped up the large box, and plunked it on the floor, already ripping the green and red wrapping paper from it. His eyes bulged, and he yelled. He yelled and yelled and yelled. He didn't stop even when he held up a large, heavy skateboard and dove back into the box to retrieve a set of knee and elbow pads in the same brilliant blue and darkest black hues as the skateboard.

Ruth shook her head at John and mouthed, "Too expensive." She was rewarded by a look so generous it took her breath away.

Esther's box contained the exact same thing, except hers was pink and black. Very, very pink—more like florescent magenta! She looked straight at John and said as maturely as possible, "Thank you, John. It's exactly what I wanted."

It was only later, in the privacy of her room, that she threw the skateboard on the bed, flung the knee and elbow pads on top, raised her arms high, and did a sort of tap dance, all by herself, where no one could see. She was just thrilled.

Barbara didn't have a package, so she thought, until John told her to wait a minute and went outside. He returned with a little wooden table and two benches. He told her to wait again while he went back out and brought in two chairs, one for each end.

Barbara smiled behind both hands. Then she sat down on the bench, patting the space beside her. John doubled up his tall frame and sat very carefully on the small space she allowed him. They both tilted their heads to one side and smiled very grown up smiles at each other.

It was as if John could not help himself, then, and he reached out an arm and squeezed her affectionately. She settled an elbow on his leg and kept it there while Mamie blinked furiously, her mouth working as she clamped a hand across it to keep her emotions in check.

Lillian had a large package wrapped in children's giftwrap with Winnie-the-Pooh all over it, dressed in Christmas reds and greens. The box held a child's vacuum, a broom, mop, and dustpan, a small ironing board, and a highchair for her doll. Very solemnly, she pulled each thing from the box, piece by piece, then stood up straight as a flagpole and asked where her iron was.

John became a bit flustered, but he got down on his knees and poked around in the box, finally coming up with an iron to go with the ironing board, relief clearly written on his face.

Lillian took it, examined it carefully, and said, "Thank you, John." She set up the ironing board and plopped it on top. She ironed for the remainder of the evening, pausing only when Waynie got in her way.

Finally John brought Ruth a brilliant sparkly gift, the light catching the silver glints in the red wrapping.

"It's heavy!" she gasped.

"Is it?"

Mamie hovered over Ruth, a protective friend and a very nosy one, John did not fail to see. He watched as the small hands carefully lifted the wrap beneath the scotch tape and folded it neatly away, repurposing it in her mind along with the bow.

When she opened the box, a small gasp of surprise escaped Ruth's lips, and her eyes filled with tears. Mamie's piercing shriek carried across the room, slammed into the walls, and ricocheted back to John's ears.

"Ruth!"

"Oh my!"

"Mam!"

"It's what you wanted!"

There it lay—the rubbed luster of the cherry wood an oval of perfection, the glass so clear and clean, the face so golden and white. It was a Swiss rhythm clock, nestled in white tissue paper with the batteries tucked in at the bottom. A clock is a traditional Amish engagement gift, but that didn't even cross Ruth's mind. All she could think to say at the moment was a simple, breathless "*Denke.*"

They carefully lifted it out of its box, inserted the batteries, and huddled around with bated breath, watching in wonder as the small castle below the face turned back and forth.

When the hands reached the eight and the twelve, the soft strains of "Amazing Grace" pealed from the beautiful clock, and Ruth lifted her face to John's, touched his arm with her fingertips, and told him it was the most wonderful gift anyone had ever given her. And she meant it.

Was it because she was older, more spiritually aware? Or was it the surprising joy of a second chance when she had felt so alone? Whatever it was, the wonder of this beautiful timepiece infused her Christmas season with the magic that is only carried by a truly grateful heart.

Chapter Twelve

CHRISTMAS EVE LASTED ON ONTO CHRISTMAS Day, as Ruth knew it would. Ephraim and Mamie and the children settled themselves in, delighted by this opportunity to become better acquainted with John.

They made hot chocolate with Mamie's recipe. When she found out Ruth had no Reddi-whip, Mamie put on her coat and scarf and marched the whole way home for some of her own, saying hot chocolate was not the same without it.

John declined the sweet drink. After all that bother, Mamie fussed at him, but he smiled and said he was a black coffee drinker, if that was okay. He certainly did not want to offend her. She said fine, drink what you like, but she was noticeably quieter than usual for the next half hour until Ruth made a big fuss about her hot chocolate recipe, which set things right.

They played Monopoly with the boys' new game. They ate candy and cookies, fruit, and Chex Mix and popcorn, until the house appeared to have been stuck by a hurricane.

Ruth winced as Waynie sat on the floor with a small chocolate bar melting in one little hand and a wedge of Rice Krispies treat in another. He was soon on his hands and knees, crawling across a braided rug that wasn't washable and leaving a trail of sugary stickiness in his wake. Meanwhile, Mamie waved her hands and exulted in her acquisition of Indiana Avenue, having finally acquired a set of three, her messy little son the last thing on her mind.

This was not lost on John, who watched Ruth watching Waynie, and knew she truly was an exceptional person.

Ephraim easily won the Monopoly game as Mamie dropped out early after spending all her money to put hotels on her properties. Unfortunately for her, no one landed on them, so she never collected any rent. She soothed her battered ego with the taco dip and tortilla chips, then made another batch of popcorn, and ate almost the whole bowlful by herself.

The children played and played. They laughed and shrieked and ran around the house until midnight, when even Esther began to yawn, and they all had to go to bed. A large air mattress was set up on the living room floor, and two children were tucked in on the couch with soft, clean sheets for each one. Soon Ephraim's children were nestled down for the remainder of their stay.

Weariness was creeping stealthily over Ruth by two o'clock, and John saw the shadows under her eyes and the heaviness of her eyelids. He stretched and yawned, saying it was way past his bedtime and he was going to call it a night.

Ephraim asked what in the world was wrong with him. The night was still young, and what was the use sleeping—that was all a waste of time. Mamie laughed hysterically at her husband and said she agreed. She was up for another game of Monopoly.

John stayed adamant, however, and Ruth told him how grateful she was as they washed dishes.

He stuffed wrapping paper in garbage bags, swept, and picked up toys for Ruth to put away. They hung the new clock on a large nail on the wall above the sofa, then stood back to admire it. It said 3:10.

"It's almost morning!" Ruth exclaimed.

"It's Christmas Day!"

"Merry Christmas!"

"Merry Christmas, Ruth."

And then, because he wanted to take her in his arms so badly, John decided to leave, and he did so rather hurriedly, leaving her with a great sense of loss and bewilderment. Ephraim and Mamie took their leave as well, prodding the older children awake for the walk home and picking up the sleeping little ones.

What had gone wrong? Why had John left so quickly, when she yearned for his arms to hold her close, embracing her in their safety and solidness? He had said nothing at all about seeing her again.

Miserably, she brushed her teeth, weariness

seeping into her bones until she collapsed into bed and cried exhausted tears of disappointment.

It was Mamie. Ruth bet anything he didn't like her and her rowdy family. They shouldn't have come. But she was only being Mamie, her dear friend, her loyal supporter, and Ruth knew she could not desert her. If John wanted to be that way, then so be it.

Everyone slept till 8:30, when Benjamin's little grunts first woke her. Ruth rolled over, opened one eye, and found Benjy's eyes peering intently at her through the bars of his crib. Immediately, she was filled with good humor and called his name in soft tones. He lowered his head and kicked his legs and squirmed with happiness, then propped himself up on his hands and watched her again.

She got out of bed, scooped him up, and nestled him in the bed beside her. She held her baby close as she breathed in the smell of him, that mixture of Downy fabric softener and Johnson's baby shampoo and formula and pacifier. She tiptoed down the hallway to the living room to rock him in the recliner for a while.

The light was grayish white. It was snowing! On Christmas Day! She stood in her nightgown, holding Benjamin, and marveled at the clean beauty of the falling snow.

"*Schnae*! (Snow)!" she told Benjy. He smiled, his eyes alight, and reached for the new wonder in his life, so she took him out to the porch and let him touch it, delighting in the amazement in his eyes.

They had sausage gravy and homemade biscuits for breakfast with dippy eggs and toasted bread, left-over fruit, and cereal.

Lillian said her doll was named Goat, and when everyone made fun of her, she threw a terrible fit, kicking against the bench and screaming so loudly that Ruth had to take her away from the table. She returned to scold the children in firm tones, telling them Lillian was only three, and if she wanted to name her new doll Goat, she guessed they'd get used to it. Then she burst out laughing in spite of herself with all the children joining in, while poor Lillian lay on the couch and sniffled.

Well, it was Christmas, but with six children,

these things happened, and no mistake about it. For a mother, it was called life—no matter what day of the year.

She was bewildered when Mamie tapped on the door, her wide face shining with exhilaration, excitement, and what else?

"Merry Christmas, Ruth!"

"Well, Mamie! What are you doing here?"

"You could wish me a nice Christmas," she said, and Ruth promptly did.

"Thanks," Mamie sniffed her indignation before announcing that she was babysitting.

"Who are you babysitting?"

"Your children."

"But why?"

"Here." Reaching into her coat pocket, Mamie brought out a sealed, white envelope with Ruth's name on it.

Completely puzzled, Ruth opened it and unfolded a plain sheet of paper. She read the words in Mamie's handwriting, but they made no sense. Please walk to this address. 11749 Gravel Road. Thank you.

Ruth looked up. "But why? Where on Gravel Road? Is it far? It's snowing."

"Oh, just go. No, it's not far. Dress warmly."

"What is going on, Mamie?"

Mamie was divesting herself of her coat, undoing the large silver safety pins as she spoke, the children watching, strangely quiet. The boys didn't ask to see the contents of the letter, which was strange. Esther and Barbara were setting their dishes on the table without any show of curiosity.

"I know. It's Ephraim. He's playing a trick on me."

"No, he'd never do that on Christmas Day. He's still in bed, sound asleep. You know how lazy he is on holidays."

And some other days, Ruth thought, but said nothing. She combed her hair hurriedly without bothering to wet it down or roll it tightly—just ran a comb through it and shrugged into her dress and apron, warm socks and boots. She donned her heavy, black coat and white headscarf and pulled on her gloves, but she couldn't conceal her bewilderment.

Mamie had settled herself in the recliner with

Benjamin on her lap, showing him a small animal book and looking as clueless as the boys.

"Don't you care that I'm venturing out in this cold snow, perhaps putting my life in danger?" she asked Mamie, who looked up at her with guileless blue eyes and didn't as much as crack a smile.

Was it just her imagination then or did she actually see the boys and Mamie peering out from the front window, glee plastered all over their faces? What was going on?

The snow was gorgeous, though, and her spirit responded to the clean stillness of it as she reveled in the hushed whisper of the falling snow. She loved how it clung to fencepost tops and tree branches. It was piling up on roofs and mailboxes and bushes, changing the drab landscape into a clean, white wonderland.

God was amazing, the way He designed each new season with the brilliance of newly fallen snow a great boost to late fall's frozen drabness.

11749. Where in the world? Oh. There was the Petersheim place. She'd have to check the mailbox.

What if there was no number on it? She looked to the left, then right, standing still at the end of Hoosier Road, indecisive.

He stood inside, peering anxiously through the windows, the trees in the front yard a filament of snowy lace obscuring his view. All morning, he'd been pacing, watching. Would she come?

11749 was the Petersheim place, but the fact that John had bought it and now lived there somehow eluded Ruth on that snowy morning. It must have been the minimal amount of sleep. Five hours of it, to be exact.

She walked along the winding driveway. It was on level ground with great trees on either side, and beyond them the whispering snow fell, creating a scene from some other world, a fictional land.

The house had two stories with a porch along the front. There was stone of brown and gray, low windows and a massive front door, alcoves, dark beige siding, and roofs of various levels.

It couldn't be the Petersheim place. It looked like an English house, almost. Oh my.

Ruth had never actually been at the house before. Her church district stopped at the end of Hoosier Road, so a neighboring district had their church services there.

There was a large barn, a shop, a stone sidewalk that had been swept clear of snow. There were pine trees and bird feeders alive with colorful winter birds. Brilliant red cardinals vied for position with bold blue jays, and anxious little black-capped chickadees twittered about, while the wily nuthatches climbed down tree trunks headfirst.

The shrubs were numerous, trimmed with a shelf of snow. Oh, what a beautiful home. Hesitant now, her steps slowed. Carefully, she placed one foot on the stone sidewalk and looked at the house.

The front door moved, opening from inside. John Beiler stood in the doorway and welcomed her to his home. Blank, her mind not comprehending, she stopped.

"But…"

His heart pounded now, afraid.

"Come in. You must be cold."

"No."

"Aren't you?"

"No. I just don't understand."

She stopped by the front door and pulled off her boots, one gloved hand going to the stone wall to steady herself. John told her to bring them into the house, and she set them carefully on the rug inside the door before looking up into his face. He was so pale, so obviously ill at ease.

"Why did you ask me to come to here? It was you, wasn't it? What did Mamie have to do with this? What's going on?"

Ruth looked so bewildered, so at a loss. John was so terribly unsure of himself, too. He knew he couldn't wait until he'd shown her around the house to say what he had planned, so he left caution behind and put his hands on her shoulders, which were still wet from the snow.

"I'm nervous, Ruth. I....oh, come here."

He pulled her into his arms, lifted her face after a few moments, looked deeply into her eyes, and slowly lowered his head. She closed her eyes as his lips met hers, hesitantly, afraid somehow, but her love spoke to him, and he kissed her with a new and wonderful love of his own.

"Ruth. Ruth."

It was all he could say.

Tears streamed down her face, cleansing her of the months of grief and loneliness, the doubts and fears, the fires of widowhood, the times when she thought she could not go on for one more day.

When he realized she was crying, John was concerned, afraid he'd done everything all wrong.

"I'm sorry. I shouldn't have. Ruth, please."

Clumsily, he handed her his red handkerchief, and she unfolded it to wipe her eyes and blow her nose, telling him she must look awful.

"But why are you crying?"

"I guess because I'm here, and you just kissed me, and it's been so long, and being alone with six children is so hard sometimes. And because I love you so much."

He drew in his breath.

"I'm sorry, John. I just do. I know you're supposed to say that first, but…"

"I love you, Ruth."

"As I love you."

Then he took both her hands and held them together against his chest and said, "Will you marry me, Ruth?"

"Yes, I will. But not till April."

"I figured." And he kissed her again with a new-found possessiveness, and she felt her whole world tilt and right itself, the stars in her eyes and heart a harbinger of things to come.

"Do the children know?"

"Oh, yes. And Mamie."

"Which means Ephraim and Hannah and whoever else she could get ahold of."

They laughed together, then, warm and comfortable, as easily as if they had known each other forever.

He took her hand and led her throughout the house. As they moved from room to room, she realized how incredible it really was. The upstairs was still empty, but she noted that the children could have their own rooms now. And there was a guest room and two—no, three—bathrooms. The kitchen was far too beautiful, and she told John so. He replied that she deserved everything, all of it. They would buy bunk beds for Elmer as Roy would still want to share a room with his brother.

Ruth suddenly stopped. She looked at John and asked if they would always remember to place their trust in God in such a place. She was afraid she'd forget to do that, living here with him.

"I mean, John, that isn't...*ach*, how can I say it? For months, I've had to trust God to help me daily. With things like the coal fire in the basement, the propane tanks—everything Ben always took care of, and now I cannot *begreif* (comprehend) the safety and security of living here with you."

She slipped her small, soft hand into his large, strong one, and he held it as carefully and as reverently as he knew how as they stood in silence. Some things just had to stay in the heart until the right time, he decided. He had a whole lifetime ahead of him to speak of his love and to distribute it over the years, enriching their marriage repeatedly and building that love into a satisfying union that eclipsed all expectations.

The snow fell around them, the pine tree branches bending with the weight of it, as they stood hand in hand on Christmas Day. Ruth's heart was full with the richness of the many sudden and unexpected blessings in her life—ones that she would never be able to take for granted following the lonely and difficult months she had endured. She knew her days as an *arme vitve* would enrich her life with John far above anything of earthly value.

The End

MARY'S Christmas GOODBYE

Chapter One

SHE STRAIGHTENED HER BACK, ONE HAND rubbing the sore spot below her shoulder blade. Still seventh- and eighth-grade stories to correct, and it was already five o'clock.

The classroom was bathed in the early spring sunlight, a pale yellow glow that turned the white walls into a golden color, the children's artwork into brighter colors as well. Another month of school, and she'd be free for the summer, or at least as free as any single, thirty-year-old Amish old maid would ever be.

Mary Stoltzfus wrinkled her nose, hiding some of the freckles that lay splattered across it. She rubbed at the end of her nose as if to eliminate a few more freckles, then gave up, allowing a tremendous sneeze to rip through her head. "Whoo!" she said to herself.

Mary was alone in the one-room Amish schoolhouse in Ronks, Pennsylvania.

She sat back, grabbed a Kleenex from the small, square box on her desk, and honked into it before tapping her desk absentmindedly with the cap of her red Bic pen. How many Bic pens had she emptied through the years? Twelve whole years of teaching Chestnut Run School. Well, all but one month to go in this school year. She'd started her first term at eighteen years of age, inexperienced, nervous, so young, her only goal to be a teacher, and a good one.

The love of the children kept her going through difficult times, the way it kept her going through the good times, too.

She was an experienced schoolteacher now. She was on the board of the teachers' class, who were asked to help young teachers and give advice, which was expected after you'd been teaching for a while. It was all right, she supposed, this prestige in the world of teachers, but certainly not what kept her going from year to year.

Before she knew it, the coming summer would end and she'd be back in the classroom with fresh yellow pencils sharpened, stacks of new tablets, and gleaming workbook covers shining in neat rows on top of the folding table. Boxes of pink erasers, bottles of Elmer's Glue, new rulers smelling of wood, it was all she knew and all she wanted.

She read Ben Beiler's story, then leaned back so far she almost tipped her desk chair, hurriedly righted herself, thumped both elbows on her desk, and snorted loudly. Now, Ben could do better than that. He should be ashamed. She scrawled a red C- across his paper, with the words, "Hey. Come on!" written below. He'd know what she meant.

This time of year, too many Lancaster County farm boys had spring fever. They wanted to ride the hay wagons or follow the plows with tin cans, picking up worms to go fishing, the sea gulls circling overhead. They thought of new colts and calves, baby goats, and squealing piglets.

Mary sighed and bit down on her pen so hard it hurt her teeth. Ah, she was tired. Her eyes felt like the plastic black and white ones you stuck on art projects, the eyeballs rolling around unattached. She needed to make an appointment at the optometrist. *Da owa dokta.* The eye doctor, as her aging father put it. He couldn't pronounce the fancy word, that was sure.

She got up, swiped her desktop with the hem of her black apron that was pinned around her slim waist, then gathered up her lunchbox and book bag. She let herself out the door and down the steps.

Her eyes surveyed the playground, looking for bits of paper or orange peels, anything the play-ground cleanup crew had overlooked. There was nothing. Good. She'd have to let the second-grade students know she appreciated them. She closed the schoolhouse gate behind her and set off on the fif-teen-minute walk home.

An oncoming horse and buggy bore down on her, the horse's head held high in the manner of Saddlebreds. She waved at John King, the neighbor man, then stepped away from the roadside to allow a car to pass. It slowed to a crawl with its window lowered as a passenger aimed a small red phone at her face.

Mary shrugged. They'd love the finished product—a tired, red-haired schoolteacher wearing a crooked covering with less than clean strings tied beneath her chin. Good for them. They could label it Scary Schoolteacher. She grinned, picking up her pace.

"Hello!" she called, yanking the screen door open. No one at home. Well, that was nothing new. Her parents were empty-nesters who loved going away, visiting, shopping, helping the "marrieds," as she put it.

The house was long and low with wide white siding, a black roof, and a porch along the front. Four round white pillars supported the roof. A white picket fence kept the household as isolated as possible from the never ceasing flow of cars, trucks, horses and buggies, scooters, and pedestrians.

Her mother's hibiscus, ornamental grasses, and shrubbery, as well as begonias and pink geraniums, made the small garden a haven of color in summer. She'd already planted a few petunias, saying they'd take the frost.

Mary's apartment, or "end," was to the right of her parents' part of the house. She lived comfortably with her own small kitchen and seating area all in one, along with a bathroom and nice-sized bedroom. It was all she needed with plenty of space for company.

Her walls were white throughout the whole apartment, with the doors and trim the same color. Her collection of various antiques and oak furniture set her taste apart. Mary was a little different, the marrieds said, nodding their heads knowingly. She hung curtains at her windows that they thought were plain ugly. She was just trying to be in style. No wonder she was still single. Without children, yet.

She put her book bag on the old wooden chair that had been her grandmother's, then went to the pedestal oak table to sift through her mail. Propane gas bill. A credit card offer. Time to renew her subscription to *National Geographic*.

All of the *Geographic*s went to school with her, with a few pages torn out if she chose to eliminate anything improper.

Hm. What was this?

She slipped a thumbnail beneath the seal on the envelope, then ripped the end of it, and extracted one page of tablet paper. Her brow scrunched into deep furrows, the red hair that escaped the dusting of the morning's hair spray, waving and quivering on her forehead.

What? Someone wanted her to teach school in. . . . Where? Maine? "MT?" No, that was Montana.

She leaned forward, thumped the heels of her gray Nikes down hard, and read it again.

"Dear Mary."

She blew out impatiently through her nose. How informal was that? They could have been a bit more businesslike and written, "To Mary Stoltzfus," or "To Whom It May Concern." Maybe that was over the top, but still.

It was a wonder he didn't sign, "Love, Arthur Bontrager." What in the world kind of name was Arthur? Was he even Amish? Did they call him Art or Artie? She'd heard of Bontragers and Weavers and Schlabachs, but they lived out in the western states mostly.

Well, Montana was west. Way west. The wild, wild way-out-yonder-clear-to-the-moon west.

Mary folded the letter, stuck it back in the torn envelope, and said out loud, "Sorry, Artie. No can do."

She went to the refrigerator and popped the top on a can of Diet Pepsi, took a long swallow, burped, and breathed, "Ah!"

Now for her Dagwood sandwich. She placed a roll right side up, lathered it with mustard on one side and mayonnaise on the other, then piled sweet Lebanon bologna, leftover turkey, Swiss cheese, hard-boiled egg slices, pickles, onion slices, and green peppers on top. She heated a can of Campbell's tomato soup until it was at the boiling point, added saltines and applesauce to cool it, then sat down to her evening meal.

Teach school in Montana? Yeah, well, this is what happened after you accumulated twelve years of experience. Everyone took for granted that you could move thousands of miles away and straighten out the mess they'd created. No wonder the children were a problem. She bet anything not one of them wanted to live at the end of civilization. Bless their transplanted little hearts.

A slice of egg squeezed out of her mouth, slid down her chin, and landed on the clean linoleum. Bending, she picked it up and stuck it back into the towering sandwich, her mind on the handwriting in the letter. Not bad, for a man.

His English was better than some Amish men she'd known. How had they even found her address? Or even knew who she was?

"Dear Mary." Now that was personal.

She scraped out the last of the tomato soup, then lifted the lid of a small wooden box, broke off half of a chocolate Kit Kat bar, and chewed methodically.

No, she wouldn't go. It was too far away. Besides, they wore those stiff coverings that stuck so far out the back, and there she'd be with her soft, organdy, heart-shaped covering, her black apron pinned about her waist, standing out like an owl in a flock of pigeons. No, no thanks. I'll pass.

She heard the crunch of steel buggy wheels turn in the drive and saw her parents seated on the spring wagon. Mam's face was red from the brisk wind. Dat's black felt hat was smashed down as far as it would go, his white hair and beard sprouting out beneath it, his cheeks ruddy with good health.

Why the spring wagon? It was too chilly. Now Mam would come down with the pleurisy, moaning and groaning and carrying the hot water bottle around like a second skin. Aging parents were sometimes as much worry as a classroom of twenty-one children.

But, of course, the powerful magnet called "parents" drew Mary to their door a few minutes later. She plopped on the worn blue recliner with the pink crocheted afghan slung across its back. Her backward force lifted the end of the afghan, flinging it over her head and thoroughly messing up her hair and covering, which hadn't been too straight to begin with.

Impatiently, she lifted the offensive throw and flung it to the floor beside her. "Why do you insist on covering all your chairs with those things?" Mary snapped.

"Now." Mam was in her early seventies, thin, and for all anyone could tell, as fit as a fiddle, in Dat's words. Her hair was white, her skin gently folded into wrinkles that showed her friendly character. She always had a smile on her face, and her hands were willing to help with whatever task presented itself.

"Mam, look at this." Mary shoved the letter into her mother's hands. Mam raised her eyebrows in question, then sat down and began to read.

Mary knew what was forthcoming before it actually came out. "My, oh," Mam said, soft and low.

Dat entered the kitchen whistling, hung his hat on a peg in the adjoining mud room, then bent to wash his hands. Hand-washing was necessary after driving and unhitching a horse. The smell of leather, horse sweat, and animal hair mingled to give off a distinctive odor.

Wiping his hands on the brown towel, he turned to look at his daughter. "School over?"

That was what he always said. Of course school was over for the day, or she certainly would not be sitting there.

"Yup."

That's what she always said, too.

Cars and trucks whizzed past the house, the steady clopping of horses' hooves accompanying them. Mary and her parents never thought about the noise. It was as natural as breathing. They lived in the humming tourist area of Lancaster County, so they had learned to adjust to the constant stream of traffic. The hustle and bustle, the gawking visitors, was a way of life. Amid all of it, including the Sunday meetings in homes, the Amish culture prospered and grew, a quiet way that remained untouched.

"Here. Read this." Mam handed over the letter. Dat lowered himself heavily into a chair, read slowly, his mouth moving as he whispered the words to himself.

"Well."

"What should I do? I'm not going so far away to teach those children."

"Then why do you ask what you should do?"

Mary shrugged. "Habit."

Mam smiled. "Aaron, what shall we have for supper?"

Mary went home, finished correcting the papers she'd brought, and prepared tomorrow's German lesson. Leaning back in her chair, she raised both arms above her head and flexed her fingers toward the ceiling, her mouth opening in a yawn of gigantic proportion. Time to shower and go to bed.

But there she lay on her side with her hands scrunched up beneath her chin, eyes closed, perfectly ready to nod off, but completely unable to stop the mad dash of thoughts in her mind.

Montana was vast without a lot of people anywhere. Weren't there snowy peaks and mountain ranges and pine forests? There were lions and wild burros and rattlesnakes called sidewinders and huge, hairy tarantulas. Or were they in Arizona?

What kind of Amish people would name their boy Arthur? King Arthur of the Round Table in medieval times, his armor clanking as his steed's hooves pounded the earth, was pretty distant from the Amish!

Those western people allowed bikes. She could picture herself pedaling along a country road, the smell of fresh pine branches in her nostrils, her skirts flapping in the breeze.

Then there were the mountain lions. Un-huh.

She'd wait a few days, think about the invitation, and sleep on it. She flipped on her back, sighed, and envisioned a row of sheep leaping across an imaginary fence, counting each one as they landed on their front hooves.

Well, it was definitely no. She was a citified Lancaster Countian, used to the comforts of home, money, having things handy. She even owned one of the newfangled electric clothes washers some genius had converted to the compressed air system. No more lifting wet, twisted clothes out of pounding, frothy water and stuffing them through a squeaky wringer.

If she felt like eating at a nice restaurant, she could. She could call a driver, the handy person who made a living hauling Amish people to places too bustling— with too many stoplights and lanes of fast-moving traffic—for a horse and buggy to go. And that wasn't very far away, just right down along Route 30 where all the outlets, hotels, motels, and restaurants vied to accommodate the thousands of tourists who descended on the farmlands of Lancaster County.

What did people in Montana do for entertainment? Probably roast buffalo steaks on an outdoor fire. Or no, buffalo were in Wyoming. What did they roast? Leg of mountain lion?

She sat straight up, lifted her pillow and thumped it against the oak headboard, folded it in half, and flung her head back down. Ow. Now she had a mean crick in her neck.

She picked up her pillow by one corner and threw it across the room, flipped over on her stomach, turned her head to one side, and closed her eyes. Now she didn't know what to do with her hands, so she stuffed them under her waist. That didn't work, either.

Thoroughly disgruntled, she sat up, put her feet on the rug and heaved herself upright, went to the kitchen, found the flashlight, and aimed it at the old schoolhouse clock above the table. 11:30. Oh, no. Tomorrow was a school day.

She opened the cupboard door above the refrigerator, brought down the box of Wheaties, scooped a generous amount of sugar on top, added a dash of whole milk, and thumped them good with the back of her spoon, then lifted a big spoonful to her mouth.

That was the thing about Wheaties. You could load an awful big bunch of them on a spoon with a bit of maneuvering and get them all in your mouth at one time, which made them twice as delicious, same as a filled doughnut. Wheaties were just delicious, she decided again, carefully getting every whole wheat flake to her mouth, then lifting the bowl and draining the sugary milk in one swallow.

There. Back to bed.

She wondered what God thought. She wished she was a prophet or at least a good person like Abraham. God told him very sternly to get out of the house and into a land that he knew nothing about, and his seed would outnumber the sands of the sea, or words to that effect. He made it very plain.

God wasn't that close or that easy to understand. In fact, he often seemed elusive. But then he might not have too much time for cranky, red-haired old maids who tried pretty hard to get their own way in most circumstances.

None of this, "Yes, Charles." "No, Charles." "Whatever you think best, Charles" kind of thing for her. Look at Ma Ingalls, dragged all over the Dakotas and Wisconsin, or wherever. Ah, well.

Please then, God, if you think it's okay to let me know, would you? Show me, direct me. You know, though, that I'm happy right here, don't you?

A truck roared past, shifted gears, and churned to the top of the low grade. Mary thought they should outlaw loud trucks but didn't think it would happen in her lifetime.

She finally fell asleep and, when she did, dreamed that every grain of sand was red like her hair.

That whole week everything seemed to go flat. Even the sunlight was tainted. She noticed the cracks in the tile flooring, the dozens of black scuff marks made by the pupils' shoes. She was irritated at the old stubborn desk drawers and cried when she couldn't find the WD40 to grease them.

The two eighth grade boys rolled tablet paper into cigarettes and almost burned the privy down, which resulted in an evening visit to both sets of parents, a splitting headache, and a sour stomach for days afterward.

Black smoke fumed from smokestacks of unbe-
lievably noisy trucks, and tourists gawked, almost
causing accidents with their sudden stops.

Mary noticed the unkempt schoolyard and the
boards that needed to be replaced on the board fence
surrounding it. The plastic cups on the shelf by the
water hydrant looked soiled and broken. She wanted
to sweep them to the ground, put them in the trash
or do something, just to get rid of them.

She decided she was afflicted with a severe case of
discontent. Once you started thinking things would
be more exciting on the other side of the fence, things
definitely soured on this side. More and more, her
thoughts turned to, "Oh, what in the world does it
matter?" Or, she'd be humming along, thinking, "Go
for it."

What if she went for it—whatever "it" was—and
she was stuck in a stinking old cabin somewhere,
committed to nine long months of teaching, and she
hated everything about it?

One thing she knew—she could never dislike
children. In her opinion, children were God's gift to

an otherwise crazy world. They were innocent, eager, funny, and painfully shy. They put in so much honest effort and were lovable, endearing, sweet, forthright—oh, the list never stopped. She didn't mind not having children of her own. She had twenty-one who were under her supervision five days a week, and she loved them like her own.

Finally Mam said that it seemed as if Mary needed to go to Montana just to take care of her curiosity, if for nothing else, because she wasn't being happy or friendly. Mary's heart leaped, then plunged with a sickening thud. "I can't travel that far alone," she squeaked.

"Of course you can. It's perfectly safe these days. I'm sure Amtrak's security system rivals the airlines."

"What do you know about it?"

"Sister Mattie was thoroughly searched."

Mary laughed appreciatively. "What about you and Dat?"

"What about us? Ten marrieds living so close? I'm quite sure we shall survive, maybe even thrive." Mam's eyes twinkled, but her mouth turned wobbly, turning down only a bit at the corners. "I'll take care of your African violets for you."

"Am I going, then?"

"I would say you should try it."

"What does Dat say?"

"He knew you'd go. Just come home for Christmas."

Chapter Two

AND HERE I AM, MARY THOUGHT. Swaying and swerving wildly on this speeding silver bullet, determined to show the rest of these passengers I am a seasoned traveler, a woman about town, completely at ease with every person on this train.

All she could think of was which person could be a bomber or a hijacker? Which one would be a terrorist, smart enough to outwit the security system? Definitely the foreign-looking youth with the pitiful attempt at growing a beard. She bet anything that huge backpack beside him contained a paint can full of nails, ready to blow them all over the state of Indiana.

Or the sour-looking individual wearing dark glasses, slumped in a corner, a questionable-looking apparatus on the floor.

Well, what about that kindly old lady with the crocheted afghan across her knees, clutching the black,
gleaming pocketbook in a death grip with gloved
hands? Suddenly she thought of Mam's afghan, the
pink color almost identical to the one across the old
lady's knees, and wondered wildly how to go about
getting off a speeding train. She'd get off at the next
stop and ride the return train home. She could do that.

She watched the young man out of the corner of
her eye and decided he was not nervous at all for
someone with an explosive device in his backpack.
She decided straightaway, then, that this fear was
from the devil, and God would not want her to waste
her time sinking into these suspicious thoughts.

After the wait in Chicago, the scenery turned into
Mary's first glimpse of endless prairie, so fascinating
she never tired of it. She slept fitfully, as if the strange
movement of the cars, as they were being pulled
headlong through an alien, spooky world, were just
about to be hurled through the vast galaxy.

But once the train actually reached the state of
Montana, Mary forgot everything else except the

view outside the window of the fast-moving car. She had read about the western states, turned the globe to find North America, and then traced towns and highways and rivers with her forefinger. She pulled down maps and showed the upper grades the great and intricate web of roadways, rivers, and mountains.

Nothing could have prepared her for this, however. The sky was a blue bowl covering an unbelievable landscape of hills and valleys, pine forests, and wildflowers. There were simply no houses anywhere for miles and miles and miles. Eagles soared as if they could spread their majestic wings and sail on forever, uninhibited or untroubled by industry, towns, traffic, and any trace of human beings.

Sometimes Mary thought the word "awesome" was overused, overextended among the schoolchildren, but here there was no other word suitable.

They passed Billings, then towns called Cascade and Antelope, but finally, Mary realized, her destination was only half an hour away. She lurched to the restroom to check her appearance, aghast to find her face chalk-white, the freckles in stark contrast as if someone had thrown a handful of mud and some of it stuck. And her green eyes, ugh.

Mary turned away. She wasn't here in Montana for a beauty contest. She was here to exercise her expertise at teaching school. It was all she had.

I may not be much to look at, but I can turn your school into an efficient learning machine, I know it.

Where the train slid to a stop, the neat brown sign said only Loma, nothing else. No population count, barely even an acknowledgment of life except for the rickety shack they called a train stop. With knees turned to jelly, her fingers shaking as she pulled out the handle of her luggage, she made her way down the steps, thanking the concerned attendant, then stood in the loose gravel and dusty weeds, thinking that if she survived the next few hours, she'd be able to survive anything.

The sun was surprisingly warm. She lifted her face to it, marveling at the ability of the sun to shine here in this forsaken place, the same time as it shone thousands of miles—well, a thousand and hundreds—away on Lancaster County.

She stood perfectly still, her hands gripping the pull-out handle on her luxurious baggage from the outlet store. Royal blue, trimmed in black, from Coach. Well, she was fairly certain no one in Montana knew the label, but here she was. Probably should have thrown her things in a green, reusable, Food Lion grocery bag.

Wind puffed up the dust, throwing a few fine grains in her eyes. She turned her back to it, rubbed her eyes, and sneezed. A few grayish-green weeds were tossed about, looking tired and sick here by the railroad tracks.

Mary craned her neck, searching for any sign of life, and decided she was the sole occupant of the state of Montana. She may as well plant her flag, the way the Mount Everest guys did. She was hungry and thirsty, so she turned toward the graying little house that served as a station. A few tall skinny pines stood behind it, as if to keep it from blowing off into the wide sky. Grasping the loose doorknob, she twisted to the left, then the right, before it swung open, revealing a dusty little room containing a wooden bench, one metal folding chair, a torn cardboard box, and two half-dead mice.

Well, one thing sure, she wouldn't starve. She could always light a fire with the cardboard and roast the mice on a spit. No Pepsi machine. No water.

She scraped the palm of her hand across the rustic bench to clean off the dust, jumped, and smacked her hand against her cheek. Ow. A splinter.

And that is where Arthur Bontrager, the school board member, found the teacher from Pennsylvania —at the window, her back turned, her head bent, earnestly digging at the palm of her hand with a straight pin.

"Hey!"

Mary jumped, emitting a low, unladylike squawk.

"Didn't mean to scare you."

Hiding the pin, the splinter, the pain, and frustration, she said gamely, "Hi!"

"Hi yourself. You got something in your hand?"

"No, no."

"You got a splinter? You were digging at it when I opened the door."

"Oh, no. It's nothing."

"Let me see."

Arthur was "terrible big," as her pupils would say. Mary bet he weighed more than 250 pounds. His face was wide and craggy and sunburned, with deeply set blue eyes that looked like half-buried diamonds. His wife must be a terrific cook. Mam had often said those western women had a way with food. His hands reminded Mary of brown paws, thick fingers covered with fine hair. Hers looked white and freckled and dead. She was terrible ashamed of her sick-looking hands.

"Boy, you've got a doozy there. Hang on."

He stepped back, reached into his vest pocket, and produced a pair of tweezers. Taking her hand, he squeezed down hard with his thumb, jabbed at the protruding splinter, and pulled, then held it to the light.

"Largest splinter in Montana! A record!"

He laughed, a deep, easy sound that was unsettling. Mary had never heard anyone laugh quite so easily, as natural as breathing. Somehow she couldn't understand the emotion it evoked in her. She was just tired, overwrought.

"You ready?"

"I am. I thought I might have to plant my flag, being the only person to have set foot in Montana."

He laughed, deeper and more genuine than before, if such a thing was possible. "Ah. Hoo. A proper sense of humor. Boy, can we ever use you! Yeah, this drop-off point is a bit questionable. I wish they'd get rid of it and dump these city folks off at a more inhabited place. But this way. I came to get you with my buggy."

He carried her luggage as if it was filled with feathers, his long, swinging stride propelling him across the barrens, as Mary thought of the weed-choked clearing. By a grove of trees, a horse lifted his head, whinnied once, then again.

The buggy was unlike anything Mary had ever seen. It was wooden, but varnished instead of painted the usual black. It had no roof and only one seat, upholstered in a flamboyant shade of red with black buttons punched along the back. The wheels gleamed as if they were wet.

"Wow. Some ride," Mary observed.

"Nice, isn't it? I made it."

"Really? You built that buggy? Even the wheels?"

"Smart lady. No, of course not."

The only way to describe the sharing of the seat was that he had three-fourths of it and she had one-fourth. Mary felt very much like an afterthought, a pale, limp version of a human being.

"Good thing you're so tiny."

"Where do you put the children when you go away in this?"

Arthur's easy laugh rang out again. "Honey, I don't have children. To have some of those, you need a wife, and I don't have one of them, either."

Mary's face flamed until tears pricked her eyelids, making her blink fast to get rid of them. She looked steadily away from him to the left until she regained some sense of control over this runaway situation. If he'd stop laughing that laugh, she'd return to her normal self. Or taking the liberty of calling her "honey."

They rolled out onto a dirt road, bits of pale stone rattling around in the loose soil. Overhead, leafy trees mingled with beautifully shaped pines, the blue of the sky cut into bits and pieces by the dark green of the branches.

"Aren't you going to say anything about that?" he asked, suddenly.

"No. I just thought any school board member would naturally be married and have children attending the school."

"You're in Loma, Montana."

"Definitely not Lancaster County."

"You know, I've never been to that metropolis in my life."

"It's not a metropolis!"

"What is it then?"

His eyes crinkled again, almost burying the blue flash, and he let out another rolling sound of good humor.

Mary smiled and said, yes, it was sort of a city in some places, but not where she lived.

The dirt road dipped into hollows, then wound its way back out of them until they came to a vast, grassy, fenced-in area, with a bluish-purple mountain rising in the background, its highest peak covered in snow.

Involuntarily, Mary gasped.

Arthur pulled on the reins and stopped the buggy, allowing her to drink in the stunning landscape ahead of them. Mary leaned forward, then scooted to the edge of the red seat, clasped her hands, and formed an astonished O with her mouth. Finally, she sighed.

"Seriously." That was all she said.

Arthur watched Mary's pale face with the splattering of freckles. He watched the widening of her green eyes, took in the way the neckline of her blue-green dress was made so differently, the delicate collarbones beneath, and wondered.

Shyness was not one of his virtues, so he blurted out, "You don't seem to be encumbered with a husband either."

She acted like she didn't hear him at first, then turned to face him rather abruptly. "No."

"Care to tell me why?"

"Not really."

"Oh, come on."

"Let's just say my red hair and freckles scare men away."

Of course, that made him laugh again. Mary sat back against the cushions, crossed her arms over her waist, and stayed silent until the most adorable little schoolhouse she could imagine came into view. It was brown, built of graying lumber that had been stained. The roof was made of weathered-looking shingles. A stone chimney was laid meticulously along the outer back wall, and a small porch was built along the front. Six windows, also brown, had been installed on each side, allowing plenty of light and air for the children.

"Beaver Creek School."

"It is for sure the cutest thing ever," Mary said, slowly, her eyes taking in the rail fence, the ball field, all familiar and dear and yet so different. A few pines created an air of protection across the roof of the school, as if God had remembered the landscaping.

"I'm glad you like it."

"Where will I live?"

Arthur looked at Mary, all the creases around his eyes crinkled up, and he said offhandedly, "With me."

"But I can't. That would not be proper at all."

"Just kidding. Wanted to see what you'd say."

"Well."

"I'll show you."

Arthur tapped the reins on his horse's back, and they moved easily up the gradual slope away from the school.

They entered a small grove of trees where the dirt road turned left, winding along a small ravine. A fence began where the ravine ended, and Mary saw a herd of Black Angus cows, calves, and a massive bull, strolling along in the thick, lush grass. Off in the distance, a house was nestled below a large grove of towering pines.

It wasn't a house, Mary decided, as they approached, but more like a fancy shed. Her heart beat erratically now, her mouth turning as dry as Wheaties without milk.

Her spirits sank lower as they stopped in front of the primitive building. There was one window and one door. A narrow wooden porch with bowed timbers supported the sagging roof. Bits of wood and sodden newspaper were scattered along the steps, as if someone had started a fire a few years previously.

"This is it. You see now why I said you're going to live with me?"

Mary nodded. "It's not much, is it?"

"Sure isn't."

"I'll make it."

"If it's any help to you, my place is just across the pasture, but whatever you do, don't ever try crossing it. Eddie isn't one bit trustworthy."

"Eddie?"

"The bull."

"Oh."

"Come on. Get down. Make yourself at home. Obviously, there's no need to lock the door, so go on in."

Tentatively, Mary stepped down, then stood uncertainly as Arthur tied the horse.

"Go on in," he called.

She wasn't about to tell him she was afraid. She— Mary Stoltzfus—afraid. She had all the gumption, the nerve, the bravado anyone could possibly need, having honed her skills well with her earlier schoolchildren and their parents on more than one occasion. But she had never been over a thousand miles from home before with only a single other human being, an over-sized teddy bear named Arthur Bontrager.

Taking a deep breath, she stepped up on the porch, wincing when the floorboards creaked and groaned. For the second time in one day, she turned a strange door knob both ways before shoving the ill-fitting door inside.

She blinked. "Well." She was pleasantly startled, which pulled up the corners of her mouth into a hesitant grin.

"It's cute! Oh, my word! It's clean! Well, look at this! Does the fireplace work? Where did someone come up with this kitchen island? This sink is so tiny! Does the refrigerator work? Oh, my! Look! The view! Aww!"

Clearly beside herself, Mary dashed from one large window to the next, opened spigots, swung doors back, then finally stopped, clasping both hands over her waist. "It's cute!" she said, suddenly self-conscious.

"The outside is pretty deceiving. I didn't get that far."

"You did this?"

"Yep, I did."

"Can I stay here tonight?"

"No."

"Why not?"

"There are mountain lions in these parts."

Mary faced him, her eyes wide.

Arthur chuckled. "Just kidding."

"Did the women clean this for me? Someone certainly did. There are clean towels in the bathroom."

"Yeah. Looks clean to me."

"I'm starved."

"Of course you are. I never thought that far. I don't know if the shelves are stocked or not. You better check. If there's nothing here, you could have supper with me."

A few basic staples were not supper, and Mary was beginning to feel extremely weak and lightheaded. She told Arthur she would accompany him to the house, but he'd have to bring her back for the night.

"You think?" he asked, his eyes almost closing when the creases folded themselves around them.

"I think."

The road to Arthur's house was hilly but pleasant, winding along low-lying ditches and gradually sloped groups of trees.

Meadowlarks and blue jays called across the pasture. He showed her where another Amish family, Kenny Yoders, lived. They had three boys in school, the troublemakers, everyone said.

"We'll see," Mary said, lifting her chin.

Arthur watched the way the evening sun set her hair on fire and thought she was probably right.

His house was built on a slope above the pasture, a huge log A-frame with mostly gleaming windows, decorated in the manner of most men—woolen blankets, elk and deer heads on the walls, rustic table and chairs, wide plank floors, scattered Indian rugs.

Mary was speechless. For the first time in her life, she felt truly inferior to another person, incapable of any pretense or swagger.

"The barn is below the house pretty far. That's one thing I'd change if I could. It was kind of shortsighted, placing the cow barn so far away." He spoke from behind the refrigerator door, banging containers. "How about some barbecue, coleslaw, pickles, and home fries?"

Mary nodded, walking slowly around the room. Suddenly she stopped. Lying flat on the surface of a small table was a photograph of a girl dressed in the typical western style of Amish clothes. It was unusual for anyone to have pictures lying around, so she touched it with the tips of her fingers, bit her lower lip, and looked at Arthur's broad back, turned to her as he let water run into the brown sink.

His girlfriend? Sister? Distant cousin? It would be rude to ask, so she didn't.

She kept a lively conversation going and accompanied him out to the front deck where they set their plates on a heavy iron patio table, pulled up comfortable chairs, and ate in companionable silence.

The barbecue was not the ground beef sloppy joes she was acquainted with, but slivers of slow-cooked beef with a sauce unlike anything she had ever tasted. The ice-cold coleslaw was a wonderful accompaniment, and the home fries, although not the same as fried potatoes at home, were absolutely delicious.

Mary leaned over her plate with the barbecue sauce going everywhere except where she wished it would, grabbed a second napkin, and swiped at her chin. Finally she sat back, caught Arthur's blue eyes, and said, "I don't know how to eat like a lady."

Arthur laughed, the same deep rumbling sound that came as easy and as natural as breathing. "I was just watching you tuck into your sandwich and wondered how in the world you manage to stay so thin?"

Mary shrugged. "My parents aren't heavy, and none of my siblings."

"How many do you have?"

"Ten."

"Wow. All thin?"

"Like rails."

"All red-haired?"

Mary shook her head, her mouth full. "No. Unfortunately. I'm a throwback. My Doddy Stoltzfus's side."

"What kind of a name is that? 'Stoltzfus'?"

"Not worse than 'Bontrager'!"

He laughed. The sun slid behind the distant purple mountain and the evening turned shadowy, but with a glow so ethereal, Mary was speechless.

Arthur said, "I don't think your red hair is unfortunate."

"Thank you. That's a compliment."

A shiver made Mary lean forward, grasping her forearms. "My, it cools off fast here in Montana."

Instantly, Arthur was on his feet. "Ruby left her sweater here last weekend. I'll get it for you."

Mary sat gazing at the scene before her, the majesty and wonder of it all. She had certainly never seen anything close to this. Unbidden, a lump appeared in her throat, again an emotion she did not understand.

A sweater was placed about her shoulders with a pat on her arm, and a resounding, "There you go."

"Thanks." Then, "I should go. Will you take me, please?"

When he didn't answer, she felt she had been too bold and said, "I can call a driver."

"You're definitely from Lancaster. A driver is likely ten miles away."

"Oh. Well, I'll walk."

"Stay awhile, Mary. You can sleep in the guest room. I'll go home with you in the morning."

Oh, well. He had a girlfriend, so no one would care.

She slept in a pair of flannel pajamas, made with yards and yards of fabric with moose antlers printed all over it, in a bed made of logs, with a down comforter and a mattress that came very close to bliss.

In Montana it was so dark and so quiet, Mary fell asleep with a smile on her face, eager to begin her new life. She'd try and make sure she was home for Christmas.

Chapter Three

THE FOLLOWING DAY MARY EXAMINED EVERY inch of her new domain and gave it a thorough cleaning with antibacterial Mr. Clean, hot water, and a rag. She polished windows and scrubbed the bathroom, then put her clothes away in the dresser with a large oval mirror.

She carefully set the few toiletries she'd brought in the cabinet above the bathroom sink, and she was finished.

The little house smelled clean but remained decidedly sterile. She looked forward to the delivery of everything she had shipped—her own quilts and comforters, towels, rugs, and some of the pictures and items she'd decorated with back home. She'd also sent clothes and shoes, but no furniture or dishes. She decided they were too expensive to ship and too unnecessary.

Her home was cozy, set under the pine and pin oak trees, just up the road from the school. It was dark brown, the vertical boards and batten stained to blend with the outdoors. Yes, the porch was small, the floorboards uneven, the steps rickety, and the posts bowed by the weather. But it was livable, if not opulent.

Now it was off to school. She tied the laces of her walking shoes, put on a clean black bib apron, and set off down the road, swinging her arms, breathing deeply, and drinking in the pure oxygen of this remote place where the hum of traffic, the smell of vehicle exhaust, paved roads, and smokestacks spewing black smoke, were unthinkable. What an assault that would be on these pure untouched leaves, dancing together in the strong mountain breeze, undisturbed by anything made by humans. It was all a wonder.

To her left, the sturdy board fence stood as a guard between her and the only threat she'd encountered so far, Eddie the bull.

Thick grasses waved and rippled in the wind, a never-ending sea of motion, rising and falling, dipping and swaying, responding to the air that swooped down from the mountains.

Mary grabbed her covering stings and tied them closely beneath her chin. Gravel crunched under the soles of her pounding footfalls as she increased her pace. She heard the children's chatter before she saw them. Three bicycles bore down on her, leaving little puffs of dust in their wake. She slowed, then came to a stop.

Three boys, like three peas in a pod, hatless, their thick blond hair windblown, their faces round, with eyes like blue almonds set in fringes of dark lashes, drew close.

They slowed, each one raising a hand, palm out, before increasing their speed, then lifted themselves off their seats to stand on the pedals of their bikes.

Without thinking, Mary called after them, "Hey!" Each bike braked to a halt, but not one of the boys turned to come back, so Mary walked after them.

"I would love to be introduced," she said.

"Yeah. We're Kenny Yoder's boys."

Aha.

"I'm the new teacher."

Silence clamped down on the boys, immobilizing them. They opened their mouths, closed them, and cast sidelong glances at each other before they checked Mary over from head to toe, taking in the red hair, the sneakers.

"How come your covering's weird?"

"I'm from Lancaster, Pennsylvania."

"See? I told you," one said loudly.

"Are you going to be my pupils?"

"Yeah."

"Good. I'm pleased to meet you. My name is Mary. Mary Stoltzfus."

She stepped closer and stuck out her hand, which each boy shook limply, but with a certain politeness.

"Your names?"

"I'm Junior."

"LaVonne."

"Matt."

"For Matthew?"

"Yeah."

"Good, good. Why don't you come with me? Show me around my new school?"

"Nope. We don't touch that place till we have to."

"Really? Why not?"

"We hate school."

"Oh, come on."

"We do." Earnestly, three heads nodded in unison, devoted to the cause of school-hating.

"Why?"

"It's boring."

"The teacher is mean as on old rooster."

"I doubt it."

"Huh! You weren't here!"

"Teachers are all the same. Every last one of those creatures is bent on making life miserable."

Mary laughed good-naturedly. "Well, you haven't met me yet, now have you?"

"Why would you be any different?"

"Hey, guys, give me a chance!"

The boys looked sideways at one another, raising their eyebrows in approval. She sounded pretty cool, actually. That David Mast would not have called them "guys."

Mary turned her head toward the schoolhouse. "You coming?"

"Nah. We'll wait till we have to go."

In unspoken agreement, they pedaled off. Mary stood and watched them go, a slight cloud passing over her features, but she turned and strode purposefully toward her new job. She had to climb over the fence, finding the gate securely locked against intruders. She wondered why Arthur had forgotten to provide a key for that first obstacle.

She unlocked the schoolhouse door, stepped into the one room, surveyed the interior with a sweeping glance, then put up a few blinds, unlocked windows, and raised them as well.

Hmm. Very interesting. It appeared as if the former teacher, David Mast, had not been able to spend all of fifteen minutes picking up paper plates and cups after the school picnic. Bits of Styrofoam were scattered all over the floor, with dried baked beans and blackened ketchup smeared over them.

Mary yelped when a small, brown mouse peeked from behind a desk leg. She dashed after the offensive animal, her foot slapping down a few inches behind the scurrying creature. When she made contact with it, she stomped down hard, lifted the lifeless rodent by its spindly tail, and flung it out the door. She killed three more that afternoon, whacking the disgusting mice with the heavy straw broom, and disposing of them as efficiently as the first one.

She made a thorough search of the baseboard, looking for any possible mouse entrances, found none, and reasoned that they must have coexisted with David Mast and his scholars. Gross. Well, consider your happy homes invaded. I do not live with mice.

She swept the wide plank floors, burned the garbage, and took stock of all the supplies, checking carefully the list she had made for herself, muttering under her breath as she did so.

The schoolroom looked a lot like the one back home except for the wooden flooring. The used metal desk was beige, like hers, the wooden seats fastened to the floor the way she was used to. The walls were white with oak wainscoting along the lower half. A round clock with large numbers hung on the west wall. There was the usual gray file cabinet, a large, cast iron woodstove, a cloakroom with hooks, shelves for lunchboxes, and a stand with a Rubbermaid dishpan for hot water and soap to wash hands before lunch.

Yes, indeed. It was all different, yet familiar. She found the parents' names and their telephone numbers. She'd call and leave messages with each one, telling them she had decided to have the school cleaning the following Tuesday.

She was surprised to find the classroom suddenly bathed in the evening glow that meant the sun was already low, and setting quickly. Hurriedly, she lowered the windows, pulled the blinds, locked the door, and let herself out, surprised to find the shadows already lengthened and deepening fast.

She scrambled over the fence, turned her head both ways twice out of habit, before realizing there was no traffic to look out for, and scuttled sheepishly up the road. She hoped no one had seen her. No one would have, since there wasn't a single soul anywhere.

A deep sense of melancholy enveloped her, silencing the song in her mind, the energy with which she'd ticked off one job after another all afternoon. She felt weary and very, very alone.

She would come home to an empty house. She could not run across the porch to her parents to share her day with them. Homesickness clenched her stomach, stopping her breathing. Her steps slowed, she bent her head, and for only an instant, nothing made sense.

Why was she here, propped up by all this false bravado? If she would have followed her instincts, she would have told those unkind boys to go home and stay there and not to bother coming to school at all with their stinking attitudes.

She had nothing to eat and no idea where there was a grocery store. Should she call Arthur? Why not?

She forgot. She had no telephone. If she did, she hadn't been able to find it. When she arrived at the small brown house, she searched along the back for any kind of shed or addition that could house a telephone, but there was none.

Well, she'd have to make do. Searching the cupboards, she found oatmeal, then carried the container to the doorway to check for bugs. Sure enough, the flakes of oatmeal were moving around as if they had a life of their own.

She found salt, pepper, seasonings, flour, and a bit of sugar in a bag that was as hard as a rock. She could soak the hardened sugar with warm water and sip it like a hummingbird. Not very nutritious. Or appealing.

Well, she had to eat. She could walk to Kenny Yoder's, but if the parents were anything like their boys, she'd probably be chased off the property by a Rottweiler or a pit bull.

She'd go to Arthur. If she didn't think of him as eligible, she wouldn't become tongue-tied and flustered. He was definitely not eligible.

Oh, she could act as unconcerned, as uncaring about her singledom as she wanted, but it was still there. She had never been chosen. She had never been asked. Never. At first, she had minded. She had hurt worse than anyone could ever tell. Rejection filled the sails that were her pride, and she moved through life with that wind propelling her, keeping her head high, a smile on her face.

Eventually she stopped caring, then stopped "running around," that time of *rumspringa* when she went with the youth. She was that young, thin-as-a-rail, red-haired girl who attended all her friends' weddings, one by one, as the young men labeled "hopefuls" in her mind turned to someone else.

She'd blamed her looks, hating her red hair. She despised her freckles, her pale skin, her too-thin body, her skinny ankles with the size nine shoes slapping like flippers on the ground as she walked. She was awkward, that was what it was, she decided. Ugly and ungainly. But not stupid or dumb.

School had been a whiz for her. She read like a starving person. Ravenously. She devoured words, mulled them around in her brain like a fine wine—or the way she imagined fancy people tasted wine.

When the school board asked her to teach, she said yes, then threw herself into her new role whole-heartedly. The children filled her heart, her thin, empty arms. She held her first-graders on her lap, shared her potato chips with them, listened to their sweet, lisping voices, and fell in love over and over again.

School-teaching became a haven, a safe, warm place where she felt no need for pretense. Gradually, the lack of romance in her life receded, stuffed in a drawer. Mary inserted the key, turned it, and threw it away. Clearly God wanted her to be single. He didn't plan for her to marry and have children. She was a leftover blessing, a real gift to the Amish community. *An goota* teacher.

In Lancaster, her guest bedroom was filled with ceramics with thoughtful-teacher slogans all over them. She had boxes of wooden plaques with beautiful verses. Towels, sheets, framed artwork, pieces of furniture, Princess House items, Pampered Chef cookware, Tupperware containers from parties held in her honor—material things, but only the finest— piled around her until she felt buried in them. They were meant to show appreciation and thanks. Thank you. Thank you. Thank you.

But never once had a young man asked for her hand.

With that thought hovering over her, she showered and then combed her wet hair carefully, wishing it would stay that deep auburn color after it dried. She dressed in a clean, although slightly wrinkled, dress that was a deep shade of brown, tied her black apron over it, put on her clean covering, and let herself out the door.

Twilight had settled across the countryside, throwing the mountains into a deep shade of velvet. The wind had finally stilled except for a few rustling leaves.

Almost she lost her nerve. It made her angry, this shrinking inside herself when she felt even remotely attracted to someone. She thought she'd successfully subdued any emotion that pertained to young men, or, since she was older, to any men.

She could not imagine, if someone as, well, as interesting as Arthur Bontrager would. . . . Well, he wouldn't. Mary, he wouldn't. A mental picture suddenly dangled in front of her eyes. Okay, God, I know. Thank you for reminding me.

Just when she thought she'd successfully squelched all emotion or attraction to him, she thought of the tanned creases around his eyes, the sound of his laugh. Oh, mercy. Mary, stop.

She hurried on up the winding, wooded slope to his house, the board fence on her right, the shadows deepening steadily. A cow's lowing, the distant yipping of a dog, an answering bellow.

A bellow? She stopped, her eyes searching the dim light of the pasture. She could barely discern the shape of the black cows. She shivered when the sound came again. More like a roar. Eddie was mad.

The last hundred yards her feet flew across the lane. She was panting, her chest heaving, when she pounded on the door. Thank goodness, there was a yellow light shining from the living room.

Arthur let her in, surprised at her agitation, listening carefully when she described the sound.

"Eddie's just letting everyone know who's boss," he said, then laughed. His eyes crinkled, and he asked her to sit down.

"I will. I'll fall over of starvation if I don't."

Arthur became clearly upset. He had never thought of her lack of groceries. He apologized profusely, over and over, then heated a large serving of ham and potato chowder and brought saltines, sour pickles, cold beef, sliced tomatoes, sliced onions, butter, mustard, and mayonnaise. He told her when he

watched her eat the barbecue he knew that she was a
real lover of sandwiches.

She bent her head and slurped her chowder and
spoke with her mouth full. She used three napkins,
drank two glasses of tea, and watched his blue eyes
appear and disappear when he laughed or when he
became serious. She ate a large wedge of apple pie,
bursting with brown sugar, butter, and cinnamon,
and topped with vanilla ice cream and caramel
syrup.

He put extra groceries in a box for her, then promised to accompany her to the local Amish bulk food
store in the morning.

"You can't walk home alone. I'll put this box on
the express wagon and go with you."

"I'll manage."

"What about Eddie?"

"I'll be all right."

"No. You're not going home alone. I let you starve,
now I won't let you be in danger. You could stay with me."

"Oh, no. I can't."

"Why not?"

"Well," Mary shrugged her shoulders helplessly. She wanted to say, what about her, the girl in the photograph? I know I'm a homely old maid, but I have never been so desperate that I would do anything to hurt someone else.

"Well, what? Just stay. I want you to hear the wolves."

"What wolves?" The words came sharply. Mary was frightened.

"The wolves."

"I hadn't realized there were wolves."

"Oh, there are."

He made coffee, laced it liberally with cream, sugar, and a shot of hazelnut flavoring, then provided his girlfriend's sweater. They sat on the great, rustic log chairs on the patio under the vast, velvet sky dotted with twinkling white stars.

They talked about his work building log furniture, the cows, the state of Montana. They wandered into conversation about the Amish who choose to live away from the curious eyes of tourists, about growing communities that are troubled by unfortunate events caused by greed or jealousy or "other maladies of human nature," as Mary pointed out. She was rewarded by a great, rolling laugh.

They fell silent. Mary sat in awe of the night, the way the stars seemed to lower themselves, blink, then blink again, before resuming their normal place. She was just opening her mouth and catching her breath when she heard the first distant sound. At first she thought it was the neighbor's dog. Arthur held up a hand, then set down his mug and motioned for her to come.

"Listen closely."

From far away across the treetops and the darkened pasture, the sound began, low at first, then building to a long, undulating howl, a wail of loneliness and sorrow, a sound of longing, a primitive, beautiful cry that was almost spiritual. God wanted them to know that He had made this night, the vast, dark sky, the blinking stars, the howling of these, his creatures.

Unbidden, a sob tore from Mary's throat. Terrified of her own weakness, she covered her face with both hands and turned away, determined to hide the fact that the wolves' howling had stirred her soul. When the sound came again, she remained rigid, ashamed of her emotion, desperately blinking back the unwelcome tears.

She felt, rather than saw, Arthur's presence as he came close. She heard his voice.

"It's always interesting to me, to see a person's response when they hear the wolves for the first time."

Even if she had wanted to, she couldn't have answered, so she stayed as she was, head bent, her hands covering her face.

"I have never heard anyone cry." Gently, his big hands held her shoulders. Slowly, he turned her around until she faced him. Miserably, she let her hands fall away where they hung awkwardly at her sides beside her size nine feet.

Mary swallowed, then whispered, "It's the most beautiful sound I've ever heard."

When he drew her against his wide, wide chest and his great arms went around her, she laid her head against the flannel of his shirt, closed her eyes, and wept. He laid his cheek on the top of her head, the way he would comfort a small child, which made Mary cry more.

Again the wolves howled, sending chills up Mary's spine. She stepped back, straining to hear, then smiled up at Arthur through her tears.

"The most overused word in the English vocabulary and it's all I can think of—awesome. Absolutely awesome." Self-conscious now, and much too close to Arthur, she tried to step out of the circle of his arms. This was completely unseemly. She was so thoroughly ashamed.

For a moment, she thought he would release her, but he only gathered her into a long, comforting embrace. She heard him sigh, and then suddenly, she stood chillingly alone.

"Mary. Mary."

That was all he said. They walked home side by side, Arthur pulling the express wagon with the box of groceries. They walked in silence, carrying the magic of the night with them.

He promised to pick her up at nine o'clock in the

morning with the team, then wished her a good night and left, the wagon bumping behind him.

Mary lay sleepless far into the night. She had never been held in an embrace by a man. She must never go to his house again. She knew deep down she could not approach him about the girl in the photograph. As long as she didn't know for sure, she could remain unaware. She would have to extricate herself before Arthur became someone she could not live without.

Chapter Four

THE AIR WAS ALREADY TINGED WITH whispers of fall by the last week in August when the bell on top of the schoolhouse rang on the first day of school. Mary stood inside yanking the rope, letting the bell peal its message across the valley, letting it roll on and on till it bumped against the mountains, unsettled the snow on top, perhaps starting an avalanche. Who knew?

She was in her element. She felt strong, in control, and capable. She had met the schoolchildren and their parents the week before and was pleasantly surprised to find them friendly, eager to be introduced, and willing to help. She was an expert at parent evaluation. Mrs. Kenny Yoder was the only rotten apple in the bunch, she could plainly tell. And even she might not be too difficult.

She had been completely enamored of the little girls with their stiff white coverings propped on their heads like neat little cups. Their hair was done so differently than Lancaster girls', whose hair was wet down flatly against their heads, the sides rolled in tightly, and the buns on the backs of their heads just as severe. These little girls' hair was combed naturally up toward the middle of their heads. And here their pinafore-type aprons were the same color as their dresses.

They were happy, well cared for, secure, and eager to learn, as far as Mary could tell.

The pealing of the bell brought the twenty-one pupils crashing through the door and sliding into their desks, after they each found their name tags stuck onto the upper right-hand corner with Scotch tape.

They watched Mary openly, unabashedly. This new teacher dressed so differently, and she was, indeed, very interesting.

The singing class was the first sign of the work ahead. The two eighth-grade boys sagged against the blackboard, their hands stuffed into their denim trousers, each refusing to hold a songbook with a girl.

Mary took notice, clasped her songbook to her chest, and said clearly, "Allen and Danny, you may go back to your seats."

They looked perplexed.

"You obviously do not enjoy singing, so you may sit down."

Snickering, they walked back to their seats. The remainder of the class watched Mary, unsure of how to proceed.

"All right. We'll start with the oldest person, and each morning three of you may choose the song you would like to sing. Alma?"

The only girl in eighth grade raised her hand. "That's not how we did it last year."

"That's all right. This year, we'll do it this way."

Mary made sure her smile reached each one. Alma chose number 248, and the room was filled with quiet and discordant strains of "Will the Circle be Unbroken?".

Halfway through the song, Mary held up a hand. Half of them were not singing, and she asked why. Mary encouraged them to open their mouths and put their hearts into the music. Then she launched into a solo, a rousing rendition of "John Brown Had a Little Indian."

Grins behind songbooks turned to titters of amusement, and then to wide smiles as Mary continued to sing at the top of her voice.

"By Christmas, we'll really bring the house down!" she chortled.

After that, Mary had the pupils' complete attention. She was experienced and knew what boosted morale, understanding that most children who "hated" school only needed to find fresh interest. Each day she set about pursuing her goal of having a classroom filled with eager children, anxious to please, happy to come to school. By the time the frost lay heavily in the hollows, the Montana community was buzzing with praise for the red-haired teacher from Lancaster. They said they'd never seen anything like it. Harley Miller's children counted the hours till they could go to school. And did you see her artwork?

Mary attended church services for the first time at Elmer Helmuth's place, transported in the back of

Kenny Yoder's spring wagon. She felt like an owl in a flock of pigeons, the way she knew she would, but she was a comfortable owl, quite secure in her owlness. She knew the parents thought highly of her, signaled by the handclasps and the fawning, the praise heaped on her shoulders.

Yes, she was indeed capable, turning the school into a lean, efficient learning machine. So she moved among these western people dressed according to a different *ordnung*, confident, smiling, pouring coffee at the dinner table. She went home with Marvin Troyers and had a wonderful evening playing Scrabble, which she won, of course. Every game, too.

Only at night alone in the little house did she let the loneliness of her heart unravel. She no longer went to Arthur's house. She told him coolly after the night the wolves howled that she could easily make it on her own, that she'd appreciated his help, but it wasn't proper to be spending all this time together.

"I've overstepped my boundaries, haven't I?" he'd said, his creases all gone, his eyes large and blue and serious.

"Well, no. Not really. I just need to stay in my place."

"Which is?"

"Alone."

He'd raised his eyebrows at that and left her alone. Every weekend his house stayed dark, until sometime late Sunday evening, he'd return.

She even went about, in her cunning way, deriving information about Arthur's weekend meanderings, finding out which other Amish communities were nearby, but never directly asking about his girlfriend's existence. She was extremely efficient at teaching school, and she told herself that she would become as efficient at removing Arthur Bontrager from her head, where he stuck like an unwanted virus. She was always in control, so she would be able to take care of this disorder, this letting down of the iron guard around her heart.

It was only at night when she relived the magic of being held in his arms, cradling the memory, nurturing it, and telling herself that if it was all she ever had, as far as a bit of romance in her life, it would suffice.

No, she had never been asked, never been chosen, but she had been held against Arthur's great chest and heard the heavy thudding of his heart. That was something, wasn't it?

When the leaves began to change their colors from many shades of green to golden yellows, reds, and oranges, wood fires were lit in stoves all over the community. Smoke rose from well-built chimneys as split wood was crammed into stoves. Warmth spread through houses, making them cozy places where adults gathered next to woodstoves, their spirits lifting.

Mary hadn't thought about her source of heat. She flipped the knob on the gas stove, turned the oven on, and let its heat warm the little house quite efficiently. She'd never given the lean-to in the back of the house much thought. She knew it was filled with split wood, but never really thought about it being her source of heat. She was too busy being capable.

So when the leaves shivered and fell to the ground, when the air turned wet and cold with the chance of snow falling, Mary woke up one Saturday morning, late, her nose like an icicle. Her legs hurt, her back was stiff, and she was, quite simply, freezing.

Well, she could lie here and be miserable, or she could get up, get dressed, and start a fire. Wistfully, she thought of home where the thermostat on the wall would turn on the propane gas heater and fill the house with quiet, efficient heat. She wanted to go shopping today and then go out for lunch with Sarah Ann, her friend.

She wanted to eat at Applebee's, a place where they served different food than she ate at home, with inappropriate music, for her, perhaps, but where anything you ordered was so good. She missed the traffic, the bustle of the fall harvest, the weddings.

Groaning, she rolled out of bed, tiptoed swiftly to the gas range, and turned the oven on. Seriously, that was like lighting a candle in an igloo, but every little bit helped, she supposed. She opened the door a crack, yelped, banged it shut, and said, "Shoo!" It was very earnestly, quite cold. Decidedly, grievously cold out there.

Shivering, she dressed in the heaviest weight dress she owned, threw a sweater on, followed by her black lightweight windbreaker, buttoning it all the way down. She put a white scarf on her head, two pairs of woolen socks on her feet, and her leather snow boots on top of them. Pulling on a heavy pair of gloves, she went to the lean-to for wood, then carried a few small sticks to the house, shivering, and complaining under her breath. She had never started a wood fire.

Slowly she opened the door of the cast iron stove and peered inside. Hmm. It was very dark in there. Going to the pantry, she found her flashlight hanging from a peg, clicked it on, and directed its beam into the stove. Looked like lots of ashes. She needed a poker. Isn't that what you called those cast iron things?

Searching the wall behind the stove, she found a short, heavy cast iron thing that had a hook on the end. Some people just had no common sense. Couldn't they see a poker needed to be a lot longer? She grasped the little thingy, as she dubbed it, and scraped away inside the stove, hurting the inside of her arm as she moved it back and forth across the rough edges.

"Ow!" She sat back on her haunches and checked the sleeve of her windbreaker, horrified to see the holes that she had just worn through it. There had to be a better way.

Going to the pantry again, she lifted the broom down from its hook, then inserted the handle into the woodstove and vigorously scraped it back and forth. That was better. When she was satisfied that most of the ashes had been pushed down through the grates, she opened the bottom door and yanked at the ash pan, then hollered as a cloud of ashes tumbled out over the pan, rolled across the clean floor, and drifted up into her face.

"Whew!" Taking the corner of her apron she waved it madly, which only dislodged more of the wood ashes, sending them flying in every direction.

Frustrated, she grabbed the pan, lurched through the door, down the steps and across the yard, where she flung the offending ashes into the wind the wrong way. They all wafted neatly over her entire body, leaving her choking and coughing, her mouth and eyes turning black where the ashes met with moisture.

Hateful old woodstoves. Lifting her black apron, she began flopping it about, trying to rid herself of all the offending ashes.

She slammed the cottage door behind her, inserted the ash pan, and stood, eyeing the door of the woodstove. Now what? Newspaper. Kindling. She had no axe. Or hatchet. Well, maybe the smallest pieces would catch fire.

Her hands stiff with the cold, her stomach rumbling, she crumpled the paper, then carefully laid the smallest stick of wood on top, held a Bic lighter to it, and was rewarded by greedy yellow flames devouring the paper.

Well, that was odd. The smoke was supposed to go up the chimney. Not out of this door. She coughed. A sneeze racked her body. Now what?

She removed the stick of wood, then crumpled more paper, arranged it carefully again, and lit the paper. More black smoke poured into her face the second time.

Stamping her foot, Mary yelled, "You dumb, ignorant stove!"

For a third time, she tried the same procedure—with the very same result. Mary slammed the stove door as hard as she could, then kicked the small door at the bottom. Pain shot through her big toe, and she sank to the brown sofa, holding the painful toe in both hands, thinking she might pass out flat on the floor.

She was licked. Beaten. She'd walk to Kenny Yoder's and ask for their help. The boys could come back with her.

But first, she had to eat. Flopping the skillet on top of the stove, she flipped the burner on, then placed both hands above it, letting the heat move through the palms of her hands. Blessed, wonderful warmth.

She fried two eggs, grilled two slices of bread, slurped down some lukewarm coffee, and set out for Kenny Yoder's, her toe throbbing painfully.

Swinging her arms while moving along at a frantic pace, she caught a movement out of the corner of her eye. A flash of brown. Mary stopped, hoping to catch sight of a deer. Or perhaps one of those elusive coyotes that was so afraid of humans. Instead, she was faced squarely by two of the largest dogs she had ever seen. Their heads were round and square at the same time, wide between their eyes, one more black than brown. Flat, wicked eyes, like serpents', looked back at her. Their huge slavering mouths, with white teeth exposed, grinned at her as they panted.

Mary backed away. Somewhere she had read not to make eye contact. Don't run. Don't panic.

She turned, walking back the way she had come, her back rigid with fear. She willed herself to keep looking ahead and not to look back.

She heard them. She heard their feet. Then she heard their breathing. Rasping breaths, coming fast.

Yet she kept walking. She wanted to break into a run, just run and run, but she knew it was futile. She would never be able to outrun these powerful creatures.

Dear God. Help. Help me. She was sobbing now.

Closer. The breathing was much closer.

Mary ran. The only instinct she could obey was to run. The heavy socks and snow boots held her back, but she kept lunging forward, willing herself more speed. Past the school. She was almost home. Her breath tore at her throat. Her chest felt as if it was on fire. She looked back.

Two more steps, and she was flung to the ground by the force of the black dog driving his body into her shoulder. She screamed and screamed as jaws attached themselves to the calf of her leg. She cowered on all fours, her head bent, and kept screaming. The grip on her boot released. Turning, she kicked out with both legs as the horrible beasts circled her.

Screaming again, she rolled, got to her feet, and turned to run as the dogs' jaws clamped around her leg again. She was thrown to the ground, bouncing with the impact. The back of her head was flung hard against the frozen soil, and she thought, "This is how I'll die."

Still she screamed, hoping someone, anyone, would hear.

When the second dog's jaws gripped her forearm, its teeth tearing away at her sweater and windbreaker, then sinking into the soft flesh, she stopped screaming. Whimpering and crying, she begged the dogs to go away.

The next hit was directly in her face, the jaws snapping on her white headscarf as she twisted away.

She covered her head with both hands and rolled onto her stomach as the dog's jaws clamped onto her leg yet again. The leather snow boot took most of the impact, saving her leg. She kicked at the solid, hairy body, then swiped at the lust in the greedy black eyes with her gloved hands.

She let out scream after scream until her voice was silenced by the impact of the dog's jaws on her cheekbone, tearing away at her face. She twisted away as blood filled her vision, turning the beautiful Montana landscape to red.

She didn't hear the shot. She felt the dog go slack, the one in her red vision, the one attached to her shoulder. He let his jaws relax, and Mary rolled away. As she rolled twice, she heard the sharp crack of a gunshot. The dog yelped, his flat eyes registered shock, and he rolled away, limp.

Mary lay curled in a tight position as wave after wave of searing pain tore through her body. She knew she was losing blood by the lightheaded, nauseous feeling that swept through her. She had to get home. Placing both hands on the ground, she steadied herself, willed herself to sit upright. She would not lose consciousness. Not now. She had to get home.

One knee was on the ground. There. She could get to her feet. With a gigantic effort, she got up on all fours. She began crying, failure seeping into her knowing. That was where Arthur Bontrager found her, saying over and over, "I can't, I can't."

Blood covered her face and soaked into her thick, red hair. Her boot was half chewed off; her coat hung in tatters. Arthur lost no time. He picked her up like an injured rag doll, strode off down the road, and laid her on the floor of her house. He went to the wood-shed where they'd installed the telephone and called the nearest neighbor, then ran to apply torn strips of cloth above her wounds. He placed a towel under her head and knew there was nothing else he could do. Mary was conscious, her eyes wide.

Wiping the blood away as best he could, Arthur asked if she was all right until they got to a doctor.

"I'll be fine," she whispered. She gritted her teeth and closed her eyes as Arthur and his helper propped her up in the middle, between them, in the old pickup truck. Not once did she cry out as the truck barreled across the ruts and potholes in the rural, gravel road.

She spoke clearly to the doctor, giving him the needed information herself, and assured Arthur that there was no need to take her to a hospital.

He waited outside, pacing the floor, as the doctor sutured the wounds. He did a good job on her eyelid, placing tiny stitches to hold it together. He repaired the hole in her cheek with nine neat little stitches. Like quilting, he told her. She smiled a very small smile. She told the doctor she supposed she was one fortunate person.

After two hours of repair work, the doctor called "her husband" back into the treatment room, which put a permanent amount of creases around Arthur's eyes for quite some time.

Arthur would not give up. It was the only sensible thing to do. She was not staying alone. She would stay with him. She stopped protesting when the truck seemed to tilt sideways and spin around in the opposite direction. She reasoned to herself, made excuses, then nodded in agreement.

Arthur paid the driver, then carried her into the house and sat her on the recliner, while he hurried from room to room, gathering sheets and pillows, blankets, a small table, a pitcher of ice water, pain pills, and a box of Kleenex.

With the room spinning wildly, her head fell back as he carried her to the wide, deep sofa. He thought she'd fainted until her eyelids fluttered and she tried to thank him, but couldn't.

When she fell asleep, he sat beside her watching every twitch of pain, every rise and fall of her chest, and wondered again at the way her collarbones rose from the neckline of her dress. Somehow, they were the only vulnerable thing about her.

Chapter Five

BACK IN HER OWN HOUSE, WITH the chimney properly cleaned, a wood fire crackled cozily. Mary's wounds healed as the weather turned increasingly colder. The snow that had waited behind protective layers of clouds tumbled down in fine, icy bits, turning the countryside into a frigid world of pure white.

Tomorrow she would go back to school. The concerned parents had taken turns keeping the school going for a few weeks, but Mary anticipated—no, *expected*—nothing short of pure chaos. Her record book would be inaccurate, if it had been kept at all. She had plenty of experience where substitutes were concerned; she would leave the house in the morning prepared for bedlam.

And now Arthur wanted her to get a dog. That was quite unnecessary, thank you very much. She had no use for those creatures, especially big ones. If they had pet day at school, she admired the yipping little nuisances from a distance, kept up false praises for the big, drooling ones, but could never feel any affection for man's best friend. They smelled, for one thing. They barked and barked, turned somersaults, and leaped senselessly in the air for no apparent reason other than their own stupidity. They shed fine hair over floors and chairs and sofas.

She had plenty of single friends in Lancaster who owned little white or black or brown dogs that leaped up into her lap, wrongly assuming they were welcome. So she grinned half-heartedly, scratched their ears once, then unobtrusively wiped her fingers on a handkerchief once the small dog had the good sense to jump off her lap.

The thing was, it was rude to push precious Daisy or Belle or Oscar off her lap. She had to restrain herself quite often, however, when every fiber of her being wanted to send the dog none too gently off her lap.

So, no, she did not want a dog or need one.

Arthur had instructed her in the ways of wood fires. She was a fast learner, quite efficiently raking down the coals with the long-handled poker, (the short one with the hook on the end was for shaking the grates) adding heavy split logs, closing the damper when she was away, and adjusting the thermostat. She felt capable now, a seasoned woodstove handler.

Marching smartly down the road, swinging her lunchbox and book satchel, breathing in the snappy, cold air, the soles of her boots crunching in the frozen snow, Mary felt on top of the world once again. Sutures removed, vitamin E capsules sent for from the store called Nature's Warehouse, B&W salve applied—it was all taken care of.

What was that? Wildly, she turned her head to the left, then to the right. Twigs snapped. Stopping, her breath coming in ragged puffs, Mary searched the trees and brush by the roadside. There it was. Oh. Oh, my goodness. A flash of brown. Unable to believe that God would ever allow more vicious dogs to attack, she remained standing, rooted to the snowy ground, as more twigs snapped.

The two deer that emerged from the undergrowth turned their heads, their wide, almond-shaped ears held erect, as they watched a heavily dressed schoolteacher hustle clumsily down the road, swinging her satchels as if they could help propel her faster.

Mary's hand shook as she tried inserting the key into the lock. She took a few deep breaths to steady herself before attempting it the second time.

As she had feared, the schoolroom was a mess. Crumpled papers were strewn haphazardly across the floor, gray stains showed where juice or soup had spilled, wrinkled aluminum foil covered leftover food forgotten on the stove, sending out a mildly burnt odor.

Her usual precise stack of corrected workbooks were thrown onto the table in the middle aisle with a half-done puzzle beside them. Markers and broken crayons were everywhere.

Mary surveyed the room, deciding that a father had likely taught on Friday. She pushed up her sleeves and set to work. She swept the puzzle into the box propped up beside it and snapped the lid down over it, then picked up crayons, straightened the workbooks, grabbed a broom, and winced at the amount of dust that puffed up with every draw.

The schoolroom was halfway in order when the pupils began to arrive. Mary greeted them all with genuine gladness, showed them her scars, then pulled up a chair to the fire and gathered the children around her for a long and detailed discussion about the stray dog attack.

They skipped arithmetic that morning, which was, indeed, the most wonderful thing any teacher could think of. They touched Mary's scars, some of them shyly, others yelping when they felt the hard ridge where the sutures had held the cut in place.

The upper-grade boys said it was necessary for her to own a dog.

Mary shook her head. "I don't like dogs."

"Why not? I don't know anyone that doesn't like dogs," Kenny Yoder's Matt said, frustrated.

"What could one dog have done to save me?" Mary asked.

"Everything!" the boys shouted, clapping their hands, then launched into a long and detailed account of Ranger, the German Shepherd's brave stand-off with a catamount.

"Whatever that is," Mary murmured.

"A lion."

"Not an African, maned lion."

"No, a mountain lion. Cougar. Panther. A big cat."

Mary laughed heartily. "I get it."

They finished their talk with plans for Christmas, which was coming fast. Mary told them they would need to begin practicing directly after Thanksgiving for the program.

Howls of protest went up. Mary could not believe what she was hearing. "Why? Don't you want a Christmas play?"

"No, no, no!" They shook their heads back and forth, denying her any anticipation of the usual Christmas celebration.

Wisely, Mary decided to drop it. She tapped the small bell on her desk, restored order, resumed classes, and marched into her usual efficient routine. She was glad of it, too.

Who could have known, she thought? How could

she possibly have foreseen that her biggest challenge to overcome was the mere walk to and from school? She was absolutely petrified, especially now when at five o'clock, long eerie shadows fell across the road.

Sheepishly, making sure no one saw her, she went to the school's woodshed and rummaged around in the blue Rubbermaid garbage can until she found a good-sized baseball bat. She picked a wooden one that went unnoticed, since the children always chose the aluminum ones with popular slogans inscribed on them.

Mary lifted it and swung it in a circle. Aha. This would do nicely. Baseball bats were efficient as far as bloodthirsty dogs were concerned, and they didn't smell and bark raucously at any small rodent or bee. Once at a picnic down at Pequea Park, Sarah Fisher's Pekingese had eaten a bee, then threw up so horribly, Mary thought she would have to stand by as the pathetic little creature met his demise.

Mary started off, her book satchel slung over her shoulder, the bat gripped in the same hand as her lunchbox. She was all set. She kept her eyes on the road and tried hard to ignore the vast shadows, the thin branches of the undergrowth, the great, deep green, pine branches drooping with the added burden of snow.

She would not look. She would keep steadfastly on course. The wind kicked up, moving the pine branches. Whump!

Mary screamed hoarsely, then dropped her satchel, whirled around, her feet apart, her back lowered, gripping the bat, the panic propelling the breath from her mouth. What was that?

Shamefaced, she lowered the bat, took up her satchel, and continued on her way. She couldn't be too aware, now could she?

With her breath coming in short puffs, she clattered up onto her porch, propped the bat against the wall, fumbled for the silver band that held her key, and opened the door, glancing back at the darkening path that led from the road to her door.

There were still a few red coals lying on the grate, which meant she'd need a few small sticks of wood. Once they burned well, she could add larger pieces.

Slapping her hands together, she rid herself of the sawdust and watched the dry bark flame up, then closed the door with a pleasing, experienced bang.

She flicked the blue Bic lighter beneath the two white Coleman mantles, turned the knob, and was rewarded by a burning white light, sufficiently chasing away the deepening gloom in the corners. For an instant, she longed for the ease of her gas heat in Lancaster, but soon let it pass, deciding there was nothing to be gained by pitying oneself, or wishing for something you couldn't have.

Oh, what was she hungry for? Nothing really. She had too many papers to correct. She put the tea kettle on the gas burner, threw a mint tea bag in her favorite mug, spread out the papers and answer book, grabbed the red Bic pen, and began.

The low moaning of the wind turned into a more urgent sound. The window by the table rattled. Mary shivered as a draft of cold air snaked across the floor. Getting up, she peeled off her black nylons, stuck her feet into a pair of old fleece socks, then pushed them into her deerskin slippers.

Very feminine, she thought, smiling to herself. But who cared? There was no one to see, no one to impress with her choice of footwear. She glanced wryly at her slippers. Perhaps they were men's slippers. They looked like it. She had always disliked her feet. They wouldn't be quite so out of proportion if she was heavier, but as it was, being so thin, her feet were big boats housed in men's slippers. She really hated them.

The tea kettle whistled, and she poured boiling water over the tea bag, added sugar, and stirred.

The sound of a diesel engine caught her attention. Quickly, she went to the door, peering out through the beige, homespun fabric. There stood an English man with a gigantic dog that looked the same at both ends. Mary squinted her eyes, looking for the difference between the dog's head and its tail.

Well, the man looked nice. When he knocked, she opened the door immediately, stepped aside, and asked him in. She stepped back much further when the man put a hand on the dog's collar and brought him along inside, too, just as if it was human.

Already, Mary felt the presence of dog hair. It would waft through the air, she'd breathe it in through her nostrils, and it would clog the air passage in her throat.

The man touched the brim of his camouflage cap. "Evening, ma'am."

"Good evening."

"Hey, Art told me you needed a dog."

"Oh, he did?"

"Yeah, I raise these 'uns.'"

Mary crossed her arms, raising her eyebrows. "Really?"

"Yeah, they're good dogs. Mighty expensive, but if you lay out the money, you know you'll have complete protection from anyone who mistreats you, any wild animal, anything. They're extremely loyal. Completely fearless. They don't smell, slobber, or shed. They're smart as a tack. They're a real highfalutin' dog. I'll let you have a six-month-old one for two thousand."

Mary eyed the man levelly, then looked at the dog, which was so black it could melt into the night and you'd never know it. The animal was huge, with hair all over its eyes. She didn't believe for one minute he didn't smell, slobber, or shed. What a salesman!

"That's all right," Mary said quickly. "I can't really afford him. I'm not sure I need a dog just yet."

The dog lifted its head. Its eyes were as black as its hair. No wonder she couldn't tell which end was which.

"He'll get bigger yet. This one's gonna be big."

"I'm sure."

"Oh, forgot to innerduce myself."

Mary took the proffered hand, her shoulders snapping forward when he shook it with the force of a sledge hammer. She wondered if her thumb would ever be the same.

"Bob Lewis Armstrong."

"I'm Mary."

"Yes, yes. Art said you were the new teacher. Said dogs got you. Mark my words, there's always them strays. Worse 'n wolves. Keeps us farmers and ranchers on our toes. We shoot 'em, so we do. Threat to our livelihood. There's plenty more where those two come from."

Mary's heart sank. She eyed the black dog.

"Well, tell Art—Arthur, I mean—I appreciate his concern, but I do not want a dog. Not now, not ever."

"Huh. So you don't want a dog. Sorry, but I thought you did. Because Art said . . ." His voice drifted off when Mary broke in.

"Yeah, well, Art doesn't know. He had no right to think I would be interested in a dog."

Bob backed to the door, snapped his fingers, and with a hasty, "Evenin' ma'am," disappeared out the door with the dog.

Mary waited till the diesel truck rounded the corner at the bottom of the slope before throwing on a coat and parading out to the newly installed telephone in the wood house, dialing Arthur's number, and leaving him a frosty message.

Arthur listened to it, then smiled, finally laughed, and told Bob the following day that her message was so cold it about froze the phone to his ear. She was something, that Mary. Independent as all get out. Bob said most old maids were fiercely set in their ways. Let her find out for herself.

The visit from Bob only intensified Mary's fear. Small beads of sweat appeared on her upper lip as she pinned her black cape to her dress. She bit down on her teeth while she pinned the belt of her apron, rolling her eyes in the direction of the schoolhouse as she spooned up her oatmeal.

Well, what did Bob know? How often were humans attacked? She should have asked him. Her chances of being attacked were very slim. Or so she hoped. When she closed and locked the door of her house behind her, she took a deep, steadying breath. Straightening her shoulders, she set off down the steps, the wooden bat firmly in hand.

It was a beautiful early winter morning, the wind chasing little puffs of snow from wires and branches and uncovering some of the brown weeds by the road. It was cold, Mary thought, bending her head to the frigid air.

The twigs bent and snapped and branches swayed, but Mary refused to give in to her fear. The dogs would not be out and about if it was this cold. A distant barking sound increased the speed of her footsteps, so by the time she reached the porch of the small brown schoolhouse, her chest hurt by the force of her exertion. Whew!

Hurriedly, she put the bat back into the plastic garbage can, then began her day. There was no use letting that bit of information circulate among the community, now was there?

She had a good forenoon, the dogs forgotten, her head filled with lessons, teaching, and dealing with problems, the way she had done for twelve school terms before this one.

The children made construction paper turkeys for Thanksgiving, along with colorful horns of plenty. They copied a good poem about being thankful and planned a Thanksgiving dinner at school for the parents and members of the school board.

As the afternoon shadows lengthened once more, and the hands of the clock moved toward three o'clock, a sick feeling of dread gripped Mary's stomach. She tried hard to throw it off by becoming relaxed and nonchalant and trying to laugh with her pupils, but her mouth became dry, and she had to lick her lips repeatedly in order to speak.

When the school van approached, she almost stopped the driver and asked him to take her home, but she put her pride firmly in place before she actually did.

After the last "See ya!" had been sung out and the last children clambered on board the van and the buggies, she closed the door and shivered with genuine fear yet again. In a way, this was ridiculous. Tentatively, she touched the tips of her fingers to the scars on her face, sometimes angry and red, other times, barely visible.

The remembering is what it was. She could still smell the dogs' mouths and feel the overpowering strength of their bodies and their jaws. Suddenly, with an urge so powerful it left her drained, she wanted to go home. She'd promised Mam she'd be home for Christmas. Perhaps she'd be home for Thanksgiving.

She missed all the traffic and waving to people she knew. How she would appreciate the safety of the traffic! She'd count herself forever fortunate to wave to the folks she recognized and even the ones she didn't. The safety of those well-traveled roads was a longing so intense, Mary felt weak. Well, as she'd told herself before, self-pity was a well-traveled road to misery, and there was no use wanting something you could not have.

She bundled up and set off resolutely for the buggy shed to retrieve the bat she mentally labeled "The Guardian." She was just lifting it from the hiding place when the sound of buggy wheels made her drop the wooden bat like a hot coal. Straightening her back, she stood, then began to walk toward the schoolhouse.

It was Arthur Bontrager. Had he seen her lift the bat? Did he know she carried it around?

Arthur slid back the door of his top buggy, as these westerners called a buggy with a top. In Lancaster County, they were known as a *dochveggly*, literally meaning a "roof wagon." Whatever you called it, it was a form of transportation with sturdy wooden wheels that would convey her to her house, a few feet above the reach of the snapping jaws of stray dogs.

She wanted to throw herself in Arthur's arms and weep like a small child that is dreadfully afraid of the dark. What she did do, though, was watch his face warily with a timid smile of apology. There was that small matter of the phone message to deal with.

"Hey!"

"Hello!"

"I thought you might appreciate a ride home."

"Not unless you were going that way."

"What if I'm not?"

"I'll walk."

"All right, then."

Arthur's eyes crinkled up, the laugh rolled out of his chest, and he chirruped to his horse, a fine black Dutch Harness.

"Wait!" All the terror welled up in Mary's chest, successfully suppressing the all-invasive pride, and she said very fast, "I do need a ride. It's late. I have a lot to do."

Once she was seated beside him, he gently put the woolen lap robe around her, patted her knee, and let the blue in his eyes twinkle at her. "You have a habit of leaving grouchy messages?"

Completely at a loss for words, she opened her mouth, then closed it again, finally saying only, "Go," jutting her chin in the direction of her house.

Again, he laughed. "So you don't want a dog?"

"No."

"But you know you'll have to have one soon. Or else I'll have to haul you to school and back. A pack of six dogs killed about half of Wes Owen's calves. Nice 500-pounders. There's a warning out for anyone walking or jogging."

Chapter Six

WAS IT SO WRONG FOR MARY to move only a slight bit closer to Arthur in his top buggy after he had finished speaking?

Gratitude welled in her heart for his endless jolly laugh, his simple acknowledgement of forgiveness. She had been quite forthright, that she had.

She shivered. Instantly, he tucked the lap robe around her even more securely.

"Warm?"

"Scared."

"So you didn't like Bob coming with the dog? You know he raises those Bouvier des Flandres dogs. I think they're French or something."

"Boo-veay what?"

"Des Flandres."

"Never heard of them."

"I think they are an extraordinary breed. I would love to see one lying by your woodstove."

"But. . . ."

"I know. You don't like dogs."

"I really don't."

"You don't like men who try to make you own one, either."

"Well . . ."

His laugh rang out.

Mary was genuinely sorry to see that they had already reached her house. Now she would be alone again.

"There you are," Arthur said, pulling back on the reins, turning the buggy wheels slightly to the right. Then, to tease her, he asked, "What's for supper?"

Mary stepped down and reached under the seat for her book bag and lunchbox. A thought pulsed through her head. She weighed the cold and the loneliness, the homesickness and fear of her walk to school, versus Arthur's face, his laugh, his big, solid strength that made a house warm and secure.

"I was thinking of making shoofly pie tonight. I have some rice and chicken I was going to make into soup."

"Do you mind very much if I invite myself for the shoofly pie? I have often heard of it but never tasted it."

"No, you can help. Or, I mean, I'll cook supper." Flustered, losing efficiency, she stumbled.

"Be right back." He drove home in record time, and Mary changed clothes because he had never seen her wear this mint green dress. She combed her hair, telling herself it didn't matter if she was a bit disheveled, and brushed her teeth because she always brushed them when she got home from school. Well, at bedtime, anyway.

Her cheeks were red, her freckles danced across her nose in anticipation, but she told herself that tonight she would ask him in complete honesty about the girl in the photograph at his house. She would finally do it.

All evening she planned on it. When she measured the all-purpose flour, Crisco, soda, and salt, when she mixed the pie dough with her hands and rolled it out with the wooden rolling pin, she meant to ask him. She spooned out brown sugar, counted eggs, and measured molasses, hot water, and baking soda. Arthur mixed the crumbs—the flour, brown sugar, and butter for the top of the pie—and all that while she truly meant to ask about the girl.

When the three pie crusts were rolled out perfectly, the wet ingredients divided among the unbaked crusts, the crumbs piled high on top, and the full pies put carefully into the oven, Mary's small house was filled with the wonderful aroma of baking molasses and brown sugar and pie dough.

She made a delicious chicken rice soup, and they ate it with chunks of good Swiss cheese, olives, and homemade Lebanon bologna she had shipped from home. She heated leftover dinner rolls and melted pats of butter across their tops. Arthur had laughed at Mary when she said she was just simply going to give up and make a sandwich. Arthur said he'd love to have some applesauce, that he always cooled his soup with saltines and applesauce, if that was okay.

She meant to ask him after the pies were finished baking and taken from the oven. She really did.

After the pies had cooled, she cut each one into fourths, then served him a wedge on one of her Corelle dishes. She sat down, watching his face eagerly as he took the first bite. She smiled when he savored it slowly, then giggled like a bashful schoolgirl when he rolled his eyes and said it was the best thing he'd ever eaten.

Even if it was an eight-inch pie, it was a bit frightening that he ate the whole thing. But then she guessed chicken rice soup was not very filling for a man his size, even with saltines and applesauce.

The house was warm from the oven's heat, as well as the crackling woodstove. Arthur chewed on a toothpick as he washed dishes at the small sink, leaving no room for her to dry them. He was so slow. His hands were so big they almost filled the sink. He added far too much dish soap and didn't rinse them clean enough, but Mary didn't say anything. She waited politely till he was done washing, then slipped into the small sink alcove, dried the dishes quickly, and put them away.

He sat on the sofa, dwarfing it. She stood uncertainly, aware of her size nine shoes, her hands hanging

awkwardly by her sides. He said he hated the thought
of going home. Mary blushed but busied herself back
at the sink rearranging dish towels absentmindedly.
She would ask him now.

Arthur looked out the window behind the couch
and said he believed it was snowing. Then, because it
was so unbearably cozy and lovely to have him here,
with the snow falling on the roof and the edges of the
porch, and the smoke from the woodstove reaching
up through the tiny snowflakes into the cold and the
dark and the wind, she knew she could not do this
again. She was not going to make a habit of enter-
taining someone else's man.

So she said very loud and clear, "Well, it's my bedtime."

"Are you asking me to leave?"

"Yes."

"Really? Don't you want to play a game of Upwords?"

"Upwords? You play Upwords?"

"I do."

"I don't know one man who enjoys that game."

"Well, now you do."

They brought out the card table and set up the plastic board game. Each reached for seven tiles and the game began.

Mary's competitive streak bordered closely on poor sportsmanship, which made Arthur chuckle constantly, inflaming her temper. When he won by quite a wide margin, she said it was because it was her bedtime and she had asked him to leave and he didn't. She was tired and not thinking right.

He got up and prepared to leave, still smiling. She could not bear to see him go, so she said if he wanted, she'd make him a cup of coffee. He watched her face quizzically and asked why.

"Well, I . . ." Then she stopped.

He waited.

Headlong without thinking, she dived into the turbulent waters of the unknown. "Arthur, I'm guilty."

"Of what?"

"I feel as if I shouldn't be spending these evenings with you. It's not right."

"What are you talking about?"

She was too ashamed to tell him, too ashamed to stop midway.

"I know you'll think less of me, but you must know this. I picked up a photograph of . . . of your friend. Your girlfriend."

Miserably, she hung her head. There were her feet, as big and obnoxious as always. Oh, why had she even started this? What made her think Arthur ever harbored any feelings for her?

Slowly, Arthur breathed out. All the creases in his eyes disappeared, and they became large and sad and very dark blue.

What he said, was, "Bring the coffee to the living room," and went to sit at one end of the sofa, his eyes unfathomable, brooding.

So now he was angry. She had done something so grievously wrong that his good-natured laugh was silenced to this moody stillness.

Quietly, Mary placed a mug of coffee on a coaster at his elbow. Softly, she sat at the opposite end of the couch, clinging to the rounded, brown arm. She lifted the mug silently to her lips, her eyes averted, unable to watch the great change in his face any longer.

"Mary, I don't have a girlfriend. Only a memory of her."

Mary waited. The snow pinged against the windowpane. The wind rattled the loose trim on the corner of the small house.

"I guess that explains your strange behavior," Arthur said gruffly.

Mary stared at her shoes. His girlfriend had told him off and broken the relationship, and he would never love again. Some men were like that.

"Well," Mary justified herself.

"No need to explain. I understand. Absolutely."

"I don't want you to think that I am thinking of you in a . . . uh . . . you know." Mary spread her hands, a great painful blush hiding her freckles. She was glad for the wan light from the kitchen. Then, because she did not know what to do or say, she got up, went to the refrigerator, opened the milk bottle and poured more milk into her coffee cup. She stirred it busily, her eyes lowered.

Arthur remained quiet, watching her.

When no words were forthcoming, Mary realized his kind heart, and since she believed he did not want to hurt her, he said nothing at all.

She knew, also, that by speaking to him in that fashion, she had shamelessly thrown herself at his feet. And he did not want her. He had never spoken to her in any romantic way or shown that he was remotely attracted to her. His kindness, that gentleness that radiated from him, was all he felt for her. It was the same feeling he had for every single person who knew him.

An obstruction built in her throat, the beginning of her defeat that would evolve into a sob, the epitome of weakness. Swallowing, she drew up the emotional shield she used so handily to protect the matters of her heart. She sat back down on the couch.

"Arthur, I was thinking of going home for Thanksgiving. I think this evening helped me to make up my mind. I will go home. I have failed here and been mauled by wild dogs, and I want to go back to Pennsylvania. I miss my parents, my way of life. I'm going back. I can never make it here." She was babbling now, a sort of incoherence flavoring her words with panic.

"You didn't allow me to finish my story."

"Well, Arthur, that's all right. You don't have to finish it. I know what you want to say, but you don't have to. I understand."

He rose from the couch and stood directly in front of her. Then he did something so alarming, so completely out of his character, that Mary gasped. He lowered his face and put a hand over her mouth.

"Be quiet. You're not making any sense at all."

Mary sat back.

"Oh, you!" Her fingers clenched into fists as she let the anger and hurt, the disappointment and remorse blaze from her eyes. "Just go home, Arthur. Go home and leave me alone. I was perfectly all right before this. I could always manage my life on my own."

"You did not give me time to explain about the photograph. You've been so busy telling me you're going home, that you have everything under control."

"Well, I do—have everything under control, I mean."

She was surprised when Arthur began to laugh.

"Yes, you do, Mary. You always do. Only your life is a mess where one thing is concerned. But the time to explain that to you is not now. So I'll go home. I'm bringing the dog tomorrow evening. I don't have time to bundle you back and forth every day to and from school."

He got his big, black corduroy coat down from the hook by the doorway and shrugged into it.

"I don't want that dog!" Mary screeched.

Arthur said very firmly, "You're getting him though. If you don't, your life is in danger."

He closed the door with a firm click.

Mary yanked the door open and called after his retreating figure, "I am going back home!"

He kept walking, spreading his hands and lifting his shoulders in an expression of complete nonchalance.

Oh, he made her so angry! She stepped back and gave the door a good hard slam.

Sure enough, the following evening, after she had made two terrifying walks to and from school, the dog arrived. He could be clipped, Bob explained. It would alter his appearance, but then she could see his eyes.

Mary nodded tersely, her mouth a thin line of distaste. She acknowledged the dog's presence by a mere look, then went to get her checkbook. Bob held out his hands, palms in front of him, and explained that the payment was taken care of. He wasted no time walking to his truck, turning it around and rattling away.

Mary inserted one forefinger somewhere around the region of the dog's neck, tentatively exploring for a collar. She came up with one made of intricate braided leather.

"Well, dog, I hope you like woodsheds, because that is where you'll be," she said, hoping he understood the efficiency with which she rid herself of Arthur and fully planned to do with him.

He would be a sort of mechanical dog to her. A robot. Eat food and drink water. Live in shed. Walk to school. Protect teacher.

"Come on."

Immediately, the obedient dog followed her to the door of the woodshed, stood patiently while she opened the door, then trotted inside, sniffing the ground floor, the pieces of bark scattered about, the rich smell of wood and sawdust.

"Here you are, dog. Your new home."

The only thing that made Mary feel bad was the biting cold. If he was a house dog, he'd freeze out here. She went to the house, debated a long time, but finally chose the knotted flannel comforter her mother had given her. She did not like the dog, but cruelty to animals was another category entirely.

When she reappeared, the dog took a step forward, as if asking permission to enter the house.

"No. This is your domain, dog. Outside. Out."

She placed the comforter on the wooden floor, flinched at the cold shed, placed his food and water a comfortable distance away, and commanded, "Lie down." The dog gave her a long look, at least that's what it felt like he was doing, then lay down obediently. She got out quickly, latching the door firmly.

She got ready for bed, first enjoying a hot shower and then a cup of hot chocolate, and felt only a twinge of guilt. This is Montana, dog. Grow up. You'll run me to school, so you'll get warmed up.

She went to bed, lost herself in the deep mound of warm covers, shifted to a comfortable position, and lay sleepless.

Of course he was warm enough, she told herself. He'd bark if he got too cold. But what if he was shivering? Cold was so harsh, so cruel. Suppose he was out there crying? Would she hear? Finally she got up, pulled on a pair of boots, clasped her bathrobe around her waist and ventured out to the woodshed.

When she opened the door, the beam of her flashlight found the big dog lying on top of the comforter, shivering uncontrollably.

"Dog!" Mary exclaimed. She was so upset. She had never planned to be cruel.

She had a notion to go right up the hill to Arthur and deliver the dog right back to him. The thought of her morning walk to school was the only thing that changed her mind.

So what was she to do? Having everything under control meant doing things her way. She did not want to give in to letting a dog—and a big, black, hairy one at that—into her clean house.

Going to the dog, she bent over and gave him a small push. If only he'd crawl between the folds of the comforter, he'd warm up. "Get off, dog. Up. Get up!"

Mary lifted a corner of the blanket. The dog rose, shivering miserably. He stood uncertainly, then laid down again on top of the comforter.

"Stupid dog. Then just be cold."

Mary went back to bed, telling herself he would get warm by himself. But she slept fitfully and woke up tired with a pounding headache above one eye that lasted all day.

The schoolchildren made such a fuss that Mary had a hard time restoring order. They petted the dog, they clipped the hair away from his eyes, they braided some of the hair on his tail and told her he had to have a name.

Blackie. Fred. Barney. Leo. Sam.

Finally, Mary said they could each write one name on a slip of paper, then put them all in a box and she would draw one. It was the only fair way she knew to do it.

Sam. That was the name written on the paper that Mary chose, so Sam he was.

Mary strode home, the dog on a leash, trotting by her side. She could see his eyes now, as black as his hair, inquisitive, searching the roadside, lifting his nose to any new or unusual scents.

It was worrisome, the amount of dog food she'd need. Where in this remote county did one go about procuring dog food? She knew how far away the closest Walmart was, and she couldn't pay around a hundred dollars for dog food at one time.

She left Arthur a terse message, and he left her one a few hours later. "The feed man will deliver it for you, Mary. Here's their number. Have a good evening." So typical of him. Didn't that man have a mean bone in his body? He was as guileless as a sheep.

So she ordered dog food and fought with herself about Sam's sleeping accommodations. When the wind moaned around the edges of the house, Mary peered at the thermometer attached to the window. Surely not five degrees and falling! It was barely the end of November. Well, she could not leave the dog by himself in

Linda Byler

the shed. That was all there was to it. But she could not let him sleep in the house without a bath either.

Grimly, she opened the door to find Sam cowering beneath the rustic porch chair, his black coat powdered with a dusting of windblown snow, shivering again. Holding the door wide, Mary said, "Come on, Sam."

The big dog raised himself to his feet, looked at Mary quizzically, then trotted past her into the small kitchen. Never hesitating, he went straight to the woodstove and lay down beside it.

"No, dog—I mean, Sam—you can't do that."

She spent the rest of the evening getting him into the small bathtub and persuading him to stay there, then using half a bottle of shampoo with a scrub brush, and finally half-drowning the sorrowful creature with a rinse from the shower.

The bathroom floor was soaked, and Mary's dress and apron were sodden. She had used two whole towels to dry all that hair, and he still smelled like a dog.

Mary sighed, knowing she could not put herself through that again. Sam was as clean as he was ever going to be.

She checked the area around the stove for stray dog hair but saw none. She almost got out her small gold magnifying glass to make sure, then decided against it. That was too overboard, as her pupils would say.

Sam explored the small house and examined each corner, sniffing at chairs and rugs and the small refrigerator set into the oak cupboards. When he licked a spot on the linoleum, Mary scolded him, saying, "No, Sam, don't do that." She opened a drawer and pulled out an old rag, wet it with soap and water, then rubbed vigorously.

Dogs were just not pleasant things to have in the house. She scoured the bathtub with Clorox bleach twice before she had her shower, searching everywhere for signs of hidden dog hair.

She spread an old rug by the door and set the dog food and water on it. She figured she could wash it every week, as she certainly could not put up with dog slobber, now, could she?

Sam settled down by the stove and closed his eyes. Outside, the wind shifted the snow into uneven drifts. The cold crept around the corners of the house, and Sam laid his massive head on his paws that had been washed with shampoo and conditioner, as he watched his new mistress with sad eyes.

Sam marked his territory around the small house, the roadside, and the schoolhouse, the way dogs do. And when the pack of wild dogs came near, they swerved around it, a small but meaningful obstacle on their way to slaughtering more animals.

Mary lay sleeping, unaware of the way of nature and dogs. She had come to the conclusion that it was a very good thing she was going home, rather than having to live with this dog she had no feelings for. The same went for Arthur.

Bossy man.

Chapter Seven

THE THANKSGIVING GET-TOGETHER AT SCHOOL was long anticipated, the children eager to give their parents a tour around the classroom, showing their artwork and stories they had written. Mary had baked eight shoofly pies. That was her contribution to the many dishes that would arrive.

She dressed carefully, wearing brown, which she thought was a Thanksgiving color. She paid special attention to her hair and wore her new, white Sunday covering.

She loaded the pies onto the sled in a cardboard box tied down with a piece of string, got into her coat and boots, pulled on her gloves, and looked at Sam. *Ach,* she'd leave him at home. He'd be underfoot, sniffing at the food and getting in the way, and she was pretty sure there were plenty of mothers who did not want a big black dog in the classroom.

Sam rose, eager for the leash. He bounced playfully, then held his head to one side, unable to understand.

"Stay, Sam."

He whined softly.

"*Ach,* you're spoiled. Well, you'll have to stay in the shed at school."

Sam trotted ahead while Mary pulled the sled with one hand, looping the leash around the other.

The air was gray and heavy, the atmosphere damp and bone-chilling. She should have worn a bonnet, but it would have smashed her new covering.

With Sam to accompany her, Mary no longer watched the line of brush and trees or the surrounding countryside. She felt protected, trusting Sam to keep her safe, so it was a bit of a shock to feel the leash in her hand go slack.

Sam stopped. Mary's eyes moved from left to right. The old fear rose in her chest, suffocating her till she fought down the panic-stricken feeling.

"What, Sam?" Sam stood erect, his forelegs

perfectly aligned, his back legs bent powerfully, his ears lifted.

Mary felt the scream forming and lost all sense of reason when she saw the low, undulating line of movement behind the grove of aspens to her right.

"No! No! Oh please, God, no!"

She dropped the string attached to the sled, then turned and ran blindly, slipping and sliding, falling, getting back to her feet, and sobbing hysterically.

Sam could not hold off the entire pack. What had Bob said? Six of them?

She ran on. She stepped on hidden ice, her knee hitting a rock as she went down hard. Pain exploded through her leg, but she rose to her feet and kept going.

Through the panic, she caught sight of her house. Would she make it before the dogs overtook her? The thought of jaws tearing at her flesh spurred her on. Her lungs were flames of pain, her breath coming in short spurts. Her ribs ached, but her feet kept pounding down on the snow.

She threw herself on the small brown porch, then turned to see if Sam had followed. Why wasn't he barking? Oh, the vicious dogs would tear him to pieces. She had deserted him, too selfish to think of anything but herself. It had been her only thought. Poor, poor Sam.

She listened. In the distance, the baying of the dogs could be heard plainly. Mary gripped the porch post, hanging onto it as tears of gratitude rained down her face. *Denke, Herr. Denke.*

Immediately, a sense of terrible shame came on her. Sam would be torn apart. He'd be bait for them. Should she try and go to him? Or call Arthur?

The baying sound remained the same, rising and falling. Why didn't Sam bark? Had they already killed him? Sam was large and powerful, but no dog could outlast six others, especially not these seasoned killers.

Unsure, Mary stayed by the porch post, watching, listening. She heard a buggy rattling by and saw Arthur's black horse. Oh, now he'd find the sled and the pies. What if the dogs had gotten Sam? Heartsick, Mary went inside, dropped onto a kitchen chair, then got up and flung open the door, as if she could see Arthur's approach.

What should she do? The parents and schoolchildren would be arriving, and she was not there. Well, this was a situation that called for calm measures, so the first thing was to realize that she was safe. And thankful. The second thing was the fact that she did care very much about Sam, which was fortunate, since she'd be here till Christmas, now that she'd decided to stay for Thanksgiving.

Oh, what was this? Sam!

"Oh, Sam! Come on, boy! Get up here! Come on!" Mary yelled, slapping her knees, then lowering herself to hug the cold, panting dog. She clung to his neck, smelled the dog smell of his black coat, and thought it didn't smell nearly as bad as she always thought.

"Good dog! Good, brave, wonderful dog!" She followed him inside and fed him a few slices of her best ham, the kind that cost $5.99 a pound at the Amish bulk food store. "Sam, you drove them off! You did!"

Sam gobbled up the ham, his eyes holding an expression of dog joy, as Mary bent to kiss the top of his head. She told him again what a brave dog he was. She took off her coat and her covering and went to the bathroom to fix her hair. Red strands had come loose and hung sloppily over her forehead.

Ugh. Sometimes it would be nice to have a different view in the mirror. Always those freckles, topped by the carroty hair. Her hands were too unsteady to draw the fine-toothed comb through it, so she sat down on the edge of the tub and took a steadying breath.

Would Arthur find the shoofly pies? The sled? It was all right that he wouldn't care. She had accepted the fact that his heart belonged to the memory of the girl in the photograph. She would be going home for Christmas, perhaps to stay. She planned on making the announcement at school after the Thanksgiving dinner was eaten.

She combed her hair, then set the new white covering carefully on top, tied it neatly, and turned to leave the bathroom, when the door leading to the porch was yanked open from outside. Mary gasped when Arthur Bontrager stood in the doorway, his face as white as chalk, calling "Mary!" in a terrible voice.

"Oh, my! What is it, Arthur?"

When he caught sight of her, his shoulders dropped as relief washed across his features. Color followed immediately, and quick tears made the ice blue diamonds in his eyes shimmer.

"Mary! There you are."

"What happened?"

"I came on the sled in the middle of the road, that's what happened. You or your dog were nowhere about. What was I supposed to think?" His voice was hoarse with emotion, his face working.

"Well, my goodness," Mary said, coolly.

"Oh, okay, Mary. You can stand there and say that. You have no idea what it's like when you care about someone, now, do you?"

What had gotten into him? This was Arthur? Laughing, easygoing Arthur? Oh, it was the dog, Sam. He'd paid two thousand dollars for him. Well, of course he cared about Sam.

"Arthur, Sam is okay. He held off the dogs, I think."

"What dogs?"

"The dogs. The pack of six. They were off a ways to the right behind that grove of aspens. I sort of lost my common sense and ran. I ran home. But Sam came soon afterward. I mean, of course you care. You paid a lot of money for him."

Arthur lowered his head to wipe his shoes on the rug inside the door. Two steps and he confronted Mary. He placed his large heavy hands on her shoulders and said in a gruff voice barely above a whisper, "I didn't mean Sam, I meant you. You, Mary. I care very much what happens to you."

His eyes never left her startled, wide green ones. As the color left her face, her brown freckles stood out in stark contrast.

Arthur lifted his hand, touched her freckled nose, lightly, and said, barely above a whisper, "Someday, I want to kiss every one of your freckles. But since you are who you are, I can wait." Instantly, his mood changed. He became lighthearted, bantering like the old Arthur she knew.

She put on her coat, her feet firmly encased among clouds. Stardust flipped and somersaulted through the air when she lifted her arms to button her coat. She almost fainted with the beauty of his words as she bent to put on her boots. When she straightened and Arthur looked into her eyes, she heard the strains of the singing she had always longed for and never found.

The Thanksgiving get-together went very well. The parents, all seven pairs of them, plus Arthur, brought so much food, the ping-pong table in the center of the room groaned with weight.

The brown paper turkeys and orange pumpkins on the wall, the poetry the children recited, the songs they sang, were all very festive. John Weaver read a special story about the Indians and Pilgrims, causing a few of the women to weep openly.

Mary moved among the people, held babies, complimented the mothers' cooking, and felt very much a part of them. Here she was, the owl among pigeons, with her heart-shaped covering and her black apron, but now there was a difference. She was an accepted owl, an honored one, she might add. She felt her place in the community keenly. She was a necessary item, part of the wheel that kept everyone together.

The ministers were the hub of the wheel, but she was one of the bolts that kept the spokes intact.

She was a teacher and a good one. She knew that. She knew a problem school sometimes lacked the voice of experience. Most folks were good-hearted, temperate, if you worked in love and understanding.

When Kenny Yoder came up to her and shook her hand, his narrow face beaming with kindness, Mary faced him squarely, taking his hand firmly. "You know, I really don't know how you do it. I have never heard my boys say they like school, and certainly not the teacher. You're amazing. They must train teachers in Lancaster."

"Oh, no. We have our share of problems. I've been a teacher for twelve years and learned by trial and error." They were interrupted by his wife, Ella Mae, a thin hawkish woman who always scared the daylights out of Mary.

"Thank you, Mary, for the good dinner."

"Wasn't me!" Mary laughed.

Ella Mae smiled. "Thank you, too, for what you do for the boys."

Flowery words of praise followed, falling easily on Mary's accepting ears. My goodness, this was the problem couple?

She tapped the small bell to get everyone's attention, then made her announcement in a clear, precise tone. She was going home for Christmas, perhaps to stay. A chorus of disbelief, a proclamation of denial, began as a murmur, then rose and swelled around her until she dropped her shoulders, raised her eyebrows, and lifted her hands in a questioning gesture.

Dave Troyer stood up. "Hey, the captain never leaves his ship."

Paul Weaver rose to his feet. "Come on, Mary. What is it? More pay? Homesick? The cold? What it is, we'll fix it."

Mary laughed, hiding the real reason from prying eyes. No, they could not fix her dilemma. For almost an hour, Mary had believed Arthur's startling words, but then she began her usual train of negative thoughts until she convinced herself that Arthur was a flirt. He didn't want her. No man ever had, no man ever would. How could they? She was nothing. Her feet were huge and flat and white, and they even had a few freckles on them. Her arms were too long and skinny, her hands big and ungainly, her hair red as fire, the freckles the sparks from it.

Many times, Mam had told her that looks has nothing to do with it. Huh-uh, Mam. Looks do have something to do with it. How many times had she been attracted to young men, even the homeliest, the least popular, and never once had one of them asked the question? Always, always, they turned to normal looking young girls with brown hair or black. With nice figures and small feet and personalities that entertained them.

She had prayed for fifteen years. She firmly believed that God controlled matters of the heart. He wrote our faith, like an author, and He finished the story, just the way the Bible said. So, it was ultimately up to God, and Mary finally figured out that she was meant to be alone.

Why, other than red hair and unfortunate freckles, was she alone? Because God wanted her to be.

That was why. So Arthur Bontrager would just have to go fly a kite.

She steadied her shoulders, dipped her head, acknowledged the praise and the begging to stay, but her eyes shimmered with unshed tears, and never once did she acknowledge Arthur's presence. She knew where he was sitting, when he moved, how easily he talked and laughed, how he was the center of attention so much of the time.

The children crowded around her after the announcement. Little Lila Mae, the first-grader, hugged Mary hard, lifted her sweet face with blue eyes as guileless as—okay, as guileless as Arthur's—and lisped, "Right, Teacher, it's not true? You'll go home for Christmas, but you'll be back? Right?"

Mary drew the little girl onto her lap, hugged her, held her sweet body against her own, and whispered, "I'll tell you a secret, if you don't tell anyone else."

Eagerly, Lila Mae nodded.

"I'm going home for Christmas. Then when I'm there, I'll see how I feel. I'll pray long and hard so God can show me the way."

"Good idea." Satisfied, she strained against Mary's arms, slid off her lap, and went to join her classmates.

Alone in the schoolroom, the afternoon fading to evening as the steel-gray turned darker by the minute, Mary hummed as she swept the floor. She smiled as she got down the dust pan and brush and whistled softly as she dumped the dirt into the trash can.

She was going home! Four more weeks, and she'd be home for Christmas. The phone calls and letters she received were only a stand-in, barely sufficient to stave off her homesickness. Now she could count the days, marking the calendar with big Xs like a child.

Her walk home was uneventful with Sam trotting obediently by her side, the leash coiled and lying on the sled. Neither of them needed it. This faithful dog was so loyal, it was almost pitiful.

Mary did keep her eyes trained on the road ahead of her to hold the fear and panic at bay. She realized Sam would stop if there was danger. Repeatedly he would dash into the brush, then back out. She'd never seen a dog who had to relieve himself so much. Maybe he had a kidney disease. She'd have to ask Arthur. He'd know. Or, she wouldn't, on second thought. She would not have Arthur in her life at all. It was far easier.

On Thanksgiving Day she was alone. There was no school. She slept late, stretched luxuriously, and put a small chicken in the oven that she had stuffed with cornbread stuffing. She ate a huge breakfast of pancakes, sausage, and scrambled eggs. She wished she had orange juice, but in these parts, if you were out of something, you were simply out of it. If you wanted orange juice, you had to have the good sense to buy frozen concentrate.

She sipped her coffee, then moved to the living room. When Sam rose to follow her, she tried not to wince, but tried instead to convince herself that he really did not shed dog hair all over her house. He didn't smell like a dog. Well, not much anyway. And he was a good companion. Mary reached down to ruffle his ears and was rewarded with a look of total and absolute devotion.

"Good Sam. Good dog," Mary said softly, then looked around, feeling silly for giving her love and praise to a dog. It was so not her.

When the chicken was tender, she made gravy and opened a can of beans. She didn't feel like peeling, cooking, and mashing potatoes. She was hungry for baked beans, so she ate them with the chicken, made a cup of tea, and then flopped on the recliner to read *The Connection*. When she fell asleep after a few pages, Sam laid his head on his paws and closed his eyes as well.

Outside, the snow finally began to fall. The world around the primitive little cabin turned from a white gray to a gray that was steadily overtaken by darkness, so when the snow began to drift down, no one knew unless they were outside. It was a deep, quiet night, the snowflakes whispering softly as they fell to the ground, covering the aspens, the pines, and cedars.

When Mary awoke, the clock's hands pointed to the seven and nine. Dark already, she thought, and not yet seven o'clock. Suddenly the evening stretched before her, long and cold and lonesome. A sense of melancholy wrapped itself around her like a smothering blanket, a feeling she did not understand. She felt almost like she had entered a void, reminding her of how parents and school board members often described the experience of a troubled child.

Sometimes the parents' misdeeds or their lack of caring created a void. Well, she'd certainly not suffered neglect from her family. She'd grown up in a world where she never questioned her parents' absolute love and concern.

She'd just take care of this senseless depression immediately and get herself to work. The foot rest of the recliner slapped down, startling Sam, who leaped to his feet, eyeing Mary uncertainly. She ignored him and went to her desk to get her pale blue stationery and her best black ink pen. Then she hustled to the small kitchen table, took off the pen's cap, put it on the opposite end of the pen, but instead of writing, began to chew on it. Who would she write to?

She had spoken to her mother and to Rachel yesterday. Liz was too wrapped up in her wedding plans. Good thing Elam didn't want to get married till spring. Otherwise, she'd have to go to Pennsylvania in November, when all the weddings, or at least half of them, took place.

Weddings. She always made a necessary appearance, but almost nothing in her life was harder, except perhaps a funeral. She was a master of deceit, she supposed. She listened to the sermon and was glad all day, happy for Elsie or Barbara or Anna or Rebecca. They each deserved a good husband.

Buried deep in her heart, she wondered how it would feel to stand beside a young man, hold his hand in front of the bishop, and pronounce the quiet, "*Ya*," that sacred promise to care for him in sickness and health, for richer or for poorer.

She would gladly have had any one of them. Reuben King was the first one she thought might ask her. He didn't. After he married her best friend, Sadie Zook, she figured probably Leroy Beiler would, the way he spoke to her whenever he had a chance. In the end, Leroy had used her to see if Edna Stoltzfus would go with him.

On and on, the story of her life. She accepted it now. But when sadness entered her life, could she honestly say there was no void? There wasn't supposed to be. God filled hearts and minds with His great unending love. Many girls were blessed beyond measure by staying single. Even the Apostle Paul said it was better to remain unmarried to serve the Lord more fully.

She knew some of the girls she was acquainted with wanted to remain single. But she honestly could not feel she was completely happy being single. But since when? She had been content in Lancaster County. She never thought much about men or marriage. Teaching fulfilled her, she believed.

Laying down her pen, she folded her thin arms on the table top and sighed. The soft hissing of the lamp faded away, then returned when she lifted her head and put up both hands to rest her chin in the cupped palms.

How hard would it be to leave Montana? She thought of never seeing Arthur Bontrager again and figured it was perfectly possible to leave Montana, knowing that meant she'd live the rest of her life without seeing him. She'd forget about him if she never heard his laugh. She'd forget his stubby nose and creases around his eyes. She'd forget all that nonsense he didn't even mean, like caring about her and. . . .

Well, now that was unthinkable, what he'd said about her freckles. She could feel the color suffuse her cheeks. *Ach,* I should not have come. I should have stayed home in good, old fast-paced Ronks, Pennsylvania. Out here there's too much time to think. The sky is too big and the mountains are too high and there is snow on top of them . . . the aspens turn yellow and the wolves howl and I want to live in Arthur's beautiful log house with all the windows that need to be washed.

For one instant she let the sweet truth fill her heart, but only for one instant.

Chapter Eight

MARY THREW HERSELF INTO HER SCHOOLWORK. The children were the fortunate recipients of every available skill she could muster. They studied for her pop quizzes, learned new Christmas songs, wrote their own poetry, and decorated the classroom with all the clever artwork they could create.

The snow was deep and beautiful, drifted high in some hollows and blown across windswept grades. The view from the schoolhouse was breathtaking— the pines, mountains, and vast, rolling acres of snow dotted with black cattle.

Mary and the schoolchildren decided that if a school Christmas play was so unpopular, they'd have an evening hymn sing. The children could recite poems if they wanted to, but they didn't need to. Everyone would sing together.

They'd finish with snacks—coffee and hot chocolate, Christmas cookies, homemade candy, snack mix, fruit desserts, and puddings, whatever families wanted to bring.

The children would wear red or green. They suggested Mary wear red, too. They were all seated around the woodstove eating their lunches and planning the Christmas festivities.

"No, I can't wear red!"

"Why not?"

Mary laughed. "I'd be red all over. Red hair, red freckles, red dress, red shoes."

"Not red shoes!" hooted little Andy, the second-grader.

"They'd shine red," Mary said.

"When do you have to go home?"

"Two days before Christmas. We'll have the Christmas singing and then I'll go back to my home near Lancaster."

"What does your house look like?"

"I already told you."

"Tell us again."

It seemed as if the children never tired of hearing about her life in Pennsylvania.

"Bet you didn't have a dog!" Betty, a seventh-grader, said.

"Oh, my goodness! Of course not!"

"Betty, she didn't need one."

"Nope. No wild dog packs in Ronks. They'd be smashed flat on the highway."

She had to explain about all the traffic again, then told the children she really didn't miss it anymore, but everyone went home for Christmas. That is what tradition required.

"But you're coming back, right?"

When Mary didn't answer immediately, the upper-graders raised their eyebrows. Betty giggled.

"What?" Mary asked sharply.

"You'll be back."

Why is it that children sometimes appear even more perceptive than adults? Mary had often experienced wise remarks coming from the sweet, guileless lips of a fifth-grader that put a situation in perspective. So, because she was afraid of where the covert glances would lead, and finding safety in the haven of denial, she dropped the subject.

On Sunday, she skipped church services because she had a bit of a headache and a scratch in her throat. The wood fire was out at six o'clock that morning, the ashes gray and dead without one red spark. How irritating.

Mary slammed the cast iron door hard, shivered, then turned and leaped back into bed. Drawing the covers over her head, she coughed and went back to sleep.

A few hours later her nose felt much like an icicle, her hip hurt, and shivers chased themselves up her back and down her arms. She knew a fever was coming on. Good thing she decided to stay home from church. The room spun when she sat up, so she flopped back on the pillows, groaning.

She hoped Dave Mast got her message on their voicemail and wouldn't drive the extra miles to pick her up for church. But when she heard a sharp rapping sound on the door, she groaned again. Her head felt twice as big as it should be. The floor tilted to the right, then to the left, as she slung her heavy fleece bathrobe around her shoulders, slipped her feet into the ratty men's moccasins, and shuffled to the door.

Dismay grabbed her when she saw Arthur standing on the porch dressed in his Sunday suit, the heavy black wool overcoat making him appear even bigger. He filled the small, ramshackle porch.

Oh, no.

"Hey, Mary. Good morning."

Mary could not say anything. She was dumbfounded.

"I didn't see any smoke all morning and was afraid there was something wrong."

Mary shook her head.

Arthur asked if she was all right because her face looked flushed. She admitted she was coming down with the flu.

"Your fire's out, isn't it?"

"No. Well, yes, sort of." She just wanted him off that porch, in his buggy, and on his way to church.

"I can start the fire for you."

"No. You'll be late for church."

"You don't feel well at all, right?" he asked, leaning closer to look at her face. The dim morning light revealed flushed, feverish cheeks and two bright eyes.

"Just the flu."

"I'll start the fire."

"No. I can take care of myself."

When he knew she meant it, he said all right, then. Mary breathed a sigh of relief when he turned and left. She needed to barricade herself from him. He had no business knocking on her door, catching her unprepared, looking her worst with the flu and all.

She yelped in disbelief when she looked angrily in the mirror. Puffy eyes, brilliant freckles, white skin, cold sores breaking out on chapped lips, and her hair in the same despicable morning state it always was. The brilliant hue of her fleece bathrobe only served as a reflector to enhance the apparition that was her face.

She was sleeping in the recliner, covered with every cotton throw and fleece blanket she owned, when Arthur's knock interrupted her fitful dreaming.

Frightened and disoriented, she threw back the load of covers and was instantly assaulted by the cold air in the room. Shivering, her teeth chattered uncontrollably as she yanked open the door. She bit down hard on her lower lip to stop the trembling and peered at Arthur with feverish eyes.

"Mary, you are really sick."

When she shook her head, he grasped her shoulders and set her aside like an annoying piece of furniture. "I'm coming in."

Sam rose to meet him, his tail wagging, his eyes glad.

"How's it going, Sam? Huh?" Arthur dropped to his knees, ruffled the dog's ears, scratched his back, smoothed the thick black hair, and told him what a good dog he was, as Mary made her way back to the recliner and rolled herself back into all the blankets.

Arthur shrugged off his overcoat, rolled up the sleeves of his white shirt, opened the door of the woodstove, peered inside, and shook his head. The house was freezing, and there she was—very ill and as obstinate as ever.

He chopped kindling, crumpled newspaper, held a lighter to it, and was rewarded by a small flame that licked greedily at the dry kindling. He filled the red tea kettle, flicked on the burner, then looked at the pile of blankets that housed Mary somewhere in the middle.

He made a cup of comfrey tea, grilled a slice of bread in the skillet, spread butter on it, and walked to the recliner, bearing the lunch on a tray.

"Mary?" He said her name softly, like a question.

From deep beneath the covers, he heard a distinct, "Go away."

"I can't, Mary. You're very sick."

Suddenly, the covers were thrown back, and disheveled, shivering Mary emerged. Her eyes sparking angrily, and between chattering teeth, she spoke in halting words. "Yeah, I've been sick before. Just leave me alone. I'll be fine."

Arthur looked at the roaring stove. He walked over and shut the bottom door, latched it, threw on two chunks of split wood, clapped his hands to rid them of sawdust, and said to the wall, "You will not be fine."

Then he turned, his ice blue eyes wide, his annoyance turning them darker by the second. "I am not going away. I'm going to stay right here with you until you are able to be up and take care of this fire. It is my duty. So don't go off on a high horse saying how fine you are. You obviously aren't."

Holding the cup to her lips, he said, "Drink."

"Stop treating me like a child."

"Drink."

"My mouth hurts too much."

Bending, Arthur saw the painful blisters on both sides of her upper lip. He placed the palm of his hand on her forehead and gave a low whistle. He went into the bathroom and rummaged around, banging things, then emerged with a tube of cold sore medication, a bottle of Tylenol, and a hot water bottle.

She swallowed the pills obediently, applied the cold sore salve, then lay back and threw the covers over her head. When Arthur returned with the sloshing hot water bottle, he lifted the blankets from her head and asked if she was still breathing in there.

She glared at him, but when his eyes flattened, all the creases appeared in his tanned face, and his stubby nose widened, her glare turned to something softer. Her face showed insecurity. She was no longer safely within her circle of mustered up courage. A very small smile appeared, and she self-consciously lifted two fingers to hide the hideous blisters.

"Sit forward."

She obliged, and he slid the warm bottle behind her.

"Your lower back aches, doesn't it?"

"How do you know?" she snapped, angry that he would take the liberty of thinking he knew how she felt.

"Oh, flu does that. Makes your back hurt. Can you sit forward a bit more?"

He placed the hot water bottle on the exact spot that had caused her so much misery all morning. It was soft and warm and absolute bliss itself.

Arthur looked at the back of Mary's head and saw the great tangle of hair with hair pins nearly falling out, ready to disappear into the creases of the recliner. He couldn't help but notice how her thin shoulders shivered, her utter vulnerability, and he held very still.

For an instant, he wondered what her usually severe bun of hair would look like, loosened and hanging around her shoulders.

Quickly, as if she read his thoughts, Mary sat back with her eyes closed, murmuring her thanks, a wan dismissal. "You can go now. I'll be all right."

He didn't say anything, just simply walked into the small kitchen, opened the refrigerator door, found the leftover Thanksgiving chicken and the broth, and set about making a pot of chicken noodle soup. He banged doors as he cooked, whistling soft and low and talking to Sam. He ate hard pretzels and slices of cheese as he worked, casting observant glances toward Mary who was once more rolled into the cocoon of blankets.

Arthur noticed the scented candles and the vase of pricey flowers that looked like silk or velvet. He observed her artwork, which wasn't cheap either. The cookware he was using was from Princess House. He raised his eyebrows. A high-class old maid. He smiled. Everything under control at all times. Yes, ma'am. He smiled again but turned quickly when the covers were flung back, the recliner groaning in protest as Mary sat up.

Reaching behind her back, she flung the hot water bottle across the floor. She kicked off the covers, lifted the handle that slapped the foot rest into place, and said she was burning up with that thing. She got to her feet and caught herself on the arm of the recliner, pushed off, then wobbled her way into the bathroom. Her face was flaming, her hairpins slithering out of the roll of hair on the back of her head.

Arthur noticed the frayed men's moccasins on her feet. Dear, funny Mary. He heard the shower while he searched for noodles. When he was unable to find some, he broke spaghetti into two-inch pieces, then seasoned the dish with chicken base, poultry seasoning, black pepper, and parsley. He glanced nervously at the bathroom door.

He drank coffee, ate more pretzels, and finished the cold baked beans he found in the refrigerator. He thought the shower was running an awfully long time.

He never knew anyone could be so proud, so self-sufficient. She was something, Mary was.

The house had warmed up to a comfortable 72 degrees. Good. He added another stick of wood, considered, then piled on two more. He'd make it nice and warm.

The shower stopped.

Arthur ladled a bit of the soup into a bowl and lifted the steaming liquid to his mouth for a taste. He added a bit more salt to the soup in the kettle, stirred, put the lid on, and turned the gas heat to the lowest setting.

He noticed the stack of school books. A black, well-worn Bible lay beside it, a blue and white journal on top, the red Bic pen beside them. He would give a fortune to know what lay between the covers of that journal. Did this woman ever think about her single status? Did she ever consider being with someone? He doubted it. But then she made his world very interesting, presenting him with the challenge of his life.

When she finally emerged, her face and lips were chalk white, accentuated by the forest green of her dress. Her hair was rolled into a white towel thrown

across the top of her head. She grasped a black hairbrush firmly in her right hand.

"Guess the Tylenol kicked in."

"Feel better?"

"Some." She sat on the sofa away from him. Lifting her hands, she unwrapped her hair and flung the
towel across the back of a chair.

Arthur was not aware of the acceleration of his
breathing. He just knew he would not allow her to see
him watching her. Down came the dark, coppery tresses, parted in the middle, the weak, shaking hands resolutely drawing the brush through the gleaming mass.

Suddenly, she laid the brush hurriedly on the arm
of the sofa and threw herself back against the cushions. "Whew! Weak as a kitten."

At least that's what Arthur thought she said. He
got up, walked over to the sofa, and offered his assistance. He was turned down quite competently with
an icy glare and a weak, "Of course not. I'm fine."

She picked up the brush and continued brushing.
Arthur went back to the kitchen. He saw her draw
the brush through the heavy wet hair, her profile

etched against the wall. She turned her face, lifted her hair, clasped it behind her head, then resumed brushing. Arthur tried not to watch, he really did. From the moment he'd seen Mary, he found her mildly amusing, not beautiful, but a charming person with a sense of humor, smart, and quick with words.

He had never felt inferior to her, certainly not bashful or tongue-tied, the way young men often were when they became enamored of a girl. But now. Now he knew he was in awe of her. It was her complete and thorough misunderstanding of her own womanly charms that was so heartbreaking. It drew him with a powerful strength. He knew he was beginning to feel inferior and shy. He was bumbling, his breathing leaving him weak in the head. Even woozy. This was a turn of events.

Finally Mary lifted her hair completely unselfconsciously, as if she'd given up trying to be beautiful and accepted the fact that she was not enough for any man's eyes. Arthur felt waves of emotion. It was her too pure acceptance of being less than others that stirred him immensely.

When she spoke, he did not hear her. She turned, watched him, and still he was not aware. "Arthur."

He jumped. "Uh, yes, Mary?"

"You can go home now."

"Would you eat some of my chicken noodle soup?'

"I thought I smelled something good."

"Soup."

She walked to the kitchen, lifted the lid and sniffed, then replaced it. She turned and walked back to the table. He caught the scent of shampoo, soap, lotion, he didn't know what all. He knew one thing only—that not another day could go by until they talked of his past. He would stay right here until she listened to him.

She ate only a few spoonfuls of the soup. She said it was good, but she'd rather have another cup of tea. He almost dropped the tea kettle in his hurry to supply the hot, sweet drink. His hands shook when he spooned the sugar into the mug. He took a deep breath to steady himself.

He spent a large amount of time talking to Sam, who seemed happy with the undivided attention.

Mary said she was feeling stronger, that it was getting on toward evening, and if he wanted to go back home to do chores, she really would be fine.

Arthur smiled at her. "How many times did you say you'd be fine?"

Mary kept her eyes averted, saying nothing. Quickly, then, she lifted her head and said, "I will be. You can go home and do chores."

"I'm afraid you'll let the fire go out again."

"I won't."

The silence that settled between them was painful, containing a new uncomfortable element, like a tic in an eye that has finally been acknowledged. Mary became unsure of herself, sensing something unusual in Arthur's face, in the way he looked at her. Perhaps it was her weakness or the effect of the Tylenol. She found it difficult to meet his eyes, or look at any part of his face, for that matter.

She drank her tea, put more salve on her cold sores, flicked the hair from her face. She coughed. Then, with the tension in the silence becoming unbearable, she said quickly, "Your shirt is so white."

"I learned how to do laundry from Miriam."

"Who is Miriam?"

When he did not reply, she picked up the mug of tea and drank quickly, with an unladylike slurp that was terrifying. "You don't have to tell me, if you'd rather not."

Arthur looked at Mary, his eyes filled with darkness, a color she had not known could possibly come from the usual light blue of his eyes that was like a diamond held to light. "Miriam was my wife."

Mary swallowed, cringing at the pain. "You . . . you had a wife?"

"I did."

A soft blush stole across Mary's face. She opened her mouth to say something, thought better of it, and closed it, incapable of speech.

"Although the girl in the photograph was my girlfriend, like I told you. First, I had Miriam. Then I dated Erma."

He let that information hang between them, a sword dangling dangerously on a thin thread, rife with the ability to sever, to maim, to hurt. Mary felt this so keenly she got to her feet, went to the double windows by the sofa, crossed her thin arms about herself, and lifted her eyes to the snowy hillsides and the pines surrounded by the majesty of the winter mountains.

Soon she'd go home for Christmas. She'd leave Arthur here in Montana with his unbearably twisted path of remembering. She was not capable of fixing his disappointments, his keenly felt losses. She wouldn't be able to lift his ton of memories. She couldn't begin to budge even one corner to allow him to be free.

Nor did she want to listen to him tell her all this. She stiffened when she heard him coming closer. She shrugged her shoulders when his hands clasped them. She stopped breathing when his hand lifted the heavy hair clasped firmly in the ponytail holder.

"Come, Mary, sit with me. We have all evening. If you feel well enough, you can hear my story."

"I don't want to."

"You don't?"

"No."

"May I ask why?"

"I can't. I don't know how to fix it."

"Oh, you're quite capable. You have it all under control."

She turned slowly, lifted her tired eyes still clouded with fever, and beckoned him to accompany her to the couch.

Chapter Nine

"MIRIAM WAS ONLY NINETEEN WHEN WE married. I was twenty-two. We lived in Indiana, one of the largest Amish settlements in the world. We were reasonably happy, but after four years of not being able to have children, Miriam was often unhappy and frustrated. I suppose I was, too. Another few years of—well, I'll just tell you, Mary—living in misery finally became a way of life.

"We went to doctors, tried gimmicks, especially anything labeled 'natural,' but nothing worked. I still wonder if Miriam's unhappiness was the root of her failing immune system. She was diagnosed with lymphoma, a deadly cancer, and died six months later." He stopped.

Mary whispered, "I am so sorry."

"Don't be. Our marriage was a burden. It took me years to recognize that sad fact. I always felt as if she didn't love me, and I really don't think she did. I'm not blameless either. My mistakes were many and frequent. I can't deny that.

"Her parents blamed me. Oh, they said they didn't, but I knew better. I came here to Montana. I made a lot of money in Indiana owning a stone mason company. I sold it, built my house here, and then lost most of my money running cattle."

He laughed suddenly, a deep rumbling release that brought back his usual good humor, which was a great relief to Mary. She wanted to throw herself into his arms and comfort him, but knew she had no power to do that. So she sat, her hands clasped in front of her primly, the way a red-haired, old-maid schoolteacher should.

"So, here I was, not rich, not poor, an ordinary guy who cooked and ate loads of good food to comfort himself and gained about a hundred pounds."

"You didn't!" Mary gasped.

"Almost."

Arthur's great laugh rang out freely as his face doubled up like an accordion. His teeth were very white in his tanned face, mirroring the white of his shirt.

Mary smiled, then she smiled wider, but the pain from the cold sores made her lift three fingers to press on them. And she stopped smiling.

"Those cold sores are mean, aren't they?" he asked, observing the way she touched them.

Mary nodded.

"So then Erma Miller came to Montana, looking for adventure, I guess. And being one of the eligible widowers and bachelors that tend to inhabit these parts, I tried to supply it. Looking back, she was too pretty, too fast, too spoiled. I was definitely not the one for her after a year or more. She told me so directly and hightailed it back to Ohio."

Mary watched Arthur shrewdly. She saw a flicker of regret, a painful confusion, but no real grief that weighed him down, as far as she could tell. But not so fast, she told herself.

"Actually, Mary, I should have known she was too much like Miriam, may she rest in peace. I did love her at first, passionately. She consumed me, filling every waking hour with her presence. I think in a way she replaced God, and I worshiped her. God seemed far away at that time. It's only since Erma left that I can truthfully say I have a close relationship with God, that I feel the warmth and protection of having Jesus Christ as my own Redeemer. So I guess everything that happens in our lives has a reason."

Mary nodded, understanding.

"Erma left over four years ago, so I've pretty much accepted the solitude. I've even come to like it."

Dumbly, Mary nodded again.

"What's your story? There is surely a reason for someone like you to be alone."

For a long time Mary did not speak. When she did, her voice was low, stripped of any false courage or pride. "There is no story."

"Come on, Mary."

"Seriously, I'm ashamed to tell you. I have never been asked out on a date."

Arthur's eyes opened wide, the disbelief stamped all over his features. "I find that very hard to believe."

"Actually, you probably don't."

"What do you mean?"

"You know."

Bewildered, Arthur shrugged. Did Mary have some undisclosed, shameful past? He had to know. "Tell me."

She pointed to her freckles, her hair.

"It's this. As far as I can figure out."

"But, Mary, the color of your hair is the most attractive thing about you."

Completely uncomfortable with compliments of any kind, Mary spread her hands wide, clasped them across her knee, and shook her head in denial.

Arthur knew there probably had been a time when pale skin splattered with freckles was not his idea of beauty. The flawless, golden skin that Miriam possessed or Erma's tanned, smooth face was what he had thought attractive.

But love had many forms. The wonder, the beauty of it, was the way God provided the real love that would last. The love that sustained a person through valleys of tears and mountains of adversity. The way God led you to see the beauty of freckles and red hair and thin arms in one extremely confident teacher who possessed not one good thought about her appearance.

Twice Arthur had fallen for the heart-thumping excitement of a shallow love. But could that be called love? Or was it really the determination to possess, to have, without consideration of the many sacrifices God expected a husband to make? Arthur had come to believe there was a very real difference in the wrong and the right way to love. If you could not lay down your own will, the determination to have your own way, love would fade away, sputter, and die.

Mary got to her feet as the silence stretched on. Arthur reached for her hand. Surprised, she jerked it away, as if she'd been stung. Real fear showed in her wide green eyes.

"Sit down."

"No, Arthur. I don't feel well at all."

"Just listen to this little bit I still have to say, then I'll go home, all right?"

Sighing, Mary sat as far away from him as possible, an elbow propped on the arm of the couch, her face held by a tightly closed fist.

"Are you listening?"

She nodded, but barely.

"I was happy being alone. I enjoyed being on the school board. The families in the community were like my own. There were a few single girls who came and went, but I felt no attraction at all. Believe me, Mary, I tried.

"When I wrote that letter to you, I simply wrote to the first person listed in the *Blackboard Bulletin* with the list of teachers in Pennsylvania. The thing I was looking for was the amount of years these young women had taught. Your twelve years were an accomplishment, I thought. Then, when I saw you digging that splinter out of your hand, I was intrigued. You were different-looking."

Mary snorted. "No doubt," she said dryly.

"No, I mean it. You were younger and much more attractive than I had planned on."

"I guess. In that dark old station."

"You have intrigued me from that first day," Arthur went on, ignoring her refusal to accept his words.

"Oddity does intrigue."

"Mary, stop it."

In answer, Mary sat up very straight. She smoothed the dark green skirt firmly over her knees that were pressed tightly together, and spoke firmly. "Arthur, I cannot accept your, your declaration of intrigue, as you call it. You know you aren't attracted to me. It's only the kindness in you, the way you pity cold, newborn calves and sick horses and dogs like Sam. You love kids and talk to old ladies and help the old men hitch up horses, and now you can add 'Boost old maids' egos' to your list of kind deeds. You know as well as I do that you do not find me attractive. Or marriageable, if you will. So save your breath. Go home and become intrigued by something else."

Arthur sighed. Then a low rumbling began in his chest, starting as a chuckle and grrowing to a full-blown guffaw of pure pleasure.

Mary turned her head sideways and watched him with suspicious eyes, and she did not smile.

Arthur finished his laugh, met her eyes, and said, "See, Mary, that is what intrigues me. Your dry sense of humor, your quick wit, and your bruising honesty. If it makes you feel any better, you are as ugly as a mud fence."

That made her laugh. She laughed quietly, sparing the vicious blisters on her lips, then said, "Hoo-eee." Very like herself. Very Mary.

Who got up first? Was it Arthur or was it Mary? Who walked the few feet first? It was as natural and as easy as if they had lived their whole lives, waiting for this moment.

His arms went around her gently, and he cradled her head on his wide, thick shoulder. That was all. They did not speak. They just stayed that way. Eventually her arms clasped his thick waist, and he sighed.

Above her head she heard Arthur say, his voice shaking with the depth of his feelings, "Thank you, Mary, for being my friend. If that's all we will ever have, I'll still cherish you as a good friend."

"Thank you, Arthur. I appreciate your friendship."

The whole way home, Arthur thought about how God worked in ordinary, mundane ways, doing what was best for his life. For what better way could have been invented than a row of miserable cold sores to keep him from placing his lips on hers? Without them, he might have declared his love to her for all time, when Mary was still on her determined path of self-hatred.

Patience, patience. This time, he'd end up with a winner, if he could only let go and let God. Indeed.

The blowing snow was beautiful but made life twice as hard, Mary decided. It drifted into every available crevice, sifting into the woodshed until it lay thickly on the split wood and melted into dirty puddles around the woodstove. If she wasn't careful, Sam would lap it up, which was disgusting. She would pounce on him immediately, scold him, and show him the water bowl—and then he tried it again. Dogs were odd creatures. Didn't he taste the sawdust?

Finally, after a week of this, she gave up and figured that if he wanted to drink melted snow with sawdust, he could. Perhaps he thought it was a fancy dish, the way the chefs gave their ordinary dishes elaborate names.

Take that picture of white bread spread with butter and sliced radishes. Mary was raised on that. It was an Amish staple in spring. *Butta brote, sals und reddich.* She'd seen a picture in *Country Living*, read the name and the recipe, then howled with laughter, kicking up her feet and bringing them down with a bang. Just look at that. Ciabatta bread, which looked like tough white bread. Butter that had a few chives in it but was still butter. Radishes sliced thin, with a bit of green stem left on, layered in decorative layers. A masterpiece. But it was still radishes and butter bread.

She even became accustomed to Sam licking up anything that fell from the countertop. Bits of bacon, a crust of bread, even a tomato or carrot or apple. She no longer bothered cleaning the floor after him. The pupils at school had informed her about the cleanliness of a dog's tongue.

Sam continued to be her guard and reliable companion. She never worried about her own safety, although she couldn't help but make some anxious searches of the distant hills at times.

She was planning her trip home for Christmas. This time she would not have to bother with Amtrak, the tickets, and the long ride alone. A van was traveling to Lancaster County, which was hard to believe, but a godsend at any rate.

Arthur told her there was a blizzard coming down from Idaho. She said she'd believe it when she saw it. He said he was worried about a few of his mother cows dropping their calves too early in the season. She didn't say it, of course, but she wanted to tell him that farmers with good management should be able to regulate that. But then, here in Montana, the cows occupied miles instead of acres, so maybe things were a little different than in tidy Lancaster County.

She considered Arthur her friend now and was so much more at ease with all this romance stuff out of the way. She figured he wasn't dumb either. Two pretty ones gone, he could keep the homely one. Well, she'd set him in his place, and she dusted her hands of any romance residue and went ahead with her life, all in the course of a week.

And then the blizzard hit.

The trees bent and swayed in its wake, creaking and groaning like suffering old men. The snow drove in, riding the powerful wind, more ice than snow, actually.

Mary staggered home from school, one hand pulling the sled, the other one held to the side of her face to avoid the stinging bits of ice. Her chest hurt from the struggle to pull the sled, but she was feeling anxious about getting home safely, the whole world turning into a vast, white, churning void that made no sense.

As usual, she was glad for Sam, who trotted ahead, his black, sturdy form reassuringly leading on. Around her, brown grasses whispered as they bent to the wind, the trees creaking and wailing from their usual positions of sturdiness.

Breathless, Mary finally reached the porch, where she had to get a shovel to dig the front door out of the tightly packed snow. When she was able to open it, she stepped through and turned to close it again but met the wind's alarming power. She struggled to shut the door.

With concern, she eyed the few pieces of wood by the fire. She couldn't admit her fear, but she dreaded opening that door again. She knew she had to. There was not enough wood to get through the night.

She almost fainted with relief when the door was yanked open and Arthur staggered in. He wasted no time in polite greetings, telling her sharply to pack some clothes. He stalked about in heavy boots, draining water pipes and turning off the refrigerator, barking orders as if she was a helpless child.

Grimly, she packed her bag, tossed in her toiletries and the book she was reading, closed it, and stood ready to go. Sam whined, begging to go. Mary snapped his leash while Arthur struggled to open the door.

Mary almost screamed with fear of the storm. She had never experienced wind of this strength. Hurricane Sandy, a year ago at home, was powerful, but this was much more frightening because of the intense cold.

Arthur was yelling, but she could not hear. He reached for her hand; she placed hers into his. The remainder of the way she tried to keep up with his large strides, but she kept foundering, slipping back down the slope. Sam lowered his head and stepped along, whining occasionally in distress.

Darkness was falling, creating an other-worldly atmosphere of whirling whiteness in a black sky as the wind slammed against their bodies, carrying their breaths away.

Arthur's house loomed out of the whirling, dizzying grayness, and Mary felt like crying with elation. The side door was away from the slamming of the wind. They fell inside and then stood, cold, breathing hard, scarcely able to grasp a place that was quiet and safe.

Slowly, Arthur unwound his scarf and pulled off his stocking cap. His mouth was still too numb to speak properly, so he motioned for Mary to go to the woodstove.

She obeyed meekly, holding out her hands to its comforting warmth. Shivering, she removed her headscarf, then her coat and sweater. She kept the black pullover on, glad for its soft warmth. Suddenly she felt ill at ease, as bashful as a schoolgirl, then chided herself. They were friends, that was all.

Arthur showed her the guest room and bathroom and told her to make herself at home, to feel free to take a hot shower, while he started supper.

She acknowledged his kindness politely. He smiled stiffly, then turned away, busying himself at the sink peeling potatoes.

He thought of cold sores, patience, and timing. He couldn't possibly have left Mary to fend for herself, and he trusted God to look out for him. But why, now, were they being thrown together like this?

Mary came into the kitchen offering to help, her face pale and frightened, the black sweater accentuating the wan circles beneath her eyes. Arthur gripped the paring knife hard and peeled potatoes with a vengeance, as he thought of holding Mary and erasing that fright from her eyes.

Politely, she inquired about the potatoes. Mashed or fried?

He was making French fries, he said. She watched from a distance as he cut the large white potatoes with an old-fashioned French fry cutter, clunking down on the handle, then dropping the oblong strips of potato in hot vegetable oil.

They were hot, greasy, and salty. A bottle of ketchup completed the meal. Arthur said they could have graham crackers and peanut butter for dessert. Dipped in milk, it was a delicious combination.

Somehow, the simple food was satisfying. It bolstered their courage as the wind struck forcefully against the large, sturdy, log house. The windows creaked as the gale mounted.

Mary helped Arthur with the dishes, stepping away self-consciously when he got too close. She often cleared her throat for something to do. He suggested a game of Monopoly, but she said no, she was too sleepy, then went off to the bathroom and had the longest shower of her life. She knew it would be more relaxing in the bathroom than in the living room with him.

She wished she would not have packed this purple robe. It was plaid and made her look like a fat hunter.

She slipped the belt in the loops and backed up to the mirror to check the back view. She decided she was as wide as the bathtub, so she pulled the belt out and stuffed it in the bag.

They sat stiffly, making small talk. Arthur said the storm was expected to blow itself out in a few days, but you never could tell. She nodded. Yes, you never could tell. Mary knew if the storm lasted longer than that, she wouldn't be able to keep her friendship with him afloat without all that emotional drama connected to romance surfacing again.

She thought she had all that taken care of, finished. She should have gone to bed straightaway after her shower. Arthur complimented the robe, and she said she didn't wear it very often because it made her look like a fat hunter.

All his reserves came down, and he laughed a long relaxing laugh and told Mary they weren't handling this friendship very well. Did she think they were? Mary said, sure they were, then lowered her eyes and kept them lowered and didn't look at him for some time.

She should not have looked at him after he got out of the shower either, with his navy blue chamois shirt and clean denim pants and bare feet. When his hair was wet, he looked so young and untroubled. The creases around his eyes made her feel as if she was having a heart attack. What did they call it? Cardiac arrest. Congestive heart failure?

He asked her why she didn't get a decent pair of ladies' slippers instead of slouching around in those men's moccasins.

Quickly, she pulled her feet in, sliding her heels up the footrest of the recliner. She said clearly, "My feet are as big as flippers."

Arthur looked at Mary for a long time. He said he'd never noticed.

Well, they were a 9 ½, sometimes 10, so she may as well slap around in flippers.

She went to bed, then, when he didn't laugh. She knelt by her bed and asked God to please give her strength to be friends with Arthur and nothing more. If the only way out of this quagmire of feelings was to go home, then please let the van leave for

Pennsylvania a week early. Otherwise, she was afraid she couldn't manage this business with Arthur with any real sense of truthfulness.

Arthur lay in his bed, shaking and laughing, thinking how she said she looked like a fat hunter in that bathrobe.

Chapter Ten

IN THE MORNING, THE ONLY LIGHT that found its way through the slight crack between the curtains was gray, dull, and not very effective in waking anyone, so it was past eight o'clock when Mary's eyes flew open, startled. The small black alarm clock gave away the fact that she had overslept terribly.

Leaping from the bed, she dressed hurriedly and brushed her teeth. Then she combed her red hair, pinned the covering neatly over it, tied on her black big apron, and opened the bathroom door slowly.

The house was empty. Through the wide, high windows in the seating area she could see a world of whirling, churning, blowing snow. The wind had abated somewhat so that the windows no longer made that frightening, popping sound of the night before. Still a sizable storm, she thought.

The house was warm, as a bright wood fire crackled and popped behind the glass in the door of the large woodstove. Steam rose from the blue granite coffee pot on the top.

Mary inhaled deeply. Had Arthur been up for awhile? He'd made coffee already. Quietly, as if she might waken him, Mary tiptoed to the kitchen and opened the pine doors of the top cupboards, searching for cups or mugs.

She smiled to herself when she found the largest, heaviest mugs she'd ever seen, the insignia of a bear imprinted on both sides. Hmm. Very masculine, Arthur.

She drank her coffee black, liking it piping hot. This was perfect coffee. She wrapped her thin fingers gratefully around the gigantic cup, stood by the woodstove, and surveyed Arthur's house. Log walls, deer horns, elk horns, wildlife pictures, a brown leather sofa and chairs. Rugs that came straight from some mail order catalog that catered to the rugged life.

She thought of her things. The impossibility of joining the two tastes, her things soft and flowery and so Lancaster County. Two different worlds.

She saw the papers thrown on top of the kitch-
en table, the pens in the wooden holder, some loose
change, a retractable utility knife. This was a man's
world, and her things would be out of place. It felt
incongruous to even think about it. Still she did.

When the door was pulled open and Arthur stumbled through it, covered with snow, Mary looked up,
not quite sure what she should say, if she should speak
at all. Quickly, she lifted her cup, taking a scalding
sip.

"Good morning, Mary! I hope you slept well," Arthur said, in a brisk, booming voice.

She nodded, watching warily as he pulled off his
stocking cap, rid himself of the heavy coat in one fast
shrug, then bent to loosen his boots.

Without further words, he got down a mug, poured
it full of coffee, took a sip, and smiled down at her.
"Good morning, Mary," he said as softly as he could.

See? That was the first mistake of the day, Mary
thought. If she would have kept her eyes on the storm
or the coffee pot or any other trustworthy place, her
heart would not have kicked up its rhythm. When

that happened, all the unwanted drama came tumbling along. That thing people called romance.

As it was, she lost herself in the new and startling gentleness in the blue glints that were his eyes, half buried in those attractive creases that gave away the goodness of his character. She felt herself hurtling through space, as she may as well have been. She had to get her feet back on solid ground, then glue them firmly with the Super Glue called reality.

To do that, she had to stop looking at him, or at least his eyes. Eyes were tricky. You had to be careful. How many times had she taken glints of humor, friendliness, laughter, or a look that lasted a few seconds longer than necessary, as meaning the young man was interested in her? Too many times to count.

Mary stepped away from him, sliding her feet softly to the left out of the circle that wasn't safe. She watched the storm, then looked at the head of an elk, its horns as big as anything she had ever seen.

Finally, Arthur spoke. "Are you interested in accompanying me today?"

"Doing what?" Mary spoke to the elk antlers. They were much safer.

"Do you ride?"

"No. I never did."

"Not too late to learn."

She shook her head.

"I need to find a few cows. I think about half a dozen are missing. I'm especially worried about the one who should be about ready to calf."

"I'll stay here."

"You sure?"

Mary looked at the whirling snow. She thought of riding a horse through it. She'd be going home for Christmas to stay and would not be back, so why not? Why pass up an opportunity like this? It was a once in a lifetime experience. One she would tell her friend Sarah Fisher, stringing it out, embellishing it like too many Christmas lights on one tree. They'd shriek and laugh at her clumsiness. Life would return to normal as soon as she went home for Christmas.

First, Arthur made pancakes, the biggest, thickest pancakes Mary had ever seen. The two-burner griddle held only two, so they really were the size of dinner plates.

She watched as he flipped them onto a plate, melted at least two tablespoons of butter across them, added maple syrup, added another layer of pancakes, and then repeated the procedure again.

He cooked sausages, thin wide patties of browned sausage that tasted so good, Mary ate two. But she could not eat all those huge pancakes. Besides, she was not used to maple syrup. It was too thin and too sweet with an odd, sharp flavor. She was used to Aunt Jemima's syrup. Or Country Kitchen. Or anything Walmart had on special. But, of course, she didn't say that.

Not once did Mary meet Arthur's eyes, which was good. She did the dishes alone, which was good, too. At least he wasn't too close. It was much easier to keep her little boat called *No Romance* afloat if she stayed clear of his eyes or presence.

She dressed warmly, putting on her black jersey pants, those fleece-lined, cumbersome, unattractive, necessary things she wore beneath her skirts to walk to school. Then she added two sweaters, a heavy black coat, a scarf, and a headscarf on her head, a pair of study boots, and her thick gloves.

Arthur remained strangely quiet as they dressed, but Mary figured he was busy and thought nothing of it. Together they floundered through the blowing snow, eventually falling through the heavy barn door, panting.

Arthur immediately set to work saddling the horses. "This one is named Tessa. I call her Tess. She's a quarter horse, small, surefooted, and so safe a five-year-old could ride her. She follows my horse around wherever he goes, so all you have to do is sit in the saddle, and she'll follow, okay?"

Mary nodded. She liked the looks of the small brown horse. She was compact with a gentle look in her brown eyes, a softness about her that instantly endeared her to Mary's heart. She stroked the side of her neck, rubbed the velvety nose. She was used to horses; she had been around them all her life. Her own driving horse, Ginger, was a high-stepping sad-dlebred who obeyed Mary completely.

Arthur came to stand beside her. Mary moved away.

"She likes you," he said softly.

"Looks like it."

"Good. I'm glad. You'll do fine. You need help up?"

Mary looked at the saddle, then at the height of the stirrup. She made the huge mistake of forgetting herself and looking at Arthur with a timid unguarded question in her eyes, completely uncharacteristic and too vulnerable. Whoa. Her boat of *No Romance* was tilted by a wave that crashed out of nowhere. Mary's eyes slid away and she lifted her chin. The boat righted itself and went steadfastly on its way. Good.

Grasping the saddle horn, she inserted the toe of her boot into the stirrup, hopped up and down a few times, and flung herself into the saddle. She almost slid down the other side, but instead, righted herself and sat solidly, getting used to the feel of the saddle. She had never seen a horse from this spot. The ground seemed so far away, the horse's ears and mane too long and too far below her. She felt clumsy, as if she weighed twice as much as usual. Lifting her shoulders, she straightened her back. She did know enough about riding to understand that slouching or sagging in the saddle was very unattractive.

Arthur tightened the cinch around the stomach of his own horse, then turned to look at her and smiled. "You sit a horse very well."

"Thanks."

"You really do, Mary."

Arthur opened the wide, heavy barn door, and Tessa turned obediently when Mary lifted the reins. She stepped out into the storm, her ears flicking forward, then back. After that, she lowered her head and bent to the task of following Arthur's horse.

Sam whined from the barn, but the sound was soon lost in the wind. He had to stay, of course. The snow came up to the horses' undersides in places.

Mary loved the snow. She had always enjoyed winter, watching motorists on Route 30 creep along, their windshield wipers moving back and forth furiously, the drivers peering anxiously from behind wet glass, honking horns, sliding into ditch-es. She loved the power of the great yellow trucks from "the state," as Dat said, their chains clanking, their immense blades shoving the cinders and salt and gray slush in a precise arc along the side of the road. Neighbors shoveled snow, called greetings to each other, spread salt on doorsteps. That was Mary's Lancaster County winters, the snow mixed with lights, black telephone poles, moving cars and buggies, and people.

Here in this moment, the solitude was awe-inspir-ing. Mary had never known you could actually hear snow fall. It whispered. It sang a haunting, beautiful melody as it rode the gale, as if some of God's angels wrote the song of the snow and God directed the symphony of nature from His throne.

The pine trees' movement rid them of their heavy layer of snow before it had a chance to settle. They looked black, so dark was the green, bent and sway-ing like restless dancers, tossed about. An occasional pine cone socked into the ever deepening snow with a barely audible sound.

Downhill was frightening. Mary fought the desire to grasp the saddle horn with both hands. Better to find the balance she needed with the stirrups supporting her weight.

Tess stopped, her nose very close to Arthur's horse's rump. He turned.

"You okay?' he shouted.

"Yes."

"You sure?"

"Yes."

"We'll be going uphill for while. There's a grove of trees over the next rise. Sometimes, cattle will take shelter there."

"Okay." Mary's voice was flung from her, carried away by the wind.

They rode up a long slope, then down the opposite side, where they located a group of five cows huddled beneath a group of bare, swaying trees. Mary saw the reason they had stayed behind. Two small calves were half buried in the drifting snow. The mothers mooed with a high shrill sound of anxiety, the wail of nature, willing their offspring to live.

For as bulky as Arthur was, he was off his horse in one swift movement. Mary remained in the saddle, watching, as he bent to check for signs of life. He straightened, looked at his horse, then back at Mary.

"They're both alive," he shouted.

Mary didn't answer him, knowing it was useless. She was beginning to feel the cold penetrating her outerwear. A shiver chased itself up her back. Her teeth began to chatter.

She reached up and pulled the woolen scarf across her mouth so Arthur wouldn't see. "I can take one on my saddle."

Arthur looked at Mary, questioning.

She nodded. "I can try," she shouted.

His horse stood perfectly still as Arthur bent to the task of tying the small hooves together, the mother cows anxiously mooing. Through the whirling whiteness he appeared, his arms cupped around the helpless calf. Suddenly a solid thump of brown weight was thrown across her lap, followed by his voice.

"You sure?"

Mary wasn't one bit sure. She was cold and shivering now. The calf smelled wet and sour. She looked down at the thick, matted hair, the terrified, bulging eyes of the just-born calf, and wanted to tell Arthur to take it. It smelled and would very likely die of cold and exposure, and then she would feel responsible. Grimly, she watched the limp tail and hoped with all her heart it would not lift and expel the unthinkable all over her lap.

"Ready?"

In answer, Mary lifted a gloved hand in a forward motion. Arthur sprang to his horse, settled himself in the saddle, turned, and started off. Tess followed immediately. Bawling incessantly, the five cows trotted beside them, falling back when they slipped, trotting, floundering, then settling into a steady walk, their heads bobbing rhythmically the way Holsteins did when they walked.

Mary remembered the farm well. She always brought in the cows, using Doddy Stoltzfus's walking cane, shouting "Hoos-sa! Hoos-sa!" The language of five generations of Stoltzfuses, Dat said. She fed calves, washed milkers, and washed the cows' teats before attaching the heavy, gleaming milking machines.

But it had been a while. Dat and Mam had moved off the farm and retired to the small ranch house along Route 30. Jonas had taken over the farm, and Mary forgot the scent of newborn calves, the bawling of anxious mothers.

Never once in her wildest dreams would she have imagined being in this faraway place, following this man through a storm of this size. God moved in mysterious ways, she thought, omitting the rest of the verse—"His wonders to perform."

Huh. No wonders for this old maid. Everything was still under control. The storm would wear thin, the clouds would open up, the blue would show in the west, and the sun would break through again. She would leave Arthur's house and go home for two weeks. She'd board the van, the long, fifteen-passenger vehicle, that would travel the 1,800 miles home to Lancaster County to resume her normal life.

She watched the sky anxiously now, dreading any sign of the storm thinning out. She wanted the snow to keep whirling out of gray skies; she wanted the wind to keep whining and howling around the barn and the house. She dreaded the blue of the clear sky, plowing the roads, the sun's warmth. With all her heart, she wanted to stay here.

Lifting her shoulders, she swiped viciously at her nose, then squeezed her eyes shut at the pain. Ouch. She likely had a frostbitten appendage now for sure.

Well, what you wanted and what you got were two completely different things usually, and this was no different. Older, she was now, and wiser. Yes, she wanted to stay, but coupled with that knowledge came the realization of the disappointment that was sure to follow. You could easily shoulder disappointment. She'd often done it. It wasn't hard after a while.

The calf slung across the saddle struggled weakly. Mary placed a gloved hand across its back, pressed down and said, "You're okay, there." She took a deep breath, straightening her back. Her legs were beginning to ache. A fine layer of snow that had settled on her scarf began to melt and drain down her back, sending goose bumps up and down her arms.

The mother cow jostled against Mary's booted foot, knocking it out of the stirrup. Mary reinserted her foot, kicked out at the anxious, bawling creature, then righted herself and kept riding. It seemed an eternity until the dark barn loomed through the gray, whirling world.

Mary heard Sam whine anxiously before Arthur dismounted and flung the barn doors wide, allowing Mary to ride through. He closed them behind her, leaving the cows behind as he latched it. He worked quickly, pulling the calves down, rubbing them with an old feedsack. He massaged their chests and listened to both calves' hearts before asking Mary to go to the house for hot water.

She was barely able to stand, let alone walk to the house. She tottered off grimly without looking back, wishing she had Doddy Stoltzfus's cane.

Sam leaped and whined beside her, cavorting in the snow, spending his pent-up energy in senseless hops and circles of needless tail-catching.

Mary plodded up the slope as if her feet were encased in blocks of ice. They felt worse than flippers now.

She returned with steaming hot water in the lidded pail Arthur had provided. Without a word of thanks, he took it from her brusquely. She stood beside him, her too-long arms with the too-big hands covered with freckles and hanging by her sides.

She watched as he mixed the yellowish powder into the bucket, his eyes squinted in concentration. When he was satisfied with the dissolved powder, he poured a portion of the liquid into a plastic bottle, then another.

When he didn't ask for her assistance, Mary leaned against the rough lumber of the box stall.

Arthur lifted the calf's nose, attempting to get it to suckle the rubber nipple, but nothing happened. The calf's head flopped into the straw. Frustrated, he tried the second calf with the same result. He must not know much about calves, Mary thought. And, if he didn't ask, she wouldn't offer. She was surprised when he sat back on his heels, shook his head, and said they'd likely not make it.

"Sure they will," Mary answered quickly.

Forgetting herself and thinking only of the calves, Mary unscrewed the cap of the bottle, placed the rubber nipple in the proper position, and tightened the ring. She inserted two fingers into the one calf's mouth and pried its jaw open. Then she quickly stuck the nipple in and let the newborn have a go at it.

She was rewarded by a licking of a soft pink tongue. She repeated the maneuver with the other calf, the way she used to as a child, until both calves were on their feet, working away at their bottles with wet, smacking sounds, the excess running out of the corners of their mouths.

Arthur watched, his eyes shining. "Hearty little orphans, aren't they?" he said, finally.

"They're not orphans," Mary corrected him.

"The mothers probably won't take them now."

"Holsteins would."

"How do you know so much about cows?"

"The farm."

"Mmm."

Arthur watched Mary while she washed the bottles with the hose in the water trough. He fed the horses, threw hay to the five cows that had returned late, and said he was cold.

When they trudged silently to the house and he strode ahead of her without speaking, she didn't let it bother her. She had to start working on accepting the end of the storm and the end of her time at Arthur's house, so she may as well begin now. She had displeased him somehow, but that was all right. If he remained in a quiet, unresponsive mood, it would make her leaving even lighter.

So when the snow thinned out, the wind died down, and the blue sky appeared, Mary was fully prepared. She went to the guest room, folded the plaid robe, found her slippers, and put everything efficiently into the Coach bag, the small one, and thought how nice it would be to go shopping again.

Arthur offered her lunch, but she declined politely, speaking to the coffee pot this time. She pulled on her boots, buttoned her coat, tied her scarf and said, "Thank you for everything, Arthur" in one hurried, flat sentence, opened the door, and let herself out.

She walked all alone, plowing resolutely through the deepening drifts, Sam bouncing and yipping energetically beside her.

Arthur stood at the big windows, watching the stoic figure that was Mary, until she disappeared behind the line of trees close to her house. He did not turn away until he saw a dark plume of smoke begin to come up out of the chimney and swirl away into the white world. She'd figure out how to turn the water system back on, he supposed. She was capable.

He had exactly two weeks left and positively no idea how to convince her that he wanted her, that he needed her to stay. Somehow he doubted his ability to persuade her of this fact.

Chapter Eleven

STRAINS OF CHRISTMAS CAROLS ROSE AND fell
in the schoolhouse the last evening that Mary would
be in Montana. The tinsel glistened in the propane
light, the red and green ribbons, drawn to the center
of the ceiling from each corner, turned and twisted slightly from the movement below. Homemade,
white snowflakes hung from the ceiling as well, with
red and white candy canes promenading across the
lower half of the windows.

The children were dressed in red and green, their
faces shining in the lamplight as they sang. "God rest
ye merry, gentlemen, let nothing you dismay, for Jesus Christ our Savior, was born this Christmas Day."

The parents were in awe of the singing. Their own
children singing like this was unimaginable. They had
never heard these songs. When they launched into

a tender version of "What Child Is This?", mothers wept discreetly into their babies' burp cloths, blinked, blew their noses, and felt a bit ashamed. When the schoolchildren formed a large circle and held hands while singing the old hymn, "Bind Us Together," they gave up and cried.

"Bind us together, Lord, bind us together, Lord, bind us together with love."

Mary was going home to stay. She told the community they would find someone to finish the school year. She felt like a quitter but not a failure. She had not failed at her teaching. She had been a success, as she knew she would be. Tonight it hurt worse than she could have imagined though, the parting so painful it made her feel oblivious to everything. While others cried, she remained stone-faced.

No one needed to know why she was going home. They all ate the Christmas meal, exchanged and shared pleasantries back and forth. For Mary, the evening was mechanical, robotic, as if she was programmed to get through this last night together.

She hugged mothers, shook fathers' hands, clasped the children to her heart, and told them she'd always remember them her whole life. They'd write. She'd write back. They'd visit someday.

Empty promises, she knew, but promises. The kind that made parting bearable.

Alone, she swept the floor and burned the trash. How many offers had she declined? But Arthur had not offered at all. So there. She had been right. He would forget about her the minute she was in that van headed for Pennsylvania.

Smart. Everything under control, easily managed. Tomorrow, her journey home. The day after that, she'd be at home in time for Christmas.

Her LED lamp bobbed beside her as Sam trotted obediently by the sled she pulled with gloved hands. Every star in the vast, black sky blinked down at her as if they wanted to remind her of her last night here in God's great sky country. She lifted her face, savoring the still, cold air, the light of the friendly stars, the sliver of moon that kept her company.

When she reached her house, she carried the boxes
of presents inside, then set the sled carefully against the
wall. Absentmindedly, she wondered why Arthur had
never finished this ugly old porch with the twisted posts.

No problem now. Perhaps in the spring he would.
She packed her presents, preparing to have them sent
by UPS with the remainder of her things. She unfolded her last paycheck, gasped at the large bonus,
then blinked. Finally, in the shelter of her own house,
away from eyes that asked questions, one round tear
hung on her lashes, quivered and splashed on the
cardboard box she was closing with packing tape.
She swiped blindly at the wetness, despising her own
weakness. She honked into a clean tissue, threw it
into the waste can hard, leaving the lid swinging back
and forth.

Arthur would be here in the morning for Sam. He
was his dog. She tried not to look at him too much,
the way he lay beside the woodstove with his head
on his paws, neatly, like a folded towel or a book replaced on a shelf. His eyes watched every movement,
as if he knew she would be leaving.

Mary showered, then checked the clock. Eleven-thirty. She'd have to get up early, by at least five o'clock if the van was picking her up at seven.

She was hungry, so she poured the last of her Raisin Bran into a bowl, added milk and sugar, and leaned against the counter to eat it. After a few bites, she gave up and set it beside the sink. She had had to choke down the Christmas dinner at school, and she'd managed only a few bites before sliding her plate into the garbage, still half-filled.

She blew out the one lone Christmas candle on the table, then turned to twist the knob of the propane gas lamp, when she froze. A knock?

Who could be at her door this late at night? Should she open it?

For the hundredth time she wished she had a door with a window in it, but since that was not the case, she had two choices. One, open the door and face the consequences. Two, leave the door shut and crawl under the bed and face the same consequences.

If someone meant her harm, they'd break in anyway, Mam always said. In a way, it was logical, but to open the door wide, facing danger head on, was just plain stupid. So she did nothing.

She dug a piece of Raisin Bran cereal out of her teeth with the toothpick she was holding and waited. She didn't know why she waited, but it was the only safe thing to do. When the knob turned from outside, and the door was pushed slowly inward, Mary froze.

As still as if she'd been made of granite, she kept her eyes on the door, watching the ever widening distance between the door and the frame. It was filled with black. No stars or porch roof were visible. When Arthur's voice filled the black space, saying her name softly with a question mark behind it, Mary's knees wobbled. She sank to a chair, grateful for its support.

"Come in," she called.

She had never been so glad to see him. There were plenty of times when she had been happy at the sight of him, but not with this relief, this sudden realization that nothing bad was going to happen to her.

"Mary?"

"What on earth, Arthur?"

"Mary, listen."

She was prepared to have him tell her he'd come to get Sam. Or anything else. She had not prepared herself for this haggard, shaking version of the man she knew so well.

"You can't leave," he burst out.

Mary was speechless.

"You can't go back," Arthur repeated, thickly.

"But . . ."

"For once, Mary, be quiet and listen. I don't know how to get this across. You have to believe me this time. I don't want you to go home. I want you to stay here. Not here, in this house. I mean . . ." His voice trailed off and he shook his head. Mary had never seen him so miserable. The poor man was in a bad way.

"I'm getting this all wrong."

Mary watched his face, surprised that she could not say a word of contradiction or denial.

Finally, he sagged in defeat. He simply walked over to her where she sat white-faced in the kitchen chair. He looked down at her and said, so soft and low it was only a rough whisper, "I love you, Mary."

He pulled her to her feet. She probably would not have been able to stand except that she was crushed against him by his strong arms coming around her.

"I can't get the words right," he said gently. He bent his head, found her mouth with some difficulty, and let his kiss speak the language of the universe, a sweet sense of possession, a conveyance of love and need.

Mary had never been kissed. She had never been held like this. All the usual denial, the normal resistance, was banished in that space of time. The little boat called *No Romance* sank immediately to the ocean floor, replaced by a white ship with every sail unfolded, accompanied by songs of love, bright lights of acknowledgment and acceptance, happiness and joy and gratitude.

Later, while his arms held Mary, Arthur found his voice, although it was hampered by small chokes of emotion. "Mary, will you stay? Will you promise to stay a while longer? At least till I gather enough courage to ask you to be my wife?"

At the word "wife," Mary drew back in alarm. "I am not a wife. I am an old maid."

"But can't old maids turn into wives?" Arthur asked.

Mary shrugged her shoulders. "I don't know," she said, completely puzzled.

As Arthur remained seated on the sofa, his arms fell away. Suddenly his whole body began to shake, his face turned red, and he burst into a long, musical wave of laughter that was so infectious Mary began to laugh quietly, then erupted into a full howl of ungraceful mirth that matched his.

He said her name three times and gathered her back into the circle of his arms, where she stayed until he released her. He slid down on one knee and took her hand.

"My dear, old maid Mary, will you be my wife?" he said, very soft and low, like a benediction.

Mary looked down at her long, thin fingers on the long, thin hand with freckles on the back of it, nestled in Arthur's thick, heavy hands. It looked exactly right. Her hands were beautiful, graceful, perfect.

She whispered, "Yes, Arthur. I will be your wife."

"Thank you, Mary," he said, as reverently as he felt.

Sam watched from his bed by the stove, blinked a few times, then went back to sleep. The fire in the woodstove burned down to embers. Mary said she didn't know what she'd do about going home for Christmas, suddenly becoming subdued and a little worried.

Arthur said the choice was hers. She could go if she wanted.

Mary's eyes never left his face. She etched every crease in her mind, folding them away in her heart. His eyes spoke the word "home." Arthur was her home. He was the haven for her bruised heart. How long had she fought her own heart?

"Arthur, I have come home for Christmas. Wherever you are, that is where I belong. I'll see my family at the . . . the . . ." Stammering, suddenly unsure if she should actually speak the word, "wedding," Mary stopped, which started Arthur chuckling happily all over again.

Their wedding was in the spring on a sunny April day that was freshly showered by fine rain. Every new leaf was washed by dewdrops, warmed by a sun holding the promise of summer.

The farm had been prepared by her frenzied family, for Mary's announcement had set them all properly on their heads with astonishment. Her sisters shrieked and held their hands to their cheeks, their eyes bulging. Her brothers laughed softly and said, "Leave it to Mary to go gallivanting off to wild Montana and return with a husband in tow, then, yet, one named 'Arthur Bontrager.'"

But when they actually met Arthur, they liked him immediately. They followed him around wherever he went, slapping their knees with laughter at his Western-accented stories. They put their heads together and decided that Mary had caught herself a very nice guy after all those years of spinsterhood.

When Mary stood in front of Bishop Joel Blank, her hand was placed in Arthur's, and the blessing followed. She had repeated her two "*Yas*" of promise, and she could truthfully say it was every bit as wonderful as she had always imagined.

Her teaching career was over after that term, of course. She moved into Arthur's house with him, and one of the first things she did was wash windows, scour, and clean the place, saying it was clean enough for a man, but certainly not for a woman.

She could wear worn, old handkerchiefs over her hair that was not carefully combed, look in the mirror, and smile. It was a wonder. She was freed of all that useless, heavy baggage called "disliking oneself," a polite version of hating almost everything about your looks. She saw herself through Arthur's eyes now. He told her over and over how beauty is in the eye of the beholder, and that God does not want us to bury ourselves in piles of insecurity.

She washed clothes in the Maytag wringer washer and hung them on the line in the summer breezes that never stopped. She cooked and baked, her feet treading lightly on clouds of contentment. And some days, she merely sat, steeped in happiness, like fine tea that improves the longer it steeps.

She had been happy before because of the school-children. She had been supremely blessed; not one year had been empty or wasted, and for that she was grateful. She knew, too, that for someone like her to be given a person like Arthur surpassed understanding. She was not worthy. He was a gift.

When their daughter was born, they named her Leah, for Mary's aging grandmother. Leah was a gift, too. Mary had never imagined having children. It would be asking too much from God, after He'd provided her with such a fine husband.

She felt a deep sadness whenever the fast-paced younger generation got married, had children, and then marriage problems surfaced. Was it really the fault of these beautiful young creatures? Maybe they had never given up hope of a happy marriage. They ran around and dated lots, not thinking about the blessings and sacrifices that are part of being married. They didn't expect struggles or hardships. Maybe they were too young. Perhaps, but who knew?

Mary watched Leah toddling across the green grass under the great blue Montana sky, and she thanked

God for her little girl, her wonderful Arthur, and even for her freckles and red hair.

They were all truly a blessing.

The End

Glossary

Arme vitve — A Pennsylvania Dutch dialect phrase meaning "poor widow."

Begreif — A Pennsylvania Dutch dialect word meaning "comprehend."

Chide — A Pennsylvania Dutch dialect word meaning "right."

Dat — A Pennsylvania Dutch dialect word used to address or refer to one's father.

Denke — A Pennsylvania Dutch dialect word meaning "thank you."

Dienna's frau — A Pennsylvania Dutch dialect phrase meaning "minister's wife."

Do net — A Pennsylvania Dutch dialect phrase meaning "don't."

Doddy — A Pennsylvania Dutch dialect word used to address or refer to one's grandfather.

Fa-recht—A Pennsylvania Dutch dialect word meaning "for real."

Fasht dag—A Pennsylvania Dutch dialect phrase meaning "fast day." October eleventh is the day most Amish people set aside as a day of fasting and prayer in order to prepare themselves for the fall communion services. Another fast day takes place in the spring on Good Friday.

Fa-schnopped—A Pennsylvania Dutch dialect word meaning "gave away" as in "revealed."

Gay—A Pennsylvania Dutch dialect word meaning "go."

Gel—A Pennsylvania Dutch dialect word meaning "right."

Gooka-mol—A Pennsylvania Dutch dialect word meaning "let me see."

G'mya—A Pennsylvania Dutch dialect word meaning "g'morning."

Huvvel—A Pennsylvania Dutch dialect word

meaning "planer" or "grater." It can be used to designate someone who works with these tools.

Ich gleich dich so arich—A Pennsylvania Dutch dialect phrase meaning "I love you so much."

Kaevly—A Pennsylvania Dutch dialect word meaning "basket."

Komm—A Pennsylvania Dutch dialect word meaning "come."

Kesslehaus—A Pennsylvania Dutch dialect word meaning "wash house."

Luscht Gartlein—A devotional book used by the Amish that can be translated as "Lust Garden" or "Love Garden" because it encourages the development of a spiritual lusting or longing after God.

Machs uf—A Pennsylvania Dutch dialect phrase meaning "open it."

Mam—A Pennsylvania Dutch dialect word used to address or refer to one's mother.

Mommy—A Pennsylvania Dutch dialect word used to address or refer to one's grandmother.

Of age—One is considered "of age" at 21 years old.

Ordnung—The Amish community's agreed-upon rules for living based on their understanding of the Bible, particularly the New Testament. The *ordnung* varies from community to community, often reflecting leaders' preferences, local customs, and traditional practices.

Rissling—A Pennsylvania Dutch dialect word meaning "sleeting."

Rumspringa—A Pennsylvania Dutch dialect word meaning "running around." It refers to the time in a person's life between age sixteen and marriage. It involves structured social activities in groups, as well as dating, and usually takes place on the weekends.

Sark—A Pennsylvania Dutch dialect word meaning "care for."

Sark feltich — A Pennsylvania Dutch dialect phrase meaning "caring."

Schnae — A Pennsylvania Dutch dialect word meaning "snow."

Schnitzing — A Pennsylvania Dutch dialect word meaning "fibbing."

Schputting — A Pennsylvania Dutch dialect word meaning "mocking."

Schtruvvels — A Pennsylvania Dutch dialect word meaning "stray hairs."

Sei — A Pennsylvania Dutch dialect word meaning "his." In communities where many people have the same first and last names, it is customary for the husband's name to be added to that of his wife so it is clear who is being referred to.

Shay — A Pennsylvania Dutch dialect word meaning "pretty."

Siss net chide — A Pennsylvania Dutch dialect phrase meaning "it isn't right."

Sits ana — A Pennsylvania Dutch dialect phrase meaning "sit down."

Undankbar — A Pennsylvania Dutch dialect word meaning "unthankful."

Unfashtendich — A Pennsylvania Dutch dialect word meaning "senseless."

Vee bisht doo — A Pennsylvania Dutch dialect phrase meaning "how are you?"

Zeit-lang — A Pennsylvania Dutch dialect word meaning "loneliness and longing."

Ztvett Grishtdag — A Pennsylvania Dutch dialect phrase meaning "Second Christmas." This is the day after Christmas when many Amish people continue their holiday celebrations with their large, extended families.

About the Author

LINDA BYLER WAS RAISED IN AN Amish family and is an active member of the Amish church today. Growing up, Linda loved to read and write. In fact, she still does. Linda is well-known within the Amish community as a columnist for a weekly Amish newspaper. She writes all her novels by hand in notebooks.

Linda is the author of six series of novels, all set among the Amish communities of North America: Lizzie Searches for Love, Sadie's Montana, Lancaster Burning, Hester's Hunt for Home, The Dakota Series, and the Buggy Spoke Series for younger readers. Linda has also written six Christmas romances set among the Amish: *Mary's Christmas Goodbye, The Christmas Visitor, The Little Amish Matchmaker, Becky Meets Her Match, A Dog for Christmas,* and *A Horse for Elsie.* Linda has coauthored *Lizzie's Amish Cookbook: Favorite Recipes from Three Generations of Amish Cooks!*

Other Books by
Linda Byler

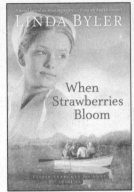

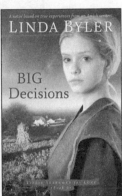

BOOK ONE   BOOK TWO   BOOK THREE

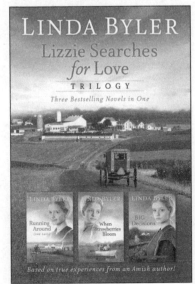

TRILOGY   COOKBOOK

Sadie's Montana Series

BOOK ONE

BOOK TWO

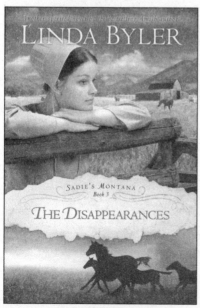

BOOK THREE

TRILOGY

LANCASTER BURNING SERIES

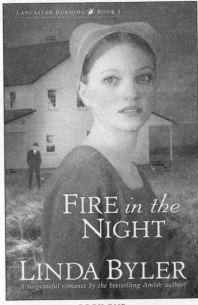

BOOK ONE

BOOK TWO

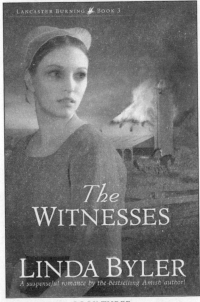

BOOK THREE

TRILOGY

HESTER'S HUNT FOR HOME SERIES

BOOK ONE

BOOK TWO

BOOK THREE

TRILOGY

THE DAKOTA SERIES

BOOK ONE

HOPE *on the* PLAINS

BOOK TWO

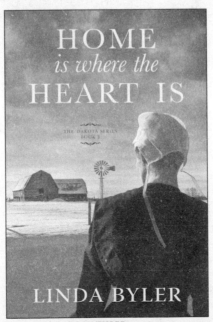

BOOK THREE

CHRISTMAS NOVELLAS

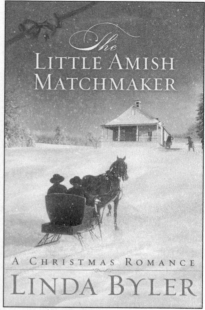

LINDA BYLER

BECKY
Meets Her
MATCH

Is Daniel Stoltzfus
really ready for Becky?

An Amish Christmas Romance

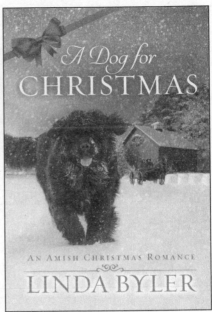

A Dog for
CHRISTMAS

An Amish Christmas Romance

LINDA BYLER

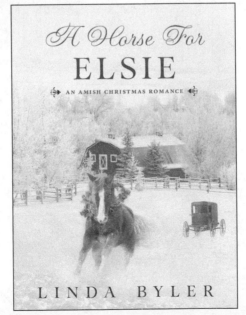

A Horse For
ELSIE

An Amish Christmas Romance

LINDA BYLER

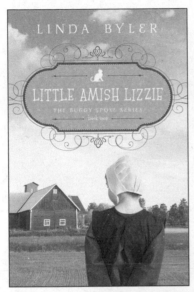